4 — While [this reader] did
NOT enjoy Coll's novel as much
she did Prep — It did bring to light
the extraordinary pressures "Kids"
and parents are subjected to and
"WILLINGLY" put upon themselves
to "secure" a place in the "right"
school.
    So much so that she only gave
her characters little gaps "to stick
their REAL heads up". So, do NOT
believe that this one is "going to
add to your reading family". It
will add to your realization that
our society is "almost" over the
edge!
[It was far much easier and [may
we say : !] FUN back in my day!

Debbi mac[Gregor]

FARRAR
STRAUS
GIROUX

ALSO BY SUSAN COLL

karlmarx.com: A Love Story

Rockville Pike

ACCEPTANCE

SARAH CRICHTON BOOKS

FARRAR, STRAUS AND GIROUX

NEW YORK

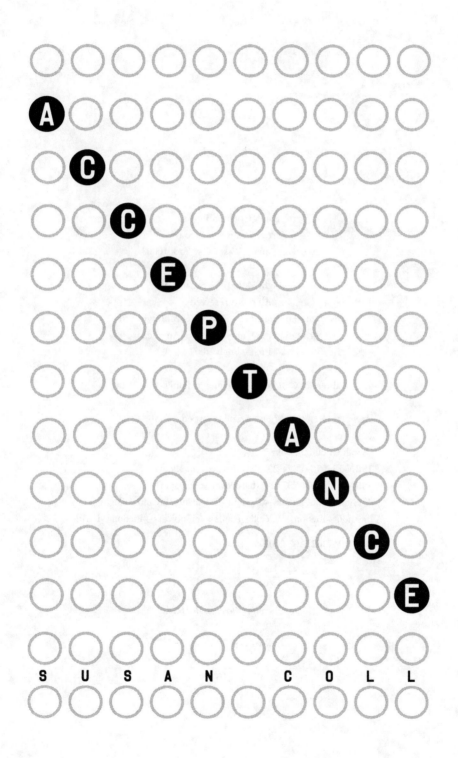

ACCEPTANCE

SUSAN COLL

Sarah Crichton Books
Farrar, Straus and Giroux
19 Union Square West, New York 10003

Copyright © 2007 by Susan Coll
All rights reserved
Distributed in Canada by Douglas & McIntyre Ltd.
Printed in the United States of America
First edition, 2007

Library of Congress Cataloging-in-Publication Data
Coll, Susan.
    Acceptance : a novel / Susan Coll.— 1st ed.
        p.   cm.
    "Sarah Crichton books."
    ISBN-13: 978-0-374-23719-6 (hardcover : alk. paper)
    ISBN-10: 0-374-23719-0 (hardcover : alk. paper)
    1. High school seniors—Fiction.   2. Universities and colleges—
Admission—Fiction.   3. College admission officers—Fiction.   I. Title.

PS3553.O474622A65 2007
813'.6—dc22

                                                          2006015896

Designed by Michelle McMillian

www.fsgbooks.com

3   5   7   9   10   8   6   4   2

For Ally, Emma, and Max,
levelheaded and inspiring guides

There is this quality, in things,
of the right way seeming wrong at first.

—JOHN UPDIKE, Rabbit, Run

CONTENTS

ACCEPTANCE

April

GRACE SAW SHIMMERING TRAILS of light, even when she shut her eyes. The scores of bulbs illuminating the enormous wrought-iron chandelier chained to the rafters of the converted barn had imprinted themselves on her brain, and bursts of white danced inside her head like the tails of rogue comets. Her head throbbed, and she wished she could slip out of the middle of the row in the packed auditorium without causing a small commotion, embarrassing her son.

As a single mother, Grace couldn't afford to actually get sick. Sick days were used to compensate for the spousal void in her family life, and she had just cashed in a week of them to accompany Harry on a spring-break road trip to tour college campuses. Surely she was just worn out from the long drive the previous day, followed by a night spent tossing and turning on a soggy, flea-ridden mattress at the bed-and-breakfast. The guidebook had advertised the Yates Inn as "quaint," but she guessed that description was nearly as old as the place itself, a nineteenth-century moss green clapboard house that had lost its charm somewhere along the way, possibly a couple of decades ago, when it appeared to have last been painted.

She and Harry had raced to this 9:00 a.m. information session and campus tour, forgoing the inn's complimentary pancake breakfast after learning it would take at least half an hour to reach the school by car.

Dinner the previous night had been an inedible sandwich from a sketchy-looking diner in Scranton, Pennsylvania, that smelled like eggs, so it was possible that her current distress was really just hunger. Nevertheless, she felt her symptoms redouble as the preppy, boyish admissions officer at the podium responded to questions from anxious parents.

"Can you tell us what percentage of the class is accepted early decision, and how much of an advantage does an early applicant have?" A female inquisitor, whom Grace couldn't actually see from where she sat, asked her question with an urgency that made her sound slightly hysterical.

"This year, 55 percent of the class was admitted early decision," said the young man, who had earlier identified himself as Soren. "So clearly, if Yates is your first choice, there's an advantage to applying early. That said, all applications are considered on an individual basis. There is no magical formula for admittance."

"What about the SAT?" another parent asked. "Is there a cutoff for scholarship eligibility? How much weight can you give to these numbers if they can't even score the tests correctly?"

"Yes, of course that's on everyone's mind. But please don't worry. We look at the application as a whole. The SATs are only one small piece of the puzzle." This answer elicited a few audible groans.

"How many applied overall last year? What is the acceptance rate? And what about the wait list?" asked a voice in the back of the room.

"This year, we've had 4,601 applications. We ultimately accepted 35 percent of those. We have a wait list of approximately 300. It varies year to year, but last spring three moved off the list."

A few people coughed and rearranged themselves in the creaky folding chairs that had been set up to accommodate the overflow crowd, causing sounds of discomfort to ricochet around the acoustically challenged room. This was an alarmingly high rate of rejection for an obscure liberal arts college tucked in the middle of nowhere, requiring more than an hour's drive off the main highway, along sixty-five miles of winding roads that snaked through fields of cornstalks and grazing cows.

Grace's heart began racing. She took a deep breath. This had to be a really bad place to get sick—were there any doctors in this tiny town? They were at least two hours from anything even resembling a city. Looking around, Grace observed that a couple of other parents looked vaguely unwell, too. Perhaps there was not enough oxygen in the stifling auditorium, which was packed so tight it had surely exceeded its fire code capacity. Or maybe they were all just having garden-variety anxiety attacks, the result of absorbing this slow trickle of disconcerting information about college admissions.

The woman in front of her, who had earlier asked which undergraduate majors helped forge a path to the most prestigious MBA programs, took off her blue blazer and rolled up her sleeves. Grace noticed that the husband also wore a blue blazer and that the two boys sitting between them were clad in identical, brightly striped, Ralph Lauren polo shirts. It had not occurred to Grace to dress up for the occasion. She had thrown on a denim skirt and a favorite Gap sweater, and her long hair, secured in a ponytail, was still damp from the shower.

Soren fielded another question having to do with recommendation letters and whether a school's music teacher counted as an academic reference. "Recommendations are just one piece of the puzzle," he replied wearily, not actually responding to the subtleties of the question. "There is no secret formula for admittance," he repeated. "We look at the applicant as a whole."

Soren raked his fingers through a shock of unruly thick blond hair that looked deliberately, even expensively, mussed, as he tackled the next question. Grace thought he didn't look like a man of much gravitas, but he did have the suggestive subliminal appeal of an Abercrombie & Fitch model. In fact, Grace had observed that the Yates University view book itself bore an uncanny resemblance to the controversial clothing catalogue, which, even in its cleaned-up, less overtly pornographic state, still featured pictures of scantily clad coeds who looked as if they'd just stumbled out of a frat party. She wondered if these images might have had something to do with Harry's reluctant agreement to visit the campus, even though he had rejected all of his mother's other non–Ivy League suggestions. But then, there was probably some other way to explain his compliance, since he was not the sort of boy who typically responded to the advertising stimuli so aggressively lobbed at his age group. Harry didn't even own an iPod.

"Mom, are you all right?" Harry whispered in her ear. "You look kind of funny."

"I'm great," Grace replied, managing to pat him reassuringly on the knee.

Another parent asked a question about the importance of grades versus standardized test scores, and then wondered aloud about how much weight would be given to her son's fluency in three languages and his forthcoming summer internship at NASA. "Think of the application as a jigsaw puzzle," Soren said. "Grades are one piece, scores are another." He sounded bored with his own answer, as though he uttered these same words several times a day, which he no doubt did. He had been asked some version of this same question at least six times in the last thirty minutes, and the schedule indicated that there were four separate information sessions being offered that day. The interrogator in this instance— a squat, wild-haired woman in her mid-fifties who resembled one of several hermit-like, mentally unbalanced chemists in Grace's office—was not this easily put off. She wanted numbers, percentile groups, statistics, solid granules of information to record in the red, three-ring binder balanced on her lap. Specifically, she wanted to know whether her son, the skinny, meek-looking youth sitting next to her with the same unfortunate hair DNA, was going to be able to use Yates University as his safety school. There was a murmur in the room, as the rest of the audience absorbed and remarked on the arrogance of this question. Her poor son slumped in his chair.

Soren winced and stabbed at his chest with an invisible knife, pretending to be wounded. A few people laughed nervously. He smiled and fiddled with his hair before saying he was sure that after touring the campus in a few moments and getting to know a bit more about the place, her son would no longer regard Yates as his safety school. He then reviewed the mechanics of his jigsaw puzzle analogy.

Grace looked around the room and noticed for the first time that it was not just the obnoxious wild-haired woman who had a notebook, but that many of the parents, and several of the students, too, were recording Soren's words. Harry also produced a small pad from his pocket and jotted something down.

Even if many of the parents in the room seemed too tightly wound, Grace still felt comforted by the sight of the kids themselves, the incoming freshmen of wherever it was they might wind up. Despite all the hand-wringing in the media about the moral decline of today's youth—a phenomenon variously blamed on violent video games, instant messaging, text messaging, indecent MySpace postings, MTV, Internet pornography, and the supposedly widespread practice of "hooking up"—Grace observed that these kids seemed pretty similar in both dress and demeanor to her own peers some thirty years ago. Flare-bottomed jeans and tie-dyed T-shirts seemed to be back in style, and there was even a smattering of turquoise jewelry. At least on the surface, these kids all seemed to be polite and focused and frankly more conservative than she and her friends had been at their age.

Grace had little opportunity to make these sorts of observations at home. Her own son, Harry, was a teenaged anomaly who went off to high school each day as if he were on his way to a job as the CEO of a Fortune 500 company. He wore khaki pants with a starched shirt and blazer and carried a briefcase as well as a backpack. This might have seemed a recipe for social disaster, but no one dared mock Harry. During freshman year, when he was one of only three ninth-graders taking an Advanced Placement history class, he was assigned the nickname "AP Harry." The teachers and the principal also knew him by this name. AP Harry had served as his junior class president and was currently campaigning to head the student body for the forthcoming school year. He was not an especially social creature, opting to spend most of his free time studying, but from what Grace could tell, he was not disliked. His classmates seemed to understand that he was golden, a mini–master of the universe at nearly seventeen; even if they didn't want to be his friend, they didn't want to get in his way.

Grace, too, understood that her son was an aberration. According to the child-rearing textbooks, Harry ought to be holding up liquor stores by now rather than apprenticing for a future in politics. Grace and her husband, Lou, had divorced when Harry was in second grade. And it was not the sort of quiet, amicable split one might expect from highly educated people living in the affluent suburbs, where parents went to family counselors and read books about how to protect the children from the emotional fallout of divorce. Rather, this was the sort of separation that involved the police, child services, teams of attorneys, the garnisheeing of Lou's salary for failure to pay alimony and child support, a kidnapping attempt, the brandishing of a gun on their leafy street, and an eventual restraining order. As a consequence, Grace's plans to stay home and be a full-time mother quickly fizzled. She worked long hours as a malaria researcher at the nearby National Institutes of Health, and Harry endured years of mediocre after-school day care. As if this were all some endless test from God, just when Grace felt things were under control a couple of years after Lou had ceased showing up drunk, in his pajamas, banging on her door in the middle of the night, the director of the afternoon child care program at Harry's elementary school was arrested on charges of pedophilia.

Against all odds, Harry had not dropped out of high school or joined a gang: he was a student leader, the principal clarinetist in the school band, a boy who kept his room tidy and helped his mother uncomplainingly with chores. Grace was proud, but she found Harry's drive alarming. She wished he would tone things down a notch and just be a kid.

Harry was extremely smart, but his transcript had a glitch, which was a piece of information he kept to himself, his secret shame. Until the fall of his junior year, he had never received anything other than an A. Then he took AP English Language, where despite herculean efforts he landed a humiliating B, a grade largely attributable to the emphasis on writing, with weekly in-class essays that factored heavily into the final grade. Harry claimed that the real problem was not with his writing skills, but with the teacher, Mr. Joyce, who he sensed didn't like him. Harry perceived the B as the beginning of a downward spiral exacerbated by his first two stabs at the SAT. While his math score was a perfect 800, despite relentless cramming and expensive private tutoring sessions they could not really afford, he could not pump his critical reading score up over a 720, and his writing score was the same. Grace's insistence that these

numbers were, objectively, extremely impressive only seemed to exacer-
bate his frustration.

Grace couldn't have cared less about any of this. Her chief ambition
for her son was that he turn out to be a nice, decent human being, as unlike his own father as possible, and on this front she was watching worriedly. In temperament he was still the same sweet kid he'd always been,
but his great march forward was sometimes disheartening to watch. She
was confident that his drive would get him anywhere, with one possible
exception. AP Harry was probably not going to get into Harvard. He was
a strong candidate, but Grace could do the math: with a 9 percent acceptance rate, according to the last numbers she had seen, a middle-class
white kid without a legacy did not have the odds in his favor. Yet Harry
had his heart set on Harvard, and the word *rejection* was evidently not in
his 720 vocabulary.

GRACE WONDERED if this session would ever end. She was beginning to
perspire. The blue-blazered father in front of her folded the Yates
brochure about freshman seminars into a makeshift fan. Campus tours
were supposed to have already begun; they were twenty minutes off
schedule, and the male model at the podium was having a hard time
stemming the flow of increasingly frantic questions—every one of them
from parents, she couldn't help but observe.

A hand two rows in front shot up, and Grace thought she must have
been hallucinating when she spied the distinctive chunky diamond ring
of her across-the-street neighbor. Nina Rockefeller's arm flailed crazily,
like she was hailing a cab in a drenching rush hour storm. How unlikely
was this? Grace had been going out of her way to avoid Nina for about
two years, sneaking out of her house at odd hours to minimize the
chances of running into her. Now she had driven more than four hundred miles to one of the most isolated college campuses in the northeastern United States, and there Nina was, just a few feet away.

For years they had been close friends, thrown together by the circumstances of geography and parenting. Harry and Nina's daughter, Taylor, were both only children, and their birthdays were just two months
apart. It was at first a natural, easy friendship even if they had little in

common besides the kids. They spent years of languid weekend afternoons parked in lawn chairs sipping iced tea, watching the children run from yard to yard, their miniature plastic ride-on cars giving way to sophisticated water guns and, later, walkie-talkies, baseball bats, and Frisbees as the summers ticked by.

As the kids grew older, however, Nina seemed to grow weirdly competitive, and Grace began to dread their exchanges. Plus, Nina was a talker, and just bumping into her outside their homes could cost as much as half an hour. There were mornings when Grace even put off retrieving the newspaper from her driveway if she spied Nina on her porch, watering her plants. Grace assuaged her guilt by telling herself she simply didn't have time for idle morning chatter or she'd be late for work. Lately, though, her efforts at avoidance had become more deliberate as Nina was edging toward insufferable, never veering far off the topic of the bright future of her remarkable daughter, Taylor.

Grace thought her neighbor was joking when she raised the topic of college the summer before the kids began eighth grade. Hoping to change the subject, Grace naively quipped that it didn't yet matter; until they entered high school, she said, they could at least enjoy life without stressing out about test scores and grades. Nina was quick to set her straight. Any high school–level classes the kids took in middle school would show up on their final transcripts, she reported. Nina explained that the county had recently changed the policy of letting students erase these grades from their records in an attempt to curb grade inflation. An A in an honors class carried a higher-weighted value than an A in a regular class, but in Verona County there were no honors classes offered in middle school. This was just wordplay, however, since the students had been tracked and then grouped according to their abilities since around the time they learned to tie their shoes, and a certain sliver of kids were working at an accelerated level regardless of the name slapped on the course. Nina's point was evidently that a straightforward, old-fashioned A, even in a mind-numbingly difficult class, could technically bring down a student's overall GPA. Grace couldn't quite believe what she was hearing. She understood the mathematical principle involved, but still, wasn't an A an A? But she nodded her head, pretending to acknowledge this grave injustice.

Grace knew it was absurd to let these sorts of conversations make her anxious. Harry was so driven that she didn't need to keep an eye on his performance; if anything she worried that he would drive himself insane trying to manipulate his already solid record. Still, sometimes Nina made her feel like she wasn't doing enough. Not only had Nina signed Taylor up for SAT prep three years ahead of the normal schedule, but she also put on retainer what she said was the best private college counseling service in the country, recently profiled in *The Wall Street Journal*. Undaunted by the fact that the consultancy was based in New York, or that their fee for two years of advice was more than $30,000, Nina opined that it would reduce family tension to have an outside party be in charge of guiding Taylor through the touchy process.

In an effort to avoid these harrowing conversations, Grace had begun to set her alarm half an hour early on weekday mornings so that she could walk her dog before Nina set out in one of her several bright pink sweat suits, yanking her overweight schnauzer along on a Burberry leash. Grace's dog, a gentle giant of a mutt that appeared to be at least part Saint Bernard, must have had some sixth sense about the Rockefeller's pet because her hair stood on end whenever he approached, which added a second layer of tension to their walks. But even a willingness to sacrifice precious minutes of sleep offered no respite; just last week Nina had spied Grace two long blocks ahead and had run to catch up, shouting for her to wait.

"Terrific news," she had said, remarkably well-put-together with makeup and jewelry at 7:00 a.m. Grace assumed she was going to deliver some encouraging update on the house next door to her and catty-corner to Nina, an eyesore that had been on the market for an entire month. Instead, she announced breathlessly, "Taylor just got straight A's."

Grace feigned enthusiasm but inwardly recoiled. Didn't grades fall into the zone of private information, along with age and weight and financial net worth? She could not imagine ever talking about Harry's grades with anyone other than his teachers or his guidance counselor. Or possibly Harry's father, although that was purely hypothetical because they were not actually on speaking terms.

Grace reminded herself that she had resolved not to get sucked into this snakepit of parental competition. Study after study showed that there was no correlation between where a person went to college and his or her future happiness, or even earning power. She knew plenty of people who had underachieved in their youth and had gone on to do great things. And she could cite many examples of the reverse—kids who burned out by the time they got to college or simply couldn't cope without their parents micromanaging their lives; she had heard of some parents who even called their college kids to wake them up for morning classes. But it was hard to step back when everyone at Harry's high school, students and parents alike, spoke of little else, and the kids were all jockeying to get into the same handful of schools. At a recent junior parents' meeting, the head of guidance had rattled off a series of sobering statistics, including the fact that from this year's class of 496 graduating seniors, 53 had applied to Cornell, 57 to Northwestern, and 59 to the University of Pennsylvania. All of them had GPAs over 3.8. About ten kids were admitted to each school, and five were accepted to all three. As Grace pondered these numbers, she couldn't help but think that ironically, this would make a good math problem on the SAT. On the subject of identifying the right safety school, the guidance counselor had referenced the terrifying, widely gossiped about, and evidently true story of the National Merit finalist who applied to twelve schools and didn't get into a single one.

Sometimes when she heard these anxiety-inducing anecdotes, Grace wondered whether she had been smart to remain in the area after her divorce. She had stretched herself financially, heavily mortgaging their house, because this was arguably one of the best public school systems not just in the state, but in the country. But lately she had begun to think she had done Harry a disservice by staying. Perhaps he would be driving himself less hard, and would have a better sense of perspective, if she had relocated to some small town in the Midwest. And even if she was wrong about that—if this college mania had reached into the most remote pockets of America—at least a community of less means might have other sorts of benefits, like fewer kids with credit cards, or a lower percentage of luxury cars in the student parking lot.

Still, Grace tried hard not to let Harry's preoccupation become her own. She knew there were hundreds of good colleges out there, some of which she had never even heard of before, like Yates. She had done just fine going to the University of Maryland, which had been the only school her parents could afford. It had never occurred to her to feel short-changed. She always felt she'd received a perfectly decent education and had not suffered, apart from the unfortunate fact that she had met Lou in an anatomy class and made the mistake of marrying him.

As it was, Harry was most definitely part of the problem, if not the most extreme version of it around. He had memorized the *U.S. News & World Report* rankings of the top fifty liberal arts colleges as well as the separate list of universities—those offering both doctorates and masters—and he frequently asked Grace to quiz him to see if he had his numbers straight. At first Grace had played along, not fully grasping the point of the exercise. But once she realized the pathos of what he was doing—obsessing about whether Pomona ranked 7 or 8 and how many points that was above, say, Oberlin (14)—she refused to play, even when Harry insisted that he was just sharpening his memory retention skills. (Yates had entered the list for the first time ever last year, coming in at number 50.) Even without her help, he had lately progressed to the point where he could provide subcategories, such as a school's selectivity rank and average rate of alumni giving.

The last time Grace bumped into Nina—another morning encounter in which Grace pretended unsuccessfully that her headphones prevented her from hearing her neighbor's noisy, chipper approach—Nina told her she was doing some reading to learn where various well-connected American women had gone to college and where they had met their spouses. Grace laughed out loud, certain she was kidding, but the hurt look on Nina's face assured her this was not a joke.

After that conversation, Grace had made an even more radical change to her schedule. She began to set her alarm a full hour early and would sneak out in the dark to walk the dog. All of these efforts had failed her spectacularly, however, because here was Nina, just two rows away. As

Grace leaned forward to stretch the muscles in her back while the admissions counselor repeated his clichés, the ostentatious diamond in Nina's ring caught a streak of sunlight, refracting it into even more bouncing specks in Grace's pounding head.

Taylor sat beside her mother, looking sullen. She seemed to be in distress. Regardless of whether Taylor was as brilliant as her mother claimed, she was no longer the happy, freckle-faced little girl who used to play roller hockey in the street with Harry and all of the neighborhood kids. Sometime in the last year, she had become transformed into a pale, haunted-looking teenager. Her once luminous black hair was now tinged with purple and hung in greasy, unkempt strands. Grace wondered if perhaps the girl was using drugs. But that didn't seem quite right, given that Taylor had become a complete loner and, while hardly fat, didn't have that heroin-chic, skin-and-bones physique one tended to equate with a serious drug habit. Grace wasn't an expert on these things, but she did assume that at least part of the allure of the drug culture was the instant camaraderie. Yet Harry reported that Taylor sat alone at lunch each day, declining his occasional invitations to join him. He also said she fled school after the final bell rang and on the few occasions that he left at the same time, she seemed to deliberately sprint ahead to avoid him.

From her slightly elevated position, Grace could see that Nina's roots were growing in darker than the rest of her blond hair. Her hand continued to wave frantically, but so many other hands competed that young Soren kept passing her over. Nina actually began to blurt out her question unsolicited, but at that precise moment Soren finally found the wherewithal to declare the information session over, instructing them to break into small groups for the campus tours. They were trying something new this year, he explained. Students would go on one set of tours, parents on another. He told them where to gather, accordingly.

"Are you all right?" Harry asked his mother again, shaking her gently on the shoulder. "You look kind of pale, Mom . . . *pale, sallow, pallid, wan . . .*"

Grace forced a smile and blotted her forehead with a piece of used tissue she found in her pocket. "*Ashen?*" she asked.

"Very good, Mom," Harry said, smiling adorably.

The synonym game was something else he liked to play, something he had read about in an SAT prep book. Grace feigned more enthusiasm than she really felt for the game, but she played along on the ground that at least it was not as obnoxious as the *U.S. News* game. Plus, she felt it was the least she could do, given his frustration with his score.

"You really look awful, Mom," he said as they filed out of the row.

"Thanks, Harry . . . Just what I wanted to hear. But if you don't mind, I am feeling kind of . . ."

"Peaky?"

"Yes. Well put. Peaked. So I think I'll skip the tour. You go ahead. I'll wait here . . ."

She pointed toward a set of armchairs in the outer room of the barn flanked by a table with two alluring pots of coffee and a platter of doughnuts. But then she saw Nina Rockefeller coming straight toward her. "Or maybe I'll find a nice bench, outside."

○ ○ ○

TAYLOR WONDERED HOW the perky tour guide managed to walk backwards without slipping out of her flip-flops or crashing into any of the small statues scattered around the campus. The weird little sculptures, almost all of animals which appeared to be either slightly deformed or maybe just weather-worn, cropped up in the same haphazard manner as the daffodils, one of which, sprouting through a crack in the sidewalk, she accidentally stepped on. Taylor was not one to notice landscaping, but there was something slightly off about the grounds at Yates. Unlike the more manicured campuses she had already visited, with geometric quads and clipped shrubbery, this campus was not just scruffy, but somehow askew. Most of the classroom and administrative buildings were shrouded in overgrown greenery, and weeds adorned the lawns. The whole place seemed to need a good trim. Still, she found the campus strangely enchanting. This was the first school she visited where she had the intuitive sense that this was exactly where she belonged, the annoying tour guide notwithstanding.

At home, just outside Washington, D.C., the temperature was already in the low 70s. It hadn't occurred to Taylor that the weather would be this different, and she wished she had brought a sweater. She wondered if it ever really got warm in upstate New York. After about twenty minutes, with stops at the library and the recreation center, Taylor had had enough of listening to this cheerful, too-thin girl prattle on about how great the social life was at Yates. She had been particularly effusive in describing the Friday night theme parties and the accompanying complimentary cocktails. Hawaiian luau night with piña coladas; California surfer night with margaritas; Caribbean night with some drink Taylor had never heard of that had something to do with pineapple and rum. Taylor wondered just how landlocked they were, how cold and dark and dreary it must get in midwinter to make students want to dress up in straw skirts and pretend there was not several feet of snow on the ground.

Anyway, Taylor was not interested in the social life at Yates so much as in the bathrooms. It was surprising how not a single one of the many college books she had pored over, including *Princeton Review, Fiske,* or even the more gossipy *Insider's Guide to the Colleges,* ever mentioned the bathrooms. The guidebooks all seemed more focused on students' fashion sensibilities. The *Insider's Guide* mentioned that everyone at Yates wore trendy North Face fleeces, for example, which she found to be a minor turnoff, notwithstanding the fact that she owned three of them herself.

She had heard there was a handful of schools that reportedly had bathrooms with special attributes—the University of Richmond, for instance, was said to have granite countertops with inlaid sinks, and Barnard boasted basins placed at a convenient height for shaving legs— but this was not her concern. She didn't especially care what amenities the bathroom had to offer; she just wanted one of her own.

As they made their way across the campus, down a tree-lined circular path, Taylor wondered hopefully if they were headed toward the dorms. This was generally her favorite part of the tour, even if it was an exercise of limited value. The schools only showed the nicer accommodations, but it at least gave a sense of the range of possibilities and might help answer the bathroom question, although getting a glimpse was sometimes tricky. She would never be the one to ask, but there was always the possibility that someone else would want to assess the bathroom situation. It was usually the parents who asked the embarrassing questions, however, and at Yates the adults had curiously been sent on their own tours. While this was a good thing in that it got her away from her mother, it did decrease the likelihood of learning anything useful. Certainly, it was not a kid who had asked to see the "hygienic facilities" during a recent tour at a school in Baltimore. Others in the group had laughed when one of the mothers made the request, but then every single person filed in to sneak a peek, a few of them even swinging open the doors to the stalls to inspect the toilets. Taylor did not need to test the flushing capacity to determine that those facilities were insufficient for her needs; not only had they not been private, but worse—coed. It was not easy for her to explain, even to herself, why she sought a private bathroom; essentially, she felt the need for a place to retreat, even within the sanctity of her own room.

From what Taylor had seen of Yates thus far, there was little reason to suppose the dorms might be any less shabby-looking than the rest of the place. She had learned to detect patterns on these visits. At one school the model dorm was so hideous, so dark and dank and smelly, that she was afraid to imagine the state of the less presentable dorms. One thing she had figured out already was that the few remaining all-girls dorms tended to be nicer; they were usually older and hence more architecturally interesting, with more gracious rooms. Many of the newer dorms she had seen looked like they had been built by Soviet-era architects or accidentally raised from blueprints for a prison camp. Girls' dorms tended to smell better, too. Presumably less partying took place when boys were prohibited from visiting after certain hours, and she guessed this explained the beneficial reduction in the foul odors she had detected in the hallways of some of the buildings.

To her disappointment, however, the next stop on the Yates tour took them to another barnlike building that appeared to house more offices. Taylor had read in the guidebooks that Yates was renowed for its Arts and Crafts–style architecture, and while she was not design-savvy enough to really know what that meant, she wondered if this explained the slightly grungy, woodsy appeal of the place. It reminded her of the summer camp in Virginia where she had been a CIT last year, before she was sent home when the girls in her cabin complained that she was stealing things.

On the outside, the building was just another tattered old barn, but the interior had been converted into elegant office space. An enormous Persian rug stretched across the lobby, and the sun streaming in through several stained-glass skylights in the vaulted ceiling bathed the foyer in a kaleidoscopic light. Sofas and comfortable-looking stuffed chairs flanked the room, and banks of brochures and blank applications were piled high on a bookshelf. This was the main admissions building, the tour guide explained, but because of the unprecedented surge in visitors this spring, they had been forced to move the information sessions to the auditorium, where they had just met.

A narrow spiral stairway led downstairs, where evidently they were headed, single-file. Taylor was relieved to see the tour guide decide to descend in the forward-facing position; even though she had already taken an irrational dislike to her, she didn't especially want to see the girl spill backwards over the handrail and splatter to the lobby below. Once they had all made their way down the cramped staircase, the guide explained that this floor housed the individual offices of the admissions staff. They were not actually going to visit these offices, but rather, they were taking a scenic shortcut en route to view the student services center by cutting through this building, down the stairs, and out the back door via some famous statue and sculpture garden. Taylor glimpsed the cute admissions officer, Soren, leaning against a wall, speaking to an older woman wearing pearls who appeared agitated. Soren saw the tour group walking by and waved.

"For those who didn't know," the guide explained, now walking backwards again, "the founder of Yates, Jeremiah Wheeling, was a locally renowned sculptor and a bit of an eccentric."

Several of the prospective students exchanged weary glances. No one really wanted a history lesson; they just wanted to know what the odds were of getting in. Tour guides were forever boring their charges with useless background information, although Taylor imagined they were probably reciting from scripts. At Colgate the tour guide had told them about the school's relationship with the toothpaste manufacturer; at

Hamilton she heard much about the generosity of Alexander himself. But really, who needed to hear biographical details about some crazy dead sculptor? This sentiment was evidently shared by a girl who interrupted to ask the tour guide what other colleges she had applied to and what her first choice had been.

"We're not really supposed to talk about that sort of thing," she said apologetically. "We're just supposed to tell you about Yates."

"Just tell us what your first choice school was," someone else begged.

This was another aspect of the school tour that Taylor generally found suspect. The tour guides invariably seemed to be either outright liars or extraordinary overachievers—kids who would let slip that they turned down full scholarships at Ivy League schools or declined starring roles on Broadway in order to attend whatever college they happened to be endorsing because they fell in love with the quirky architecture or the spectacular cafeteria food.

In this case the tour guide looked around to be sure no one official was close enough to hear and replied, quietly, "Yale."

A few people nodded their heads, but no one actually spoke. This was such a startling answer that there was really nothing much to say. Now everyone was probably even more curious to learn the specifics of the girl's profile. Had she been delusional in applying to Yale in the first place? And if not, if she had perfect credentials plus some other edge, like a niche sport or a legacy, and she had still failed to get into Yale, were there not better buffer schools along the way? Had she been too cocky to bother applying to in-between safeties? Were they all doomed to share this fate? Maybe, Taylor mused, she had already stocked up on Yale T-shirts and Yates was at least a close phonetic second.

The guide then led them into another common area that branched off into about a dozen offices. In the center of the room, surrounded by a low circular gate, was an enormous, somewhat shocking stone-carved depiction of a naked Native American woman who stood at least fourteen feet tall. The peace pipe she clutched in her giant hands poked through the second floor of the building, which seemed to have been designed specifically to accommodate the dimensions of her oversized breasts.

"I'm going to tell you a brief story about *Yashequana Woman*," the tour guide announced. "This statue was a gift from an elder of the Yashe-quana tribe to our school's founder in about 1859. It was passed down through a couple of generations of the Wheeling family until Jeremiah's great-grandson, Jeremiah IV, presented her to his friend Franklin Delano Roosevelt, back when he was governor of New York, in about 1925 . . ."

Someone yawned conspicuously as she continued, and a few people clustered in the back began to giggle.

"Believe it or not, FDR liked *Yashequana Woman* so much that he brought her to the White House when he became president. But legend has it that Eleanor, his wife, didn't like the statue and ordered her into storage in the basement. Years later, when Richard Nixon became vice president . . . brief history quiz here . . . does anyone remember who Nixon served as vice president?"

No one replied. Taylor thought she knew the answer but didn't want to sound like a brownnoser. "Okay, don't worry. I didn't remember either until I took my tour guide orientation . . . The answer is Eisenhower. Dwight D!" she exclaimed. "Anyway, Nixon was poking around in the basement of the White House looking for something one day, and he found the statue. He suggested they get it out of the White House and reunite it with its rightful owner. Somehow they traced it back to Yates, and here it is. The entire building was renovated in 1958 in order to make the statue the architectural centerpiece. Pretty neat, huh?"

Someone asked the tour guide what her SAT scores had been.

Taylor was completely mesmerized by the statue, even though she couldn't really explain the appeal. *Yashequana Woman* was actually vaguely misogynistic, and with her erect nipples, more suggestive of pornography than art. Still, Taylor felt a certain kinship with this woman that she couldn't quite explain.

Taylor hadn't realized she'd fallen behind, that most of her group had already passed through the double doors that led out into the sculpture garden, until she looked up and saw a different group of kids file into the room. She thought she glimpsed a familiar figure chatting up the tour guide, but her view was obscured by the statue, so she figured she must have been imagining this. It was something of a local urban legend that it was impossible to visit a college campus without bumping into someone from Verona High School. While this could not possibly be true, she observed that this person was wearing crisply pressed khaki trousers and had his shirt tucked in, a high school fashion faux pas distinctive of AP Harry. She felt a little wave of panic when she realized it really was him. Her instinct was to turn away, but then they locked eyes and it was too late.

Even though they had been friends since preschool, lately Taylor had begun to feel an unsettling blend of guilt, dread, and a tiny bit of longing whenever she saw him. For years there had been an almost sibling-like quality to their relationship, but that was before Harry had become so obsessive about school. It was also before they had played a momentous game in his dark basement one day, back in seventh grade. Taylor still cringed when she remembered this. What could she possibly have been thinking, letting him stick his hand up her shirt, encouraging him, even, to fondle her breast? She had touched him, too, she thought with a shudder, remembering the hunting dog boxer shorts she'd glimpsed in the dim bit of light that had seeped in through the window wells. And *he* had been the one to end the game, even when she was willing to take it to the next level. "Doctor's office is closing," he'd said, zipping up his pants. She still wondered what that had been about. Was it something she'd said? Had she done something wrong, or hurt him somehow?

They muddled along after that, still walking to school together sometimes, until Taylor couldn't stand the embarrassment anymore and began to avoid him. Harry did not appear to notice: he seemed to float inside a little bubble, oblivious to normal social cues. Harry persisted in smiling and saying "hi" to her in the hallway, and he frequently invited her to join him at lunch, even though she had replied impolitely on more than one occasion that she preferred to sit alone.

Taylor waved feebly at Harry and quickly turned away, to no avail. "Your mom ran into my mom," he said. "They are back at the auditorium, talking."

"Oh, awesome," Taylor said, trying to be nice. But this was not good news. Lord knew what stupid things her mother would have to say, things, she suspected, that would eventually be reported back to AP Harry, and then possibly disseminated throughout the entire junior class.

Yet another tour group entered the room, creating a small logjam at the doorway. There were about a hundred and fifty prospective students visiting, broken into tour groups of roughly twenty-five. By now Taylor had lost track of her own group, and would be forced to tag along with Harry or would have to risk trying to find her way back through the maze of trails and overgrown shrubbery. Even though the campus was small, she was turned around and there were few landmarks along the dark, winding trails. Plus, she thought she had heard someone say the word "bear."

Taylor watched the other kids file in. It seemed impossible, but there, striding affably, gorgeously, at the end of the next group was her next-door neighbor, Maya Kaluantharana.

This seemed a cruel joke. She had driven all this way only to run into two kids not just from her high school, but from her quiet, boring neighborhood. Was it not torture enough to live in the literal shadow of Maya Kaluantharana's four-story McMansion? Now she had to contemplate her presence at college?

One problem with Maya was that she was impossible to hate. She was not just beautiful and gifted, but exceedingly nice. She was also obscenely wealthy—the house her parents built when they demolished the rambler that had stood on the lot for fifty years was so enormous that it sucked up all of the afternoon sunlight on the two adjoining lots. It was also out of proportion to the other houses in the modest neighborhood, earning it the nickname "the hotel." The owner of the house behind the Kaluantharanas lodged a complaint with the neighborhood association claiming that her once lush sun garden had withered and died from lack of light, and that she had been forced to replant all of her perennials at a cost of more than $1,000.

What were AP Harry and Maya doing at Yates? Taylor had no idea what sort of grades Maya got, but she assumed she was a genius—all of the Indian kids at the school were brilliant, from what she could tell. Anyway, Maya's grades were beside the point, given that she was a star of the swim team who had tied the state record in the butterfly relay or something like that. Taylor wondered if Yates even had a swim team.

Living beside Maya presented a daily psychic challenge: Taylor had to walk to and from school each day watching her neighbor prance ahead like some long-legged woodland creature. Maya scaled the steep hill that led from their subdivision to the school three blocks away without pausing to catch her breath. Then, just last year, AP Harry began appearing with Maya as she made her way home. His friendly advances were almost certainly uninvited, but nevertheless there he was by her side, like a boy suitor in a 1950s sitcom. This meant Taylor had to either walk slowly or take a detour to avoid running into them. The whole situation had become so depressing that Taylor had recently begun to race home at the sound of the first bell, arriving on their street before the other two had even gone to their lockers to collect their books. Because the county used the same set of buses to transport all the kids in each cluster, the start and close of each school day was staggered accordingly. High school, which began at the ungodly hour of 7:15, ended half an hour before middle school, and an hour before elementary school, so there was a brief period when the neighborhood was almost completely quiet, where apart from the occasional dog walker or stay-at-home mother pushing a stroller, the place practically belonged to Taylor, if she got home fast enough.

Still, there was nothing all that intriguing to do in this staid landscape. It wasn't like she was going to vandalize cars or steal anyone's garden ornaments, even if it was tempting to do something that might discourage one neighbor's regular rotation of brightly colored and seasonally appropriate flags. But it did occur to her that if she were so inclined, she might do a bit of snooping. She could take a quick, innocent peek at the contents of her neighbors' mailboxes, for example.

She never meant to actually *take* any of their mail; it just sort of happened one day when she climbed the steps to AP Harry's front porch and squeezed behind a green Adirondack chair to reach the mailbox, where she found a flier intended for Harry's mother. It was just an invitation to a science fair, and she only snatched it as an experiment. She had taken little things before and had felt this same compulsion that horrible summer at camp, but those were items she had only meant to borrow, like T-shirts, soaps, and in one case, gold hoop earrings. She had fully intended to put everything back, but then some nosy girl staged a stakeout and had Taylor sent home. She hadn't borrowed anything since, even if she thought about it often.

The sensation of reaching into Harry's mailbox proved strangely pleasurable; it gave her a bit of a rush, as well as an odd sense of relief, at least for a while. Over time her little reconnaissance missions began to increase in boldness. An unintended consequence of her snooping was that she began to learn a thing or two about her neighbors—what doctors they had recently visited, what brand of car insurance they subscribed to, and from the time she swiped a UPS package from Maya's front porch, what Speedo size she wore. Taylor had meant to seal the box and put it back again, but then she lost her nerve. Now she sometimes donned the one-piece purple racing back and stood in front of the mirror in her bathroom, pretending she was perched at the edge of a pool, waiting for the referee to blow his whistle. She could pretend that she was Maya Kaluantharana, 5 feet 7 inches, 110 pounds, living in a house with a three-car garage and a heated swimming pool, an exotic-looking mother, and a locally renowned plastic surgeon father. The game made her feel good for a few minutes, but the suit was too tight and the elastic cut into her flesh, leaving red marks after she took it off.

Each night she vowed to stop the business with the mail, but then the afternoon would roll around and she'd find she couldn't help herself. Plus, she was beginning to feel a personal connection to her neighbors that gave her a sense of camaraderie with people she had never even met. She knew who subscribed to which magazines, who was partial to certain furniture catalogues, who needed to renew their vehicle registration. She meant no harm, and reasoned that nothing that important ever arrived in the regular mail anymore, anyway.

MAYA SEEMED to finally notice Taylor and AP Harry standing together, and she waved and smiled.

"Hey, guys! What a coincidence!" she said cheerfully as she approached.

Harry looked slightly flustered. Maya wore a short corduroy skirt that showed off her athletic legs and brightly colored sneakers that looked like soccer cleats. Her sweatshirt said CORNELL.

"I really love this place," Maya enthused. "Mr. Joyce said they have a great English Department. Did you know Fritz Heimler is on the faculty?"

Actually, Taylor did know that Fritz Heimler taught at Yates—she had been impressed by this herself. Heimler was a Pulitzer Prize–winning poet, and their English teacher, Mr. Joyce, had read aloud some of his heavy, dark poems, full of symbolism about death, the apocalypse, and sheep.

"I wouldn't know," said AP Harry. "We only stopped here because we are on our way to Harvard. My mom wanted to break up the trip, and it seemed like a good place to stop."

Taylor studied Maya's face for some reaction to Harry's obnoxious comment, but her expression was inscrutable. "I've heard great things about the school," she replied instead. "The student-teacher ratio is supposed to be one of the best at any liberal arts school in the country. Mr. Joyce said I would like it here," she added.

Half of the girls at Verona High School were in love with Mr. Joyce, and Maya was evidently among them, Taylor deduced from the fact that she had dropped his name twice in the space of a minute-long conversation. This was a largely meaningless revelation, but it made Taylor bristle. It seemed to touch a nerve in AP Harry, as well.

"I'm here because I heard the bathrooms are nice," Taylor said, thinking this was the only possible response to Harry's Harvard pronouncement. As if Yates was not completely out of the way, no matter how you mapped the route from Washington to Cambridge!

"You are so funny, Taylor!" Maya quipped. "Doesn't she have the greatest sense of humor, Harry?"

Harry nodded, but Taylor was skeptical. She'd known Harry for sixteen years and had never seen evidence that he knew what humor was, beyond the definition in the dictionary, which she'd bet he could recite, word for word.

May

AFTER A DASH TO the campus coffee bar for a midday jolt of caffeine, Olivia returned to her cramped, paper-strewn office to find a cheap bouquet of flowers wilting on her desk.

She was restless now that the seasonal admissions crunch was over and felt something like spring fever taking hold despite the chill that still hung in the air. The last of the snow was melting following a freak late-April storm, and the sky was a brilliant blue. The tulips had finally begun a shy, late bloom; she thought on her way home she might even snip a few, if no one was looking.

Contemplating the sad bouquet before her, she briefly indulged in the fantasy that she had a secret admirer—she and Fritz Heimler had enjoyed a flirtatious, tipsy exchange at a poetry salon a week earlier, where he read from his celebrated if dusty collection, *Nuclear Summer*, in an effort to extract money from some deep-pocketed, literary-minded alumni. But he was far too bohemian for her taste, as possibly evidenced by this shabby floral arrangement, and he smelled slightly odd, like he had a bunch of mothballs tucked in his beard. Or maybe Ari Horvitz, Yates's vice president for Institutional Advancement, had finally come to his senses and was ready to return to her for good, leaving his wife and their ridiculous number of children behind.

This particular floral arrangement consisted of a dozen red carnations with a spray of baby's breath in an oblong vase. Olivia began opening the envelope slowly, savoring every last second of possibility, until a knock at the door broke the spell.

"There were some calls for you, ma'am," reported a frightened-looking student intern, handing her a thick stack of telephone messages before making a quick retreat. Olivia was known to snap at support staff, and she was aware that almost everyone who worked in the admissions office was afraid of her. Seconds later another intern appeared, wrestling an enormous Balloongram that she had trouble squeezing through the door.

Olivia's mood plummeted as she read the card. She had no secret admirer, and apart from the visits he routinely paid her late at night, Ari probably only thought of her when he stopped by her office to register admissions-related complaints. It was just that time of year again, and the fact that the gifts were still trickling in a month after rejection letters had been mailed indicated that this spring was in line to become the most floral yet.

The sender of the carnations identified herself as Brittany Henderson from Orlando, Florida. She wrote in purple ink, in a loopy cursive. As she read, Olivia began twisting the string of pearls around her neck.

Yeats remains my first choice school. Please give my application a second glance, a second chance.
"I sought a theme and sought for it in vain, I sought it daily for six weeks or so . . ."

Olivia took the vase and set it on the least cluttered corner of her desk, then stared at it for a moment, scowled, and placed it in the trash. She jotted down the name Brittany Henderson on a Post-it note, and crumpled the card from Yates Florist. It took her a moment of reflection before she remembered why the name rang a bell. Refusing to admit this girl had been Olivia's most recent flirtation with career suicide. Brittany Henderson was the granddaughter of a major donor, a contributor at such an elite level that the development office not only electronically flagged her file for automatic admission, but sent a secretary from upstairs to personally affix a note to her application that said "AH/yes." Which was to say that Ari Horvitz did not want to hear about her atrocious grades, her low SATs, or her one-year stint in juvenile detention. He just wanted the girl admitted.

Olivia had been put temporarily in charge of the admissions office when her immediate boss, Ray Salazar, called in sick one day in early December and never came back. Rumors ran the gamut from Ray's being squeezed out for political reasons by the new college president, to his possibly having a fatal illness. The official reason was posted as "family emergency," two words that were always surrounded with air quotes when spoken aloud.

As long as Olivia was sort of the boss, she felt she could use her discretionary powers to reject anyone named Brittany from Orlando, Florida, for reasons she considered entirely self-evident and did not feel compelled to justify. But more to the point, Brittany had misspelled the name of the college and erroneously assumed there was some connection between Yates University and the Irish poet W. B. Yeats. The Yeats mistake was a perennial. Every year, along with a handful of essays about how Mahatma Gandhi was the single greatest inspiration in these kids' lives, or how the historical figure with whom they most closely identified was Harry Potter, there were at least three essays about how W. B. Yeats was their favorite poet. Then, like Ms. Brittany Henderson, they would pluck a completely random and invariably irrelevant couplet from the *Collected Poems*, which they had probably copied into a notebook while drinking lattes with their friends at some bookstore café, and consider themselves clever.

Olivia didn't feel unduly worried about the Brittanys of the world. If the system of capitalism ensured there would always be social divisions, college admissions guaranteed pretty much the same. There was a place for the Brittanys, who could surely muddle their way into state or community colleges and wind up in the sorts of jobs for which they were probably best suited.

The fact that this particular Brittany was still lobbying in May for the chance to attend this tiny, unremarkable college was surely another red flag, a sign that she had probably been rejected from every place she had

applied to and was now completely desperate, showering half-dead carnations on admissions officers across the nation.

Even in her cynical, calcified heart, Olivia did feel bad for some of
these kids, who had every reason to be stunned by the receipt of slim envelopes the previous month, informing them of either an outright rejection or a spot on the wait list. Yates had fielded an unprecedented crush
of applicants this year, many of them surprisingly, even shockingly, overqualified. Two years earlier, Yates had won a spot on the influential *U.S.
News & World Report* annual list of the top fifty liberal arts colleges. Applications the next fall increased by 50 percent, overwhelming the small
admissions staff and elevating the profile of Yates incoming freshmen
overnight.

Olivia learned from her ex-husband's cousin, whose son's fiancée was
an editor at *U.S. News*, that a series of inputting errors coupled with a
software glitch had landed Yates on the magazine's list. By the time the
mistake was discovered, the issue had already gone to print. A small college in the foothills of Tennessee was relegated to the second tier as a
result of the mistake; their president hired an outside statistician and
presented its findings to the *U.S. News* legal counsel, threatening to sue.
The aggrieved college was eventually pacified with the promise of special
mention in a forthcoming article and inclusion on an as yet undeter-
mined specialty list the next year—"undiscovered gems" perhaps, or "ten
hot schools."

Olivia attended three separate champagne toasts with Basil Dickerson, Yates's president of two years, to celebrate this achievement. A Yates
alum, class of 1977, Basil had served as an executive vice president at
Enron, overseeing the trading of charity futures. It seemed a good time
to transition to a new career, he said; he left unscathed just before the
place imploded. He then moved to Vermont, where he began raising
money for political campaigns. The board of trustees decided that his
impressive networking and rainmaking skills outweighed any possible
stigma associated with Enron. Basil was inheriting a minor financial crisis: one of the school's most famous alums, a well-known analyst of tech
stock who for a while had a regular gig on CNBC, had convinced the
school's trustees to load up on Yahoo at $230 a share in December 1999,

which had resulted in an erosion of the school's endowment by 10 percent.

Yates then made the *U.S. News* list again, still holding steady at number 50, the apparent explanation being that once the school achieved some small measure of recognition, even if that had been in error, good things began to happen. Proud alumni opened their pocketbooks, colleagues at rival institutions became effusive in their praise, and more kids applied, which meant fewer could be accepted, and so the statistical profile of the incoming freshman class continued to improve.

Basil had just this week treated the entire admissions staff to a steak dinner at the nicest restaurant in town, Yates Steaks, to mark the occasion. This festival of self-congratulation made everyone in the office slightly uncomfortable—they all felt tainted by the *U.S. News* mistake—but no one argued with the free meal. More unsettling was the unspoken fact that Basil had originally decided to enter the world of academia and deflect attention from his former place of employment by making a name for himself as a renegade, railing against the ranking system as a corrupting influence in the world of higher education, one that forced a small school like Yates to put marketing concerns ahead of educational values. He had already published op-ed pieces in both *The Wall Street Journal* and *The New York Times* to this effect. But now, like a relapsed gambler, his attempts to boost Yates to number 49 had a frightening, manic edge.

In her initial briefing when she was informed of Ray's leave, Basil let her know that priorities had changed.

"The trick, Olivia, is to feign indifference to the rankings while at the same time being enormously attentive," he'd said, leaning back in his black leather desk chair and mauling a pen with his molars.

The mandate that trickled down to the admissions office was relatively straightforward: Pump up the numbers. SAT scores and class rank both factored into the rankings, and these figures were not that difficult to boost, especially with the help of a little merit scholarship money thrown the right way. Ray, before his disappearance, had always emphasized looking at the complete picture, and under his steady, ethical command, money was reserved for the needy.

She couldn't quite believe what she was hearing, but in a way, Olivia was privately encouraged. She'd been waging her own private campaign over the years to revamp Yates, although her concern had less to do with rank than image. The whole place was a bit too crunchy for her taste; people were always bragging about their fuel-efficient cars, for example, when this seemed one of the few places in the country a person could actually justify driving an SUV. And the faculty seemed consumed by esoteric concerns. Just before Basil had come on board, for example, a committee vetoed plans to ask Donald Trump to speak at graduation, opting instead to hear some dullard head of a Washington think tank bloviate about global warming. People at Yates tended to dress badly, too, showing up at school functions in ratty blue jeans and sporting earthy, ugly sandals that made them look like trolls. Despite ten years in this fashion-challenged environment, Olivia had not surrendered, continuing to show up for work each day in a suit and heels, as well as her beloved string of freshwater pearls, a present from her parents for her sixteenth birthday, before they'd shut her out.

One admissions officer had recently spent a long session with a calculator and determined that if he tallied the numerical profiles of Yates's new crop of freshmen, they ranked in the top 15 percent of students nationally. This was a huge leap from the first year Olivia had been on staff, when pretty much anyone who could manage to get the right postage on the envelope had a reasonably good shot at getting in. In truth, however, Olivia had come to the conclusion there was very little difference between the previous batch of Yates students and these supposedly new, improved kids, with the rare exception of the off-the-charts brilliant kid, or the exceptionally stupid kid who misspelled the name of the college.

In this new competitive atmosphere, if there was any hope of persuading Olivia Sheraton to reconsider an application, it had to come in the form of a serious achievement—or at least something more amusing than whatever Yates Florist was likely to have in stock. Straight A's the first semester of senior year might catch her eye if accompanied by a phone call from an influential guidance counselor—preferably at a fancy private school, so long as it wasn't the one recently in the news for doctoring transcripts—or maybe something along the lines of the publication of a novel, or the production of a film. Having grown up on a horse farm in Middleburg, Virginia, she had an irrepressible soft spot for equestrians, but no application to cross her desk had ever mentioned riding skills. She made a secret pledge to herself that she would lobby to admit the first student to write an essay about a horse regardless of the applicant's other merits, notwithstanding Yates's deplorably low minority enrollment figures, unlikely to be corrected by such a strategy.

All of this was largely irrelevant, because this year, nothing short of a miracle was going to get a kid off the wait list. They had already accepted five hundred more students than there were spaces, working on the assumption that a significant number of them would decline Yates's offer. A final tally would be available at the end of the week; postal delivery was notoriously slow in Yates, and a few deposit checks were still trickling in. But early indications were that the incoming freshman class was already over capacity by 20 percent. One explanation for the surprising rate of subscription was simply an all-around increasingly competitive environment, but another factor was that some especially cute boy on a popular MTV reality show was evidently a freshman at Yates.

Forecasting acceptances had always been a rough science at best, and the recent trend among students to hedge their bets by applying to more schools was only further complicating efforts to estimate yield. Olivia had heard of cases of kids who sent off more than two dozen applications. Not surprisingly, the fact that more kids were applying to more schools had the effect of making it harder for everyone to get in, ramping up the general climate of hysteria.

Olivia's miscalculations were almost certainly going to result in a housing crunch. Urban campuses had alternatives: they could kick upperclassmen out of dorms, encouraging them to find off-campus lodging, or they could rent nearby apartment buildings or even lease wings of hotels, but at Yates, options were severely limited. They could turn single rooms into doubles and doubles into triples, but after that, there was not much else to do but pitch tents in the woods.

They desperately needed to build new dorms as well as renovate several of the older buildings, one of which had failed a recent fire safety inspection. Basil agreed this was a priority, yet he seemed much more focused on seeking financing for a huge new student services center with a state-of-the-art fitness center and a twenty-four-hour food court with an impressive range of gourmet options.

Each May, after the admissions process was largely completed and the class selection for the following year was finalized, Olivia vowed she would leave. The lead-up to decisions was always grueling and vaguely depressing: two months were spent in virtual isolation in her drafty house, reading applications while drinking endless cups of tea. Apart from Ari's brief visits this winter, her only reliable companions were the mice that constructed a small metropolis behind her stove; she was forced to make peace with them when a blizzard dumped so much snow on Yates that she was unable to leave her house for four days to buy glue traps or poison. By the time the plows reached her street, she had diagnosed herself with a late-in-life onset of adult attention deficit disorder. After reading three hundred college applications without a break, she found the words blurring on the page. No matter how hard she tried, she could not keep track of these applicants, who all sounded the same. She tried to keep herself engaged by digging into her stash of office supplies—different-shaped Post-it notes and brightly colored pens—but they failed to amuse. Her symptoms were punctuated by apathy so deep that it had begun to veer toward rage. For the love of God, couldn't a single one of these kids write a lively essay? It was in this frame of mind that she had moved Brittany's application, with its missive about the plight of homeless people, which the girl evidently thought was bad (among other things, they sullied communities and brought down real estate prices) to the reject pile. She was fully aware that it would come back to haunt her.

Once March rolled around and she was forced to attend endless meetings with some of her insufferable, idealistic colleagues to finalize decisions, however, she began to long for the isolation of her freezing little house. She knew she cared too little, but she could not understand how some of her fellow admissions officers cared so much.

All of her colleagues in admissions were very young. Some of them were fresh out of college themselves, and clearly better temperamentally suited for the job than she was. The most recent recruit, a young man named Gavin, actually *volunteered* to answer the phones and lead information sessions, tasks normally assigned on a rotating basis that the rest of the staff maneuvered to avoid.

By now she had been at Yates so long, she feared she was going to take root in the bottom floor of the admissions building, then just wither and die. She pictured herself a corpse at the desk, a pen in her hand and her ear to the phone, legs crossed, high heels dangling from her swivel chair. She had just celebrated her thirty-ninth birthday, and she felt pale and brittle from the long, cold winters. Each morning she detected an additional strand of gray, but was afraid to hand herself over to the only colorist in Yates for fear of winding up looking like an actual resident of the run-down clay-mining town, hair permed to the texture of a Brillo pad, then streaked in awkward brassy chunks.

The first time Olivia visited the Yates campus, she'd thought of the Jack Nicholson horror movie *The Shining*. The unpaved road leading from the main gate to the first sign of life was two miles long. There were occasional wild animals sighted in the woods, and once she glanced outside her office window and locked eyes with a moose.

She was willing to wager that this was one of the least idyllic spots on earth. The long, dark winters were one part of the problem; the remote, depressed, and nearly abandoned ghost town of Yates, another. Back when Jeremiah Wheeling wrote the charter for Yates in 1840, the school was intended primarily as an art college, with a specialty in pottery. The town of Yates had once been rich in clay; hence the attraction for potters. Only twenty or so years ago, before the clay reserves had dried up, Yates had been a summer retreat for New York artists, she'd been told.

Olivia couldn't have cared less about pottery, never mind clay, and even though the reserves were long gone, there was still the occasional Yates resident who insisted on droning on about it: it had been popular as a mid-fire hydrous alumino-silicate earth, rich in alkalites and irons, the head of the Art Department told her on her first visit, as Olivia had stared at his potting wheel, wondering if it was possible to sit on it and spin oneself to death.

Over the years the school had expanded its offerings, but it still had a strong bent toward the arts. Written into the bylaws was the requirement that each student take a pottery class before graduating. This had been the subject of debate for years. Olivia was in the anti–pottery class camp, insisting that it alienated a certain sort of student, precisely the kind Yates needed to attract if it was going to move in a new direction. But even the few people on campus who shared Olivia's worldview were not in full agreement. Many thought the pottery requirement lent the school a certain eccentric charm. If Columbia University still had a swimming requirement, why couldn't Yates ask students to spend a few weeks playing with clay?

Olivia's sister-in-law, Nadine, had finagled this job for her as an associate admissions officer. No particular experience was required, she had said. They were just looking for a fresh pair of eyes, for a well-rounded "youngish" person with a few years of real-world experience under her belt. Olivia feigned enthusiasm, but by the time Nadine called with this offer, she could not really pass herself off as well-rounded so much as completely flat. Within the space of just two weeks, she had finalized her divorce and received rejection letters from the only three law schools to which she had applied on the grounds that there were only three schools worth going to. She had made this same mistake seven years earlier, receiving the identical batch of rejections, her mother unhelpfully admonishing her about how it was a sign of insanity to repeat the same mistake twice, expecting a different result.

Interactions with her parents had been chilly for years; she still saw them when they visited Nadine and Ben, Olivia's brother, to drool over the grandchildren, but charitable gifts had long ago stopped flowing in her direction. Olivia thought being frozen out of the family was a bit harsh; she hadn't killed anyone or broken any laws—all she had done was marry her father's best friend! And anyway, not only had they been divorced for ten years, but now he was dead.

Besides, in a sense, her parents had helped facilitate the mess. After college, after that first round of law school rejections, her father called his friend and former law partner to ask whether he could use an extra pair of hands. Evidently he could, in more ways than one, and he and Olivia were married within a year, a thirty-five-year age gap and the preexisting condition of his wife and daughter, notwithstanding. Things soured within the first few months: Preston turned out to be a control freak; plus, Olivia quickly discovered him philandering. Still, they went through the motions for six more years and did enjoy the occasional special moment: they regularly went to the races, for example, where he always grew aroused, remarking that her thick dark hair and toothy smile reminded him of his favorite childhood horse. Olivia had never been sure if this was a compliment, but she had heard such comparisons before and wondered if she'd taken on a certain equine air as a result of growing up around the animals.

Daughter Amy was seventeen when they divorced, by which time she had dropped out of high school and taken up residence in a fancy clinic for girls with eating disorders. She had a breakthrough in group therapy one day: Olivia, by virtue of being an emotionally cold and unusually thin stepmother, was the reason Amy was breaking down. She evidently received a standing ovation and some sort of plaque for this epiphany. Amy shared this insight each time she saw Olivia, which was the closest the two women ever came to bonding.

Olivia truly felt awful about the whole thing. She had been young and naive, she said—only twenty-two at the time!—but no one had much sympathy. Two years earlier, at Preston's funeral, Olivia tried once again to reach out to Amy. She was now a married woman with two small children, and she looked settled and content. But when Olivia extended condolences and a heartfelt apology, Amy spit in her face.

Olivia remained grateful to Nadine for helping to arrange this completely random job. Moving very far away had been the right solution at the time, although she'd never meant to stay. Being an admissions officer was definitely not her life's calling; plus, living in such close proximity to her more domestically successful sibling forced her to constantly suffer the spectacle of his happy family life. Nadine and Benjamin married shortly after Olivia divorced, and everything about their lives was appallingly idyllic. Benjamin was chairman of the English Department at a prestigious college in Vermont, and they had settled in a town halfway between the two schools, where they bought a charming refurbished Victorian with a swing on the front porch. They had two cute kids and a slobbering golden retriever who had destroyed at least three pairs of Olivia's shoes.

Observing her sister-in-law, Olivia had to admit that all of her snotty thoughts about the school and the town aside, the quality of education available at Yates was probably just as good as the one she had received some twenty years ago, at Barnard. Yates had always lured great faculty, in part because of all of the other highly regarded schools in the region, and they were able to hire some of the professors who were denied tenure at these other institutions. Inevitably, many fine teachers were let go, such as her sister-in-law had been, for the simple reason that the number of overqualified faculty was rivaled only by the number of overqualified students applying to these schools, many of whom aspired to one day be faculty themselves.

Olivia initially worried that the appearance of nepotism might bar her employment, but Nadine assured her that having a family connection was definitely not a problem. The more she came to learn about Jeremiah Wheeling and his intimate family relations, the more she understood how nepotism might be a part of Yates's tradition. The legend was that Wheeling had fathered a child with his own daughter and had later died in mysterious circumstances. His body was found behind where the freshman dorm now sat, and while the cause of death was never determined, one of his hands was missing and there were unsubstantiated rumors he'd been tied to a tree. To add to the ghoulishness, Wheeling had left his mark all over campus in the form of these little stone creatures that cropped up everywhere you looked. Some of the statues had paws outstretched—friendly animal beckons, perhaps, but they were widely used as ashtrays. Nonsmokers were in the minority at Yates, both in the town and on the campus. Olivia wondered if news of the hazards of nicotine had somehow failed to reach these parts, or if things were just so dull around here that no one feared an early death.

OLIVIA WAS rooting around in her drawer for an object, a letter opener or her long-lost scissors, to slice through the many layers of tape that bound the balloons together. She found several tubes of half-empty lipstick in various shades of red, but nothing remotely sharp. She picked up the phone and ordered an intern to bring her a knife, a request that she knew would cause much giggling and speculation in the outer offices.

She was not really a balloon person, and she planned to give them away, or maybe release them in the lobby and hope that some colleagues would take them home to their kids. If it were left to her, she would simply pop each one and stick them all in the trash with the flowers, but she didn't want to add to her reputation as a generally sour sort of person. Oddly, the Balloongram had not come with any sort of card. She supposed if she were a more responsible admissions officer she would ask one of the students to follow up with the florist, or whoever sent Balloongrams— balloonists?—and find out who had placed the order. But in truth, she really didn't care.

When her office door swung open, she was about to bark at the intern for failing to knock, but instead she saw the smiling face of Basil Dickerson. Olivia could never decide if Basil seemed jolly all of the time simply because he was ruddy and pudgy, which lent him an air of being slightly drunk, even though she had never seen him consume a single drop of alcohol. She had actually conducted an amateur investigation into this subject recently, watching him hoist a glass of wine in his left hand as he worked the room at a welcome party for Arnold Hutch, the new head of the Environmental Engineering Department. Actually, Arnold Hutch—a much celebrated hire, a MacArthur Fellow snagged from Caltech for a salary reportedly in the mid six figures—*was* the Environmental Engineering Department, but given that at least 80 percent of the requirements just drawn up for the major overlapped with those of other departments, Yates was able to fudge things for a while. Basil had proposed multiple toasts, but he never took a sip.

"Congratulations again on a job well done," Basil said, moving a pile of folders to the floor and squeezing himself into the chair facing her desk. "Seems all I do at this job is eat," he remarked. "I've got a dinner scheduled just about every night for the next three months." He patted his bulging stomach for emphasis.

Olivia forced what she knew was a not very convincing smile. She didn't like surprise visits, even from the college president.

"I hear the acceptances are flooding in. You are literally breaking records!" He swept an arm to emphasize his enthusiasm, accidentally overturning a small stone horse on her desk, causing its hind legs to stick up in the air.

Olivia stared at the animal. She knew that she made Basil nervous, but did nothing to set him at ease. She also knew that he was almost certainly here for some reason other than to congratulate her, which made her wary of his compliments.

Basil leaned over and righted the horse. His eye caught on the flowers peeking up from the trash can.

"Would you like the flowers, Basil?" she asked. "Help yourself. Take them home."

"Lovely carnations," he remarked, but made no attempt to retrieve them. "I was just looking over the data and can't help but marvel at how spectacular the numbers are this year. Are these kids getting smarter, or are there just more of them?"

"More kids," Olivia remarked dryly. "Plus proportionally more insane parents. This equals smarter kids. On paper at least. In reality half of them need shrinks."

"Good one, Olivia. Anyway, if we keep steady on this track, who knows, in a year or two we'll be catching up with Amherst!"

Olivia faked a laugh. As if Yates was ever going to catch up with Amherst. Amherst had been the number 1 liberal arts school on and off for several years running. Basil's competitive streak seemed to know no bounds, which she supposed was not a bad trait in a college president. It was arguably a more productive attitude than the one held by the former president, who spent much of his twenty-five-year tenure writing mystery novels under a pseudonym while the campus withered under his apathetic rule.

Over Basil's shoulder Olivia saw Ari walk past her office, pausing beside *Yashequana Woman* to talk to two female students. A rush of adrenaline caused her to sit up straight in her chair. It seemed every time Olivia glimpsed him he was in the presence of curvy young coeds, but then, this was a college campus, so admittedly, they were hard to avoid. He had a seductive Israeli accent that Olivia knew she was not alone in finding irresistible. They had been together for four years and were talk-

ing about marriage when seemingly out of the blue he decided to reconcile with his wife. Olivia had been devastated. Was she destined to a lifetime of law school rejections and doomed relations with married men?
How could she be quite so unlucky? she wondered.

Ari came to Yates just a few weeks after Olivia arrived, and they met
when they were randomly seated next to each other at an uneven campus
production of the 1940s musical *Brigadoon*. Ari proposed a drink at the
Yates Pub after the play ended, and they'd never looked back. Olivia
imagined he'd been as swept away as she by the romantic idea that Yates
was their very own Brigadoon, an enchanted village in the Scottish high-
lands mist, but when she'd brought this up once, he said he'd fallen
asleep during the first act of the play and had no idea what she was talking about.

Still, it had seemed the real thing. She and Ari even looked alike, both
dark-haired and small-boned, and she mused that their children would
be perfect clones. She never told Ari, but she'd taken the radical step of
driving an hour and a half to the nearest synagogue to talk to the rabbi
about conversion. Only one week after she'd thumbed through the Old
Testament thinking this seemed a not unreasonable religion, there came
blond, buxom Belle, Olivia's—and Ari's—opposite in every way. Like a
British memsahib arriving at a summer hill station in India trailed by
teams of luggage-bearing elephants, Belle returned to Yates with a big
moving van and three children, and she and Ari immediately began to re-
sume reproducing. With at least two pairs of twins in the mix, there were
now too many small Horvitzes in the world to count, and no greater in-
sult than to have her lover return to the wife he'd spent four years complaining about. Ari insisted that he still loved Olivia, but family was
family and he simply had to do the right thing.

"LISTEN, OLIVIA, . . . I've got a couple of things to talk to you about," Basil
said, but she was still focused on the scene outside her office. She saw
Ari jot something down on the back of a business card and hand it to one
of the girls. He was wearing jeans and a tweed blazer with patches on the
elbow that looked right out of central casting. He had not always dressed
this way. He'd worked as a bond trader for five years before coming to

Yates, and when she'd first laid eyes on him, he was wearing an elegant, pin-striped suit, which had perhaps been part of the initial attraction.

"The first thing is about Ray," Basil said. He sat up stiffly in his chair before continuing. "I'm afraid he's asked to extend his leave. He's not well . . ."

"Not well?" Olivia asked worriedly. She had always liked Ray, even if she hadn't treated him as respectfully as she might have.

"Privately, Olivia, and this is just between us"—he paused, seeming to search for the right words—"he's had some sort of breakdown . . . His wife checked him into a private clinic in Connecticut. The stress of the job got to him, I suppose. I don't have a lot of details, other than that his wife said they were trying some experimental therapies . . ."

"Experimental therapies?" she asked, her voice pitching higher. "What, like shock treatment?"

"I honestly don't know. It didn't seem like the right thing to ask. Obviously, we are all hoping for his speedy recovery, but in the meantime, Olivia, you've been doing a great job filling in. We'd like you to become interim dean while we sort this out. We can't begin an actual search until we know Ray's status. And if we do begin a search for a replacement, of course we hope you will toss your name into the ring. But anyway, for now we are hoping you will stick around . . ."

"Of course," Olivia said uncertainly, trying to absorb the many implications of this news. For one thing, who was "we"? Plus, her brain seized on the word *interim*. She wasn't sure if she was just being paranoid, but it seemed that *interim* suggested she was definitely only filling in a gap rather than possibly bridging one toward a new future, as might be implied by the words *acting dean*. She pulled on her pearls and glanced out the window into the hallway again. Ari was gone.

"Terrific," Basil said. "I don't have time right now, but obviously we'll need to sit down and talk this through. Probably Ari should be there, too, so let's line up our calendars. Maybe we can start with a lunch this week. Of course you've already been filling in, so it ought to be a smooth transition."

Olivia nodded, already contemplating the awkward lunch.

"Anyway, let's not dwell on this. We'll just carry on, business as usual.

There's just one more thing, Olivia," he added, looking suddenly uncomfortable. "I had a phone call this morning. It has to do with the wait list. An alum. Big donor to the school. Granddaughter did not get accepted. Clearly there was a mistake—she'd already been cleared for admission by Development. I spoke to Ray about this months ago before he . . ." His voice trailed off as he searched for the appropriate word, to no avail. "Hate this sort of thing, Olivia . . . bend over backwards to stay out of this . . . have to make an exception. I personally promised him we'd fix this ASAP . . . whole thing makes me queasy. Anyway, if you don't mind, have someone call this girl this afternoon and tell her a mistake has been made."

"Letters were mailed a month ago. Why is this just coming up now?"

Basil shrugged. "I can only imagine that she's exhausted all other options," he said matter-of-factly. He slipped a piece of paper into Olivia's hand and rose from the chair. Olivia thought it amusing that he found it less distasteful to pull a favor this way, in sentence fragments accompanied by a passed note, rather than speaking the name aloud. Olivia didn't bother to look at the note. They both knew who he was talking about.

"Just so you know, Basil, the girl couldn't even spell *Yates* correctly." Her eyes darted guiltily toward the trash can.

"F. Scott Fitzgerald couldn't spell, either," Basil said.

Olivia started to say something about how F. Scott Fitzgerald hadn't done time in juvie before entering college, but then she stopped herself, uncertain if this was true. Anyway, the conversation was pointless. Brittany would be moving into a Yates dormitory in the fall even if she was discovered torching homeless people over the summer.

"What are you doing in August?" Basil asked.

"Haven't thought that far ahead. Why?"

"Come to my house in Vermont," he said. "I'm having a small gathering. Some of the trustees will be there. I'll get my assistant to e-mail you the details."

Vermont! She was not a big fan of the state. Too much land, too many cows, and the whole place was even "greener" than this patch of upstate New York, probably full of ticks, too. Nor was the idea of spending any portion of her vacation time with a bunch of Yates trustees especially appealing. Not that she had any real choice as interim dean but to accept the offer.

"Thanks, Basil. That sounds lovely."

He had barely left the office when the admissions secretary came in. "Olivia, Ari Horvitz is on the phone. He said it's urgent. He needs to talk about a girl named Brittany."

"Oh, for goodness' sake . . . Tell him to get a grip. Tell him she can come to Yates and he can continue to collect his so-called *donations* from her grandfather," said Olivia. "And close the door on your way out."

The secretary tried, but she got tangled in the mess of ribbon streaming from the balloons and accidentally popped one loudly when it got caught in the door.

June

MAYA TRIED TO STAY focused, or at least appear to be engaged, as the admissions officer catalogued the good times to be had as an undergraduate student at MIT. It seemed to her the woman was going a bit overboard in the number of superlatives she used to describe the campus social life, but this was of no real concern to Maya. She had no intention of applying, and since her sister, Neela, was an MIT senior, she already knew quite a lot about the school, possibly even more than this young representative, who confessed that she had just graduated from Brandeis and was new to the job. Maya was only at this meeting to appease her parents, who seemed to be in denial about the fact that both her grades and scores were tragically below the MIT threshold.

A glance at the clock confirmed that it was getting late, and she hoped to make it back to English class before the final bell rang. She had just begun to fidget with her hair when she heard a strange buzzing noise. She looked around worriedly for a bee and saw AP Harry flinch, as well.

Justin Smelling, whose chief distinction, apart from being off-the-charts brilliant, was that he was AP Harry's best friend, raised his hand and asked whether the oft-repeated tale about the student prank during Al Gore's 1996 commencement speech was really true. The very pretty MIT representative shook her head affirmatively. "I wasn't there to see it," she said, explaining that she would have still been in high school, "but

I heard it was really hilarious. Someone passed out bingo cards with certain buzzwords on them, and every time Gore said something like 'information superhighway' or 'knowledge worker,' you could mark the spot on the card."

"That is *so* funny," Justin said, laughing too loudly. "That is just about the funniest thing I've ever heard!" he added, holding his stomach, presumably to emphasize that the hilarity was giving him a bellyache. Justin's personality was a bit off, and Maya hoped the MIT woman wouldn't think he was representative of kids at their high school.

There was something so socially awkward about the group assembled in the school library this afternoon that Maya found it difficult to believe the admissions officer's claims of fun. She had heard there were wild fraternity parties and that students had a reputation for heavy drinking, but her sister never talked about normal college things like roommates, boyfriends, or cafeteria food. Neela's voice did switch an octave, however, when she referred to weekends spent either in the lab or the library. The most animated she had ever heard Neela was when she called to report she had been selected as the research assistant to a renowned neuroscientist who had possibly discovered a way to boost brainpower via a tiny molecular change in the brain chemistry where long-term memories are stored.

Surveying her peers, among them the reclusive and somewhat paranoid Gail Fiora, a not unattractive girl behind half-an-inch-thick plastic eyeglasses who always sat alone at lunch playing chess on her laptop, and the inseparable, wild-toothed Bradley twins, who had memorized the school telephone directory as well as all Amtrak train routes and would randomly inform you what time the *California Zephyr* was due to arrive in, say, Omaha, Maya was reminded of a controversial article that had appeared in *Wired* magazine a few years earlier and had caused a local stir. The author posited the theory that high incidences of autism and other related behavioral disorders could be traced to the new mating patterns of brilliant social misfits, many of them tech nerds, researchers, and academics who, under previous societal conditions, would have been too introverted to ever marry or breed. The Verona community was implicated because of its proximity to the National Institutes of Health, which supposedly attracted a disproportionate number of extremely smart people to the area, a suspicion somewhat confirmed by another article, elsewhere, that cited the suburban enclave as being the best-educated U.S. city of its size. The problem, apparently, was that the more bumbling of these brainy men met equally bumbling brainy women in the warm petri dish that was Verona, and they managed to reproduce. The result was the occasional offspring that might have caused Darwin to rethink.

Maya had considered this theory—oft recounted in the school newspaper—so mean as to be perverse, even possibly libelous. Yet looking around at these MIT wannabes, she couldn't help but wonder if it contained perhaps the tiniest grain of truth. Or maybe it was just that Justin Smelling's mother was so weird that she tainted the rest of the assembled crowd by association. She was a local pediatrician who was forever offering unsolicited diagnoses at school sports events, running onto the field to help whenever a player went down, and usurping the coach's authority by ordering players with questionable sprains off the field. Dr. Smelling had a dark moustache that Maya thought could have easily been fixed with bleach or wax, and today she wore a horribly mismatched skirt and blouse, set off by scuffed white pumps. The problem with Justin Smelling's mother this afternoon was not one of personal presentation, however, but was specific to her inappropriate physical presence in the school library. Maya had sat through about ten of these in-school information sessions with visiting admissions officers and had never once seen a parent attend. But Dr. Smelling had evidently graduated from MIT herself, and her attachment to the place was so fierce that she greeted the admissions representative with a hug, even though they had never met before.

Maya heard the weird buzzing sound again and looked around anxiously. It would have to be a rather large insect to make that level of racket, she thought, cringing at the memory of the time she had been attacked by a swarm of angry bees when a baseball-bat-wielding kindergarten classmate knocked a hive out of a tree on the playground. Several bees had become trapped inside her shirt after somehow managing to enter through her baggy sleeve, leaving her with no choice but to strip in front of her peers, a recollection that was still scarring all these years later. A couple of other people also looked up at the fluorescent lights and toward the windows, failing to identify the source of the noise.

Jing Xiang, president of both the debate team and the Spanish Honors Society, seemed oblivious to the buzzing noise as he posed a question Maya did not entirely understand, but had something to do with the level of student access to the school's renowned grating fabrication technology. She had nothing but admiration for Jing, who was not only supersmart, but exceedingly nice, yet she had a vague suspicion that his professed interest in grating fabrication technology was not really genuine, and that he had worked to craft an obscure question in order to impress the MIT officer, who would presumably make a notation in her file folder about the brilliant young man with the lyrical name from Verona High. Instead, the young woman giggled and reminded them that she herself had not gone to MIT, but had been an English major at Brandeis, and that she didn't have any idea what he was talking about, but would happily contact the department head—once she figured out what department oversaw grating fabrication technology—and report back.

Maya looked again at the clock. If this session ended soon, which it might if people would stop asking questions, she would make it back to English class before the last bell rang. Usually, when these sessions wrapped up, a new round of competition began, as students jockeyed for the opportunity to make a personal impression on the visiting admissions officers. From what she had observed, the goal of this particular phase of the blood sport of admissions was to be the last man standing, the last body in the room alone with the rep. Maya wondered if this was really important, and whether it was better to make no impression at all, rather than a possibly bad one. In any event, she was too reserved to insert herself into the scrum.

She was always slightly stunned by the stupid questions posed by otherwise intelligent kids, as when students rattled off their scores and grades and then asked whether they had a shot at getting in. Didn't these people understand the game? The more kids that applied, the more kids the school could reject. Rejection was good for the school; it made the place appear more selective. But then, perhaps Maya only knew this because she was the youngest of four children and talk in her house had been of little else for nearly a decade.

Maya had pleaded with her mother the previous evening, saying that she couldn't afford to keep missing classes to attend these largely pointless sessions with visiting admissions officers. She had no interest in applying to a single one of the schools her parents had on the list they had painstakingly assembled for her, filling college guidebooks with annotated Post-it notes. She was already struggling to keep up with the end-of-year flood of schoolwork while attending exhausting swim practices. This morning she had to be in the pool by 5:00 a.m., which meant waking at 4:00; the coach had insisted she attend practice even though she could not swim in Saturday's meet because she was taking two SAT subject tests that morning, neither of which she'd had time to prepare for.

The head guidance counselor sent out a weekly e-mail to parents informing them of which colleges would be sending representatives to the school each day, and her mother regularly reminded her to attend. She had not actually visited with representatives of any of the schools she herself thought she might want to apply to, and the only campus she had toured that was on her own list was Yates, where her skeptical parents agreed to stop only because they were already in upstate New York after visiting Cornell.

Unlike most of her classmates, who seemed unable to talk about anything but college, grades, and test scores, Maya was not really that absorbed by the subject. Of course it was impossible to ignore, given that talk of college admissions dominated almost every conversation she had had with her peers since the previous fall when they took the PSATs, and the whispered comparisons of scores a few weeks later was only a harbinger of worse things to come. One friend on the swim team confided to Maya that she missed that morning's practice because she and three other girls—all freestyle swimmers—had spent four hours sitting on the floor in the basement of Barnes & Noble poring over college books the night before—and had become so engrossed they forgot to feed the meter and Verona's notoriously aggressive parking control officers had towed the car with their backpacks and swim kits inside. By the time they discovered the problem, it was too late to retrieve the vehicle until the next morning.

Intellectually, Maya understood what the fuss was all about, but she did not personally share the obsession about where she went to school. She planned to go to college as the next logical step after high school, and then she would do something else . . . get a job or go to graduate school, or maybe fall in love and start a family. Should she be tearing her hair out because—even though she had a transcript of mostly A's and B's—she was not in the top 10 percent of the class? Her parents seemed to think so. Her father reacted to her nonchalance about the future as if she planned to drop out of high school to mop the floors at Target. When she pointed out that she had a 3.7 grade point average, that she actually spent every minute that she was not in the pool studying, and that she had A's in nearly all her English and history classes, they just smiled pitifully at their youngest child. And yet their attitude was baffling, because at the same time that they were disappointed in her grades, they didn't seem willing to adjust their mindsets about her college options. Perhaps that was because everyone in her family, and extended family, and so far as Maya knew, every single person to have been born with the surname Kaluantharana, was an overachiever.

Maya's life thus far was marked by a sort of reverse discrimination that she was only just beginning to understand. But it also had its benefits: teachers who had known her siblings tended to give her the benefit of the doubt—the time she botched a relatively simple chemistry lab in which she was meant to observe soluble compounds change the boiling point of water, for example, the teacher simply assumed this was because she had taken the experiment to the next level of observing acetone instead of sodium chloride, and not because she had simply begun with the wrong numerical boiling point. The downside was that teachers frequently called on her to consult when they had trouble operating their overhead projectors, or when their printers got jammed. She had tried to pick up a bit of technological know-how over the years just to keep from disappointing them on these occasions.

"At least Maya is a looker," she once heard her mother gossip to her aunt on the telephone. "Maybe we should have sent her to supermodel school." Her father, in turn, was invested in the idea that her swimming prowess would get her in somewhere impressive, despite what he sometimes described to people as her learning disorders. But he always smiled lovingly when he said these sorts of things, like Maya was his favorite puppy even if she was having trouble being house-trained.

She knew that her parents only wanted the best for her. They sometimes tried to make her feel guilty by reminding her that they had come all the way from India to give their children opportunities they themselves had been denied, although the reality was that they met at the University of Chicago and were both from prominent, wealthy families. Maya's paternal grandfather, originally from Sri Lanka, emigrated to India and became the head of the largest steel company on the subcontinent, and her mother's family owned a chain of high-priced boutique hotels. Unlike some of her friends who spoke disrespectfully about their parents, however, Maya was a polite and dutiful daughter. She had been born in Cleveland and had never set foot in South Asia, yet she found certain aspects of American culture somewhat shameful, particularly this strain of disobedience she observed in some of her peers. Maya did as told, but she also practiced a bit of self-preservation by filtering her parents' remarks. It was a delicate balance, especially with the added challenge of living in the shadows of her gifted siblings. The sister currently at MIT, for example, had been accepted to every school to which she had applied and was then forced to make the excruciating decision about whether to attend MIT, Harvard, Yale, Stanford, or Reed. Neela actually gave her parents quite a scare by visiting Reed over her spring break senior year and professing to like it best, before ultimately coming around to MIT. Maya had never learned if there was something about Reed that had appealed to Neela, or if this was her sister's idea of a practical joke.

Maya envied her best friend, Pam Goldfarb, whose parents were delighted by everything she did. Even when Pam came in last place in a swim meet, her parents made a huge fuss, and when she did poorly on a test—a rare event—they told her not to worry about it. Of course it was easy for the Goldfarbs to be relatively low-key: Pam had a nearly perfect transcript and had also just been selected as the school newspaper's managing editor for the next academic year. She already knew that she wanted to go to Georgetown and planned to apply early. Given that both of her parents had gone there, she was almost certain to get in.

Whatever Maya's parents had in mind, one critical aspect of the college admissions game was out of her control. She was a horrible taker of standardized tests. Her math scores were not just disappointing, but alarmingly low. She was technically one of the few people eligible for the money-back guarantee from Kaplan Test Prep. Not only had her scores failed to improve, but her math score had actually gone *down* 50 points. Her mother railed at the course rep who had offered to send her a refund, claiming that she had never been so insulted in her life. As if the Kaluantharana family needed money! As if anyone in the Kaluantharana family might somehow be deficient in math! Clearly this new SAT test was poorly designed! While Maya wished her scores had been better, she was not unduly discouraged; she wanted to be a writer, notwithstanding the fact that her reading score was less than dazzling and her writing score, similarly low to begin with, had also plummeted 20 points after weeks spent crafting practice essays.

THE MIT representative fielded a question from Angie Lee about class rank—their high school didn't actually provide these numbers; it gave only percentile ranges, and since the competition was so intense, there was almost no way to distinguish among the top fifty or so students, all of whom had weighted GPAs of over 4.5. Angie wanted to be sure she wasn't at a disadvantage because of this, and wondered if there was any way to let MIT know that she was quite sure she would be the class valedictorian if her school awarded such distinctions. A couple of students eyeballed each other, possibly thinking *themselves* valedictorians. The MIT woman assured her she would not be penalized, that the admissions officers were familiar with the various high schools in their assigned regions and understood that some of the larger public high schools had abolished class rank.

"I have another question," Angie quickly interjected as Justin Smelling's mother began to speak. Angie was brilliant but lacked common sense and was reportedly such a bad driver that she had totaled her father's car the first day she had her license and had been in three more scrapes in the nine months since. "I wonder if you think it would be better to write an essay about cancer—like how my cousin's death last year has made me realize that I want to find the cure—or should I do something about growing up in a racially mixed family? Or should I write about the class rank problem, do you think?"

"Those all sound like great ideas," the MIT rep said, checking her watch. "Maybe you could combine all three."

Maya shared a brief sympathetic glance with Courtney Ruben, who from what she knew of her grades from the group labs they had done in chemistry, also had no prayer of getting into MIT. Then again, Courtney's mother was a famous former *Jeopardy!* contestant who had lasted seven weeks and earned about $100,000, so perhaps Maya was underestimating her potential.

This time, the strange buzzing sounded more like a small vibration. Maya wondered if this presaged not a wayward bee but an impending earthquake or some other form of biblical punishment for all of this self-absorption. She looked around and saw AP Harry sheepishly retrieve a cell phone from his briefcase, where it was vibrating noisily against the leather. He tried to be discreet as he glimpsed the screen, which lit up blue.

"Sorry," he mumbled, his face turning red.

The head of the school's guidance office, Mr. Roberts, inconveniently chose that very moment to stop by along with Louis Gonzales, the newly appointed county coordinator of Systemwide Continuous Improvement, who was auditing Verona for the week. Mr. Roberts looked hard at Harry, his eyes widening.

"I'm really, really sorry," Harry said again. "It's not what you think. It's this SAT service . . ."

Harry dug a deeper hole as he continued. "I accidentally subscribed to this service—it sends me a text-message question every day. There was a free trial period and now I really don't want it and I've tried to cancel it, but it just keeps coming. Anyway, it's supposed to come at 3, so there must be some mistake, 'cause it's an hour early today. I honestly don't know how to make it stop."

"You might try turning off your phone, for starters," Mr. Gonzales suggested, evidently on the lookout for improvement.

"While we're here," Mr. Roberts suggested, "perhaps you could share the question with us."

Harry tapped at his telephone keyboard for a moment and looked around nervously, as if this was some sort of trick. "Their ideal was to combine individual liberty with material equality, a goal that has not yet been realized and that may be as [*blank*] as transmutation of lead into gold."

Before Harry could continue, a small girl wearing orthodontic head-gear blurted out the answer: "A, *chimerical*."

Several pairs of eyes turned to her, confused. It was not just that Harry had not yet read the list of possible answers, but no one had ever seen her before. Mr. Roberts asked her what grade she was in.

"Oh, I go to Sparta," she explained, referring to the local middle school. "My mom wants me to go to MIT, and she thought it would be good if I get a head start in learning what classes I ought to take in high school and stuff. She called the guidance office, and they said it would be okay."

Maya considered this the interlude she had been waiting for. "I'm really sorry to run," she said, rising from her chair, "but I just need to stop by my English class before it ends to be sure I get the assignment."

"Me too," said AP Harry, grabbing his backpack. He ran to the door and held it open for Maya, who eyed him suspiciously. It was not like AP Harry to leave an information session early.

The MIT woman thanked them both for coming and sent them off with a thick wad of admissions propaganda which Maya was actually grateful to accept; she could hand it off to her mother as proof she had followed instructions.

MAYA BOUNDED into the classroom invigorated from sprinting up the three flights of stairs, even if her spirit had been somewhat sapped listening to AP Harry talk about how he preferred Harvard to MIT, and how he was struggling to get the footnotes properly formatted on his computer for the end-of-term English paper. He had chosen to write about female archetypes in *Beowulf*. The assignment was due next week, and Maya had not even finalized her topic. It had not previously occurred to her that one could squeeze an entire essay from this subject, given the dearth of women in the poem.

Maya handed Mr. Joyce the yellow slips that formally excused their late arrivals, but instead of locking eyes meaningfully with her, as he often did when they spoke about poetry after school, he stuck the passes on his desk and continued speaking. He was evidently mid-rant. It seemed the SAT question of the day had just landed in another student's text-message in-box and had caused that particular phone to not just vibrate but actually ring.

Mr. Joyce had lectured them on multiple occasions about the consequences of allowing one of the insipid devices to disrupt class. He bemoaned the fact that he was not legally allowed to take a hammer to them, or at least force kids to leave them in their lockers. Phones and pagers had once been prohibited at school, but the county relaxed the rules after September 11 and a local sniper ordeal caused parents to lobby the board of education for change. The new liberties were supposed to allow parents instant access to their kids in case of emergency, but in reality the lines all jammed the last time there had been a minor scare, which occurred when the school was evacuated while the fire and rescue squads scoured the air ducts for anthrax after a fine white powder was discovered in the choral room. The substance was eventually determined to be powdered sugar from a doughnut.

In Mr. Joyce's opinion, which he made known about once a week, bringing phones to school only encouraged kids to zone out during class as they played games, or text-messaged one another. Still, Mr. Joyce had some limited discretion, or at least he claimed it, and he announced at the beginning of the school year that if anyone's cell phone rang during class, everyone seated in the row of the offending device would have 20 points deducted from their next in-class essay. This policy was revoked by the principal when he received a barrage of angry phone calls from parents the day after nine innocent students received point demotions. One of the parents who complained was a well-known lawyer and a frequent commentator on CNN. He used the word *litigation* in reference to wanting his son's otherwise perfect grade point average restored. Verona's administrative staff worked long enough hours as it was; even if the prospect of a Supreme Court battle over the constitutional rights of teenaged cell phone users might prove a useful civics lesson, no one, apart from Mr. Joyce—who complained that the administration failed to support him—was interested in the fight.

The offender in today's case was Marty Stoddard. He was almost two years older than most of his classmates and at eighteen a nearly full-grown man. His parents had held him back twice, putting him into a private kindergarten for two years before enrolling him in first grade. They were quick to let everyone know this was not because he was in any way intellectually deficient, but because he was so big they felt it was to his disadvantage to be considered more mature than he actually was. People generally nodded even if they didn't understand exactly what was meant by this. Why was it better to be the biggest kid in the class *and* be two years older than everyone else? No one tried too hard to grasp the logic, since it seemed fairly obvious that the real point, no matter what cockamamie explanation was on offer, was that Marty would one day dominate his peers in athletics, and that aspect of the plan had worked out beautifully.

"Although this announcement has no direct bearing on the fact that Marty finds playing video games more interesting than *Beowulf*, let's just say the issues are not entirely unrelated . . ."

"It's not a video game, sir," Marty said. Marty called all of the teachers "sir." He may have been larger than the Redskins' new right tackle, but he was an unfailingly meek and polite churchgoing boy. "I'm very sorry, sir," he continued. "My parents signed me up for this SAT prep service, and it came an hour early. I don't really have much time to study right now because of lacrosse, so while I had the time I was just responding. It was wrong, sir. I should have been listening to you talk about that monster."

"Grendel," Mr. Joyce said without emotion. "That monster's name is Grendel, but never mind." Mr. Joyce glanced at the clock before continuing. "Honestly, if you people want to waste your time learning by rote, far be it from me to interfere. What I was going to tell you is that I have made a rather sudden decision to stop teaching here at the end of the term. I've just signed a three-year contract to teach overseas. I'll be working at a small village school in Laos. I leave in a month. I know this puts some of you in a bind . . ."

Maya could not believe this. *Laos?* That seemed rather extreme. Had they really pushed him that far? And why should *she* be punished? She never even brought her cell phone to class!

A hand shot up in the back of the room, and Sarah Lipinsky blurted out a question before he had the chance to call on her. "What about recommendations?"

"Yes, Sarah, that's what I'm about to discuss . . ."

The bell rang but no one moved.

"Given that this is all happening very quickly, what I have decided to do—and I've already cleared this with Mrs. Craig, who is taking over as department head while Ms. Olsen is on maternity leave—is that I will write recommendations for twenty students. I will then leave them in sealed envelopes with Mrs. Craig. When it comes time to apply, you will give the college forms and the envelopes to Mrs. Craig, who will fill in the paperwork and send out the recs."

Maya felt like she might actually start to cry. This simply could not be happening. Mr. Joyce had been the greatest single influence in her life. He had changed the course of things for her; he alone believed in her, had coaxed from her soul the inner poet. She knew it was hopeless and stupid, but she had fallen in love with him. Of course he was married, and she didn't contemplate ever actually *doing* anything; her love was, while not quite platonic, somehow pure, a romantic love that transcended physical need, if that was possible. She swam faster thinking he might be there, in the bleachers, cheering her on, even though that would never happen, given his pronouncements about the evils of competitive sports. Sometimes she thought about him when she dressed in the morning, wondering whether he might notice the subtleties of her wardrobe decisions, such as whether to wear small gold post earrings or go with something of the more funky, dangling, beaded variety. She agonized over every word choice in the essays she wrote for him; at least he seemed to notice this.

She was so tired she could barely process this information. *He was leaving her.* Maybe she was dreaming; perhaps it was still early morning, and she had fallen asleep swimming laps. This would at least explain the sensation she had that she was sinking.

Another hand shot up in the back of the room, and Mr. Joyce nodded in the direction of Federico, the son of the deputy head of mission from Chile.

"I wonder if you could tell us how many points the final exam is worth, in terms of the overall grade and the final research paper."

"We'll talk about that tomorrow, Freddy. Right now I want to explain that given my own personal time constraints, I am only going to be able to write these twenty recommendations, and I will have to do that before I leave, since I have no idea what sort of conditions I'll be encountering in terms of computer access and the like. And I want to be fair about this. I don't want to play favorites. The best system I can think of will be that I'll write recs for the first twenty people to ask . . ."

Twenty-five hands immediately shot up, but he kept on speaking.

"Of course I teach three other classes, and the same rule applies for everyone. And then there were some who had me last year who might want to ask for a recommendation, and in fairness they also deserve a shot. I've been wracking my brain about how to do this . . ."

Raymond Wiley blurted out a suggestion. "Why don't you just write recs for the twenty kids with the highest grades in the class?" he asked. Maya had not previously noticed how deep Raymond's voice was and wondered if perhaps he was just now going through puberty. Some stubble on his chin suggested that she might be right. He was a small boy with red hair who was obsessed with grades and had once stormed out of class when he received a B on a paper.

Mr. Joyce shook his head. Normally this would have set him off on a rant about how they all paid too much attention to grades and scores, but he had the nonchalance of someone who had already moved beyond these Verona-centric concerns.

"What I'm going to do to be fair—and I admit this may not be the best system, but after much soul-searching it seems better than playing favorites—is that I'm going to write recs for the first twenty people to ask beginning tomorrow morning. I'll be here, in my classroom. So think about it, and if you want me to write a rec, just come in a few minutes early and ask."

Maya's mind was racing far beyond the problem of college recommendations. She thought through the list of teachers who taught senior year AP English Literature and couldn't think of a single one she liked. Was it possible that this newfound love of literature was tied entirely to Mr. Joyce? She wanted to speak to him privately, but a small crowd formed at his desk before she could even stuff her spiral back in her bag. A few boys gathered around Marty to give him crap about the text message. She saw her neighbor Taylor Rockefeller alight from her desk in the back row where she was seated next to Raymond, and watched her rush out the door, looking unwell.

○ ○ ○

GRACE WAS ROUSED from a deliciously deep sleep by the sound of a slamming door. She sat up in a panic, thinking of Lou. What a twisted sort of luxury it would be to live with the general fear of random crime, as opposed to the more specific threat of an unhinged ex-husband; the odds of being victimized by a stranger had to be statistically much lower than being harassed by Lou. She had changed the locks years ago, and he didn't have a key, but he was a devious son of a bitch. Since he couldn't hold a steady job, from what Grace could tell he spent most of his free time devising ways to make her miserable. Once he hired a private detective who sat in front of the house for two weeks watching her come and go, for what purpose she had no idea, unless it was to eat up her would-be alimony. The detective was surprisingly good-looking, and he turned out to be pretty nice as well: he apologized that his humongous vehicle made it difficult for Grace to see when she backed out of her driveway, for example, and he offered to walk the dog for her once when she was running late for work. Shortly after they swilled Coronas together, leaning against his big Ford Bronco, Lou must have pulled the plug, and the detective disappeared, replaced by Lou himself, who evidently forgot that she had a restraining order prohibiting him from coming near the property. With little criminal activity in Verona, the police responded to her call within minutes and seemed very excited about having a perp to put in handcuffs.

While she knew that Harry occasionally met with his father, Lou hadn't come around the house for at least a year. Her high-tech alarm system had recently been dismantled in a cost-cutting measure, but she still had the warning signs on her windows and on the front lawn, and she liked to think that they kept Lou at bay. She fretted that it was a breach of ethics to still display the signs, but then, she reasoned it was unethical for the courts to have let Lou out of jail the last time he'd been arrested for breaking and entering.

Grace rolled over and looked at the clock: 3:45 a.m. She bolted out of bed and went to the window, where she glimpsed a figure just as it crossed in front of the streetlight. The long shadow appeared humped, and the rectangle dangling from an arm could only be a briefcase, which made the weird shape identifiable as her son, bent from the weight of his backpack. Was Harry really going to school at three forty-five in the morning? Another twisted luxury would be to think he was possibly sneaking out of the house to meet a girl. Of course she would not actually want him to be doing that, but the idea of Harry lightening up a bit, having a little fun, was somehow less worrisome than the thought of him voluntarily heading off to school in the dark of night.

Grace crawled back into bed and tried to fall asleep. She could never quite figure out when to worry about Harry. Every time she believed they were on the verge of some disaster, things would suddenly normalize. Navigating his teenaged years was not unlike keeping an eye on the thermometer when he was little, prepared for full-scale panic if the mercury rose just one notch higher. Not that it ever did: even as a baby Harry seemed to have everything under control. The chief difference nowadays was that she was alone on the roller coaster. Harry's pulse never seemed to quicken, and his spirit rarely flagged; he just kept pushing forward. Of course he had weathered minor disappointments. Apart from what he perceived as the ongoing SAT debacle, for example, he had failed his driving test twice when he was unable to successfully parallel-park. He remained stoic as they spent weeks practicing backing the bloated station wagon between strategically placed cones in the school parking lot on weekends. When he finally passed the test, rather than pump a fist in the air or cheer, he simply emerged from the car and instructed Grace to park the vehicle while he stood in line to get his picture taken.

Somewhere inside him she assumed he must be storing anxieties—at least she hoped he was, because his cocky confidence seemed dangerous. And on this occasion Grace thought perhaps she really *should* be worried: her son had just left the house before dawn! But then, her son was AP Harry, and he seemed to be operating in some parallel universe that demanded Grace, and everyone else around him, rethink the rules.

The dog usually slept with Harry, and she must have been confused by the early wake-up; she parked herself at the foot of Grace's bed and began whining to go out just as Grace finally drifted back to sleep. This time the roller coaster went into freefall, as it occurred to her belatedly that the school was almost certainly not open at this hour. Now she was mad at herself, thinking perhaps she had tempted fate with her silly wish that he was up to no good. Was Harry possibly involved with drugs? Not for recreation of course, but for enhancement, like Ritalin or Adderall or some kind of speed. It wouldn't shock her to discover that Harry might try to give himself an edge. But then, he seemed too calm to be under the throes of any sort of addiction. With her mind racing like this, she was clearly not going to fall back to sleep. She threw on the clothes she had laid out for work just a few short hours earlier and headed downstairs to his room to see if she could find something that would make her mind stop spinning.

Whatever he was up to, it didn't detract from his general straight-arrow behavior. Harry was quite possibly the only teenager on earth who made his bed before leaving for school in the morning, even when his departure happened to occur in the middle of the night. Then again, for all she knew, he might never have gone to sleep in the first place. She turned on the light over his neatly arranged desk, piled high with SAT study guides and textbooks. A draft of a paper on *Beowulf* sat on his desk with notations penciled in the margins. Another paper, written entirely in Spanish, sat atop a dog-earred copy of *One Hundred Years of Solitude*, also in Spanish. She had studied the language in high school, but had never taken it to the advanced level of near fluency that Harry had reached. But then, she hadn't taken anything to his level.

She looked around for signs of delinquency, but the only offending item she could find was a bulletin board full of 2004 Bush-Cheney memorabilia that included an autographed photograph of Donald Rumsfeld. Her son's conservative politics made her cringe, but she could hardly haul him into a child psychologist for being a Republican.

Propped against the wall in the corner were Harry's three lacrosse sticks, the sight of which made Grace at once weepy and freshly enraged. She had never really figured out the game, beyond the obvious objective of getting the ball into the opposing team's net. She had failed to learn why some sticks were longer than others, and why sometimes it was okay to charge at an opposing player, seeming to deliberately hit him in the ribs with the end of a stick, and sometimes that was called a foul. Also, no matter how hard she tried, she could not keep track of the fast-moving ball.

The handles of all three sticks were still wrapped in white tape of a particular texture meant to produce a better grip. She remembered losing her patience the day Harry called her at work and dispatched her, in rush hour traffic, to an obscure store along Verona Pike to get a new head. His month-old head, for which she had just received the credit card statement with the charge of $104, had snapped during practice in thirty-degree weather. Evidently, four kids lost their sticks that day to the cold, further evidence, if any was needed, that lacrosse was not a winter sport.

When Harry showed enough interest in the game to spend a second year on the JV team, she took the extremely radical step of trading in her sedan for a used station wagon so that she could fit more kids and equipment when it was her day for car pool, and she even rearranged her work schedule so that she could leave early when it was her turn to drive. Grace hadn't fully appreciated at the time what wherewithal Harry showed by remaining on the team. Evidently, Harry was the very opposite of a typical lacrosse player—even if they were all good kids, the LAX boys tended to be superjocks who liked a good party. Harry apparently felt the need to play a sport in high school in order to appear well-rounded. After studying his options, he determined that he stood a better chance of making the varsity cut in lacrosse than in baseball or soccer.

She remembered those balmy spring afternoons when she would rush to the practice field promptly at 5:00, only to sit in the car and watch the boys practice for another forty or so minutes. Some mothers buried their faces behind newspapers or magazines as they waited, or chatted noisily on cell phones. But Grace had wanted to absorb every speck of detail on the field below. Even when Harry was only in ninth grade, she was acutely aware of the passage of time, perhaps because he was her only child, perhaps because once he left home she would be decidedly alone. She didn't really understand what the team was doing, but she did see a beauty in their precision drills, an outdoor ballet of cleated, helmeted boys in orange jerseys running up and down the field with sticks.

Still, she could have done without the mandatory volunteering and the seemingly endless fund-raisers. Certainly, she had never enjoyed getting up at 7:00 a.m. on Sunday mornings to get him to a practice field forty minutes away. But now she felt guilty about any private griping, because Harry had put in two dutiful years only to be cut from the team this spring.

Not surprisingly, Harry handled the cut with a resilience that she couldn't believe he possessed at such a young age. Grace had fantasized about calling the school to scream at someone, but she refrained—that was not her style; plus it would surely have reflected badly on her son. But only two boys had been cut! How could there not have been room on the team for just two more boys? It would have been one thing if the coach had cut a dozen players, or even half that number, but to say that only two out of forty kids did not pass muster seemed un-American. Or maybe she had it all wrong and that was entirely American. Was the current mandate to build character or self-esteem? It was hard to keep track. All she knew was that she had had her fill of the lacrosse coach over the years, who came to the twice-a-year sports booster meetings, yelled at the already overextended parents about their lack of commitment to the team, and then instructed them to write hundreds of dollars' worth of checks. He scared them, threatening that their boys would be punished for missing a single practice for anything less urgent than a death in the immediate, nuclear family, and not so subtly insinuated that parents who did not put in hours manning the snack bar during games might see repercussions in the amount of time their sons saw on the field. Lacrosse took precedence over academics, internships, doctors' appointments, jobs, and any other school-related activity like drama or music, he said, sounding like a Marine drill sergeant. The only acceptable excuse for missing a Sunday game was church. Grace was tempted to point out that this placed an unfair burden on non-Christians to get up early on weekends and carry the slack, but she was pretty sure this observation would not help Harry's cause. Yet look where all of her Friday nights spent selling hot dogs had landed him, she thought bitterly, staring at the $100 helmet hanging on the bedpost. Except that Harry himself had not shed a tear. He only said it would help him resolve to work that much harder at the next thing that came along and that he pitied the coach for having to make such a tough call. Maybe he really was on drugs, Grace thought, and whatever it was he was on, she could use some herself.

A flash from outside caught her eye. Through the blinds in Harry's window she could see the lights flicker on in the Rockefeller's house. She guessed it was the front hallway that was illuminated, but just as quickly the lights went out again and she saw their front door open. It was too dark to clearly identify the figure that emerged, but it was almost certainly Taylor.

Where in the world could these kids be going so early? Had Taylor and Harry arranged a secret rendezvous? She wouldn't really mind if that were the case—she had always liked Taylor, but she seemed so gloomy lately it was hard to imagine what Harry might see in her. Anyway, it was now 5:00 a.m., and Taylor would be over an hour late for any supposed assignation.

The instinct to pick up the phone and call Nina Rockefeller was so strong she had to stop herself. It wasn't that long ago that they had run their homes like a commune, with their doors always open and kids drifting between the houses. Some mornings Grace would wake to find Taylor at her kitchen table, helping herself to a bowl of cereal and watching cartoons. (Grace refrained from saying anything at a recent neighborhood coffee when she overheard Nina brag that Taylor had never watched television as a toddler and had become partial to National Public Radio at age four.) By the time the kids were in middle school, she couldn't even remember who had originally purchased things like the portable goalie nets they used to drag into the street, or the wheelbarrow that both families once used to throw mulch on the flowerbeds back before the Rockefellers hired a gardener and Grace had simply given up. It was really awful to consider the level of estrangement Grace felt from her former friend. Anyway, Grace told herself, it was best to not drag Nina into this on the one-in-a-million chance that Harry and Taylor were up to something romantic. She didn't want to contemplate them engaged in intimate relations, but nor did she feel they ought to suffer the humiliation of having parents descend on them like bounty hunters.

She had heard other parents say that they kept an eye on their kids' activities via the instant-message fragments they left dangling on their computers. One colleague at the lab told Grace that she regularly scrolled through her son's messages to see what was going on in his life. Evidently, the boy knew this, yet he still couldn't be bothered to shut the computer down at night. It was hard to imagine Harry wasting time mindlessly chatting with people when he could be doing something useful like studying. Plus, it seemed unlikely he'd ever be so negligent as to leave his computer on.

She touched his keyboard on a whim, and to her astonishment the screen on the monitor lit up and the machine purred to life. What she saw at first glance appeared to be a bunch of math problems, but it turned out to be somewhat more worrisome. She looked at the formula at the top of the page and saw the letters *SAT*:

$$AI = \frac{[SAT\ (V) + SAT\ (M)]}{2} + \frac{[SAT\ II + SAT\ II + SAT\ II]}{3} + CRS$$

And below that, another formula:

$$Z = \frac{(2 \times absolute\ rank) - 1}{2 \times class\ size}$$

And then below that, she saw the first formula repeated, except this time, plugged into the SAT spots, were Harry's actual scores. She wasn't sure what *CRS* stood for, but kept scrolling down the page, where she saw a few more equations that finally enabled her to understand that it had something to do with his class rank. She still wasn't sure what this was. Then she noticed a book sitting next to the computer, *A Is for Admission*. She opened the book and a note fell out. It was printed in large block letters. Simple and to the point: DEAR HARRY. MAKE YOUR DAD PROUD!

She felt a rush of rage and dread. Had Lou always been such a jerk? she wondered. Perhaps she had contributed to his worsening behavior by shutting him out. Yes, she knew she was probably overreacting—he had only given Harry a book. But still, she wondered how much of Harry's incessant drive was coming from Lou pressuring him. Thirty years later, Lou still grumbled about how his own sad, mucked-up life would have been different if only he had matriculated at Harvard, where he said he had been accepted, but couldn't afford to go. Grace had never heard such a claim when they first married and was somewhat skeptical this was true.

She leafed through the pages until she saw a bunch of stars Harry had made around the entry "The Academic Index," which was evidently what these figures were: this was a formula used by the Ivy League schools to boil everyone into a single number. Apparently Harry couldn't settle on a precise number because of Verona's refusal to provide a rank, and because the formula did not take into account the fact that the new SAT was divided into three sections or that SAT IIs were now called subject tests. To compensate, Harry had devised a number of possible formulas.

This was what her son was doing with his free time? Calculating his mathematical chances of getting into the Ivy League almost made memorizing the *U.S. News* rankings seem like a creative activity.

Grace sat down in his chair with the book and began to read. "For the most part, Ivy League hotshots are *not* the ones reading your application. You will note the conspicuous absence of Rhodes scholars or well-known educators on admissions staffs . . . What I am trying to say without shocking you too much is that the very best applicants will often be brighter than many of those who will be evaluating them."

She read this three times, hoping it was a joke. When she realized the author was serious, she felt a vague stirring in her stomach and wondered if there was some number she could call, some emergency hotline to help stage an intervention for her son, to pull him back from the brink of becoming the sort of person with an ego so inflated he might one day think the sorts of thoughts contained in these pages.

The dog had finally given up whining and had escalated her tactics to clawing painfully at Grace's bare leg. Grace figured this was probably a good time to just give in and get the walk over with. Technically, she was Harry's dog—a gift from Lou for his thirteenth birthday, one as ill-conceived as this college admissions book. She didn't suppose Lou had actually taken the time to consider that the gift would pretty much convey to her once Harry left for college, a little twice-a-day reminder, rain or shine, of her ex-husband's generosity. Anyway, an early walk this morning would serve the dual purpose of getting a head start on Nina and giving her the chance to pass by the school to see if there was anything she might learn about Harry. She put the dog on a leash and donned a sweater, although as soon as she stepped outside she realized this was unnecessary—it was at least ten degrees warmer outside the house than in.

The dog started yanking hard in the direction Harry had set off in almost two hours earlier, as if she could still track the scent. At 140 pounds, the dog outweighed Grace, and it was hard to keep up as she pulled. Three cars drove by, headed toward Verona High. One of them had the windows open, and rap music was blaring from the jacked-up sound system. She saw two other students walking toward the school from the opposite direction. Maybe it was some sort of senior prank day? But Harry and Taylor were still juniors, so that didn't do much to further the theory. Was there a junior prank day? An early exam scheduled for some reason?

Grace turned the corner and was greeted with a panoramic view of the school parking lot, which was about a fifth full. She could see a group of kids lined up at the front door, like they were waiting to buy tickets for a rock concert. Many of them were sitting, a few were sprawled on the ground, tucked into sleeping bags. Harry had a flashlight and appeared to be reading, although the sun was just breaking through the clouds making additional illumination unnecessary. She couldn't begin to imagine what was going on.

The dog suddenly began to growl, and Grace looked around, worried. Racing toward her was Nina Rockefeller, talking on her cell phone.

She ended the call and greeted Grace excitedly. "How about these kids?" she asked. "What devotion! I've brought Taylor a thermos of coffee from home. Would you believe I drove to Starbucks and it's not even open yet? I mean, what are they thinking? *Hello? Earth to Starbucks management!* These kids need caffeine!"

"They should have you run the place," Grace said, hoping that came out sounding more supportive than sarcastic.

"You know, they should!" Nina agreed. "I'd get them to deliver! I mean obviously they are not thinking, those Starbucks people. There are kids out there like Harry and Taylor! Kids so driven they'll get up at the crack of dawn to get a recommendation for college."

Grace hated to let on that Nina was more on top of things than she was, but in this case her need for information outweighed concerns about appearing clueless. "What are you talking about?" she asked.

"That gay English teacher they both have. That Mr. Joyce?"

"Oh, him. Yes. I thought he was married."

"Whatever. I hear he's leaving at the end of the school year—no great loss if you ask me—and he said he is going to write recommendations for the first twenty people to ask. It looks like our kids are close to the front of the line, so it shouldn't be an issue, but I think this is awful. There must be a better system. These kids shouldn't have to lose precious sleep to get college recommendations."

"Are you sure that's what they're doing?"

"Positive. I had to haul Taylor out of bed this morning to do this. She didn't think it was worth it, said that Mr. Joyce didn't even like her, but I think it's important that she have a recommendation from her English teacher. I'm going to take it up with the PTA. After he writes Taylor's letter and leaves the country, that is!"

Nina suddenly stopped speaking and turned in the direction of their homes, from where Maya Kaluantharana was approaching. With her dark, clear eyes, and her athletic build oozing good health, she was breathtaking. It made Grace think that in some odd way she had not previously considered, she was lucky to have a son. Surely it was easier to ignore her own aging process when she didn't have a teenaged girl in the house, someone to remind her on a daily basis that she was past her own prime. They stood silently while she approached.

"Don't tell the coach," Maya said half-jokingly, but I'm skipping swim practice to get to school early to get a recommendation from my English teacher."

"I hate to be the one to tell you," Nina said, "but you're a little late. The line is already about sixty deep."

"It's only just after 5:00," Maya said, checking her watch to confirm the time. She surveyed the parking lot and looked as though she might start to cry.

Grace felt sorry for her and wanted to distance herself from Nina's cold remark. "You should go on ahead. You never know. Maybe some of these other kids are there for something else. Maybe there's another teacher offering to write recommendations this morning."

"I doubt that," said Nina, but then she softened a bit. "Certainly give it a try, honey. You've got nothing to lose!"

Maya adjusted the heavy bag on her shoulder and continued toward the school. Once she was out of earshot, Nina let out a little laugh. "As if that girl needs any help getting into college. With all this affirmative action she'll go to school anywhere she wants. And they'll probably give her money, too, even though her parents could buy up half the neighborhood."

Grace was so stunned by this comment she couldn't think of anything other than a lame reply. "I don't know why you'd say that. She's such a sweet girl," she said irrelevantly.

Nina looked at her and shrugged her shoulders. "Sweet or not," she said, "you watch out. These people are going to take over the world! And then they'll convert us all to Islam. And it's not just the Indians—have you noticed all the Chinese or Koreans or whatever they are moving into the neighborhood?"

"I believe the Kaluantharanas are Hindu, actually," Grace replied, a much sharper response poised on the tip of her tongue. She was not a confrontational person, and her first instinct was to always keep the peace. Starting a fight with Nina would do little to change the world and would only make their interactions even more unpleasant. She wondered how she could have spent so many years with Nina without recognizing all this venom just beneath the surface. Or was it possible that Nina had not always been this way, and that like Lou, something inside was turning toxic as she headed into middle age.

"Oh, whatever," said Nina. "I guess I have to confess that I don't really know the difference. There's just so many foreigners in this neighborhood. Like that guy who just moved in up the street, the one with the thing on his head."

"He's a Sikh, Nina," she replied. "He works for the IMF." Now she felt herself about to explode. "You really ought to listen to yourself—you sound like a racist!"

She couldn't believe she'd just said this. The remark felt uncharacteristically bold as well as incredibly stupid. Nina *was* a racist! She waited for Nina's angry reply, but none was forthcoming. She'd forgotten Nina was a master of denial. Instead, Nina checked her watch and let out a little gasp. "It's so late! I'm gonna just dash over there and give Taylor her coffee. I'll tell her to give Harry a swig!"

"Thanks, Nina," she said, somewhat thankful to skirt the issue, even though she did regret the next lame sentence out of her own mouth: "That's really nice of you."

July

TAYLOR HOPED HER MOTHER would go away. Nina had been talking to her through the door for the past five minutes. "I have a great idea," Nina pleaded. "If you'll just let me in, I'll tell you about it. It's really terrific!"

Her mother sounded bright and cheerful, nonchalant, the same tone she struck when proposing jaunts to Saks Fifth Avenue, or tennis and lunch at the country club, something she persisted in suggesting at least once a week even though Taylor had refused to set foot in the place since Nina threw her a surprise pool party when she turned thirteen. Taylor had spent most of the party weeping in the locker room and claimed she didn't even know at least four of the girls who had been invited, daughters of women she accused her mother of wanting to impress. Her mother didn't deny this was true, but she did scold Taylor for always being such a drama queen.

"Really, Taylor, you'll like this!" she said again when there was no response, but there was a weariness in her voice that betrayed a possible wavering of faith in the fabulousness of her own idea.

Her mother persisted in bringing up the subject of college on average twice a day even though Taylor always bristled. Nina complained that she didn't understand why they couldn't have reasonable conversations about this, but then, Taylor couldn't remember the last time they'd had a reasonable conversation about anything. Certainly, the conversations about college counselors had not gone well, if you could call her mother's unilateral decisions to hire two different advisors "conversations." First, there had been the "premium-plus package" with the fancy counselor in New York—two years of monthly advice plus a once-a-week phone consultation—which Taylor had refused to utilize, the promise of shopping sprees in SoHo notwithstanding. Then her mother hired a local counselor just a few blocks away; Taylor was supposed to visit with her six times over the course of the next few months, but she had no intention of doing that either, especially since the woman was the mother of someone in Taylor's Spanish class and she couldn't bear the thought of the girl eavesdropping on their conversations.

In the past, Taylor's refusal to follow her mother's instructions would have resulted in some lively verbal jousting, and there were times when she felt oddly nostalgic for their fights. She and her mother had never really gotten along, but at least their battles had been a form of engagement. These days much of what rolled off her mother's tongue left her too flummoxed for words, but every once in a while she couldn't help but react.

Taylor calmly pointed out that it was only July, for example, when Nina railed that they were on the verge of an impending crisis and that *someone* had to take control. She was just doing her job egging Taylor along, she insisted, and she needed to keep raising the subject of college even if it upset her daughter.

"You'll be applying in just a few months," she said on one occasion. "This whole thing is imminent, like pregnancy. Thank God that's not our problem, but at least it would be more straightforward!"

"So you would rather I was pregnant than applying to college?"

"Of course not, darling. I'm only pointing out that at least that's something you could just take care of and be done with! It's less complicated."

"Unless I wanted to have the baby. I think I might want to, actually."

"You can't have a baby! You're only sixteen. You need to go to college!"

"I'm nearly seventeen. And I could have a baby and go to college. Lots of people do."

"You are *not* having a baby at age sixteen. You would ruin your life. Trust me."

"Did *I* ruin *your* life? Is that what this is about? Anyway, it's my body and I can do what I want," Taylor had said at the time, retreating to her room and slamming the door. She suspected that her mother had been drinking, and she took a perverse pleasure in twisting the conversation like this.

Undaunted by these sorts of exchanges, or possibly just forgetting they had ever even occurred, Nina took it upon herself to order catalogues from a number of schools she thought might best suit Taylor, and she had even called admissions offices and set up interviews and campus visits for the end of August and throughout the early fall. She was big on Vassar, because that was where Jacqueline Kennedy and Katharine Graham had gone, and they had both married well, she explained. Wellesley was also high on her list for similarly turning out name-brand female alums, although she was conspicuously silent on the nuptials of two of the school's most famous graduates, Hillary Clinton and Madeleine Albright. Picking up on that train of thought, Taylor saw the opportunity to point out that Condoleezza Rice had not gone to a fancy school, but rather to the University of Denver. "Condoleezza Rice is conspicuously single," her mother replied. "And anyway, darling, the point is not to become the National Security Advisor."

"She's actually the Secretary of State now, Mom," Taylor had said, but Nina seemed unimpressed by the distinction. No one in Nina's family had even gone to college, she reminded Taylor, and she therefore couldn't understand her daughter's blasé attitude about the tremendous opportunities available to her. Taylor knew that her mother's heart was in the right place, that she had grown up harboring a confusing blend of envy and disdain for the wealthy, blue-blooded families that employed her as a nanny until the day that Wilson came to visit his young cousins at the home where she was working, looking jaunty with a tennis racquet slung over his shoulder and a cigarette dangling from his lips. It was love at first sight, her own personal Cinderella story, except that from what Taylor could piece together after the passage of so many years, her mother had been less a princess-in-waiting than a crude, loudmouthed party girl, and while her father may have looked like a prince in his designer tennis whites, he was really an aimless, troubled young man with severely strained family relations. Bad omens notwithstanding, such as Nina's getting drunk and passing out on their first date (a story frequently recounted as amusing family lore), they married two months later, and then moved to Washington where he began a consulting career. Taylor was born within the first year of marriage, and her own best guess was that her parents had not slept together since.

Nina rapped on the door again.

Taylor realized that her mother was unlikely to go away without eliciting some sort of response, but there was no way she was going to open the door. She was in the middle of reading a new batch of entries on her favorite blog, and she had just been victorious in logging on to a neighbor's unprotected wireless network after several failed attempts. Among her mother's many rules, she was now forbidden to use the Internet unless it was for the purposes of homework or college applications, and Nina had the cable company disable the Ethernet connections from all the upstairs rooms. Happily for Taylor, her mother didn't understand the first thing about wireless technology.

"I'll come downstairs in a few minutes," she lied. She was pretty sure her mother wanted to talk to her about the essay for her college applications, which was her latest obsession. Nina had seized on the idea that Taylor should be spending her downtime crafting the perfect essay almost immediately after losing her bid to orchestrate Taylor's summer.

"We need to find you a passion," her mother said when she initially introduced the idea that Taylor should spend six weeks working with Project Hola Amigos, helping to build houses outside Tijuana. Taylor was pretty sure that particular great idea occurred after Nina heard through the grapevine that Maya Kaluantharana was spending the month of July in India, visiting relatives and working with a charity that rehabilitated leprosy patients by teaching them to raise broiler chickens and weave hand-loomed cloth. Everything about the Kaluantharanas seemed to set her mother off; her latest rant was that all of this affirmative action and loosening of the immigration laws and even the outpouring of sympathy for impoverished hurricane victims put people like them—people with a name like Rockefeller—at a new disadvantage. "There should be affirmative action for disadvantaged Rockefellers," she once declared.

The family drama about what Taylor should do this summer was so prolonged that her vacation was half over and no plan had ever gelled. At the heart of the months-long argument was her mother's desire for her to do something résumé-enhancing, and her father's insistence that she get a job. Taylor had entered the debate with a somewhat open mind although she did veto Project Hola Amigos. It was not that she thought it unworthy in principle so much as that it seemed somehow manipulative. She knew at least five kids from her school who were going to build houses in Mexico. One of the girls, Lara Kagan, had been featured on a local television news program about superficial kids. Lara proudly revealed to the reporter that she owned nine pairs of designer jeans, which retailed for over $150 apiece, and that she had UGG boots in every available color. The segment showed her walking down a Verona High hallway wearing a Burberry jacket and carrying a $300 Coach bag in lieu of a backpack. She had been so ridiculed in school the day after the program aired that she had gone home in tears. Taylor wondered if her wardrobe could withstand the rigors of a summer construction job.

After listening to her parents spar about her summer for a couple of weeks, all she wanted to do was lock herself in her bedroom.

"These kids are spoiled rotten," Wilson Rockefeller had said within his daughter's earshot. "They have no work ethic. No incentive. She should spend the summer scooping ice cream or pumping gas like we did when we were young."

"*Oh, please!*" her mother said. "Believe me, that's overrated. As if anyone in your family has ever held a gas pump or an ice cream scoop!" Taylor entered the kitchen mid-argument and, for deliberate dramatic effect, walked over to the freezer, took out a pint of chocolate chip cookie dough, and began to heap ice cream into a bowl. No one appeared to notice.

"If you want to talk about gas, what about the fact that we must pay an extra $200 a year because you won't pump your own gas? You just waste money. It's like you can't be bothered to even *think* about it."

Taylor pulled herself onto the granite counter, where she sat, staring at the ice cream that she didn't really want.

"When did you become such a cheapskate?" her mother snarled.

"About the time that you started throwing our money out the window. You haven't taught Taylor a single thing about values. What sixteen-year-old has a gold American Express card?"

"Just about every kid in this town," Nina answered.

Taylor sensed that her father's anger was not directed at her, that all the bad energy in the house almost certainly stemmed from her parents' marital problems, but that didn't mean that he made any effort to reach out to her. He never stopped by her room to talk, and she couldn't remember the last time she and her father had had any sort of meaningful interaction. He spent most of the time he was home tapping on his BlackBerry, and Taylor wondered if he was having an affair. That he might have a girlfriend seemed almost logical, but it pained her to consider that the woman on the other end of the e-mail exchanges might have children who he went out of his way to be nice to, or even a dog that he actually liked. On the upside, he wasn't nagging her about college. Still, she couldn't recall ever feeling like part of a normal family, the sort that went out for Chinese food on Sunday nights or watched the Super Bowl on TV. The one time they tried the latter at Taylor's insistence, they ordered pizzas and sat down to watch the game only to realize they had missed it by a week.

She actually wasn't sure what her father did all day, as a year earlier he had taken a buyout offer from the consulting firm he worked for and she had never understood what it was he had done in the first place; so far as she could tell, "consulting" was a euphemism for something else. She had no idea what their current state of finances was, but got the impression that money flowed somewhat less freely than it had in the past. Her father still left the house each morning dressed in a suit and tie, and he seemed to keep normal business hours—normal for Washington anyway, which meant several late nights each week. But Taylor sometimes wondered if he had become one of those people she sometimes glimpsed at corner tables at Starbucks who spent their entire day staring at their

laptops, giving the probably false impression that they actually had something to do.

She didn't feel any particular hostility toward her father, nor did
she disagree with his suggestion that she get a job. She wouldn't have
minded getting a job, but by the time the arguments ceased, she assumed it was too late. Certainly, it proved too late to join Project Hola
Amigos; her mother learned that all of the summer programs were full,
some even with long waiting lists, notwithstanding the fact that the cost
of the program was more than $5,000. And she didn't know *how* to get a
job. Her mother usually did all of the talking for her. She had never really learned to assert herself, only to stand beside her mother and cringe.
This would have been a good opportunity to take a stab at independence,
to break the family stalemate by acting, but the thought was overwhelming. Could she muster the courage to simply walk into the ice cream
shop and ask if they needed help? Who would she talk to, and what
would she say? Should she stand in line, as if she was going to order a
scoop of caramel fudge, and then casually ask if they needed help? Or
should she ask for the manager? Part of the problem was that a lot of the
people who worked at the shop went to Verona, and the thought of nego-
tiating this rite of passage with any of her classmates was completely
mortifying.

By default Taylor was prepared to spend the better part of the summer in her room. Already she was bored, but lethargy seemed to breed
lethargy and she couldn't do anything about it. She thought about paint-
ing, but would need some new supplies as her brushes were crusted and
the tubes of acrylic were mostly empty. Her mother had discouraged this
activity; she said Taylor didn't have the talent to ever paint professionally
and she didn't want her to become "too artsy." Taylor pointed out that
she was unlikely to ever play the flute professionally, either, so perhaps
she should quit the school band, but Nina said that was different. Taylor
didn't really understand how.

For lack of anything better to do, she spent a fair amount of time on
a blog she had discovered: highschoolconfessions.blogspot.com. She'd
been logging on to the site for about a year, and had come to view it as
her mental health reality check. People posted photographs with their

confessions written below, things like "I hit someone and I just kept driving . . . now I can't sleep at night" or "I don't believe in abortion and I
don't know what to do." That latter confession had a picture of a torso
with a gun pointed toward the swelling belly. Taylor felt queasy just looking at the photo. Yes, maybe she was in a bad place, and maybe her problems were pretty abnormal, but she was not as bad off as some of these
people. She wasn't sneaking into the girls' locker room after school to
smell dirty gym clothes, for example, although she suspected that was almost certainly a boy sort of problem. And she wasn't as desperate as the
person who wrote, "I spend most of my time at school daydreaming
about different ways to kill myself." She had no desire to kill herself, and
on the occasions when she considered this, she always came back to the
conclusion that she couldn't bear the thought of people rifling through
her personal items, or talking about her behind her back at the funeral.
Still, she found herself drawn to a photograph of a wrist with a sharp
blade pressed to the skin. Beneath the jarring image were the words "I
think my mother would be happier without me around." She found the
photograph so weirdly compelling that she kept logging on to view it. She
couldn't say why, but somehow she found that looking at the picture was
cathartic, and she finally saved it onto her computer as background wallpaper.

When she wasn't on the computer, or when her connection occasionally faltered, she spent much of her time staring out the window, watching her neighbors come and go. That morning she had watched AP
Harry set off on his bicycle. The thermometer outside her window had
read 85 degrees at 9:00 a.m., and there was Harry, wearing his khaki
pants and a long-sleeved Harvard polo shirt. She watched a group of
middle school boys ride their skateboards down the street, flying over the
speed bumps, incurring the wrath of drivers. When she was bored with
these activities, she slept. She also began to watch a few soap operas, although these made her feel depressed and anxious. All of the drama in
these people's lives only emphasized her own emptiness. It was hard
to concentrate, even on the undemanding story lines. She found herself
contemplating some things she might do to make the pain go away,
which always brought her back to thinking about the razor-blade photo-

graph. Perhaps she should post a confession of her own. "I see inside the envelopes," it might read. But that was oversimplifying things. Maybe the more accurate confession would be the one that described her sense that a little nick with a knife might help the other problem go away.

She had come to the conclusion that taking her neighbors' mail wasn't really the worst thing in the world she might be doing, especially now that she knew about how other people cyber-stalked old boyfriends, or were obsessed with pornography, some of it pretty twisted. She had brought a steak knife up from the kitchen, but she hadn't put it to her skin. Her favorite character in her favorite novel, Esther Greenwood in *The Bell Jar*, had cut herself once, on the calf. But that was different. Esther was suicidal and Taylor was only looking for a way to feel less awful for a minute or two.

She remembered the scene in *The Exorcist* when the possessed girl wrote "Help Me" on her chest, the words rising from the skin like raised welts. Taylor always thought that if only the letters could push forward a bit more until they burst, then the demon might bleed out. That was the image that stuck in her mind when she envisioned a trickle of blood seeping from her arm and onto the floor. She didn't really want to cut herself, but the knife was there, a perverse sort of safety net in case things got really bad.

SHE DIDN'T realize that her mother was still at the door. Nina must have been in a rare contemplative mood, standing silently for so long. "Taylor, listen. I've got an appointment to get my nails done. I'll be back in an hour. Unless you want to come . . . I'll treat you to a manicure and pedicure? Or some highlights . . . I can see if they can squeeze you in."

Taylor didn't reply. Her mother was forever bouncing between the extremes of irrational anger and excessive generosity. She watched this dynamic played out with the dog on a daily, and sometimes hourly, basis. First, Nina would yell at her for exhibiting animal-like behavior like barking when the doorbell rang, and then she would apologize by giving her treats, resulting in a dog who was so fat she could barely make it up the stairs. In Taylor's case, she would fly into a rage about her being too apathetic or antisocial, and then a minute later she'd sweetly offer to take her shopping. Taylor did consider her mother's current offer, wondering if she would fund a transition to orange or blue hair, like the character Clementine in the movie *Eternal Sunshine of the Spotless Mind*. She was always in awe of these slightly unhinged, flamboyant female characters, like beautiful Nicole Diver in *Tender Is the Night*, or Holly Golightly in *Breakfast at Tiffany's*. She remembered how Holly would go to Tiffany's to neutralize her mood when she had the "mean reds." Taylor had tried that once, but it had no effect; plus, the salesgirls kept asking if she wanted any help, and after a while she got the feeling that the security guards were eyeing her. Sometimes she feared that her destiny might be to go crazy without anyone to find it romantic, yet she realized there was nothing very romantic about feeling like you might go crazy.

"Call my cell if you change your mind," Nina offered after an awkward silence. "By the way, I had a good idea for an essay. It has to do with overcoming hardship, making the best out of a bad situation, like when your great-great-great-grandfather used the first Great Depression to his advantage . . ." Taylor wished her mother was kidding. She understood that her father was in no way related to John D. Rockefeller, that the shared name was purely coincidental, but her mother insisted on maintaining the illusion that they had a common bloodline.

"We can talk about it later, I suppose," Nina said hopefully. "Also, I've got this thing I wanted to show you from yesterday's paper, so I'll slip this under your door. Just take a look at it. I've highlighted a school that has come up three times. If you read the articles, you'll see that these girls all went to the same school and have interesting jobs *and* they all look really happy."

Taylor knew without looking what her mother would be attempting to slip under the door, and she also knew that the style section of the Sunday *New York Times* would almost certainly not fit. Only her mother called the wedding announcements "articles," and only her mother would leap to the conclusion that the smiles plastered on prospective brides' faces were genuine reflections of emotional well-being. Nina Rockefeller herself was a striking example of the falsity of that assumption.

Taylor waited until she heard the garage door close before she set down her laptop and opened her door, making a private bet about the school du jour. From what institution might three girls have graduated, found spouses, and then exuded such happiness that tangible droplets of joy leapt off the gray *Times* newsprint? It was a rhetorical question of course, because there was a new answer every week. For the sake of amusement, she guessed Stanford, based on her own personal feeling that the farther she could get from home, the more radiant she might be, herself. But she was wrong. The winner of this round was Vanderbilt, where by some fluke of nature (or perhaps a connection to the editor of the social page) all three girls had not only gone to college, but belonged to the same sorority. She had no interest in sororities and definitely none in going to school in the South, yet she found herself reading the profiles. She didn't want to, but she couldn't help it. It turned out that only one of the three was marrying a college classmate, so she wasn't sure how that spoke to her mother's matchmaking theory. The name of one of the boys was familiar, and sure enough, he was from the area. She realized with a shudder that it was probably the older brother of a cute boy in her class, a fact she would be sure to keep from her mother, who while generally forgetful about day-to-day stuff, had a habit of seizing on socially useful tidbits and inserting them into conversation, often irrelevantly.

On one occasion she had foolishly alerted her mother to the fact that a new boy in her class was the son of a freshman senator from Arizona, for example, and ever since then Nina had found a way to bring up his name whenever she was in the presence of someone she wanted to impress. More often than not, that someone was the parent of a child who went to private school. This was her way, Taylor supposed, of letting others know that the wealthy and important, like the children of U.S. senators and people named Rockefeller, went to public school, too. It enabled Nina to sound like the sort of person who supported the idea of public education, when in truth Taylor knew that the cost of private school tuition had been the source of another family meltdown when she was in eighth grade. Her mother had prepared applications to six schools without mentioning it to her father. Taylor never learned whether she would have been admitted because her father went ballistic and cancelled the checks that had been sent to cover application fees. The process was aborted before she had to endure the first round of interviews, which was a huge relief.

Her public school might as well have been a private school, and in a way, it was. There was no tuition, per se, but irrational real estate prices served to filter out most of the rabble and lend it a somewhat exclusive air, or so she'd heard her mother say.

The demographics were less a concern to Taylor than the horrendous workload; the academic standards and amount of daily homework seemed impossible to exceed. Pressure for the school as a whole to succeed was fierce; the principal even quizzed random kids she passed in the hallway to see if they could define the vocabulary words she drew from cards in her pocket, and she handed out certificates for free burritos if they could correctly answer five in a row. On the downside, with nearly two thousand kids attending and operating on a shoestring county budget, the school was too large to give students much personal attention. Guidance counselors were severely overburdened, each one responsible for the welfare of nearly four hundred kids. There had been numerous attempts over the years to reduce the size of the student population by redrawing the catchment boundaries, but every time legislation was proposed, even the most apolitical residents practically took up arms—if an area were cut out of the Verona school district, its real estate values would plunge, and that was enough to get even retirees without school-aged kids out in front of the county executive's office waving placards. The building itself had recently been renovated in order to accommodate a new bulge of students, although the latest demographic figures suggested the crowds in the hallways would soon be thinning. The new, improved façade resembled the sleek headquarters of a high-tech start-up, and had in fact been nicknamed "Microsoft" by rival schools who taunted them at sports events, yelling "scoreboard, scoreboard" to highlight the fact that invariably Verona was losing whatever game was in progress. Verona students, in turn, shouted "SAT scores" to emphasize that they at least had the advantage in brainpower.

TAYLOR STARED at the pictures of the beautiful couples in the *Times* for a few minutes before crumpling the newspaper and tossing it against the wall. She tried to imagine herself in lace and pearls. If she ever married and deigned to let Nina mail a marriage announcement to a major newspaper—two enormous and unlikely *ifs*—she would sport some new outrageous hair color that hopefully would still shock in black and white, and she would snuggle against some scruffy backpacker type, or better yet, someone with an ethnic background specially selected to unnerve her mother.

In her brighter moments, she did look forward to moving on to the next phase of life. She knew it was not that unusual to be somewhat miserable in high school and had heard stories of kids who floundered in their teens but went on to thrive in college. Yet everyone around her seemed so well-adjusted, or at least so motivated, while she felt like she was the only one unraveling.

Still, she felt more enthusiasm than she let on about the prospect of going to college, and she had her heart set on Yates. After the campus tour had ended that day in April, she worked up the unprecedented nerve to wander into the all-girls dorm, where she knocked on a door. The girl who answered was in many ways her ideal of a college student; she was cute but not in an annoyingly fresh-faced, rowdy, full-of-school-spirit mtvU sort of way. She wore sweatpants and fluffy slippers and had a wool scarf tied around her neck. A Virginia Woolf novel rested on her desk beside a mug of tea. She agreed to show Taylor her bathroom without indicating that she thought the request was weird. Inside was her very own quaint Victorian pull-chain toilet and a pedestal sink. Taylor felt her work was done, notwithstanding the fact that the girl said the toilet frequently clogged.

Even if she didn't wind up at Yates, she suspected that going to just about any college would improve her general mental health. She had actually experienced something approaching a sense of peace when she spent a recent day at Georgetown working on a research paper at the library, for example. It had been pouring outside, and as she wandered through the gray Gothic campus, she stumbled upon a coffee bar, where she ordered a cappuccino and sat by herself at a table, watching the sea of people come and go. It seemed a place a loner with stringy purple hair might actually feel at home, even if at least half the girls she saw were athletic and blond. Anyway, Georgetown was not on her list; she needed to put much more than twenty minutes between herself and her family, and besides, between her slippage in grades and a D in tech ed last semester, she knew she had little hope of getting in.

She often thought that if her mother weren't driving her so hard, and for all the wrong reasons, she might take a bit more initiative in the college search. Or at least she might widen the scope of her interests beyond bathroom conditions. It simply came naturally to her to resist her mother. She understood this went against the laws of physics, that giving in to her mother would reduce friction and quite possibly even up her happiness quotient, but she found it impossible to do, even when she tried.

Another aspect of the problem was that her mother was not aware of her poor academic performance second semester of junior year and had believed her when she said she'd earned straight A's. "Why hasn't your report card arrived in the mail?" Nina asked. "Who could say? The mail delivery is so erratic!" Taylor replied. There was a new computer program that allowed parents to monitor their kids' performance online, but fortunately for Taylor, her mother could barely figure out how to check her own e-mail.

Taylor wondered if she was developing strange special powers where the mail was concerned, because while reflecting on her missing report card, she walked to the window and saw the squat postal truck rumble down the street and park on the corner. It seemed to be plagued by a muffler problem, as it was inordinately noisy and puffed smoke like a steam engine. She liked the mailman, and thought of waving to him, although he could not possibly see her standing in an upstairs window in her pajamas, with the blinds partially closed. But when he emerged from the truck, she could see it was not the regular carrier. She hadn't seen him for a while and wondered if he was possibly ill. The substitutes were generally so hopeless that mail *was* often misrouted. Just last week the Rockefellers had received all of the mail for the old woman across the street, and frequently they would get the mail intended for the street directly behind them, where the numbers followed the same general pattern. Her household's missing mail for the past six months had been

blamed on the inefficient U.S. Postal Service, and while Taylor felt somewhat guilty about that, she figured it was probably at least a little bit true.

○ ○ ○

HARRY KNEW THAT envy, like jealousy, stress, and anxiety, was entirely
counterproductive. Many a mortal might harbor some resentment about
pulling weeds in his best friend's garden on his one day off, but AP Harry
was a rational person who had resolved long ago to never be petty. Justin Smelling was lucky to be summering in New Zealand, working for
an international biotech firm conducting research on a rogue herd of
oddly hoofed sheep, and Harry wished him well. And bravo for Justin
Smelling's younger brother, who might be able to pull a weed or two
himself if he didn't have better things to do, like attend some six-
thousand-dollar summer camp, honing his soccer goalie skills.

Harry was in no position to complain: he had secured a highly
coveted internship working three days a week for an up-and-coming Republican congressman from Texas. Even though the job didn't pay, he
loved putting on a suit and tie and riding the Metro downtown, reading
the newspaper and generally imagining himself a member of the ruling
class, albeit it one without his own car. Already he had been invited to
lunch in the Senate dining room, where he spied not only Hillary Clinton
and Ted Kennedy, but one of his personal heroes, Trent Lott.

He knew he was lucky to have this gardening gig on the side, which
was as flexible as it was lucrative. Surely it was guilt that led Dr. Smelling
to pay Harry about five times the going rate for yard work, but he was not
above taking the cash. It was not as though there was any great class war-
fare at work in his community, certainly no economic divisions worthy of
a proletarian revolution, and yet things were not quite equal. Harry fell
somewhere between the Justin Smellings and Mike Lees of the world.
Mike Lee's father was a Korean immigrant who owned a small conve-
nience store in downtown D.C. and had scraped together the down pay-
ment on a dilapidated old rambler so that Mike could attend Verona.
Mike was required to practice piano at least two hours every day, attend

Korean school on weekends, help out behind the cash register five nights a week, and study every remaining waking moment. Somehow he still found time to satisfy his insatiable appetite for American pop culture, which meant keeping up on all the latest television shows. He was particularly fond of *Fear Factor* and dreamed of being a contestant someday. He practiced by occasionally eating bugs and other bizarre and possibly toxic concoctions at lunch. Mike once raised his hand in AP Psych and asked whether he was the only one in the class whose dreams were always in the form of cartoons, a revelation so bizarre that his friends still teased him about it. Harry wasn't hugely surprised Mike dreamed in animation: he pretty much assumed Mike's mind had been warped by all the celebrity gossip he absorbed—he ran home each Friday to read his *Us* magazine and was always going on about the breakups of minor movie stars Harry had never even heard of. Yet Mike still managed to get straight A's with what appeared to be relatively minimal effort.

The problem, as Harry saw it, was that there were simply too many Mike Lee types at Verona. The cluster of brainpower at the top was packed so tight, it was like the inner loop of the Beltway at rush hour. There was no room to move, hardly any way to get where you were going. Your run-of-the-mill very smart person, even if he was as driven as Harry, could give up sleep entirely, study 24/7, sign up for every available extracurricular activity, and still pale beside a kid like Mike Lee. And yet if one were willing to take things down just one single notch—to aim for B's instead of A's—it meant a sea change in lifestyle. Harry's friend Kevin Connor, for example, was a bright, well-adjusted kid who was perfectly content with his 3.0 grade point average. He never studied, explaining nonchalantly that he preferred to spend his free time playing Halo and writing songs on his guitar. When Harry asked him if he was worried about college, Kevin replied that even if he gave up his mellow afternoons in pursuit of a seat at a top-ranked school, he would never get in, what with all the brains at Verona already engaged in some unspoken duel to the death. He figured he would settle on a perfectly good but less competitive school—preferably somewhere near a beach—and he'd buckle down and study then.

Harry thought Kevin was slightly mad. But he also understood that the competition at Verona was itself insane. Harry could work until his brain began to bleed while Kevin played video games, and it was possible they'd still wind up rooming together at Maryland. At some level it didn't really matter how a kid like Harry stacked up against all the Harvard wannabes in the rest of the country; the kids at Verona were engaged in their own internal battle. Any one college was going to take only a handful of kids from the same high school, even if there were twenty kids from Verona who might be better qualified than the valedictorians at twenty other high schools scattered across the country. The way he saw it, the competition consisted of Justin, Mike, and a few quiet, nondescript girls he didn't really know, but one of whom had won the Westinghouse science competition the previous year with an entry that measured gaseous fumes on Saturn. Another had straight A's and perfect scores, and played cello with the National Symphony Orchestra. Rumor had it she was being wooed by Juilliard, but had her heart set on Harvard, where her father had gone. And then there was Mandy Shapiro, who was the school's captain on *It's Academic* and had led the team to the state championship for three straight years. There was also Keith Johnson, one of only three African-American boys in their grade and a National Merit scholar semifinalist. Keith was also an aspiring actor who had snagged the lead role in every student play—dramas and musicals. While Harry had no idea where Keith planned to apply to school, he wouldn't be shocked if he entered the Harvard fray as well, although if the subject ever came up in Harry's presence, he thought he might name-drop all of the famous actors who had gone to Yale, even though off the top of his head he couldn't name a single one.

HARRY SLAPPED at a mosquito on his wrist and watched it ooze blood. He thought of his mother's many years of malaria research at NIH and wondered whether she would ever find a way to really eradicate the disease. Then he found himself thinking of Maya, who was currently in India. He wondered if Maya was taking any prophylactic—and then blushed at the intimacy implied by the word.

He didn't know what to make of his feelings toward Maya. He figured his interest in her was just a biological thing, like malaria itself. Just a boy reacting to a pretty girl, producing some chemical reaction that made him do things like follow her around without really meaning to. Yes, she was very attractive and she also smelled very good, like lavender soap, but he didn't have time to deal with this sort of distraction. He'd watched his friend Bill Segal, who had just graduated, spend his senior year in various states of distress that seemed to Harry to be bordering on psychosis. Bill's girlfriend kept severing their relationship and then showing up at his house in tears, wanting to reconcile. Bill would go into an emotional tailspin every time this happened. Harry didn't have room in his life for a girlfriend if it was going to involve a lot of time-consuming hysterical behavior.

Still, he had to admit an involuntary infatuation. He had even looked her name up in the dictionary once, justifying the act on the grounds that it might improve his reading and writing scores. He learned that Maya, also called Mahamaya, was a Hindu goddess who personified the power that creates phenomena. Creates phenomena? He wasn't sure he understood what that meant, and had yet to see it appear on a standardized test.

Her house was big and ugly, and he thought the Mercedes SUV she had been given for her sixteenth birthday was atrocious. It had sat in the Kaluantharanas' driveway for a week with a red bow on the hood. Maya rarely drove it, and she continued to walk to school on the mornings that she didn't have swim practice. He couldn't help but think about how she and Justin were jetting around the world over their summer breaks while he, in turn, was trying to liberate the Smellings' rosebush from about three years' worth of angry bindweed. He had heard rumors of a subtle backlash among admissions officers who were sick of hearing about kids' exotic, supposedly character-building, career-enhancing summer vacations and had to think there might be some hidden benefit to being a congressional intern–cum–itinerant gardener.

He wiped the sweat from his brow and stared at the mess of vines, for which the delicate pruning tools Dr. Smelling had given him were no match. He needed something more powerful, like an axe, or maybe a hacksaw.

His bite began to itch, and he wondered if, in this age of globalization, it might again become possible to catch a mosquito-borne disease in the United States. Yellow fever had once been a problem in the South, he had heard, or maybe he had read this in a book that explained the origins of Tulane's School of Tropical Medicine. A person could learn a lot from college guidebooks, he'd decided. He was wearing the long-sleeved Harvard shirt his father had sent him and long trousers, and gardening gloves shielded his hands, but it was impossible to protect himself entirely. He was so hot and sweaty he was tempted to strip and jump in the Smellings' enticing pool, malarial mosquitoes notwithstanding.

He mentally calculated how much he had made so far today and decided he would call it quits in about an hour. His mother rarely talked about money, but he had a sense of how stretched they were financially. Certainly, there was food on the table at night and their living conditions were better than 98 percent of the rest of the world, but that didn't mean his mother's paycheck went much further than covering the basic cost of living in Verona, which she frequently quipped must be quadruple the national average. Any bit of house repair that needed to be done, he once heard her complain, cost four times whatever you had set aside. When their driveway had disintegrated to the point that it could no longer be ignored, Grace budgeted $2,000 for the repair, only to learn that there seemed to be just one contractor operating in the entire southern part of Maryland—or at least only one who returned her phone call after weeks of trying to solicit competitive bids—and his baseline price for a new driveway was approximately $10,000.

While Harry knew his mother had been socking away money for college, she had not factored in the costs of *applying* to college, which they had both falsely assumed were negligible. They had spent hundreds of dollars touring campuses, even though he limited his search to the East Coast and they traveled only by car. Just a few nights in a hotel room and meals on the road added up pretty quickly. But then, all of this campus touring was at her insistence. He didn't really think it was necessary, since he was pretty sure where he was headed. He would apply early to Harvard, and then when the time came, he'd pick a handful of lesser schools—Dartmouth, perhaps, or maybe places like Princeton, Stanford, and Columbia—as backups. Even though he was well aware of the competition, and his deficient reading and writing scores stuck in his craw like one of the many thorns in this strangled rosebush that kept tearing through his glove, he was fairly confident that his summer internship, as well as a stint as student body president, would lift his application above the rest of the pack. He was also grateful to have a slight edge as a member of the last class allowed to apply early action.

Then there was the cost of testing. The last SAT fee hike meant the basic test now cost $41.50, and Harry had taken it three times. He planned to take it again in the fall, but was a bit concerned—Grace reported back to him after the last Verona college-planning parent meeting that one of the guest speakers joked that taking the test too many times made a kid look "desperate." That caused a brief crisis of introspection, but then, Harry decided that he *was* desperate—desperate to get into Harvard—and couldn't imagine he would really be penalized for trying to realize his dreams. On top of that was the cost of at least three SAT subject tests, requiring an $18 registration fee plus anywhere from eight to nineteen additional dollars depending on which test you took. The AP tests cost $83 apiece. And then there were reporting fees—the College Board provided four free reports, but only if you selected the schools when registering for the test, or shortly after the test date. What if you didn't know where you wanted to apply until you saw your scores? And four schools? Harry didn't know anyone who planned to limit his applications to four—or even eight or ten for that matter—except maybe the handful of kids who were headed to Verona College. "VK," the principal had recently called it over the loudspeaker during morning announcements, in the context of telling kids that if they did not spend the summer wisely and start getting organized, they might well be headed to community college, her misguided stab at humor implying that anyone headed to a two-year school would not know how to spell the word *college*. She issued an apology the next day.

For those planning to apply to more than four schools, each report was an additional $9.50. And if you were anxious to find out your scores as soon as possible, you could pay $26.50 for a rush report by phone.

There were all sorts of ways to keep racking up extra fees, some of them not really optional, in Harry's view, like forking over $50 to have them verify his score by hand and another $50 to double-check the essay. Given all of the egregious scoring mistakes that had been made recently, Harry didn't see that he had much choice.

None of this was even taking into consideration the actual application fees, averaging roughly $50 apiece. Most review courses ran about $800, and the private tutor Harry had talked his mother into hiring charged $200 per hour. He had glimpsed an e-mail from the tutor in response to his mother's query about how to most effectively maximize the six sessions she had allotted for Harry's preparation. The tutor had written back that they should schedule all of the sessions as close to the test date as possible, that normally she might spread them out a bit more, but given that she had only just come to understand that "money was a problem," they would try to do the best they could under the circumstances. Harry could only imagine his mother's reaction, which she hadn't shared with him. He felt bad having her spend so much money on him—she worked incredibly hard and rarely complained, and he couldn't recall the last thing she had done for herself. He knew other mothers went to spas and bought themselves nice clothes and even midlife-crisis convertible sports cars, but he was also convinced that if he could just boost his scores, he would lock in a spot at Harvard, and then one day he would pay her back somehow with . . . he wasn't sure what, but maybe a Caribbean cruise or a full-time housekeeper or some big hunks of jewelry.

When he and his mother had met with the guidance counselor at school, a woman in her early twenties who had grown up in Australia and seemed to know far less than Harry did about college admissions (and who Angie Lee's older sister had reportedly bumped into at a club downtown at 2:00 a.m., slightly drunk, about a week earlier), the counselor had suggested that Harry consider the honors program at the University of Maryland or look at any number of schools that would happily give a kid like Harry a merit-based scholarship. She was big on promoting St. Mary's, the highly regarded state liberal arts school, and went on about it so much that Harry wondered if perhaps she was getting a kickback for each student that applied. He knew he was probably being overly sensitive, but still, he found this insulting. On what basis did this woman assume that they needed money? As if he had worked this hard to go to a state school in Maryland!

Inevitably, his mother thought these were good ideas, and she suggested they drive out to College Park the following week. He couldn't blame her for being so enthusiastic—Harry had been one of fourteen students from his class to win a $3,000 per year Distinguished Scholars award, which was applicable only if he attended a Maryland college or university. Grace even hinted that she might be able to buy him a new car as a graduation present if he went to Maryland. She asked Harry to at least call the school to reserve a spot on one of the tours, but he conveniently kept forgetting to do this. It was not just that he didn't want to go to a state school, but he happened to live in a state with what he considered to be a second-rate state university. The fact that Maryland's numbers had actually become quite competitive—more than half of the freshmen were in the top 10 percent of their high school class—did little to persuade him.

They finally compromised with a self-guided tour early on a Sunday morning, sparing Harry the ordeal of attending a formal information session where he would no doubt bump into someone he knew. But even strolling through the virtually empty Maryland campus on a weekend morning in mid-July he had the misfortune of running into someone from Verona. Samantha Ruth, who had been in his AP World History class when she was a senior and he was a sophomore, explained that she had transferred after finding Middlebury too insular; she was taking summer courses to get some of her mismatched credits in order, she said. Although Harry didn't ask, Samantha volunteered that she initially had an attitude about attending a large state university, but now that she had experienced both, she preferred Maryland.

He had trouble imagining how transferring from one of the most picturesque campuses in the country to a huge school in suburban Maryland was a quality-of-life enhancer. Surely there was more to the story than that, Harry thought privately. He found Maryland pretty architecturally uninspiring, and thought College Park was hardly the quintessential college town, despite its name. He'd heard of a few kids who had gone away to college and then had minor breakdowns, or been placed on academic probation, or suffered some other variety of maladjustment, such as landing in the emergency room a few times too many with alcohol poisoning, and all of them wound up at Maryland. From what he had heard, there was a clique of Verona kids at Maryland who still hung out together, like it was just an extension of high school. Perhaps Samantha had struggled academically, although that seemed unlikely given that she was very bright and Verona kids generally claimed they worked so hard in high school that they were well prepared for college. Harry wished Samantha would just go away, but then Grace asked her which dorm she was living in, and the next thing he knew they were sitting with her at a campus coffee shop hearing about the Terps' awesome season and how she was part of the pep squad and got to travel with the team when they were in the playoffs against Duke. By the time they parted, Grace was practically weepy with nostalgia.

HARRY HAD had enough gardening for one day; he needed to use a telephone almost as badly as he needed a drink of water. He had brought his cell phone and his mother's credit card for the purpose of calling the College Board at precisely 2:00 p.m., when in theory he could retrieve by telephone the scores for the AP exams he had taken in May. But when he tried to call, he realized he was in what must have been part of the only 2 percent of the country where his wireless provider had no service. Looking up, he saw a monstrous cell phone tower looming overhead and wondered if, counterintuitively, his proximity to the tower might be blocking his signal.

Dr. Smelling would certainly have let him use the phone, but he was covered in dirt and sweat and he didn't want to ask. Plus, he didn't want to report on his slow progress with the bindweed, or remind her that Justin's scores were available, although it was hard to imagine she wouldn't already have that marked on her calendar. And he didn't want to discuss his scores with Dr. Smelling. It was bad enough that he and Justin were always at each other about grades—there was at least an edgy playfulness to their constant jockeying—but to have Justin's neurotic mother involved in the competition would push the situation into a new realm of ugliness, even for Harry. He and Justin had been friends and rivals since third grade, when they both took the test to apply to the county magnet school. Even though they had scored perfectly on the test and had the third grade equivalent of straight A's ("above average" check marks in all subjects), they were both denied admission, which seemed an early blow for eight-year-olds. Still, given that their school was actually considered as good as the one that contained the magnet program, it didn't much matter, so long as they were in the same boat. They had been in virtually every class together since. They cemented their bond as freshmen; both boys had late growth spurts, which meant that when they first entered high school, neither one of them stood taller than five feet, which made them conspicuous in classrooms full of nearly fully grown kids.

While he didn't know for sure, he assumed Justin's SAT scores were better than his. They usually compared notes, but in this case Harry didn't want to ask, and he feigned an attitude that he was somehow above discussing these sorts of things. He had just received the results from his most recent stab at the SAT and as before, he couldn't budge his numbers. He was tempted to fill in the bubbles to form the outline of a duck and write a bunch of gibberish for the essay to see if this was some sort of curse. It seemed unfair that no scoring errors had turned up; two Verona students from the class above him had their scores raised 100 points when it was discovered they were part of the group of five thousand or so test-takers whose scores were incorrectly reported, so it was not completely delusional to suppose that the College Board might be eating his missing 160 points. They claimed otherwise. Whatever the explanation, he thought he ought to get some sort of bonus for consistency. But even if Justin had perfect 800s—so-called "collect calls"—he wasn't student body president, and Harry had to think that weighed heavier than a couple more right answers on a piece of paper.

HARRY PUT his bicycle in the garage before collecting the mail. There wasn't much there: an electric bill that looked as though it had already been opened and, oddly, bore a postmark of two weeks earlier, as well as a circular for a local garden store. His mother had recently complained to the post office that something was wrong with their mail service. Bills arrived late, and some never came at all. He and Justin Smelling had been playing a game since they first took the practice PSATs sophomore year, collecting their piles of unsolicited college junk mail to see who had the most. They had been in a dead heat until Harry's solicitations became sporadic and then suddenly stopped, making him slightly paranoid. For more than a year, he had received some sort of mail from Washington University in St. Louis just about once a week, for example, and while he had no real interest in the school, their frequent solicitations had begun to feel like a form of affection. Justin was getting mail from a wide range of schools, including tiny colleges in western Pennsylvania that neither one of them had ever heard of. Harry wasn't even on *those* lists. Meanwhile, he had requested a Harvard catalogue three times, and it had never arrived. He was able to bring home catalogues galore from the school guidance office, and of course any information he needed was available online, but still, it had been a real ego-boost to get a daily torrent of mail, and it was somewhat unnerving to imagine that a unilateral decision might have been made by admissions offices across the nation to cross him off their lists.

Even more unnerving, however, was that the automated system at the College Board had transferred him to an actual human, who then left him on hold. He had been hanging in telephone limbo for about twenty minutes trying to access his English score. The other scores had come through fine—all 5s, of course—and retrieving them had been straightforward. It was a good thing he had waited for a landline or he might have used up the monthly remainder of his precious wireless minutes. The man, who had identified himself as Mel, finally came back on the line and said that something was wrong and could Harry please continue to hold. Harry took a few deep breaths, forcing himself to remain calm. He paced around the kitchen and absentmindedly began to put the dishes piled in the sink into the dishwasher. He stacked the newspapers lying around the room and brought them into the garage for recycling. He gave the dog her medicine—the vet had recently put her on estrogen supplements, another painful expense for a family already teetering on the financial brink. All that accomplished and he was still on hold.

Now he couldn't remember whether he had dealt with an actual human being last year. Maybe this was really the norm, and the computer automated system the exception. How could he not recall such an important detail? Had he done something wrong? Maybe he had forgotten to code in his social security number when he took the test, or perhaps he had gone over the credit line of his mother's Visa card. He had the sudden wild thought that maybe he had maxed out on the number of AP tests allowed by the College Board. But of course that was nonsense given that surely someone was making money off this racket. They currently offered thirty-seven different AP tests, and he had only taken eleven so far. His plan back in sixth grade had been to take every single AP test, figuring this would set some sort of record that could not help but guarantee a Harvard acceptance, but that was before he understood the practical constraints. Even if he gave up lunch, there were only eight class periods in a day, and he was therefore not going to be able to take the tests in French, German, or Latin given that he had not had time to actually learn these languages. Another problem was that he didn't know the first thing about art, which forced him to cross both Art History and Studio Art off the list. It had been his original intention to sit for the Psychology exam even though he had not taken the class, figuring that it was sort of a joke of a subject, but then he overheard Mike Lee discussing the test and realized that he might be overestimating his ability to wing it. Additional scheduling complications arose when he learned that certain AP classes like Biology and Chemistry were actually two periods long. Harry was still determined to find a way around this, but was eventually persuaded by his counselor, who had taken to cringing when he appeared in her doorway, to let it go.

While he continued to languish on hold, his cell phone rang. Harry flipped it open and saw a text message. It was the SAT question of the day.

Choose the word or set of words that, when inserted in the sentence, best fits the meaning of the sentence as a whole.

The dramatist was _____ over his lack of funds and his inability to sell any of his plays, and his letters to his wife reflected his unhappiness.

1. despondent
2. supercilious
3. prudent
4. encouraged
5. fortified

It was an easy answer; this was not the sort of question that might result in a penalty on his would-be perfect score. Number 1 accurately filled in the blank, but it also described how Harry felt when Mel came back on the line to report that there was some sort of problem, that they could not find Harry's score, that actually they were having trouble finding any of the scores from Verona High, and would it be all right if they called him back in a couple of hours?

August

THAT BASIL DICKERSON'S AFTERNOON barbeque would turn out to be an elegant affair was another in a long series of miscalculations Olivia had made in the last few years. Tired of being ridiculed for being chronically overdressed, she deduced incorrectly that attire for a backyard barbeque might be somewhat casual. She was not so gauche as to wear shorts and flip-flops for an event involving trustees, but still she felt horribly tacky in a simple khaki skirt and sleeveless checked blouse, which she now feared only emphasized the atrophying muscle groups in her upper arms. She had even swapped her pearls for a whimsical hand-crafted cow on a chain that some wait-listed would-be studio art major had sent in the mail. She hung this hideous ornament around her neck thinking that it might help her look more Yates—part of a campaign to position herself for a promotion that she wasn't really sure she wanted. Meanwhile, almost all of the men were wearing natty ties and jackets despite the oppressive heat, and most of the women had donned their summer best, a few of them even wearing fussy hats as though they were here to take tea with the queen.

She had always dreamed of a life of invites to fancy garden parties like this, where she'd mingle with beautiful, important people. And here she was, accepting champagne from a white-gloved waiter who passed her the flute from a silver tray. So why did she not feel as though she'd arrived? she wondered. It probably had something to do with the pop psychology notion that she was responsible for her own misery: if she took her own job more seriously, if she gave a bit more credit to the institution that employed her, it might have occurred to her that being invited to a trustee barbeque at the home of the college president was actually something of an honor.

Of course this was hardly her first taste of the good life. She'd been raised in great wealth, but her parents were stuffy and dull, the sort who preferred sipping brandy and watching *Masterpiece Theatre* to being photographed at soirees. She'd had a second shot at society: she and Preston had in fact enjoyed their first romantic moment at a party much like this, their relationship inaugurated with a session of indecent groping behind the barn at a colleague's restored eighteenth-century farmhouse at the annual firm picnic. She had imagined, as he'd crudely thrust his ancient, garlicky tongue in her mouth, a life spent attending functions as a bride on Preston's well-tailored arm. Her dream was partially fulfilled, but she failed to foresee that once she married, she would be considered such a social pariah that she would no longer feel welcome at these fabulous events.

Her heels sank into the soggy soil of a steeply curving slope of the small hamlet of President Dickerson's so-called summer cottage, which she guessed spanned about forty acres. She was having a hard time staying erect with the champagne in one hand and a plate of food in the other, and thought she might actually pitch backward as she tried to adjust her stance. She had seriously underestimated Basil Dickerson, who was evidently very rich. Although she privately disparaged the school, she had to admit that from what she'd seen over the years, Yates graduates tended to land on their feet.

Remaining vertical was proving difficult, but the greater challenge was maintaining her equilibrium while conversing with the annoying Arnold Hutch. She could see Ari from this perch on the hill; he was standing with an unusual-looking older man who was wearing some sort of military uniform, a stark, steel-gray crew cut, and a chest full of medals. Beside them was a younger man in pressed designer jeans and an expensive camel-haired, double-breasted blazer. He had a ponytail and a thick silver stud through his ear. At least she was not the only one who had underdressed.

Just beside them, in another cluster, was the redundantly named Belle, wearing a sexy chiffon number with a plunging neckline. She was holding a chunky toddler on a hip, so perhaps it was only her awkward stance that made it appear she was possibly pregnant. And yes, that was indeed Fritz Heimler with his back to Olivia, leaning in close to whisper something in Belle's ear, causing her to laugh hysterically. Olivia felt a pang of jealousy too complicated to deconstruct without the help of therapy.

Arnold Hutch was nattering on about the design of the New Orleans levees, and she was pretending to be engaged. Olivia knew she was supposed to treat Arnold with respect, but she had truly had enough of celebrating this man, regardless of his genius status, as had just about everyone at Yates except, evidently, Basil Dickerson.

There had been a huge uproar on campus when Dickerson was hired; the two other serious contenders for Yates's top job boasted impressive academic credentials—one was the Harvard-educated, African-American dean of students at a prestigious liberal arts school in Minnesota, and the other, a Hispanic woman, was the president of a small but ascendant college in Florida. Dickerson, a fat white male with a sketchy corporate résumé, inspired dread among the faculty, who assumed he would be insensitive to their needs, chief among them them the demand for higher salaries.

To dispel the notion that with his Enron past he was removed from the concerns of a small liberal arts college, Basil held several informal meetings with department heads, and then threw a lavish party where he said he hoped to get to know the faculty on a more intimate level. This didn't go well. He set out a spread of fresh sushi that he bragged had been specially flown in from a famous Japanese restaurant in Manhattan, but one of the biology professors in attendance said that some of the fish in the mix had almost certainly been caught using methods that were known to endanger sea turtles. He also served a wine that had been the subject of a recent boycott stemming from the oppressive working conditions of the migrant farmworkers employed by the California vineyard. Then there was the poorly timed delivery of a new Viking range for his kitchen, adding fodder to accusations that he was tone-deaf to matters of money. His wife was a gourmet cook, he'd explained as the deliverymen wrestled the appliance through the crowded living room, and Mrs. Dickerson could not possibly manage with the ancient stove that had conveyed with the house.

But the most controversial matter was the hiring of Arnold Hutch, who was rumored to have come with a jaw-dropping price tag. Fritz Heimler was sloppy in containing his resentment that evening, when the news of Hutch's appointment had first surfaced. He had had too much to drink, and began to rail loudly about the lack of respect paid to poets. He then said something regrettable about a still life hanging over the fireplace, which turned out to have been painted by Basil himself.

Heimler was widely regarded as both a pompous windbag and a second-rate poet, but he was also the only member of the faculty to boast a Pulitzer, which served as a not inconsequential promotional tool. To keep the peace, Basil now invited both Heimler and Hutch to every important school function, where they were frequently the only faculty in attendance. Meanwhile, Hutch seemed to be soaking up his celebrity status, and was not afraid to opine on subjects as far outside his field as U.S. foreign policy in Iraq. He had already graced two covers of the Yates alumni magazine. Olivia had had lunch with him once, and it hadn't gone well. She found Arnold creepy, and suspected that underneath the smug, macho veneer was a once-scrawny nerd, a man who had spent a frustrated, horny adolescence in his rec room playing with a chemistry set, and then had undertaken a self-improvement campaign lifting weights and gleaning seduction tips from men's magazines in an effort to make up for the lost years of his youth.

For the last ten excruciating minutes she had stood in the searing midday sun pretending to be engaged by the engineering obstacles faced in rebuilding New Orleans. Then Basil appeared, his own version of party chatter having to do with money. He was in negotiations with various drug companies about having them underwrite a $10 million state-of-the-art science lab, he said. She was calculating the right sorts of dean of admissions things to say in response, like how a new lab would help attract strong science candidates to the school, but personally she thought there were more interesting things to talk about, like the surprising size of Basil's wife, evidently his third, who easily weighed over three hundred pounds and was in the process of shoving a melting chocolate cream puff in her mouth. Ari had recently filled her ear with gossip about how Basil's second wife had been bulimic and his first had run off with her yoga instructor. Olivia knew she was supposed to be shocked, but really this made her warm to him a bit. She liked that she was not the only one with a complicated past.

This shift in the conversation inspired Arnold Hutch to start blathering about the beaten-to-a-pulp subject of the dearth of women in the math and sciences, opining that this reflected a genetic predisposition to perform poorly in these subjects. Olivia was about to attack him, possibly physically, just as Basil interrupted with a startling disclosure.

"This is not for publication, of course," Basil began, lowering his voice, "but we've had a few preliminary discussions over the summer about the idea of abolishing the SAT requirement. Of course we will form various committees to look into this if we decide to move forward. It's just something we're contemplating at the moment."

Olivia and Arnold were momentarily united in their astonishment. Again Olivia wondered who the "we" referred to. How could even preliminary conversations be taking place on such an important subject without involving the interim and possibly future dean of admissions? This seemed to not bode well for her future. She reminded herself that above all, she hoped for Ray's speedy return to health, even though a promotion would be nice.

At least she had been part of the committee that met over the summer to design a new view book, although their conversations had sounded more like brainstorming sessions to sell a car than a college. Following the recommendation of the expensive consulting firm Basil had put on contract, instructions were given to the art director to eliminate all pictures with snow in the background and to give the impression that "At Yates, it is always fall."

"Drop the SAT requirement?" Arnold asked, perplexed. The look on his face suggested he believed that the school would be overrun by a horde of ignorant barbarians if the SAT floodgate was opened wide.

Olivia thought she knew where this idea was coming from. Another nearby liberal arts school had just abolished the SAT requirement, and within two years it had climbed 2 points in the *U.S. News* rankings, a result of the fact that the reported scores were self-selective, and therefore higher. If Basil adopted the same approach, it would allow him to continue to look like a trailblazing maverick by taking a public stand against the SATs while actually propelling Yates on its great march forward toward number 49.

"Have you considered the possible drop in the retention figures?" Arnold asked worriedly.

Olivia watched Belle walk over to Ari and thrust the child into his arms. She could see, even from this distance, the cranberry stain on the toddler's white dress, an accident that had occurred earlier in the day when Olivia slipped past Belle to say hello, accidentally knocking into her and causing her to spill juice on the little girl's head. Ari began to bounce the thing on his hip, and then turned and began speaking to a woman Olivia recognized as a reporter from the local NBC affiliate, a perky gal with a trademark ponytail that seemed to sprout skyward from the center of her head. She had a pen and pad in her hand, and was taking notes. Olivia wondered what was going on.

Now standing beside Ari, making amusing animal faces at the little girl, were two gorgeous men who resembled a pair of preppy models from a Ralph Lauren ad, or some freshly scrubbed Doublemint twins from another era. She assumed they were trustees, not just because they were here at the trustee barbeque, but because they appeared to be extraordinarily rich. As Olivia stared at them, she marveled that despite their good looks, they had zero sexual appeal, and in fact they looked a little off. They were so exquisite-looking, so finely featured and chiseled, that they appeared to be crossing some invisible line back toward ugly. This seemed meaningful in some complicated way she would have to contemplate when she was less distracted.

"Retention figures?" Basil asked, snapping her back to the mind-numbing reality that was her life.

"If you drop the SAT requirement you will be attracting an entirely different breed of animal," Arnold said. "You will have no indication of whether these people will be able to perform in college. Any rise in the rankings from the higher SAT scores will be offset by a drop in reten-tion."

Basil seemed slightly shocked by this remark. Olivia was shocked, too, not by his observation, but by the fact that Arnold would so blatantly re-fer to the rankings. Evidently, he needed an etiquette lesson; like his bloated salary, the subject was at the very heart of things, and yet com-pletely taboo.

"Actually, Arnold, studies have shown no correlation between a stu-dent's SAT scores and his ability to perform in college," she said, sur-prised to hear herself taking this position.

There was a time when Olivia might have shared Arnold's fears about retention rates, but she had just recently begun to view all this in a differ-ent light. These higher-scoring kids were not discernibly different in terms of mental prowess either in person or on paper, but she did catch a subtle whiff of entitlement, as if many of them believed it was only an unfortunate convergence of unfavorable circumstances that had landed them at Yates, a school that just a few years ago hadn't appeared in any of the major college guidebooks, and still didn't appear on most maps.

She used to take a lot of crap from Ray for emphasizing test scores. Perhaps the most egregious case—the one that made her cringe when she recalled the details—was when she had first arrived a decade earlier and voted to reject a straight-A student from an elite private high school in San Francisco who had low SATs. When her baffled colleagues asked her what she might possibly have been thinking—the girl was the editor of the school newspaper and had glowing teacher recommendations, among other things—Olivia replied that the kid was obviously a grind. She would be working round the clock to make up for her mental defi-ciencies, Olivia said, and she'd have nothing to contribute to the collegial community generally since she'd be toiling in the library all the time. The girl was admitted by a committee vote of six to one, and Olivia read in the alumni magazine that she was now a senior editor at *The New York Times*.

Olivia managed to take a bite of the shrimp thing on her plate; then she swirled the champagne around in her mouth, trying to dislodge the bit of food that stuck between the gap of her two front teeth. She was not one to spend much time worrying about class division in America, and yet there seemed to be something so glaringly wrong with the system that it was threatening to turn even a snob like herself into a woman of the people. How had a test originally intended to give a smart kid stuck farming pigs in the Midwest a chance to compete with the children of the Northeastern elite morphed back into a tool to help the rich stay on top? (Of course, she knew that was oversimplifying things; there were ugly assumptions about race and intelligence embedded in the blueprints of early standardized tests.) Even she, who had scored well herself and had once regarded it as an instant way to gauge a person's brainpower, was coming to the conclusion that the test was useless as a way to assess either potential or intellectual curiosity. It seemed an inconvenient time to be having this epiphany, given that she was gunning for a job that, on Basil's watch, required bowing to the numbers.

Olivia looked once more toward Ari, who this time noticed her and lifted his chin in acknowledgment. She looked away, and then, without meaning to, she looked at him again. He seemed to wink, which gave her an innervating jolt. She wondered again why he was talking to a television reporter, and why she was taking notes. She looked back at Basil, who had his back to this weird, Felliniesque, tableau of Doublemint twins and now more of Ari's brood, playing with soap bubbles. She was pretty sure something was wrong.

"Basil," she said, but he put a finger in the air to indicate he wasn't quite finished with his thought, which had something to do with allowing kids to submit SAT subject test scores in lieu of the so-called reasoning test. He also mentioned a couple of schools that had begun allowing students to withhold their scores if they were willing, up-front, to waive scholarship eligibility. This, too, seemed a win-win situation, he said, since then you were guaranteeing yourself kids who could pay full tuition, even if they might not be the brightest crayons in the box.

The television reporter and the two men were moving toward them. Olivia felt a now certain foreboding and tried to get Basil's attention again, without success.

The thing between her teeth would not budge despite vigorous

machinations of her tongue, and she tried to keep her mouth from opening too widely. As a kid she had chosen to forgo braces; Lauren Hutton
had gotten pretty far in life with that same imperfect smile, she had reasoned. But she understood she was not a natural beauty, and over the
years the space attracted more food debris than modeling contracts. She
tried to be discreet as she stuck the fingernail of her pinky into her
mouth and pried the slimy substance free; a television reporter was approaching, it seemed imperative that she not have an unsightly glob
stuck in her teeth in case there was a camera crew lurking somewhere
out of sight. Arnold looked at her with what might have been disgust and
then excused himself, claiming to need the bathroom, heading off toward
a cluster of middle-aged men who were smoking cigars, tapping their
ashes into the freshly mulched soil of Mrs. Dickerson's carefully tended
rosebushes. Olivia thought they looked like bankers, although she realized that was an outdated observation. These days bankers wore blue
jeans and sat at computers doing i-banking or e-banking or something.
These guys looked more like old-fashioned, pot-bellied railroad tycoons.

"So what do you think, Olivia?" Basil said at last. "About the SAT."

Olivia wasn't sure what to say. Cynical views were not career-
enhancing. In fact, she probably ought to have sounded more sincere
when she spoke to the earnest young man who had interviewed her over
the summer at collegeboard.com, a job she had applied for as a self-
protective measure should the dean gig fall apart. He'd said he'd call her
back, but he never did. A job as an editor at Princeton Review had fallen
through, as well, even though she thought she'd nailed it after she had
made the final rounds and been flown out for a daylong interview. She
didn't know what had gone wrong, although she speculated that maybe
her contact there, a former colleague at the law firm where she'd met
Preston, had just been humoring her from the start.

"I think that's worth looking into," she told Basil, deciding to be deliberately demure. It was better not to worry about these things, to just do
your job and not overthink the implications. Look where all this hand-
wringing had landed Ray! He was forever agonizing about the merits of
potential candidates, hesitating to put a kid in the reject pile because,
say, her sister had attended and it might cause family tension to reject

one sibling and admit the other, or accepting a kid because of the number of times she had visited the Yates campus. He'd actually comment about things like the extra hours a candidate had put into community service, as if that made a whit of difference about how smart she really was! To top it off, he'd then lose sleep bemoaning the lack of integrity of the deals that were inevitably struck to accommodate the spawn of these men with cigars who were brutalizing Basil's garden.

"Basil," Olivia finally said more insistently, when the reporter and the two men were just a few feet away, "there's someone who looks like that television reporter, the one with the crazy hair, approaching."

Basil's red cheeks turned redder, and he turned around to glance. "Actually, Olivia, we have a bit of a situation," he said, lowering his voice. "I'll fill you in, later."

"Ah . . . Mr. Dickerson," said the younger of the two men, approaching with his hand outstretched. "It's so nice to see you again. As I mentioned, I've brought along my father, Mr. Jaycee Bear. Dad was one of the most highly decorated fighter pilots to have flown in 'Nam. Dad is also our tribal chief . . . and this is Loretta Bear. Perhaps you recognize her from YNBC news? She's my second cousin."

"Please, call me Basil! My goodness, we were practically classmates. The honor is all mine," he said, shaking three sets of hands and introducing Olivia. "This is Joshua Bear," he explained, referring to the younger man. "He's one of our most distinguished alums. You have probably heard of the New York law firm Bear and Bear."

"Of course," Olivia replied. She hadn't realized Joshua Bear was a Yates alum. She recognized the name, but couldn't remember why. They did not have many famous alums, so they usually milked the few they had, inflating their ongoing relationships with the college. Sadly, two of the most successful alums, including a U.S. senator and the head of a major software company, had transferred elsewhere after their freshman years, but this didn't stop Basil from exploiting the connections, inviting both of them back to the college the previous year to bestow honorary degrees. She wondered if Joshua Bear had something to do with Enron and the expensive-looking lawyers who sometimes paid mysterious visits to Basil's office.

Olivia was less puzzled by Joshua Bear than by his intimidating-looking father, however. His craggy face made him appear much older than his Vietnam record suggested, yet he still looked sturdy and formidable with his uniform full of shiny medals. She tried to think of something clever to say but only blurted out a boring question, the one she held in reserve for when she was stymied at dinner parties or trapped in conversations with people who she couldn't quite place. "What are you working on these days?"

Joshua Bear's dark eyes sparkled. "Funny you should ask," he replied.

"Yes," Basil agreed unconvincingly. "Funny, Olivia, as it has to do with Yates. Joshua contacted me a few months ago. You may have seen this in the news. Mr. Bear is an elder of the Yashequana tribe."

Olivia instantly sensed that her standard question was, in fact, the wrong one. "Oh, what an honor!" she said. "We have *Yashequana Woman* right in our admissions lobby, so I kind of feel a real connection to the Yashequana." She worried this must have sounded patronizing, and yet she surprised herself with the realization that her sentiment was a little bit sincere, even if she didn't much care for the statue itself.

"Actually, Olivia, the two Mr. Bears are of the opinion that our esteemed founder, Jeremiah Wheeling, violated the Yashequana Treaty of 1815 when he erected the first building on campus, which happened to be the admissions building, of all places. Evidently, there was a long-standing dispute about the land, and hard as it is to imagine, they are suggesting that Mr. Wheeling did not act honorably."

"Oh!" Olivia replied, trying to think of something positive to say. "This could prove fascinating! Unearthing the history, that is . . ."

"Yes. Fascinating!" Basil agreed. "Good for our U.S. history students . . . And there is also an issue to do with *Yashequana Woman*."

"Oh?"

The elder Mr. Bear spoke for the first time. His voice was soothing, even if his words were not. "We are of the opinion that *Yashequana Woman*, along with the land that she sits on, was taken from our ancestors under false pretenses." He said this in a monotone, like he was delivering a declaration of war, which he evidently was.

"I thought she was a gift . . ." This was starting to sound vaguely familiar. "Wasn't there a similar claim in the news not too long ago? About a land grant having to do with the nearby resort on Lake Masepakwa? Wasn't the attorney general involved?" The look in Basil's eye made her realize she should probably stop talking.

"Yes," said Joshua Bear, smiling. "That was my case."

"Aha!" Olivia said. "That's why I recognize your name!" She tried to remember the outcome of the dispute, which had made headlines for months. The whole thing seemed to have quietly faded away, and she had no idea what had become of the land. She wondered if that was where a giant new resort was under development, and she entertained the fleeting image of Yates being turned into a casino. Instead of books in the library, slot machines. Then she entertained some other ideas: prolonged litigation; high-priced attorneys; an erosion of the school's already meager endowment; *a plunge in the rankings!* . . . Then again, a few fistfuls of casino income might solve some of the larger problems.

The elder Mr. Bear suddenly hoisted his glass of orange juice in the air and proposed a toast. "To *Yashequana Woman*," he said.

They all held their glasses aloft and agreed. "*Yashequana Woman*," each person said, slightly out of sequence. Olivia contemplated a job that did not involve viewing a somewhat sordid, voluptuous, naked woman several times each day; it was not all bad.

Fritz Heimler appeared and lifted a glass of beer, putting an arm on Olivia's shoulder. "What are we toasting, my friends?" He had a rich baritone, and everything he said seemed to come out in a lilting iambic pentameter.

"*Yashequana Woman*," Jaycee Bear answered.

"I'll drink to that!" Heimler said, giving Olivia a squeeze.

Ari walked over and put his hand on the small of Olivia's back and steered her away from Heimler. "If you don't mind, gentlemen, I need to steal our dean of admissions for a moment. There's a trustee who would like to meet her."

Olivia began to follow him against her better judgment, with the certain knowledge that they weren't headed in the right direction, no matter which way they went. They had only moved a few yards when they smacked into Belle, trailed by a bunch of exhausted-looking kids, one of whom was crying. Again she thrust the toddler into Ari's arms. "You promised you'd help if I came along!" she snapped.

"Sorry, darling," he said. "I just had a bit of business to take care of."

"Yeah, isn't that always the case. Sorry to seem so bitchy, Olivia, but honestly you can't imagine how hard it is to deal with all these children."

"I'm sure it's a complete horror," Olivia said.

Belle began to stare hard at her, which was mildly unnerving. "My God, Olivia! That is the most stunning necklace!"

Olivia fumbled with the chain, trying to remember what was hanging from it. "Oh, the cow! Would you like it? It's a gift from a prospective student, some girl who wants to be an art major at Yates."

"It is absolutely exquisite," said Belle. "Look at the intricacy of the design!"

"Seriously, it's all yours," Olivia replied, trying to unhook the chain. Ari looked at her strangely.

"Oh, no no no no no. I'd never take it from you. It's a reward for all that hard work you do."

"No, Belle, you have the harder job, just being a mom." Olivia wasn't sure if her own words contained sarcasm, but she genuinely wanted Belle to take the cow.

"Tell me, did the girl get in?" asked Belle.

Olivia hesitated before answering. "I have no idea."

○ ○ ○

"I CAN'T DECIDE which dorm I want to live in," AP Harry said. "I like the architecture of Matthews Hall the best. But Weld is nice, too. Both are right in the middle of Harvard Yard, so that's good, because you know how cold it can get in Cambridge in the winter."

"Hmmm," Maya said as she put on her turn signal and glanced over her left shoulder before switching lanes. "That must be a hard decision." Her knowledge of weather in Boston was limited to what she saw on television, although she agreed that the winters looked pretty cold. She had been there twice, but only in the summer, once when they moved Neela into her dorm at MIT, and before that, when they settled her brother into Harvard. She didn't recall that Ashok had any choice about where he lived, but then, she had been in middle school at the time, blissfully oblivious to things like dorms.

A little gray Mercedes cut in front of her, precariously close. Maya recognized the driver as Cathy Roberts, who had been given the convertible sports car for her sixteenth birthday. Cathy had just sat in front of her during the three-hour test, and as Maya looked around the room, panicked, she couldn't help but notice that Cathy was scribbling away, while her own brain, and pen, were frozen. This gave her plenty of time to concentrate on Cathy's precision haircut, and to observe how her light brown hair was offset by streaks of perfect blond. Cathy had a reputation for, among other things, driving like a maniac. She partied hard and had once been suspended from the field hockey team when she was cited for underage drinking. Maya watched in awe as the tiny car swerved recklessly in front of a truck before ducking again into the left lane of the Beltway. Maya was a timid, cautious driver who clutched at the steering wheel with sweaty hands. She hated driving generally, and especially disliked the responsibility of having passengers.

She knew she was in no position to have an opinion about Cathy and her fancy car given that she was behind the wheel of a Mercedes herself. She had begged her parents to get her an old used Toyota when she first got her license, claiming that she'd feel less pressure about the inevitable scrapes she would incur as a new driver, but her father said that made no real economic sense.

Maya listened with envy as Harry continued to weigh the costs and benefits of various Harvard dorms. If anything, she felt her own aspirations spiral downward after repeating the three-hour makeup test. She knew she had not done well. The multiple-choice section had been so difficult she'd wondered if she was taking the right test; she was sure she'd botched every one of the questions. She didn't think she'd fared much better on the essays, either, and upon reflection was almost certain she had misunderstood the prompt that had her synthesizing passages about marriage from various works of Victorian literature.

She glanced in the rearview mirror and saw that Taylor was mercifully asleep in the backseat. She was grateful to not have to make awkward small talk, particularly after the jarring episode in the bathroom just a few minutes earlier, after the test had ended.

There had been no traffic when they set out that morning at 7:00 a.m., but by now it was approaching noon and they had just come to a sudden halt. As if it were not bad enough that their original AP English Language scores had been lost, they had been reassigned a makeup test date on a Saturday morning in August, at 8:00 a.m., at a recreation center more than thirty miles away. Evidently, this was the only facility available in the county that morning because of a mandate by the county coordinator for Systemwide Continuous Improvement to cut the electricity to all school buildings on the weekends, summer school and makeup tests notwithstanding.

No concessions were made to the inconvenience of either having to repeat the test or having to drive all this way other than that the makeup was free of charge, a boast which Maya had trouble appreciating since the original tests had been lost through no fault of the students. More than two million AP tests had been administered in over fifteen thousand schools, they were told in a letter that seemed more defensive than apologetic, and the AP English Language tests from Verona High School were the only ones that had gone missing.

She wished she could turn up the radio to avoid having this conversation with Harry without appearing rude. She liked Harry, but she didn't want to talk about school or college, and she wasn't sure that he ever talked about anything else. Harry had called at 6:30 a.m. that morning to say his mother had been unexpectedly summoned to work and therefore needed the car, although of course she could take the bus if it was too much trouble for Maya to drive. Taylor had called the night before: she had been grounded and her car keys confiscated after her mother learned she had received a D in tech ed, she reported nonchalantly. Her mother planned to drive her to the test, but Taylor said that she might kill herself if she had to spend an hour in the car with her mother. Maya had laughed politely, but after what she had just observed in the bathroom, it occurred to her that perhaps Taylor wasn't kidding.

Maya was relieved to hear Taylor's tech ed news and confided that she had also received a maddening grade of C in the class. She thought that sharing her anecdote might make Taylor less morose, that they could bond and have a good laugh about the teacher being a misogynist, but it seemed to have no effect. Maya explained that she thought she was doing fine, good enough anyway, when she received an F on the clock project. This seemed unfair. She had worked pretty hard, slicing her finger when she struggled to carve the block of wood into something resembling a timepiece. She had even stayed after school to try to get some extra help. "This clock has no arms," Mr. Keller had written on the grade sheet marked with a giant F, thereby sinking her grade and critically dragging down her GPA. Of course she knew the clock needed arms, and she would have put them on, eventually. This seemed as minor an infraction as not putting a title on an English essay, she said boldly. Evidently, he did not see it that way, and he lectured her on how telling the time was the essential feature of a clock, like a tail was an essential feature of a dog. She wanted to point out that there were some dogs without tails, breeds where the tails were routinely docked, hence there might be some aesthetic that preferred clocks without arms, but Mr. Keller was pretty scary. He was a former professional wrestler, and he always had a sharpened X-Acto knife peeking out of his pocket, which seemed like it ought to be against school safety regulations.

Maya's story did not elicit so much as a chuckle. Taylor only replied flatly that she didn't really care, and she had willingly handed over her car keys. There was no place she wanted to go anyway, she said.

Maya glimpsed Taylor in the rearview mirror. She looked pale, and her hair was what might be politely described as in transition. The streaks were mostly gone, and it appeared as though it had been styled with a pair of children's safety scissors, then dyed so many times it looked fried. Once she might have thought Taylor was veering toward grunge, or possibly even Goth, but really now it looked more like sheer apathy— which sounded catchy enough to be a shade of lipstick in the MAC product line. Complementing the depressing hair were nondescript blue jeans and a long-sleeved sweatshirt—odd choices given the oppressive August heat. Blue eye shadow and bangles on her wrist seemed the only concessions to a look that otherwise suggested she had just rolled out of bed.

Maya was relieved that Taylor's eyes were still closed. Maya had been terrified, and even now that the immediate crisis had passed, she still felt there was something she ought to do or say, although she didn't know what. At the time, a rush of adrenaline must have caused some dormant maternal skills to kick into gear, and she knocked on the door to the bathroom stall when she observed that Taylor had been in there an unusually long time. The exam had seemed far more grueling this second time around, and she wondered if perhaps Taylor was feeling as woozy as she was from sitting in the stifling room, thinking too hard about the Santa Ana winds, which was the prompt for the second essay they were instructed to write.

> . . . the hot dry Santa Ana wind that comes down through the passes at 100 miles an hour and whines through the eucalyptus windbreaks and works on the nerves. October is the bad month for the wind, the month when breathing is difficult and the hills blaze up spontaneously. There has been no rain since April. Every voice seems a scream. It is the season of suicide and divorce and prickly dread, wherever the wind blows . . .

She saw the familiar print pattern of Taylor's Vera Bradley bag propped by the door inside the stall, and while she didn't want to put too fine a point on it, the position of the feet did not suggest that the person inside was actually using the facilities. Plus, she thought she heard a strange noise that might have been a moan. Upon reflection, Maya wasn't sure what she imagined was wrong in that split second before she acted, beyond the vague notion that perhaps Taylor had some medical condition like diabetes, and perhaps she was giving herself an injection.

Maya had called to her, eliciting no response. When she knocked gently on the door it swung open, to their mutual astonishment. The two of them locked eyes, then Maya's gaze drew downward to the jeans bunched at Taylor's ankles. She was wearing polka-dot cotton briefs from Victoria's Secret, and Maya was on the verge of blurting out that she had the same pair, but stopped herself just in time, realizing the observation might be a little inappropriate. Pressed to the fleshy, milky skin of Tay-

lor's inner thigh was what appeared to be a serrated bottle cap. And then
Maya uttered quite possibly the most stupid, mortifying sentence she
had ever said in her life. "Be careful," she advised, "you might want to be
sure you've had a tetanus shot."

Could she have possibly said such a thing? She had evidently caught
her neighbor in the act of some sort of self-mutilation, and like a mother
hen, she was advising her to watch out for tetanus? For all she knew, Taylor was trying to kill herself. Wasn't there some important artery in the
thigh? She would hardly care about infection!

But then, somewhat reassuringly, Taylor replied, "Don't worry. I had
one last year."

Maya swung the door closed again, advising her too cheerfully that
she and Harry were ready to leave whenever Taylor was finished. *Finished with what?* Each sentence that rolled off her tongue seemed more
ridiculous than the last. Taylor thanked her and said she'd be right out.

"**ARE YOU** going to apply anywhere early?" Harry asked as they came to
yet another brake-gnashing halt. They had finally begun to move again,
but now the three right lanes were suddenly closed for construction,
meaning five lanes of vehicles had to squeeze into two. Between Harry
and the traffic, she felt like she might be on the verge of some sort of
anxiety attack. Maybe it would be better if Taylor was awake to defuse
the situation. She really didn't want to talk about this.

"I haven't decided yet. I'm still looking and thinking."

"Well, what's on your list?" he asked, not getting the hint.

She no longer had a list. After her pathetic performance on the SATs
she had taken in April, she had moved even further away from having
any idea of where she wanted to go to school or, rather, where she might
get in. Yates had been at the top of her list, but between her C in tech ed
and her latest math score, she was not optimistic about her chances of
acceptance.

A recent perusal of the newest *Insider's Guide to the Colleges* had
confused her even further. It seemed like she didn't know herself in
some possibly fundamental way. Was she a J.Crew girl or an Abercrombie girl? The college guidebooks seemed to suggest this level of self-

awareness was important in selecting a school, akin to knowing whether you wanted a large or a small school, or one that was urban or rural. She had actually gone to both of these stores in the mall recently, in search of an epiphany. The visits turned out to be more expensive than illuminating. J.Crew was having a huge end-of-summer sale, and she bought three short skirts and a striped T-shirt. At Abercrombie she found a pair of jeans that fit perfectly. The trip didn't clarify anything other than the fact that this was a stupid way to think about schools. And yet, how were you supposed to differentiate among a bunch of schools that seemed the same? Although she hadn't conducted a scientific study, colleges that didn't affiliate themselves with any particular clothing line instead were said to have a preponderance of smokers, skaters, nose rings, and lesbians. Maybe she wasn't really ready to go to college after all.

Maya wondered if perhaps part of the problem was that she had always thought of herself as an athlete. It seemed possible that the decision to stop swimming was not only the source of this identity crisis, but might be having an adverse effect on her overall well-being. Just after the school year ended, she whined to her father that the pressure to compete was too much, that she was always exhausted, and that she had no time to concentrate on her schoolwork. She hadn't actually meant to suggest that she was quitting—really, she was just letting off steam. But her father assumed the worst, and once Maya realized it was really within her power to drop off the team, she embraced the idea. Her coach had been so upset that he called Maya's father, and a two-hour arm-twisting session was convened at her house with the two adults and the captain of the swim team. She held her ground for possibly the first time in her life. Three e-mails to Mr. Joyce outlining this bold move had gone unanswered, but she told herself it didn't matter, even if his disdain for competitive sports had been in the back of her mind when she made her decision. Meanwhile, she hadn't swum a single lap since June, and it was only now occurring to her that all of the physical energy she once put into propelling her body through the water was bottling up inside.

On top of that was a wrenching experience she'd had in Delhi over the summer. Ironically, it was not the volunteer work that was trying—she didn't actually interact with any lepers and was only asked to do paperwork in the air-conditioned administrative offices. It was at her aunt's fancy swim club that Maya was challenged; she was asked to teach a little girl, orphaned in the 2004 tsunami, how to swim. Seven-year-old Manju's village near Chennai had been destroyed, and she was sent to Delhi to live with cousins, who happened to be friends of Maya's aunt. Manju had developed such a profound fear of the water that Maya had trouble coaxing her into the pool, even when she promised to hold her in her arms. She had also been instructed to urge her to talk about her experiences, and while she was reasonably successful in getting Manju to open up, she was less certain about what she was meant to do with her tearful disclosures. By the end of the month, Manju had practically adhered herself to Maya and had begun to call her "mummy." She never succeeded in convincing the child to put her head in the water. Maya found herself longing for the release of the water at the same time that she was beginning to absorb Manju's fears.

This test had just dredged all that anxiety back up. In the spring, when she first took the AP English Language exam, she had felt almost soulful as she penned her essays. She had been uncharacteristically confident that she had done well, unlike today, when she was pretty sure she had botched the whole thing, choking on each word, veering off on tangents. She thought about the prompt for the Joan Didion passage, where she'd been instructed to discuss in "a coherent, well-written essay" the author's distinctive style and how it revealed the purpose of the writer. Now, as she drove home, it was all beginning to click, but at the time, she had stared at the sheet of white paper, her mind completely blank. She had never heard of the Santa Ana winds before, and it took her a while to understand what this Didion person was driving at. She suspected she was missing the larger point.

Now that she had turned off the air-conditioning, realizing she was low on gas, and with AP Harry quizzing her about college and with her emotionally disturbed neighbor stirring to life in the backseat, she felt a sudden sense of clarity. That knife-edge feeling the Santa Ana winds provoked was not unlike having to repeat the AP English Language exam on a Saturday morning in mid-August. It made an otherwise happy, stable girl feel like she was going to burst into flames.

"I can't really decide where else to apply," Harry continued. "Dartmouth might be a good backup for me, but it seems like there's too much partying, too much emphasis on fraternities. I'm not sure if I want to go Greek or not."

Maya was tempted to share with him some of her other observations from her trip to India, the ones that made her feel like all of their Verona concerns were not really that big of a deal, but she stopped herself. She knew she was becoming a bore; even Pam's eyes glazed when she referred to her summer, even when she was merely talking about the food and shopping, or telling her about a cute guy she had met.

Still, she wanted to tell Harry about her cousin who was in his first year studying philosophy at the University of Delhi. When Maya asked him how he liked school, he replied that he liked the academics fine, but he had one complaint: there were too many Taliban in his class. He said this so matter-of-factly, like he was identifying a minor annoyance akin to, say, not liking the weather in Buffalo. She couldn't stop thinking about this. She and her peers were focused on things like the comparative sizes of big-screen TVs in dorm lobbies and the availability of Starbucks on campus, or how many times a week housekeeping services were provided. Meanwhile, people living in the rest of the world had to actually think about . . . the rest of the world.

"The thing is," said Harry, suddenly sounding somber, "even if I got into Harvard, it would be a huge financial burden for my mom."

Maya was surprised to hear this. She wasn't sure what to say. It was almost as if he'd read her mind. "Well, what about scholarships? Or aid?" she asked. She had to confess that money was one aspect of reality she didn't know much about herself, as her family seemed to have limitless financial reserves.

Harry frowned and explained that he was unlikely to qualify for either, at least not at Harvard. "I'm really smart but I'm not a genius," he confessed, which struck Maya as a surprising admission.

"But don't schools have a lot of money to give to kids who can't afford tuition? What about all these merit scholarships I hear about?"

"Yes, I imagine I'd get money at some schools, but basically I'm a dime a dozen. White, middle class, no special talent. I understand that, and I'm not angry or anything. Besides, we can probably figure out a way to pay. We're not *poor*; it's just that it would be a real stretch, whereas I've been awarded this scholarship to go to a school in Maryland. I could go for practically nothing. It would make life a lot easier."

"So? Why not do it? They have a great honors program at Maryland."

"The thing is, if you can go to Harvard, you should go to Harvard, whatever it takes," Harry replied. "That's what my dad says."

"You have a dad?" she asked before realizing what a dumb question this was. Somehow she hadn't ever considered the possibility of there being an AP Harry, Sr., out there. She wondered if he was at all like Harry.

"Yeah, he lives in an apartment just outside Baltimore," he said, and then he seemed to start staring at her. Maya worried that perhaps the thought of his father had sent him into some weird trancelike state like Taylor there, in the backseat. She glanced in her mirror again, and saw that Taylor was now fully alert, gazing out the window without speaking.

She turned up the radio to break the awkward silence. An old John Mayer song came on, "Why Georgia." This brought back memories of the road trip she and her dad had made over Memorial Day weekend to visit Emory, another school she would never get into. She had liked the school, even if she was put off by the nickname the tour guide had mentioned, "Coca-Cola University," so named for the massive endowment made by the corporation. She was lost in thought, trying to remember what the median GPA had been at Emory and wondering if she stood half a chance in hell, maybe if she applied early, which they claimed to appreciate more than many schools. She wondered if Emory was more Abercrombie or J.Crew. Emory attracted a lot of pre-meds, so maybe they would look kindly on prospective English majors, although presumably not ones with low scores who couldn't write eloquently about the Santa Ana winds. This was what she was thinking when Harry reached over and put his hand on her leg. She couldn't imagine why he did that. Maybe he was trying to brush away a bug or something. Or maybe . . . she had never thought of Harry that way. He was cute but he was so . . . she wasn't sure what word she was searching for . . . one-dimensional, maybe? Before she could react, however, he removed his hand with such alacrity that she wasn't sure it had really happened at all.

September

GRACE UNDERSTOOD THAT AT least some of the college hysteria she'd
been recently observing had to do with her perspective; because the
subject was on her mind, her antenna was finely tuned to all collegiate
references. It was like embracing Christ and then noticing a sudden preponderance of crucifixes dangling from people's necks. College seemed
to be the only thing people ever talked about, and the reminders were
everywhere. She began to notice that certain colleagues used e-mail ad-
dresses to forever bind them to their alma mater, for example, or that a
couple of neighbors, whether digging in their gardens or out for their
morning jogs, always had the names of their kids' schools splashed across
their chests. One neighbor who had been unemployed for at least two
years—evidently let go in vaguely scandalous circumstances by a local
wealth-management firm—wore what seemed to be the same Columbia
T-shirt every single day. In the grocery store just the night before, she
overheard two women comparing notes about where their kids were
planning to apply while their carts sat obtrusively in front of the lobster
tank, clogging supermarket traffic. She found that even her once restora-
tive trips to the YMCA had become stressful, as discussions about things
like the use of the common application could be heard over the whir of
elliptical machines.

So it didn't strike her as especially surprising that every conversation she'd had so far in the hallways on back-to-school night had to do with college, or that the senior parents crammed in the classrooms seemed a little bit tense.

"As I'm sure you are well aware, Verona had the highest standardized test scores in the state this year," Mr. Leon, the young AP English Literature and Composition teacher, reported as he handed out copies of the syllabus to parents. Actually, they did know this, because the principal had just reminded them of the same fact over the public address system moments earlier.

Justin Smelling's mother raised her hand and asked what percentage of the class could expect to get 5s on the AP exam. Mr. Leon replied that he'd get to that in just a second.

Grace had said hello to her in the hallway just before the bell rang, but got the impression that Dr. Smelling didn't remember who she was. She didn't take offense: Dr. Smelling had a busy practice and couldn't be expected to recognize the multitude of characters who passed through her life, even if one of them happened to be the mother of her son's best friend, someone she had known for over twelve years.

"You as parents are largely responsible for maintaining that distinction," Mr. Leon continued. "I mean, let's face it. There are schools in other parts of the county where the parents are not as involved in their children's lives."

Grace wasn't entirely sure this over-involvement was such a good thing. It seemed to her these kids might be better off if they learned to fend for themselves a bit, or even had a little more downtime to just hang out. She remembered finding a small creek in the woods behind her house when she was a kid, and she and her best friend spent weeks skipping rocks and catching frogs after school. What would Harry's childhood memories consist of? Homework? Of course there probably were no more woods or creeks in Verona left to explore, as every inch of land had been developed. Besides, she had to confess that this whole line of thinking about parental involvement being responsible for stressed-out kids was not particularly useful: she did not consider herself overly involved in Harry's life, yet he'd still turned into an academic Frankenstein.

She looked around at her fellow parents and saw a sea of attentive

faces—fathers in pinstripes straight from the office, helmet-haired mothers in navy blue suits, stay-at-home moms at both ends of the spectrum
of the harried/unkempt and pampered/well-coiffed varieties.

Mr. Leon was the coach for the girls' field hockey team and had a
bit of a reputation as a ladies' man, or so she had heard through the
grapevine at work; one of her colleagues had a daughter who was a
Verona freshman, and she seemed to be completely plugged into, if not
directly mainlining, all the school gossip. Grace never gave any indication
that she wanted to hear these reports, which always left her feeling
vaguely unclean, but they had become as much a part of her daily briefing as the updates on the malaria vaccine trials she was overseeing. She
had once viewed work as a refuge from home—never the place she preferred to be, but at least an interlude in the day when she was reminded
of concerns larger than her own. Increasingly, however, it seemed that all
anyone did at work was talk about their kids, and no matter where these
conversations began, they invariably seemed to wind their way back to
the topic of college.

The subject had even come up that morning in the lab as she and
Serena, her research assistant, took notes while observing their test rats
quiver with malarial fevers. Serena's daughter had yet to begin kindergarten, but she wondered if Grace had an opinion as to which of the elementary schools in the Verona cluster best prepared a child for college.
It struck Grace as somehow disrespectful to have this conversation while
documenting delirious rats crashing into the sides of their cage. Evidently, their experimental vaccine needed some refining.

Grace claimed that from what she had heard, all six elementary
schools were pretty much the same. This was not a completely honest
answer, however. One of the schools did have a reputation for . . . for
what she wasn't actually sure, but whatever it was—a better-stocked art
supply closet or a 1 percent higher student-teacher ratio—it caused real
estate prices to go up an average of $50,000 on the side of the street that
marked the boundary.

Grace guessed that Mr. Leon was probably about twenty-five, which
struck her as too young to be this test-absorbed. But then, she almost
certainly had it wrong. It was probably just her generation that still har-

bored some quaint notion of learning for its own sake, and it was kids Harry's age, as well as these twenty-something teachers, who considered learning a competitive sport. She was probably the one who needed the attitude adjustment: why *not* go to school to get the highest grades and scores and then get into the best possible college and then land the job that paid the most money—not that she really believed these things were necessarily related—rather than sit around and drink black coffee, smoke cigarettes, and deconstruct philosophy? Now that too much of her daily life was consumed by worrying about bills, she had to wonder why she'd been so drawn to the relatively low-paying field of medical research when, if she'd had any sense at all, she probably would have been better off just sitting for her real estate license.

It was 8:30 p.m., and she was tired after a long day of work. These years and years of back-to-school nights were starting to blur in her mind, distinguishable only by rough eras. She recalled sitting at tiny desks in elementary school, admiring Harry's finger paintings, for example, but could no longer recite the names of all of his teachers. Of course there were certain memorable moments: she remembered the mortifying question she had asked of Ms. Morrisey, who had been Harry's third grade teacher. Ms. Morrisey kept referring to some of the students being shifted into GT reading and math programs. Almost certainly because of her work orientation, Grace assumed the initials stood for "government-tested" and asked a convoluted question to this effect, only to be informed that *GT* stood for "gifted and talented." Several parents had looked at her as if she had just beamed in from another planet, presumably one where, tragically, offspring were only of average intelligence.

She had another particularly vivid memory, this one of sixth grade back-to-school night, which had featured a highly anticipated viewing of the toothpick bridge project. Harry's prize had taken a disappointing second place to Andrew Kumar's, whose bridge (built with the help of his architect father, he later confessed) was such an astonishing feat of glue and toothpick engineering that it had withstood the weight of their two-hundred-pound science teacher.

Although the official point of these back-to-school nights was to chart the course of Harry's academic progress, in her mind's eye the years blurred into a painful chronicle of her deteriorating marriage. Lou had behaved belligerently even back when Harry was in kindergarten, asking inappropriate questions and frightening the earnest young teachers. Worse, perhaps, were the years after the initial split, when he persisted in showing up at these events, suddenly acutely interested in the minutiae of Harry's education. He would sit across the room glowering at Grace, his questions to the teachers about various standards of third grade learning both obnoxious and incomprehensible. He began to volunteer in the classroom, even when his services were not wanted, and on a couple of occasions he was politely asked to leave the building, then forcibly removed. It became harder with each passing year to remember the sloppy yet dashing, brilliant yet moody young man who had sat beside her in the library and blown her mind with his theorems on turbulence. She fell in love with his equations, as arcane as hieroglyphics, always printed in the neat, assured hand of a calligrapher, and his passionate ramblings on stochastic property changes dazzled her like poetry. If only she'd been sharp enough to see the obvious; this obsession simply reflected his inner mess.

While she was unequivocally glad to have Lou out of her life, she still felt a twinge of sadness when she looked around the room and saw that many, if not most, of the parents were there as couples. She sensed in her gut that raising a kid in a two-parent household was preferable to muddling through on her own, yet she knew from absorbing the complaints of her peers over the years that even marriages considerably healthier than her own did not always translate into familial bliss. At least her house was tranquil; she and Harry peacefully coexisted, and she didn't have to deal with the sort of stuff her colleagues griped about, like touchy ego problems related to erectile dysfunction in middle age, or nasty fights about credit card bills. Another benefit was that there was no one around to observe the extra few pounds clinging to her hips, or the gradual drooping of her eyes, but then, there was no one to give her reason to suppose she might still be in any way desirable, apart from Harry. Harry encouraged her to date, insisting she was too young to be alone, and he kept an eye out for a suitable mate. Matchmaking was not his forte, however: he had sent her on two blind dates with divorced fathers of classmates, and both evenings had been so spectacularly awful that she lied to Harry about the outcomes. On the first occasion she actually got out of the car and walked home from downtown Verona when her date proposed they cap off the evening with a visit to a sex club in D.C. The second date was less awful but not especially promising, as the man had cried throughout much of the dinner, reminiscing about his ex-wife, who had recently left him for her gynecologist. A couple of details alerted Grace to the fact that she went to the same gynecologist, and the evening left her feeling vaguely queasy.

SHE HAD gone to six of Harry's eight periods so far—he didn't have a lunch this semester, since forfeiting a free period was the only way he could cram Symphonic Band in with his full load of courses. It occurred to her as she listened to Mr. Leon talk about preparing for the AP exam in May that he hadn't made any reference to the books they would read this semester, although she figured it was possible that they had had so much assigned reading over the summer—Harry had read eighty pages every day of his vacation in order to get through the four books for this class, plus two for his history class—that they would spend the remaining time this semester digesting these assignments. She couldn't tell, because the handout Mr. Leon distributed referred only to major assignments and test dates. None of the teachers in the preceding periods had spent much time addressing the curriculum either, other than to say how it reflected whatever final exams were in question. The Physics with Applied Calculus teacher had bragged about her students' scores on the last round of subject tests; the AP European History teacher, about the breakdown of scores on the county exam. In band, the teacher proudly pointed to the display case full of the trophies he had garnered over the years, and rather than naming any particular pieces of music, he talked only about which grade levels they would be tackling and how advanced the compositions were, as well as which competitions they would be traveling to that spring. He also reminded them that music took precedence over sports (which was of course the opposite of the message from the lacrosse coach, but at least this was one problem she could cross off her list).

While Grace had mixed feelings about last year's English teacher given the grief he had caused Harry (although privately she thought the reality check of a B was good for him), at least Mr. Joyce had spoken enthusiastically about the curriculum at back-to-school night. He had even read aloud some of the more amusing responses to an assignment that instructed his students to choose a new literary form for the tale of the tortoise and the hare. Harry had written his as a sports broadcast, which had evidently been deemed "unoriginal," but among the celebrated essays was a rap, with a few memorable lines such as

Yo yo yo.
What?
I was chillaxing in my crib when I looked outside.
And to my surprise. I saw these two hoodlums about to ride.
I went up to them and I say:
Yo yo.
What you folks down doin out hurr?
My name Tee-urtle he replied . . .

The rap sparked a countywide controversy when one girl in the class asserted that it was racist. The author of the rap, a wispy blond girl who probably weighed about eighty pounds, defended it as "urban poetry." A debate then raged for two weeks in the op-ed columns of the school newspaper before progressing to the pages of the *Gazette* about whether this was racially offensive. Somewhat belatedly, a reporter from the local Fox news station interviewed the three African-American students in the junior class and learned that, curiously, none of them was offended. They each claimed to be amused by the popularity among rich white kids of not just rap, but so-called ghetto styles—baggy jeans and $150 sneakers, as well as otherwise ordinary-looking baseball caps but with a certain "ghetto" color scheme—all available at the local mall at specially inflated suburban prices.

Mr. Joyce had spent the entire ten minutes allotted to him that night describing how proud he was that he made the kids think. At the time, Grace had wondered why they weren't memorizing Shakespeare soliloquies instead, but tonight, as she listened to these test-obsessed, results-oriented teachers, she was nostalgic for his quirky creative approach.

Earlier in the evening, as she entered Verona's front door, she noticed an electronic board suspended from the ceiling of the vaulted lobby that flashed the words SUCCESS, SUCCESS, SUCCESS. Grace stopped for a minute and thought she was imagining this. Surely she was just being overly sensitive, exaggerating what she perceived as too much emphasis on achievement. She stopped and looked up again, and indeed, a steady stream of teletype words ran across the board like the news scrawl on CNN. Except that these words were not information so much as mandate: SUCCESS . . . SUCCESS . . . SUCCESS . . .

"Last year," Mr. Leon continued, "out of my two AP classes, which would be fifty-two kids, 90 percent earned 4s and 5s on the AP test. I'm assuming you all know that 5 is the highest possible score."

Even in her cynical, or perhaps just burned-out, mind-set, Grace had to agree these were pretty impressive numbers for a large public high school. Harry had received 5s on all the APs he had taken thus far, although he said he felt less confident about the makeup test he sat for in August. A father who looked at least sixty-five years old raised his hand and asked whether the teacher could be more specific. "How many received 4s, how many received 5s, and what were the other scores?" he asked. She searched the faces of her fellow parents for reaction—personally, she couldn't understand why this was important information—but all she saw was Nina Rockefeller sitting catty-corner behind her. A cell phone rang and Dr. Smelling reached into her purse, apologetically reminding everyone in the class that she was a doctor and this was probably an emergency. She stepped into the hall, from where she proceeded to talk so loudly to what sounded like a kitchen contractor that it was hard to concentrate on Mr. Leon's words.

Mr. Leon opened a folder and rattled off some numbers. "Forty kids got 5s; seven kids got 4s; four got 3s; one got a 1."

Someone in the room laughed at the mention of a "1," reminding Grace of the comment made by the head of guidance at the last college planning meeting she attended in the spring. He was warning parents to be sure the kids had safety schools on their lists and was in turn encouraging applications to Maryland. "Last year, we had about two hundred kids apply to Maryland," he explained. "The school has really improved over the last few years. You should urge your kids to consider it." After a brief pause he continued, "Of course, for some of our students, even Maryland is a stretch"—at which point he let out a little laugh. The last time Grace had checked, the median GPA of Verona freshmen attending Maryland was over 3.5, so she wasn't sure what was so funny about a kid who couldn't get in. But of course she was absorbing all of this angst for no reason. She was the mother of AP Harry! What no one seemed to appreciate, however, was that being the mother of an overachiever only meant that her angst was of a different sort.

At another college planning meeting the previous winter, the students had been given ID numbers enabling them to log in to a new computer program where they could view, via a scattergram, the fate of Verona applicants at any given school. A graph plotted the number of kids from Verona who had applied to that school over the previous few years and showed the GPAs and scores of all who were accepted, wait-listed, and rejected. It also showed the fate of early decision and early action applicants. It was like peering into a guidance counselor's secret files, a startling reality check that felt a bit like snooping, somehow. But it also felt like you were being snooped *on*, because already loaded into the database was each student's academic record. A little circle plotted Harry on the map according to his numerical coordinates and showed, in completely unmistakable terms, where he stood in relation to past candidates. Harry was not outside the Harvard acceptance cluster; it was just that he had way too much company inside. From what she could tell from the chart, thirty-two kids had applied from Verona the previous year, five were accepted, and the rejects seemed to have pretty much the same academic profile as the admits. Obviously, this picture didn't explain things like legacy and extracurricular activities, but it at least gave her a general idea of whether he was even in the game. She deduced that despite his best efforts to get a leg up on his peers, at the end of the day a Harvard acceptance was really just going to boil down to the luck of the draw.

Grace actually thought they would have been better off if Harry was visibly outside the Harvard range; then he might be persuaded to move on. She honestly didn't care where he went to school—and she didn't think Harvard was the best place for him anyway—yet she'd been experiencing that same sick, anxious feeling that she'd heard another one of her colleagues refer to just recently. Her coworker's boy was a senior at a nearby Catholic school. An otherwise excellent student, his scores barely broke 1500, and the mother couldn't identify a single college that she had heard of that he could be sure of getting into. She got excited when he expressed an interest in studying at some obscure school in Boston. Since the name was unfamiliar, she figured it might be less inundated with applicants, and he might stand a chance. But when she called to set up a campus tour a month ahead of time, she was told that the information sessions were already full, but his name would be put on the list for an "overflow" tour if they decided to schedule one.

The colleague told Grace how lucky she was not to have to fret about these things, having a son as gifted as Harry, but in truth Grace had just as much reason as anyone to worry, given that Harry's expectations were unrealistic. Not surprisingly, Lou was continuing to aggravate this problem, taking him to visit only supercompetitive schools. She feared that Harry was turning into the worst sort of snob. He said disparaging things about every campus they set foot on that was not within the Ivy League, and even bad-mouthed some of the schools within. When they toured the University of Pennsylvania, Harry pointed out that at Penn-Princeton football games, the Princeton students shouted taunts of "Safety school" to the opposing team. One small liberal arts school he dismissed as too earthy, several others as too remote. He refused to look at one school because he didn't like a couple of kids who had gone there from the previous year's senior class. Two kids from Verona High School had died at one university she took him to, both in freak accidents, and this was enough to sour him on that front, which was at least a little less irrational than some of his other reasons. She had logged so many miles trying to help him find alternatives that she wished there were some sort of E-Z Pass program that would reward her for racking up tolls. And despite all her efforts, he continued to show no enthusiasm for a single Harvard alternative.

Meanwhile, she was enthralled by just about everything they saw. She was so moved by their visit to Syracuse that she burst into tears during the information session when the promotional video showed elated graduates moving the tassel from one side of their mortarboards to the other. She later ascribed that embarrassing incident to exhaustion stemming from one too many poor nights' sleep in roadside hotels. Harry had sulked throughout the entire visit—they had agreed to meet his second cousin there, who was contemplating applying early decision to the School of Communications. When Grace and her cousin realized they were both going to be in upstate New York at the same time touring colleges, they decided it would be fun to rendezvous and let the boys get to know each other, as they had last met in elementary school. Grace thought Harry might also take note of Syracuse—she thought it was a lovely campus herself—and possibly he'd even like it enough to apply, if only as a safety. The idea backfired, however, as Harry made it a point to let everyone within earshot know that he was Harvard material and was essentially slumming on the Syracuse tour. Grace couldn't have been more embarrassed.

When she pushed him on the subject of safety schools, he only replied that everything was "under control." She had been momentarily excited by his quip about Penn being a safety school until she investigated and learned that the odds of his getting into Penn were not really any better than of his getting into Harvard, given the number of qualified candidates applying from Verona. The scattergram cluster in which Harry would hypothetically sit was so crowded that it looked like ants swarming a crumb at a picnic. She couldn't even distinguish the details of one candidate from the next, except to note a preponderance of rejection symbols.

She asked him what he'd thought of Yates, and he shrugged, which was actually a more positive response than she had reason to expect. She didn't know what went on in Harry's head much of the time, but suspected that the presence of Maya Kaluantharana when they had toured the school last spring might be the only reason he hadn't rejected the place outright.

The honors program at Maryland seemed to her the best solution, particularly given his award, but Harry didn't say much when she tried to engage him on this subject, other than that he didn't want to go to a party school, at which point Grace, exasperated, couldn't help but think that it wouldn't be the worst thing in the world if he lightened up and downed a beer. But she didn't say anything to that effect, as her mind always leaped ahead a tick to what Harry might repeat to his father, even in jest, and how quickly a phone call from child services might be forthcoming.

○ ○ ○

NINA ROCKEFELLER SAW her neighbor round the corner along the third-floor hallway after AP English was dismissed. She tried to intercept her as they filed out of class, but Grace had a head start squeezing through the crowd. Nina called her name and raced to catch up, a feat that re-quired throwing herself like an offensive tackle into the parent-clogged artery that led to the math wing. The student population was 2,012 this year, they had just been told over the loudspeaker, and since many par-ents had come as couples, that meant there were somewhere between 3,000 and 4,000 people currently jammed in the building.

Even as Nina pursued her neighbor, she could not say exactly what complicated, subliminal set of motivations compelled her to run, to shout Grace's name, to almost knock another mother to the ground as she bull-dozed her way through the crowd. When she thought about it, there was actually nothing she had to say to Grace, and anything she might think to share with a friend—or, perhaps more accurately, a former friend who had grown inexplicably chilly over the last couple of years—was better left unsaid. Maybe it was just her natural inclination to be social, which she couldn't help but think was good. Wasn't it normal to want to say hi to someone you knew? It seemed to her that the art of being friendly was fast fading from modern life. She was always spotting people that she had known for years at the dry cleaner or in the grocery store, and they looked the other way. She really didn't understand it. Was this just a Verona thing? Was everyone so busy that they didn't have time to stop and say hello? Or was it just that most women her age were losing their memories and didn't remember that their daughters had played recreational basketball on the same team for seven years, or they had been in a baby group together? Nina never forgot a face, so maybe she was assuming that was true of others as well.

Her hypothesis was that there had been a radical decline in manners not just in Verona, but in society at large, and she thought that just about everyone she knew could stand to get a copy of *Miss Manners' Guide to Excruciatingly Correct Behavior* in their Christmas stocking this year. Certainly, Taylor would be getting one, although she wasn't sure if Miss Manners had thought to include a section on how it was impolite to not acknowledge your mother when she was speaking to you, or to put a padlock on your bedroom door.

Nina tapped Grace on the shoulder. She was instantly reminded that talking to people did not always make her feel better, and actually sometimes made her feel worse. Grace looked so pretty and so serene. How was it possible that they were the same age? Grace was a single working mother with messy marital and financial problems, and it seemed to Nina that her neighbor ought to at least have a few gray hairs. Just the night before, Nina overheard the vice president of the PTA suggest to the gossipy gaggle assembled for a meeting about the controversial new sex education curriculum that Grace had probably been an unwed teenaged mother. Grace's name had come up when someone mentioned that the student body president, AP Harry, supported the new curriculum despite his reliably conservative politics. Working backwards from her specious assumption, the PTA vice president calculated that if Grace was thirty-four, she must have given birth to AP Harry when she was about sixteen. It was evidently easier to accept this possibility than to consider that Grace might simply be aging more gracefully than the rest of them. If only Grace knew that Nina had rushed to her defense! She had known Grace since Harry was a baby, she said, and in fact Grace was in her late twenties when he was born and married at the time.

"Hey, neighbor," Nina said brightly. "What class do you have next?"

"Oh, hey, Nina. It's so nice to see you!" Grace kissed her on the cheek and smiled sweetly before consulting the slip of paper in her hand. "Let's see. I've got . . . AP Statistics. Room 316 . . . E . . . wherever that is."

"Too bad," said Nina, looking down at her own schedule. "I've got

Multivariable Calculus and Differential Equations . . . Maybe we could cut class and go have a smoke!" Grace didn't respond; she was momentarily distracted by a father who shouted something to her about a Music Department bake sale as he pushed by. Nina felt a small flush of embarrassment as her stupid joke withered unacknowledged. Her feeling of mild idiocy was compounded by the realization that she had no business bragging about Taylor's mathematical proficiency when Harry was clearly taking Statistics only because he had already taken Multivariable Calculus and Differential Equations, as well as every other math class offered at Verona.

Taylor had actually done quite well on the SATs, and Nina was convinced she could do even better if she simply had more time. She had planned to have her diagnosed with a minor learning problem over the summer so that she could take the test again under special circumstances. But Taylor, always contrarian, refused to even talk to the people who were going to administer a few quick tests in an effort to help her find a disability.

"Is Harry taking the SATs again in October?" Nina asked, wondering if this might help her get an idea of his scores, or possibly prompt Grace to inquire about Taylor's.

"I hope not," said Grace. "I've told him he shouldn't bother. He's got enough on his plate as it is, but knowing Harry I wouldn't be surprised if he does."

Nina wasn't sure what to make of this vague reply. "How did Harry find the writing section?" she asked.

"Okay," Grace replied, noncommittally. Nina was not getting much satisfaction from this exchange. She wanted an opening to boast about Taylor's high score on the writing section, but this conversation wasn't veering in the right direction. Anyway, there was no point in trying to keep up with Grace. While the kids had been on the same accelerated path throughout elementary and middle school, Harry had jumped at least a year ahead of Taylor once they hit ninth grade. Nina hadn't thought that it was even possible to skip a level once they were all tracked in high school, but she later learned that Harry had spent the summer at school tackling the math and science curriculums that lay ahead.

Nina knew, and suspected that Grace probably knew as well, that whatever level math Taylor was currently taking was likely to be the least of her problems. Her decent if imperfect scores aside, she was doing poorly only three weeks into the semester, and Nina had just been asked to sign a grade sheet acknowledging that her daughter had failed the last test. Taylor's once stellar grades were plummeting; the attendance office had called four times already this semester to report that Taylor had not come to school; and that irritatingly pretty Indian girl, Maya-what's-her-name, had called one day when she must have known Taylor was not home to report to Nina that she was worried about her. She said something about a supposed incident that occurred in the bathroom during the AP exam. It was such a horrible thing this Maya girl suggested— something to do with Taylor cutting herself in a bathroom stall—that it couldn't possibly be true. Nina thought about calling this Maya-what's-her-name's aloof mother to tell her that her daughter was spreading malicious rumors. But then, she didn't want to make the whole thing worse by involving another person, although of course it was possible and even likely that Maya had already confided in her mother. She waved to her sometimes from across the street, and while the Indian woman smiled warmly and waved back, Nina couldn't help but think she had an attitude, looking so regal wrapped in her colorful shawl, her head held high with a whiff of arrogance like she was Sonia Gandhi or someone like that, Sonia Gandhi sentenced to a life without servants in the bland Verona suburbs. She knew all about Sonia Gandhi because this was another high-profile marriage that resulted from a serendipitous college choice: she and Rajiv had met at Cambridge.

Of course she had every right to be arrogant, Nina thought, with her big house and her plastic surgeon husband and her fleet of Mercedeses, not to mention three kids who had gone to top universities and a fourth on the way to God-knows-where. What motivation could her daughter possibly have for spreading such vicious rumors? she wanted to ask. Sure, there had been small warning signs along the way, aspects of Taylor's behavior that perhaps she had been missing or, really, choosing to ignore. That a seventeen-year-old girl might be moody and withdrawn was not the sort of thing that set off alarm bells. Still, it was perhaps a mistake to view behavior in relative terms. Yes, Taylor spent most of her free time alone in her room with the door locked, but wasn't this better than having her out all night, driving around with God-knows-who? At least she didn't have to worry about Taylor going to unsupervised parties where alcohol might be served or doing drugs or having unprotected sex.

Nina figured that in the absence of other signs of trouble, she needed to respect her daughter's privacy. But if she was honest with herself, there *were* other signs of trouble. Taylor had lost almost fifteen pounds since last spring, although given that she was a bit heavy to begin with, this was not all bad. The weight loss did not seem to indicate any interest in a health campaign, however, so much as a complete disinterest in food. And then there was that awful hair. At least back when she was dyeing it a hideous array of colors, it demonstrated that she had some energy, enough of a life spark to get in the car and drive to the drugstore to purchase a box of L'Oréal. Now that she had let it grow out into a shaggy, chemical mess, it just looked disheartened.

This morning Taylor had goofed, however. The chain around her door knob was slack, and although the complicated if low-tech security mechanism was still elaborately rigged around the leg of a giant mahogany dry sink, it served no purpose. Nina felt guilty as she turned the knob, but she justified her entrance on housekeeping grounds. She was not really intending to snoop, she told herself, so much as to see what was doing in there—how many dirty dishes and glasses might have accumulated in the last few weeks, whether the toilet paper needed replacing, if the bulbs still worked in the overhead fixture. She honestly did not believe what Maya had told her, and even if what she said was true, poking around in her daughter's room was not likely to yield clues about the awful thing she was insinuating.

When Nina entered the bathroom to empty the trash, the first thing she saw was a steak knife, gleaming theatrically as the bit of light that streamed in through the blinds illuminated the silver blade. She had to admit this was not a good sign in light of Maya's disclosure. Then she

spied two wobbly towers of paper of various shapes and sizes in the corner. It was mail—actual U.S. mail replete with stamps and return ad-
dresses. There was more of it under the skirt of the sink, hidden by the
piece of gingham cloth she had tacked up after reading an article about
sprucing up the bathrooms in *Real Simple* magazine. She opened the
narrow linen closet and more came spilling out, a torrent of mail, packed
tight on every shelf. A heavy Express Mail envelope spilled from the top
shelf and smacked her on the head.

Her hands trembling, Nina gathered a few armfuls of mail and
brought them into her daughter's room, where she sat on Taylor's antique
canopy bed and began to sift through the cache. Almost all of the mail
was addressed to houses on their street, with a few pieces meant for the
lane behind them. Two other pieces seemed to have been intended for
an identically named street in Verona, New Jersey. Most of it was junk,
although there were a few bills and magazines, as well as dozens of college catalogues and about forty letters addressed to AP Harry from
Washington University in St. Louis. Something was extremely wrong
here.

She began to cry, and she felt the strong urge for a drink. This—
whatever *this* was—was almost certainly not *her* fault. She knew she had
made mistakes; she may not have been the most enlightened mother in
the world, but she had certainly tried. She had devoted her life to Taylor,
never wrestling with any of these ridiculous career versus mothering de-
bates everyone was always wringing their hands over in books and on
television. She personally felt the whole work thing was vastly overrated.
Apart from her time on the golf course and in other club- and school-
related activities, she had been available to her daughter 24/7 and had
never denied her a single thing. So what had she done to deserve this?
And if Taylor had to be disturbed, why couldn't she be so in some
straightforward, socially acceptable kind of way, like having an eating disorder, or abusing her credit cards? Even teenaged drinking had come
into vogue, or so it seemed after watching a couple of episodes of *Dr.
Phil*. On one of the college visits with Taylor, she had overheard someone
quip that the metal in the sinks of one of the dormitories had corroded
over the years from all of the acid in vomit, although there was evidently

some debate about whether this was a result of too much heavy drinking, or the high incidence of bulimia.

She knew her relationship with Taylor was not that close, and truly wished it was otherwise, but she never quite knew how to connect with her daughter. She envied these mothers and daughters she saw playing doubles tennis, who then laughed over salads in the restaurant at the club. Someone once asked her and Taylor to join her mother-daughter book group, but even back in fifth grade, when the invitation was extended, Taylor had refused. There was a brief period in her early teens when Taylor agreed to shopping sprees, and sometimes Nina could squeeze a lunch into the outing, but then she seemed to have lost interest in clothes, most days wearing the same pair of ill-fitting jeans.

She felt like she was always walking on eggshells around Taylor, lapping up whatever crumbs of affection were offered. If she asked Taylor how her day had been, for example, and received a simple if sarcastic "Awesome," she figured that was better than no response at all.

Nina had always been clear about one thing: she wanted Taylor to have everything she'd been denied as a child. She had suffered through these unhappy years with Wilson for the sole purpose of giving Taylor a stable home, although she supposed she had to admit that there were other reasons as well, such as lethargy, money, and a lack of any alternative plan.

Wilson was probably responsible for whatever awful crisis she had just unearthed. She sometimes thought that if he hadn't been so cheap, Taylor might have been better off in private school, but it was obviously too late to revisit that particular drama. Still, Taylor had so much going for her. She was bright, pretty, and privileged. She had her own car and her own credit card. Nina had never once said no to any material request, even though the once generous wad direct-deposited into their bank account each month was slowing to a trickle now that they were reaching the end of Wilson's severance pay. When a *Newsweek* cover story suggested showering children with material goods only created unpleasant and narcissistic kids, resulting in a weeklong period of soul-searching and discussions of credit card canceling among her fellow PTA moms, Nina did not waver. Taylor could have anything her heart desired, and Nina would find a way to pay, even if it required deceiving Wilson. This was mostly just an ideological position, however, since there was very little Taylor wanted, other than to paint, which was not only a waste of time, but very messy.

Her hands began to shake, and she couldn't seem to stop the tears, so she nipped into her bedroom to get a bottle of vodka from her bedside table. She felt a brief resolve as the liquid burned through her system—they would get through this, whatever this was! Bad things sometimes happened to good people! But then she returned to Taylor's bedroom, and when she sat on the bed, a heap of mail spilled to the floor. She bent over to pick it up, and more came raining down. The next thing she knew she had thrown it all on the floor and was lying spread-eagle, making snow angels in the mail, which proved strangely cathartic. When she sat up to take another pull of vodka, a return address caught her eye. It was from the bank, and it looked ominous. She had only just had her nails done and didn't want to chip the polish, so she retrieved the steak knife from the bathroom to slice open the envelope. She had bounced a check, the notice informed her—three months ago.

Why couldn't she have married a real Rockefeller? Even an illegitimate Rockefeller would have been better than this. At least if Wilson had descended from, say, the family maid, they might have been able to sue their way into claiming a piece of the pie! Anyway, there was no harm in giving the impression that they were related, and who knew—there was always the remote possiblity that they really were. She had done a fair amount of reading about the family when she first met Wilson, hoping to find some way to connect the genetic dots. When she learned that John D. Senior had evidently suffered from alopecia, a rare condition that resulted in periods of complete hair loss, she grew excited, thinking that Wilson might have inherited the same trait somehow. But Wilson just looked at her like she was raving mad when she made this suggestion, and explained that he was simply going bald.

Now she wondered if she ought to take a look and zero in on any possible incidences of Rockefeller-related mail-hoarding. Certainly this condition—whatever it was—wasn't traceable to *her* side of the family.

As she stood chatting with Grace, it occurred to her that, for the first time in her life, she might actually want a bit of advice. She had been feeling unusually low lately, even before her awful discovery. For a patch of several nights in August, Wilson had not come home at all, and when he did, he just sat in a chair, absorbed by his BlackBerry. When she asked where he had been, he didn't answer. When she picked a fight, he didn't engage. They hadn't been close for years, but his recent behavior seemed to be ushering in a new phase of marital decline. This was distracting, and she was suffering from a certain lack of focus. She found herself losing her passion for golf, for example, and didn't even enjoy the Sunday-evening drinks gala in the club bar, which for years had been the highlight of each week.

She entertained the radical idea of saying something about this to Grace. Even if the women had drifted apart, Grace seemed the kind of person in whom one might confide, someone who would offer sage advice. She was on the verge of asking her if they could talk privately sometime, but before she could choke out the request, Angie Lee's mother, Lena Bell, appeared and gave them each an air kiss on the cheek.

"Hey, girls!" she said, always bubbly, presenting like an airhead, just like her brilliant, dizzy daughter. Although Nina had never met Mr. Lee, it seemed obvious that Angie must have inherited her brains from his side of the family. "How are the kids? How is Harry doing? And of course . . . Hunter."

"Taylor," Nina corrected.

"Taylor. Has Harry decided where he's applying yet? Angie already finished her applications, thank God, because with her schedule this year, I don't know how she'd possibly get it all done. But she's only sent two of them off so far, just the ones with rolling admissions."

Nina felt a wave of panic. Angie had finished her applications? It was only the second week of September. So far as she knew, Taylor hadn't even written her essay yet, her efforts to encourage her on this front notwithstanding. She had assembled for her twelve folders with view books and assorted materials about the schools she thought best, but so far as she could tell, Taylor had not even touched the pile. She would have to talk to Taylor about this when she got home and let her know that Angie Lee was already done. Maybe she ought to ground Taylor until she filled out all the applications. But then maybe that was too harsh? Maybe she should just ground her until she wrote her essay. Or ground her until she agreed to visit one of the two college counselors she had lined up for her. But given that Taylor spent most of her time locked in her room, doing who-knew-what with the knife and the mail, perhaps grounding her was not the right answer. Parenting was very complicated sometimes.

Grace shrugged her shoulders. "He's got a little time," she replied calmly. "I'm still hoping to take Harry to visit a couple more schools before he makes a final decision."

Nina waited for Lena Bell to ask about Taylor so that she might have an opportunity to mention her impressive SAT writing score, but she didn't. Instead, she said that they were fielding phone calls from admissions officers from a couple of schools *begging* Angie to matriculate. Nina wondered why no one was calling Taylor. Perhaps she really *should* ground her.

"Girls," Lena said, mercifully changing the subject. "I wonder what you think about this sex ed business."

Lena Bell was an active member of both the PTA and the Guidance Advisory Committee and seemed to have a hand in just about everything that went on at school.

Grace looked at her watch and shrugged. Nina didn't really want to get started on this subject, either. E-mails had been flying back and forth for weeks about the new controversial course outline that included a videotaped instructional segment showing how to put a condom on a cucumber. The video evidently included frank discussions about oral and anal sex. Even in mostly liberal Verona, there were those who believed the curriculum went too far. As evidence they pointed to the fact that the automatic censor feature on the county's Web server blocked e-mails containing language describing the sexual acts in question. When strung together, the list of rejected words read like vile spam mail. The subject seemed to be pitting friends against neighbors, producing vitriol unrivaled by even the last presidential election.

Nina didn't really understand what all the fuss was about. Whatever this video was, it had to be less perverse than the film the kids had been watching in health class called "Am I Normal?" where a young boy, fretting about the size of his penis, asks a zookeeper whether something is wrong with him. Happy to oblige, the zookeeper takes him aside and speaks to him frankly about the variations of penis size in the animal kingdom. When Nina viewed the film during a PTA meeting, she couldn't help but wonder if this boy's mother knew what her son was doing, and whether anyone had thought to check whether the zookeeper was on the national sex offender list. Anyway, someone was going to have to talk to Taylor about sex, and she was happy to be let off the hook. She wasn't comfortable talking to her about intimate bodily functions; plus, she didn't know how to put a condom on a cucumber, so she was just as happy to leave that to others.

"What do you think of the stress management controversy?" Lena Bell now asked, using her long pink nails to place air quotes around the last word.

Grace and Nina both replied that they weren't aware of any stress management controversy.

"Oh," said Lena, seemingly excited to be the one to impart the details. "We arranged to have a special meeting for kids that are feeling really stressed out, and we asked parents to bake some cookies in order to entice them to come, and then we'd have a speaker talk about how to handle stress. But now there's this whole countermovement saying this is somehow 'too intrusive,'" she said, pausing to make some more air quotes. "They say that the school should not be mucking around with our children's minds without parental consent. And there's this other camp that says that their kids can only attend if the parents can come, too. Can you imagine?"

Nina couldn't decide which of these aspects she was supposed to have trouble imagining. Her only thought was that anyone dealing with the sort of stress that could be alleviated with a one-hour meeting and a plate of cookies was in pretty good shape.

A bell rang and Nina noticed that the crowd in the hallway had already thinned. Grace glanced at her watch again and said she'd better hurry, or she'd be late for class. For a moment Nina imagined that she was back in high school, although she reminded herself that it hadn't been that happy a time. Even back then she had been in awe of girls like Grace, and even then, she got the impression that when they spoke to her, they were only being polite.

October

HARRY TOOK PRIDE in being a fiercely rational sort of person. He was
not the sort to read tea leaves, but he was starting to wonder if there was
some admissions office in the sky full of wizened old deans who were trying to tell him something. Never mind his stubborn SAT scores, or the
astonishing intelligence he had picked up about the number of fellow
Verona classmates planning to apply to Harvard; there were other things
messing with his mind.

His guidance counselor had just quit, for example, and she had not
yet written his college recommendation. He'd never had much confidence that she would write a compelling letter on his behalf, but on the
other hand, an important piece of his fate, and that of about one hundred
fellow classmates whose names fell in his range of the alphabet, was now
in the hands of someone he had just met for the first time this week. At
least the new counselor, Mr. Kushner, had seemed interested in Harry
and the question of where he was planning to apply to college, which was
a pleasant surprise. He'd grown used to his previous counselor's indifference and had come to regard her as a mere gatekeeper, or a twitchy
armed guard, whose chief objective was to prevent him from entering
her office to muck with his schedule, generating more paperwork. On
the downside, Mr. Kushner's desk was piled so high with folders—each
one representing a letter of recommendation that he had to write within

the next two months, he explained—that Harry could barely glimpse the friendly, bearded face peeking from behind the stacks.

The problem that was causing him the most angst, however, had less to do with Verona than with Harvard. He had visited the campus three times and had yet to take a formal tour. He knew this was a minor and almost certainly insignificant blip, and yet perhaps because it signified the first step in the college admissions process, he found himself concerned about its possible meaning.

The first time that he visited Harvard didn't really count, as he had only been in seventh grade, and just happened by with his father when they were driving back from seeing Lou's deadbeat brother who lived in a trailer outside Worcester. Since it was late on a Sunday in August and the admissions office was closed, they wandered around the campus on their own. Lou said they probably didn't give tours to kids in middle school anyway, even though he thought they should. His dad said that maybe an early visit to Harvard would have motivated someone like his slacker brother to work hard in school to make a better life for himself. Harry remembered thinking that there was something not quite right with this analysis; his uncle seemed to have a lot of problems, and it was difficult to imagine they might have been avoided by a visit to Harvard at age thirteen. Uncle Burt had been divorced three times, for example, and he had once shot a neighbor and spent ten years in jail.

Harry never questioned his father. A lot of what his dad said was so confusing and illogical that he went into some trancelike state when he was around him; his brain shut down but the essence of Harry still lurked inside, sort of like when his computer put itself to sleep. This mental sleep mode served him well when his parents divorced. He didn't waste energy overthinking things, and simply did as he was told. If his mother instructed him to pack a bag to visit his father, he stuffed his pajamas and a toothbrush in his backpack. And when things got ugly and the police came around and his mother told him to unpack the bag, he did that, too.

His father had been talking to him about Harvard for as long as Harry could remember. Lou had spoken of the place with such reverence that Harry had come to think of it as having magical properties, like Disneyland, or maybe Oz. On that first visit he was surprised to see that the

campus, while still somehow rarified even in its late summer abandon-
ment, was essentially just a collection of buildings and trees.

Although Lou had always been unnaturally attached to his video
camera, he was not an especially talented filmmaker, and the resultant
footage of that visit, with most of the buildings badly out of focus and a
long stretch of Harvard Yard upside-down, made Harry slightly nause-
ated when he watched. Lou had spliced that visit together with another
unsettling milestone: Harry's first day of nursery school, which in retrospect, also had its own special pathology. Lou had evidently sat behind
the lens as the children and fellow parents participated in "circle time," a
morning ritual when each child shared some supposedly telling piece
of information, such as what book he had read the previous night, or
relayed some amusing pet-related facts. At the time, Lou had been in-
between jobs—a condition Harry would later realize was chronic—and
was therefore available to do more than his share of parenting duties.
When it was Harry's turn, Lou spoke instead, saying that Harry was a
math prodigy who began doing long division in his head at eighteen
months, helped with the household budget, loved to tour Civil War bat-
tlefields, and had read biographies of every U.S. president. Lou added
that he wanted to see his son spend his time in nursery school honing the
skills that would get him into Harvard. Even the teacher started laughing
before Lou had finished speaking.

Nowadays Harry couldn't completely separate which memories were
real, and to what extent he was projecting his current perspective on the
past, but he seemed to have a dim memory of something clicking that
day. Like even though he vaguely understood that they were laughing *at*
his father, he didn't especially care. He somehow knew that he was just
doing time among his peers, some of whom still wore diapers, drank
from spill-proof plastic cups, and spent a lot of time crying and wiping
the resultant globs of mucus that dripped from their noses into their already filthy sleeves. Harry imagined himself special somehow, like whatever it was that his father said set him apart from this song-singing,
finger-painting crowd, even if his boasts were not remotely true.

One thing he did remember well, even without the help of videotape,
was that he didn't have a lot of friends when he was little. He wondered

if his peers kept their distance because they could translate his aspirations—or perhaps his father's aspirations for him—into toddler-friendly terms, like being greedy at the toy store. Although he spent very little time dwelling on it, even now, in high school, he wished friendships came more naturally, and he envied the kids he saw hanging out in the hallways at school, all laughing and goofing around like they were living inside one of those teen dramas on television that everyone was always talking about. He sensed that Taylor didn't like him anymore, and he couldn't really think why that might be. He seemed to be having a chilling effect on Maya as well. His only reliable companion was Justin Smelling, and even though they had been best friends for years, he did not entirely trust the relationship. Most of their time together involved studying; they had spent every weekend for two months preparing for the SATs, agreeing ahead of time that they would take the same subject tests. Even when they did normal kid things like going sledding, there seemed to always be some form of competition involved. There were times when Harry suspected Justin was the sort of friend who might leave him wounded on the battlefield, or nudge him out of the lifeboat so that he could eat the last ration.

DURING HIS junior year, when Harry and his mother began to seriously discuss his college options for the first time, she practically kidnapped him to visit schools he had no real interest in, and one night, seemingly out of the blue, she insisted they attend a program at the Verona Public Library called "Seeing Beyond the Ivies." In the end Harry was glad he had gone because the lecture only reinforced his initial instincts. For two hours the speaker admonished the capacity crowd that they would get a decent, if not better, education at a lesser-known school where the professors actually taught their own classes and were not just famous figureheads who spent most of their time on the road, promoting their books. In Harry's mind, the speaker's entire argument was negated by the fact that he, himself, was a Princeton graduate. Evidently, Harry was not alone in this perception because the question-and-answer session snaked its way back to discussing strategies about how to get into an Ivy League school that went on so long the librarian finally had to flip the lights on and off several times to get people to acknowledge that it was time to go home.

A one-hour motivational speech about the virtues of a bunch of schools he had never heard of was not likely to have much effect on a plan some seventeen years in the making. He had spent his young lifetime listening to his father blame all of his own problems on an inferior education. Lou said he constantly watched people in his office get promoted when they were clearly less capable than him, simply because he had gone to Maryland. Now that Harry was older, he thought there might have been more to the story. For one thing, his parents had met in college, and so far as he could tell, his mother was pretty successful in her field. Another thing was that by the time his father lost his third job, he had begun to look and smell a little funky.

THE SECOND time Harry visited Harvard was back in April, when he failed to notice in the fine print on the school's Web site that while info sessions would take place as usual, there would be no campus tours the week he was visiting because the student guides were on their own spring break. He couldn't imagine how he had let this happen, given how hyper-organized he was, and he feared it was perhaps representative of a Freudian slip—Freudian slips being something else, like tea leaves, in which he did not actually believe, but was nonetheless having to rethink his position on. He had sat in on an information session that day, and the woman conducting the talk nonchalantly mentioned that the size of the crowd was *triple* anything she had ever seen before.

Now, to top it all off, he and his mom had driven all night in order to arrive in time for the Saturday morning tour and the tour was, for the first time in recent history the woman at the reception desk in the admissions office reported nonchalantly, cancelled because of the weather. Harry's nerves were frayed from the long drive, but he collected himself and calmly suggested that it wasn't that bad outside, even though he knew it was. They had turned on the local radio station while they were driving and heard the newscasters compare the thrashing winds and driving rains to the "no name" storm of October 1991—the one that had inspired the book *The Perfect Storm*. Grace begged him to let her pull off the road and seek shelter in a motel, but Harry was worried that they wouldn't make it to the tour in time if they stopped. He began to doubt his own judgment when they maneuvered past an eleven-car pileup on I-95, but he kept coaxing his mother forward, exit by exit.

They arrived in Cambridge almost exactly on time and found a perfect parking space smack in front of Radcliffe Yard, which housed the admissions building. But when they went inside to register, they were told that there had been some sort of electrical incident in Harvard Yard and that the fire department had actually cordoned off the area. In addition, the power was out in several of the main buildings, including Widener Library and the science center, which were two of the stops on the tour.

As long as they were there, Grace agreed that they might as well sit through another information session, even though Harry had found the one in the spring to be mildly depressing. He had imagined that the level of discourse at a Harvard information session would be devoid of the usual banal questions about test scores and teacher recommendations, and had even fantasized that he and his fellow aspirants would spend the hour engaged in a Socratic dialogue about the purpose of education and its role in a meritocractic society. But the questions had proven no less sophomoric than those at other schools. One girl asked whether it was better to submit her French or her Spanish subject tests—she let slip that both scores were 800s. Another said she was attending community college since she had already taken everything offered at her high school even though she was only fifteen and wondered if it was better to apply as an incoming freshman or a transfer student. The admissions officer seemed unimpressed and replied to each question with some version of the jigsaw puzzle analogy: they looked at the application as a whole, no one piece was more important than another, etc. Harry wondered if admissions officers were trained at some secret Virginia farm, coached perhaps by former CIA case officers, where they learned these methods of linguistic deflection. Or maybe he had been right in his earlier thinking: all of these places were like Oz; they ran on a currency of illusion, with buzzwords being part of the scam.

The student representative at the last Harvard information session had proven similarly uninspiring and certainly didn't strike him as a future world leader; not only was she wearing short shorts and a shirt that seemed to deliberately showcase her bra straps, but she had been one of the ditziest girls he had ever seen—right on par with Angie Lee. He wondered at the time if she had been admitted as part of some sort of affirmative action campaign, with a few precious spots set aside for the airhead, otherwise a victim of discrimination in society at large. When it was her turn to speak about why she had chosen to go to Harvard (as if such a story were really necessary, given her disclosure that her other choice was Arizona State), she told a long, convoluted story having to do with the day her acceptance letter arrived and then chronicled the completely irrelevant screwball visit to campus that involved getting on the wrong flight. Her story was punctuated by at least five "Ohmygods!"

Another disappointment at the last session was that the admissions officer had spent the first ten minutes discussing the merits of Boston—its proximity to both skiing and beaches and the number of fun things to do in the city itself, as if he might have worked this hard for so long to go to Harvard in order to hang out in pubs or catch Red Sox games! Unlike the session Maya said she had gone to at Vassar, the Harvard person spent virtually no time stressing the difficulty of getting in. Maya reported that she had found the Vassar admissions officer hugely discouraging and left feeling that she shouldn't even bother applying since she hadn't taken all of the most difficult classes offered at Verona. Hearing that would have actually made Harry feel good, like at least he was sitting in the right room.

Harry tried to buck Maya up when she mentioned this as they walked home from school a couple of weeks earlier. It struck him as absurd; surely she could get into Vassar! The last time he'd looked, Vassar was only number 12 in the *U.S. News* rankings! Still, he had to confess he had heard rumors of a flurry of rejections received by Verona kids who had applied to Vassar from last year's senior class, difficult as that was for him to believe. He asked her what her grades and scores were, trying to help her figure this out, but she'd looked at him in a funny way and hadn't answered. Once again he felt like he'd done something wrong, but he wasn't sure what.

When he reflected on that last Harvard information session, though, he did recall that the admissions officer let slip certain worrisome numbers: some 23,000 applications had been received the previous fall for a class of 1,650 freshmen, but she said that in a quiet way, as if this sort of information was not very important. In the same tone she also mentioned that 80 to 85 percent of the applicants were completely qualified to come to Harvard and do "perfectly good academic work." Harry understood that these numbers were supposed to make people feel less bad about their forthcoming rejection letters. While he absorbed this information and understood the implications, he sensed he'd be okay; going to Harvard was, for him, somehow preordained.

Harry could only conclude that the whole tenor of any college visit depended on the luck of the draw pertaining to tour guides and information session leaders. He felt he had possibly been gypped because Justin's visit had yielded much more satisfying statistics along the lines of how Harvard could fill its freshman class with valedictorians alone.

At least the questions Harry listened to were a little less loopy than some of the others reported by his classmates. Courtney Ruben said that when she visited Hampshire College, she asked the tour guide—who was dressed in all black with a dangerous-looking, spiked choker around her neck—to describe the sort of person that went to the school. At first she refused and said it was impossible to pigeonhole kids, that the school attracted all types—which evidently Courtney said she found hard to believe given the preponderance of pierced noses and Birkenstocks she spotted on campus. Courtney was persistent, and finally the tour guide relented and said that people tended to use the "Scooby-Doo" analogy to distinguish the personality types at the five schools in the area: kids who went to Smith were like the prim Daphne character; kids at Mt. Holyoke were like the artsy, more intellectual Velma; Amherst kids were blond, preppy Fred types; Hampshire kids were like Shaggy; while UMass was full of Scoobys.

Mike Lee said that when he visited Boston University, someone asked how the school stacked up against Harvard and MIT. Mike said the otherwise seemingly unflappable admissions officer was actually stumped for a moment before he cobbled together a bland nonanswer along the lines of how each school had its own special attributes. In that same info session, Mike reported, one mother raised her hand and asked what these SAT subject tests were that the admissions officer kept talking about, and said that her son was a rising senior and no one at his school had ever mentioned that such a test existed. Harry thought the real question was, *What was Mike Lee doing at a Boston University information session?* but he kept that to himself. One could always dream that there was some secret blemish in Mike Lee's transcript that caused him to stoop so low for a safety, but he certainly wasn't going to be the one to ask.

Harry had heard someone speculate that the most obnoxious questions could usually be heard in the baptismal wave of tours over spring break, when everyone was first getting their minds around the whole college thing. At least now it was October, and those in attendance had presumably sat through a few sessions already, so perhaps the questions would be somewhat less insipid.

Harry settled himself in one of the ancient, creaky chairs in the small auditorium. The room was filling up fast, severe weather alerts notwithstanding. Harry looked around and had to reluctantly admit there was really nothing all that remarkable about the experience of visiting Harvard. While he observed small differences in dress and demeanor, for the most part kids looked the same at every school he had seen. On this occasion he was the only one in the room who had even bothered to dress properly; most everyone else looked like they were en route to a weekend sports event. At least when he had attended a combined information session at the Verona Marriott just a few months earlier, where Harvard, Stanford, Penn, and Georgetown all sent representatives, the style of dress had been more collegiate. About 80 percent of the boys in attendance were wearing dress shirts and ties. Harry had worn a tie himself, even though his mother suggested that was unnecessary. She observed later that the Verona Marriott was situated between two private schools with dress codes, which almost certainly explained the more formal attire. Still, Harry felt more comfortable in a nice starched shirt, and he thought it showed a real lack of respect on the part of his peers that they wore ratty jeans and T-shirts when they set foot in the hallowed hallways of Harvard. If they aspired to be members of the ruling class, he believed that they ought to get in the habit of dressing the part.

He pulled two books from a wet plastic bag that crinkled noisily, and looked around, embarrassed. He tried to interpret his mother's expression as he flipped open the first book, *50 Successful Harvard Application Essays*. After learning that the tour was cancelled, they had wandered into Cambridge to get some lunch and kill time before the information session, and had ducked inside the co-op bookstore to get out of the rain. Most of the stores were shuttered because of power outages, and the brightly illuminated bookstore was consequently jammed with soggy people toting dripping umbrellas. Then he saw another book, *The Guide to Getting In*, written by Harvard Student Agencies. He *had* to have these. He looked at his mother imploringly; they conducted the rest of the transaction entirely through silent gestures. He picked up the book and nodded toward the cash register. Grace raised her eyebrows. Harry shrugged his shoulders. Grace lifted her chin in assent, although the look on her face was, while not upset, along the lines of what he might classify as . . . resigned. *Resigned, reconciled, submissive, acquiescent* . . . He had just taken the SAT a week earlier and was done with the test for eternity, yet he suspected he'd be thinking of synonyms for the rest of his life. Not that the exercise had done him a bit of good. He was pretty sure that he would have gotten a 720 on the critical reading and writing sections if he'd taken the thing back in middle school, and he'd get the same scores ten years from now, even if he spent the intervening years literally memorizing the dictionary and writing practice essays.

He opened the essay book to a random page and began reading about a banana. Evidently, the author's favorite teacher at his fancy prep school always had a bowl of slightly wilted bananas on his desk. Harry thought this was kind of a risky way to begin an essay and couldn't imagine where the applicant was going with this. Wouldn't the admissions people be more interested in learning about this kid's participation in the chess club, his work with migrant farmworkers, his plan to become a diplomat? Why would they want to know about a bunch of fetid rotting bananas? Maybe something was going to happen at the end of the five hundred words that would illuminate the student's achievements. Or maybe this somehow qualified as *literary*. People were always going on about being literary, although Harry never really understood what all the fuss was about. What was the point of being literary, when there were practical concerns in the world like curing diseases or making money? Maya seemed to be interested in this whole literary thing, too, but then that was probably just because she had been in love with Mr. Joyce. Even if Harry was not *literary*, he was logical, so he understood that his inability to appreciate an essay about these stupid bananas probably had something to do with the hostility he still harbored for the teacher who had given him a B.

He had just begun to read another essay about friends who held a contest to see who could get the higher SAT score. Now *this* he could understand. He was only into the first paragraph when someone called his name.

"Harry, is that you?" asked a soft, but otherwise nondescript, female voice.

He flipped the book over on its back hoping to disguise its content, and looked up. It was Lily Wong, who he'd known since kindergarten, and his very first thought was that he'd been a moron for not realizing she, too, would be jockeying for a spot at Harvard. He wasn't sure how he'd missed her when he'd gone through the school directory back in September, putting asterisks next to all the names of seniors who would be likely contenders.

"Lily!" he said, feigning enthusiasm. "What a coincidence. Where have you been hiding?" It dawned on him that he hadn't seen her for a while.

"We moved," she explained. "We moved into D.C. the summer after sophomore year, and now I'm going to Klee."

"Klee?" Grace asked, looking up from her newspaper, sounding subtly surprised. Klee was one of the most troubled high schools not just in the area, but in the nation. The school had been closed for weeks at a time over the last few years for reasons ranging from teacher shortages to lack of heat.

"We went to see a college counselor," Lily explained, sounding remarkably unembarrassed by what came next, "and he said that if I wanted to stand a chance of getting into Harvard, I needed to get out of the Verona school district and also do something to counter the smart Asian kid stereotype. So at Klee, I'm class valedictorian. And I'm also head cheerleader."

Harry wondered what the head cheerleader at Klee did, given that all of the sports teams had been indefinitely suspended since the new school budget famously eliminated the athletic program. "Do you still play piano?" Harry asked, remembering how she always dazzled the parents at the annual spring talent shows. Each year there would be at least five groups of blond girls in sparkly leotards wearing too much makeup and dancing provocatively to pop music, and then there would be about five noisy rock bands doing bad Creed covers, and then there would be about five kids like Lily Wong who wore long black skirts with lacy white tops and played their instruments with such grace and sophistication that it seemed they belonged at the Kennedy Center, notwithstanding the fact that the production values of a Verona High School talent show actually rivaled any professional performance. Now it seemed Lily Wong had become one of the girls in sparkly leotards, which was a surprisingly arousing thought given her voluptuous body, which Harry was just noticing for the first time.

"I do play, yes. In fact I'm playing in the Verona County Youth Opera as an accompanist," Lily confessed sheepishly. "But the counselor thought it would be better to bury that in my profile and do more sorts of regular, fun activities."

Harry nodded and agreed that this made total sense, while he silently calculated that one space for the incoming class of 2011 at Harvard had just been claimed.

The wind outside had been raging loudly while they spoke, and suddenly the walls began to rattle as if they were being shelled by enemy forces. The sound of a small explosion was followed by noises that Harry was pretty sure were popping fuses. All at once the windowless room went black. No one said a word at first, perhaps fearing that an inappropriate response might negatively affect their chances of admission. After a moment someone began to issue violent screams, which was far more alarming than the dark, and seemed to be the catalyst that caused another person to cry. A few minutes later the receptionist appeared with a flashlight and led them back up the stairwell and to the front door, explaining the information session had just been canceled. She offered her apologies, saying that so far as she knew, nothing like this had ever happened before.

In that admissions office in the sky, Harry was pretty sure the deans were laughing at him.

○ ○ ○

"I HAVE THE PERFECT first sentence," Nina announced as Taylor headed out the door. "I had a brainstorm while I was watching Larry King last night. Martha Stewart was on and she said something about . . ."

Taylor didn't pause to absorb her mother's latest pearls of wisdom. It was chillier outside than she'd expected, and she considered turning back to grab the jacket hanging on the stair post. But she didn't want to hear any Martha Stewart–inspired essay ideas, even if they only had to do with baking cookies, so she decided to brave the morning frost wearing just a sweatshirt. Nina was still obsessed with Taylor's topic, constantly lobbing ideas at her, and even going so far as to begin drafting essays herself: "The game of golf is a metaphor for life . . ." and "Family lore has it that my first words were 'Standard Oil . . .' " were among the most recent results. Fortunately, Nina had little patience for the exercise, so she rarely got beyond composing the first sentence or two.

Taylor thought that her mother's ideas were cracked, but she wasn't having much success coming up with something on her own. "I see inside the envelopes," the sentence that had been banging around in her head since she'd first discovered the highschoolconfessions blog, didn't presage a topic likely to sit well with Mr. Leon, for example.

Taylor wondered if she was the only one in the class to have her draft college application essay, the first mandatory writing assignment of the school year, handed back to her three times for revision. She had tried several different approaches and was only just beginning to understand that it was the theme of the essay that Mr. Leon objected to, and not its execution. He was evidently suggesting that her complicated relationship with the U.S. Postal Service, however compelling, was not the best vehicle for helping her get into college. But his notations in the margins were initially too subtle, and Taylor thought the problem could be fixed with a little buffing of grammar. Finally, Mr. Leon asked her to come in and see him after school; she feared she was in some sort of trouble, but it turned out he was just looking for a gentle way to urge her to scrap the essay and start from scratch.

"Why don't you go with something more routine," he suggested. He seemed to be avoiding eye contact, like whatever he found disturbing in her essay might be contagious. "You could describe your favorite character in your favorite novel, for example. Or you could write about a role model." Mr. Leon was young, like Mr. Joyce, but his opposite in demeanor. While Mr. Joyce had been an educational renegade, Mr. Leon was a taskmaster, a stickler for rules, the sort of teacher who would not round an 89.5 to an A. Or in Taylor's case, the more relevant detail was that he would not round a 69.5 to a C, which was the grade she had received on the first quiz. Also, while Mr. Joyce had looked a bit like the part-time poet he advertised himself to be—slightly unkempt in a wild-haired, dreamy kind of way—Mr. Leon looked more like a straitlaced insurance salesman in his jacket and tie. He was kind of cute, which made a private meeting with him slightly awkward. Taylor hoped no one would get the impression that she had sought him out to flirt. She wondered why so many of her male teachers were very young. Did something happen after a few years that sent them screaming into the night?

Mr. Leon waited for her to respond, but she hesitated, afraid of saying the wrong thing. She looked around the room and noticed for the first time that the alphabet was stripped across the top of the chalkboard in both print and cursive writing. She wondered why this was. How could she have sat here for nearly six weeks without noticing the artwork on the walls—posters from various theater productions of *Hamlet*, travel promotions from Spain, and a totally random framed movie still from *Chicken Little* mounted on the back wall. Evidently, the room had other lives outside the time Taylor logged here each morning, listening to Mr. Leon from her perch in the last row.

"Do you have a favorite novel?" he finally asked.

"I do!" she said, brightening. *"The Bell Jar?* By Sylvia Plath?" She had read it again over the summer, for the third time.

Mr. Leon nodded his head but didn't speak, causing Taylor to suspect this was the wrong answer. She was probably supposed to say something like *Little Women* or *The Call of the Wild*.

"Let's skip the novel and concentrate on another idea. How about a role model . . . Does anyone leap to mind?"

Taylor tried to think of a role model, to no avail.

"How about Mother Teresa?" he suggested. "She's an excellent example of the sort of person you might want to choose to emulate."

"Mother Teresa?" she said wearily. "I'm not Catholic."

"That doesn't really matter. Mother Teresa's good deeds symbolized much more than just religion." He said this with an intensity that made Taylor assume he was either Catholic himself, or had some other close affiliation with the nun, like maybe they were related.

"I guess I can give that a try," Taylor said, disappointed. She had worked hard on her essay, and so far as she could tell, it conformed to all of the parameters that Mr. Leon had set out. At a most basic level, at five hundred words, it was the right length; it passed "the litmus test for originality" and was likewise "revealing," which were two other specifications in the book *Accepted!*—portions of which Mr. Leon had photocopied for their reference.

"A key to writing a successful essay is that it must be original," the book explained. "One of the best tests is employed by an admissions officer who calls it the 'Rule of Thumb.' Basically, if he can cover the name of the author with his thumb and insert the name of any other applicant, then the essay is not original." Taylor was pretty sure she was on safe ground on this front.

"I'm not sure I completely understand what's wrong with my essay as it is," Taylor said boldly.

Instead of answering right away, Mr. Leon walked over to his desk and retrieved his dog-eared copy of *Accepted!* He flipped through it for a few minutes before finding the page he was looking for and read aloud:

"Besides having an original essay, you need to make sure that it reveals something about you. It cannot just be a mere description of a person, place or thing. You want to reflect on an aspect of your life, preferably one you are *proud* of."

Taylor noted his emphasis on the word *proud*. Then he looked her in the eye for the first time. Taylor felt her face heat up. She understood what he was driving at, but she also tucked away the observation that the book prefaced the word *proud* with the word *preferably*. She was not sure she really agreed with Mr. Leon's assessment of her essay, but she understood that he was only trying to help. Besides, this was just a routine English assignment, a straightforward transaction worth at most one-tenth of her semester grade. At the end of the day, the decision about what set of words to attach to her application was entirely her own.

Anyway, she was not entirely sure she understood what the problem was and wondered if perhaps Mr. Leon was reading something into the essay that wasn't really there. Verona was one big rumor mill, so it was possible that he had heard things about her and was therefore not very objective when he read her work. On paper, she was pretty sure she had stuck to the theme of bonding with her neighbors, albeit through unconventional means. Still, she supposed it was possible she had not been as opaque as she thought, and the suggestion of bad behavior might have sprung like weeds through her carefully selected euphemisms.

In her essay, or in her conversations with Mr. Leon, the word *mail* was never even mentioned. Never mentioning the unmentionable was part of the plea bargain she had struck with her mother, the terms of which allowed her to redistribute all of the neighbor's mail in the dark of night (although actually it took several nights, as so much had accumulated) in exchange for agreeing to see a therapist twice a week and removing the padlock from her bedroom door. Her mother said they were going to refer to the incident as "the thing that never happened." She said that it was possible to set a bad chapter of one's life aside in this manner, that she had done so herself when she was in high school, when she and her best friend Charlene had gone into downtown Boston one night with fake IDs, had had too much to drink, and had picked up three strange men. The next morning she and Charlene realized how badly they had behaved and vowed that they would never discuss this with another living soul. They would henceforth refer to the evening as "the night that never happened." Taylor cringed a couple of times during this little heart-to-heart. She wanted to tell her mother a few different things, along the lines of this was way too much information and that she had essentially negated the point of her story by bringing it up in the first place.

Taylor tried to craft the essay around the theme of self-discovery and about the experience of sometimes feeling on the outside of things. She wrote that learning more about her neighbors in a nonthreatening manner, which she did not actually describe, helped her to feel more connected to the world. She drew a reference to Annie Dillard's *Pilgrim at Tinker Creek*—required summer reading freshman year, which was followed by a tedious assignment asking students to be an observant pilgrim at a place of their own choosing. Most of her classmates selected spots where they could do a bit of socializing, like the fountain in downtown Verona, which was a popular local hangout. Taylor had chosen her bedroom and titled the resulting essay "Pilgrim at a Window." She unearthed the original essay written back in ninth grade to use as a reference and was stunned to see that it had been full of veiled references to the mail. Somehow she had imagined this weird impulse came upon her suddenly, and was startled to see she had premonitions of this compulsion two years before she first crept onto Harry's front porch.

At least Mr. Leon had been sensitive in his remarks. Her guidance counselor, never one to mince words, saw a copy of the essay and scrawled a succinct message at the top of the page: "This makes you sound like a psychopath." It was possible that she meant this in a humorous sort of way, rather than the statement of fact Taylor believed it to be.

MR. LEON'S cell phone rang. He checked the caller ID and punched a couple of buttons before putting it back in his pocket and wrapping up the meeting. Taylor briefly considered the alien concept of Mr. Leon having a personal life—might he have a girlfriend, or even a dog? She wondered where he had gone to college, and whether he'd written an essay about Mother Teresa.

"Why don't you go home and take another stab at this, Taylor," he suggested. "My advice would be to go a little less dark."

"Do you mean less dark in the essay? Or less dark generally?" she asked.

Mr. Leon seemed to think for a minute before replying. "Both."

SHE TRIED to brighten up, but it was hard work. She pulled from her closet some of the pink and green preppy clothes her mother had purchased for her over the years, and downloaded some cheery girl-group music, but the experiment left her feeling vaguely ill, like she'd been sitting in the sun for too long. She tried her hand at an essay on Esther Greenwood, from *The Bell Jar*, but this did not turn out well, either. Obviously, the author herself was not a beacon of mental health with her suicide attempts, her irascible depression, and her morbid poem about a cheery bowl of tulips, yet somehow Taylor had never really appreciated what a mess she was and had perhaps just seized on her creative success. Guest editor at a New York magazine! Published before even graduating from college! Now she saw the character of Esther Greenwood in a different light, and it proved impossible to write about Esther without mentioning the many ways in which she could relate to her, like always feeling on the outside of things, like feeling every little thing acutely. Taylor had to admit that *The Bell Jar* essay made her sound like the kind of disturbed person a college admissions officer might possibly want to avoid.

She then tried her hand at an essay on Mother Teresa, instead. It began well enough: Taylor once had a flute teacher who had been born in one of Mother Teresa's orphanages before being adopted by an American family, so she was able to relate her personal if somewhat tenuous connection to her work. She then wrote something about the great circle of life and how everyone is separated by only six degrees that did not really work very well in the context of what she was trying to say, which was something she was slowly losing sight of, herself. She didn't really want to mention religion, but that proved awkward given that Mother Teresa was a nun. While Taylor was respectful, she couldn't relate to Mother Teresa's proclamations about seeing Jesus in every living being; privately she thought that sounded nearly as wacky as enjoying a peek at her neighbors' mail, but she understood that most readers, whatever their religious beliefs, would not see it that way.

She was desperate to feel normal. For a while she felt like she was progressing toward the goal of being a well-adjusted teenager, but every time she moved a little bit forward, she also moved a little bit back. The day of the makeup AP test qualified as a huge step back, if only because Maya Kaluantharana had stumbled into the bathroom and probably misunderstood what she had seen. If she ever talked to Maya about it—not that she ever would!—she would explain that the incident had been cathartic, really the beginning of the end. She was so miserable after taking the test (although in retrospect she wasn't sure why she felt so doomed as she had scored a perfect 5) that she began to fantasize about some sort of release. She was thinking about going home, about how the mail would probably be delivered around the time they would arrive, and how good it would feel to stick her hand inside a postbox. But then she realized it was a Saturday, and of course all the neighbors were around. She fought a little wave of despair as she realized there was no way she could find relief until Monday.

She had finished the test about an hour early and was looking around the room, weighing her options. Her eye caught on a bottle cap on the floor, and she had an idea. She had only been experimenting when Maya found her, unsure of whether you could even break the skin with the top of a Sprite bottle, although it turned out that you could. The shock of being caught just as the first drop of blood appeared was so traumatic that it negated whatever good feeling might have been forthcoming. Plus, Maya was right—she wasn't sure if she was up to date on her tetanus, even though she said she was. She remembered reading about lockjaw from her history class, and thought that sounded pretty nasty, even more of a deterrent than the possibility of scars from slashed skin.

While she suspected it was wrong to view mental health in relative terms, she still found it comforting to compare herself with her anonymous blogspot friends. Some of the entries were light and amusing, if somewhat twisted: "I've had enough of the school mascot," one read, with a picture of an astronaut hanging from a noose. And some were disturbing but not in a desperate sort of way: "I don't really love my dog and I wonder if this makes me a bad person" was the confession, accompanied by a photograph of a pretty adorable golden retriever. Taylor sometimes fretted about this, herself: she didn't *dislike* her dog, but she couldn't help but think of it as her mother's dog, and frankly she didn't feel any special bond. She suspected the feeling was mutual. But these were nothing compared to the confession about hooking up with boys for money: "I might not be smart but I know how to make a buck."

It was hard to tell where stealing the mail fit into the hierarchy of such problems, or whether she was improving after regular visits with the psychotherapist, who kept urging her to open up. She wanted to open up, sort of. On the one hand, she longed to be relieved of her burden and wondered if it might be helpful to talk things through. She and her mother hadn't actually addressed the question of *why* Taylor had the neighbors' mail; Nina seemed to regard the stash in her room as a matter of mere logistics: how might they most efficiently get the mail from point A to point B without being caught? Tiptoeing around what lay at the heart of the matter was fine with Taylor, because she still had the gut feeling that she wanted to keep this to herself. Her relationship with the mail was private, and whatever brief rush she got from her surreptitious missions might vanish if she talked about it. This was why she hadn't sent a photograph to the blogspot, even though she spent a fair amount of time mentally composing her message and thinking about the picture she would post: piles of sliced-opened envelopes with gorgeous stamps, maybe a sharp letter opener resting beside it, for good measure. But after Mr. Leon read her essay, she felt strangely violated, and realized that the idea of sharing her secret with a wider audience might make her feel even more of a mess.

She had decided, however, that she was not going to share her innermost thoughts with Dr. Zimmer, who in her view was a cliché of a psychotherapist, a stuffy man in a bow tie who happened to be a friend of a friend of her mother's. He kept assuring her that their conversations were confidential, but she didn't entirely believe him. While she didn't know what sort of privacy rules technically governed their sessions, she assumed that since she was a minor and her mother was footing the bill, he probably told Nina everything. Under other circumstances, she might have been willing to talk about the fact that her father had essentially disappeared and that she took his absence personally. She understood things were not great between her parents, and even empathized with the idea of needing to get away from her mother, but what about from *her*? Did her dad even remember that he had a daughter? She was sure she had helped to drive him away; she knew this was an almost laughably compliant textbook reaction to parental marital woes, but the knowledge did little to alleviate her guilt.

Dr. Zimmer made Taylor very anxious, and sometimes she thought it was possibly better to have an absentee father than one like her psychotherapist. She had overheard him talking to her mother on a couple of occasions, complaining about his own daughter, who was evidently a senior at a local private school. Dr. Zimmer told Nina that he was unhappy with his daughter's decision to apply early to Duke, as he had his heart set on her going to his alma mater, Rice. He was also disappointed with her grades from spring of her junior year—she had received two B's. Plus, he was angry that she had quit working on the school newspaper as he was certain that would have made her a more attractive candidate. Once, at the very beginning of a session, technically a couple of minutes before the clock began to tick on their forty-minute conversation, he asked Taylor if she would have given up an editorial position because she was "too busy." Taylor was afraid to respond. She couldn't tell if he really wanted her opinion or if this was a trick question, some sneaky kind of Rorschach test of her own mental health.

Taylor mostly humored him when she spoke of the dark impulses that had driven her onto Harry's front porch the first time. She knew he would find it clinically satisfying if she pretended to find links between dramatic events, like having a fight with her mother and then walking across the street and filling an empty Bloomingdale's bag with mail. She was actually comforted by this creative analysis: it made sense to her to view the mail problem as one of impulse control, something that could be remedied with a twelve-step program or a little anger-management training. In truth it was nothing like that. It was slow and deliberate. It was the culmination of an entire day spent obsessing. It was like planning for twelve hours what you were going to eat for dessert, except that you were not a mentally healthy person who could eat just one piece of chocolate cake without ingesting the entire cake and then deliberately throwing it up, which happily was not her issue.

With Dr. Zimmer she pretended they were talking about her problem as if it was in the past, as if they were deconstructing a crime scene where the victim was already dead. She didn't tell him that the desire to walk across the street and flip open mailboxes was so strong that she had actually fallen off the wagon a couple of times in just the three weeks they had been meeting. She was grateful that she had never begun drinking or doing drugs, because without any help from Dr. Zimmer, she was pretty sure she had what they called "an addictive personality."

After her most recent session, Dr. Zimmer had asked her to step outside while he spoke privately with her mother for a few minutes. No one was in the waiting room, so Taylor pressed her ear to the door. She was only able to decipher a few key exchanges, however, before the next patient arrived and she was forced to retreat to a chair and pretend to read an issue of *People* magazine, which, with its gossipy reports on the lifestyles of rich and famous mostly anorexic-looking women, struck her as possibly not the best magazine to have lying around in an office meant to promote emotional well-being.

"In my experience with this sort of thing—which is admittedly not a lot, as far as the particular issue of mail hoarding is concerned—Taylor is behaving this way to relieve anxiety and/or mild depression. Is Taylor feeling any stress at home?"

"At home? I can't imagine why she would feel stress at home," she heard her mother say defensively.

"Well, the good news is that we have a high rate of success with patients when we catch this early . . . We can talk about prescribing antidepressants, or we can consider some radical change in circumstances. It's possible that when she leaves home, the behavior will be easier to control. But of course the opposite might prove true, as she might find herself under even more stress . . . Either way it is good that we've caught this now . . ."

Taylor hoped he was right, but she was somewhat skeptical. Maybe they had caught it early, but so far the discovery hadn't changed a thing. Now that she was theoretically allowed nowhere near the mail, it was pretty much all she could think about. Most of her dreams had mail-related themes, even if they had no plot. Just the night before, she had dreamed she was swimming through a sea of mail wearing Maya's purple Speedo. It was actually a beautiful, calming dream, a mailscape dotted with colorful stamps and postmarks from all over the world, shimmering in the water's reflection. Most of the mail dreams were good, but once she had a nightmare where she was chased by an angry eel and she had woken screaming, her T-shirt soaked with sweat. In other versions of the dream, the mail rained hard from the sky, landing on lawns fronted by wide suburban treeless streets where no one was ever home. She saw herself with wings, flying over this mail-drenched landscape, dipping down to rescue stray pieces and returning them to their rightful owners like some angel of the U.S. Postal Service. It was beautiful and quite moving, and she incorporated this into her college essay, trying to lend it a coherent narrative.

Ironically, despite her mother's endless nagging, the thought of going to Yates was just about the only thing that got her out of bed in the morning. She thought Dr. Zimmer might be right about a change in circumstance: if she could just get out of this house, she might be able to leave her problems behind. She had less than a month to decide whether she was going to apply early decision somewhere and was certain that Yates was her first choice. She kept envisioning the spacious private room she had glimpsed after the official tour had ended, the old marbled bathroom with its quaint facilities. She especially liked the isolation of the campus; it seemed a good place to hide for four years, or maybe just three if she spent her junior year abroad, somewhere even farther away, while she pulled herself together. She also reflected on the mesmerizing naked Indian woman in the admissions lobby—she thought about it so much that she wondered if it had possibly cast some kind of spell on her. And imagine taking a class with Fritz Heimler! Maybe he could finally explain that poem about the radioactive shepherd that she'd had to deconstruct in English class. These seemed like valid enough reasons to fall in love with a school, better reasons, really, than what some of her class-mates could be overheard talking about, like reports of great frat beer bashes or crazy tailgate parties before games. Her mother was practically forbidding her to apply early to Yates, claiming that she didn't want her to waste her best shot on a school she could easily get into, which was perhaps another reason why it held appeal. She imagined applying early to Yates might preempt the next few months of this unpleasantness. Her scores were well above the Yates median, and even with her slippage in grades last semester and her D in tech ed, she had to think she was still near the top of the applicant pool and likely to get in.

Because she wanted this process to go smoothly, she listened closely to Mr. Leon, even if she wasn't completely sure what to do with his ad-vice. One day she arrived a few minutes early for a follow-up meeting and noticed a few of her classmates' essays stacked on his desk. Naturally, she couldn't help but take a peek, and anyway this felt like child's play compared with her usual methods of snooping. At the top of the pile was an essay that began, "They call me AP Harry . . ." She quickly averted her eyes; everything Harry did was perfect and she found this depressing, al-though she did notice that Mr. Leon had scribbled a note in the margin about rethinking his tone, possibly coming up with something "a bit more heartfelt." She began to flip through the rest of the pile but heard Mr. Leon's footsteps approaching, so all she saw of Maya Kaluantharana's essay was that it had something to do with India. She liked Maya fine and hoped that she got into whatever school she wanted—so long as it wasn't Yates! But she couldn't help but think that even though she didn't share her mother's ugly xenophobic sentiments, Nina was right about one thing: spending the summer helping lepers self-actualize by working on a chicken farm in India was pretty hard to top, and possibly even trumped the girl who had spent the summer assembling cameras in a Chinese sweatshop, and then went on to Yale.

Taylor remembered her mother's pronouncement that she needed to find a passion. The thing was, she *had* a passion. And she was able to write more passionately about her passion than about Esther Green-wood, or stabs at an essay about how her parents' endless fighting had made her self-reliant, or even about how affected she was by the death of her dog who had been hit by a car when she was nine. These sounded . . . passionless. And she didn't need Mr. Leon to tell her they were also too dark. Somehow she had even managed to turn the subject of Mother Teresa into something slightly depressing, which she imagined was the sign of some unique, if unenviable, ability.

November

HARRY HOPED HE HADN'T dug himself too deep a hole in his attempt to capitalize on the serial position effect. A few weeks earlier he had seen among his mother's papers a Carnegie Mellon study entitled "Those Who Perform Last Finish First," and a lightbulb went off in his head. The study tracked performances of the likes of *American Idol* contestants and not college applicants, but he figured the general principle was probably the same: *Those who appeared near the end of contests earned higher marks from judges than those who performed earlier.* He had to reschedule his interview.

He invented a couple of what he thought were legitimate-sounding excuses to postpone meeting with the ominously named Mr. Kevorkian, the Harvard alumni interviewer who he had come to associate with the identically named doctor of death. The appointment was originally scheduled for Monday. At first he felt somewhat smug when he heard Justin complain that he couldn't get on Mr. Kevorkian's calendar until late in the afternoon that Friday, but then the day before the scheduled interview Harry saw the report sitting on the kitchen table and cancelled his meeting, feigning the flu. He rescheduled it for the Monday after Justin's interview, but then at lunch he overheard Keith Johnson and Angie Lee talking about their interviews later that week. Harry wasn't going to stand a chance of making an impression if he came before a brilliant African-American thespian and a bubbly female math and science genius, so he called again to reschedule, this time claiming that his mother was ill.

The day was finally here, and now he worried, belatedly, that he might have already earned a black mark in his file for erratic behavior. Prior to turning his energy toward agonizing about the interview, he had spent an equal amount of time fretting about the application itself— whether to apply online or whether to trust the postal service. This sent him into another frenzy of overanalysis: his gut said it was better to send it through the mail, that going through the ritual of sticking it in an envelope and adorning it with stamps demonstrated more of a commitment somehow, even if everyone in the know insisted that it made no difference. Harry briefly entertained the idea of hand-delivering it himself, but his mother went slightly berserk when he casually mentioned the idea of driving the application to Boston, and in the end convinced him that there were ways to track the envelope on the off chance that it went missing. She also insisted that the problems they had with the mail seemed to be only on the receiving end.

He then moved on to agonizing about precisely *when* to send it. He wanted everything timed just right, so the various pieces of the so-called jigsaw puzzle would arrive in good order. The Verona transcripts took three weeks to process, as did the scores from College Board. While he had no control over when his teachers sent their recommendations, he did try to impress on them that the situation was urgent. He didn't want the application itself to arrive too early or too late; nor did he want it to arrive in the midst of a torrent of other applications. He wasn't sure if it was good or bad that when he went to the post office to mail it on the date he arrived at as optimal based on a complicated formula that even he had to confess made as much sense as sticking pins in a voodoo doll, he ran into Justin Smelling, who was also clutching a 9 by 12 clasp envelope with the same preprinted mailing label addressed to Byerly Hall.

In the end all Harry could really do was hope the various narrative threads of his academic life converged at the right place at the right time. He had heard some disturbing stories, like the one about a friend of a friend of Justin's who overheard someone in line at an airport say that her

first choice school had screwed up her application. A couple of weeks after the January deadline, she reportedly called to check on the status of
her paperwork and was told that her transcript was missing. She supposedly spoke to her high school guidance counselor and was assured that
everything had been sent. Weekly and then daily phone calls to the college turned up no sign of her transcript. Finally, with the admissions office on one phone line and her high school guidance office secretary on
another, she coordinated the faxing of the transcript and received verbal
confirmation that it had arrived. But when April rolled around, she got a
postcard saying that her application could not be considered because her
file was incomplete. Harry never heard the final outcome and didn't
know whether she was allowed to appeal her case, or whether the story
was even true, and if so, whether she had had any prayer of getting into
this school in the first place.

Harry wasn't about to let some technical snafu get between him and a
Harvard acceptance. Although he understood that certain things in the
world were simply out of his control, this only made him fiercely determined to micromanage the parts he could. He had double-checked that
his references had been sent, including the one from the congressman
he had worked for last summer, plus those from four teachers including
the now far-flung Mr. Joyce, and the reference from his pediatrician, who
didn't seem to understand at first that Harry was asking for something
other than a copy of his most recent physical. Harry had heard the adage
"The thicker the file, the thicker the applicant," but as with the wisdom
about not taking the SAT too many times, he found it impossible to believe that he might really be punished for caring too much.

He had also ignored all of the well-meaning if misguided suggestions
about the subject of his essay. Mr. Leon advised him to scrap his missive
on the cruel fate of his SAT scores and to go with something more "hu-
manizing." His mother had agreed when he reluctantly showed her his
essay. He appreciated their advice, but really, what did either one of
them know about getting into Harvard? His father liked the essay, and he
seemed to be the only one who truly appreciated the importance of an
Ivy League education.

His topic had been inspired in part by the book of successful Harvard essays he had purchased that stormy day at Cambridge: it was the same essay that had caught his eye as he waited for the aborted information session to begin, about two friends and their academic jousting. When the author of the essay lost the contest to see who could get the higher SAT score, he decided to try his hand at the ACT and landed a perfect 36. This was evidently such a rare occurrence in his town that he became a local celebrity and was even invited to appear on *Good Day Alabama*. Harry assumed the point of the essay had to do with the trite observation that friendship is more important than test scores, but what he took away from it was that he had been tragically misguided; no one ever told him it was possible to get a perfect 36 on the ACT when his SAT scores were subpar! He considered scrambling to take the ACT in the fall, but the test was only offered on a weekend when he had already promised his mother he would attend his cousin's wedding somewhere outside Toledo. The look on Grace's face when he proposed missing the wedding, and then, when he devised a complicated plan that had him driving an hour from the hotel to take the test at a school in Ohio, was enough to get him to scrap the idea. He wrote an essay describing all of this, hoping that the "meta" effect of his Harvard essay being inspired by a book of Harvard essays might earn him a bonus point or two. Then he wrote two more essays, and sent them as well. The Harvard application supplement seemed to acknowledge the fact that there were some kids, such as Harry, who had so much to say about themselves and their accomplishments that they needed extra room.

HARRY CHANGED into a fresh shirt and just-ironed khakis and fretted about his choice of tie. He was meeting Mr. Kevorkian in the lobby of the Verona Country Club at 5:00 p.m. and had arranged for his mother to leave him the car. He patted his pockets to make sure he had the keys. Locking himself out of the car and the house, and then missing the interview, was just the sort of thing he could imagine doing, given the way things were going on the Harvard front so far.

In any event it was Mr. Kervorkian who was late—or so it seemed. Harry had been sitting in the country club lobby for over twenty minutes now, which was, by his own definition, five minutes past casually tardy.

He worried that perhaps he had gotten the time wrong, or even the place. He had given Mr. Kevorkian his cell phone number, and he checked to see whether he had missed any calls. He had not. He went back to pretending to read the newspaper while he glanced around, wondering if any of these people might be Mr. Kevorkian.

The nicely groomed families loitering in the lobby gave him a moment of pause. Were a couple of kids, a pretty wife, and admittance to a prestigious country club such as this one the grand prize for years and years of hard work? The carrot at the end of the master of the universe stick? While he had known in his gut since that first day in nursery school that he wanted to go to Harvard, there were moments, such as this one, when he realized that he couldn't say *why*.

He wanted—no, *needed*—to rise to the top of the heap for reasons that he couldn't quite articulate. Harry knew that his mother blamed his father for applying undue pressure, and he suspected that she blamed herself for not doing more to intervene. In his limited, seventeen-year-old way, he understood that he was probably being driven by certain demons, propelled by forces he did not entirely understand, but on another level he felt that all these stabs at analysis really missed the point. His need to succeed was pure. What made a painter paint, or a writer write? Why were *those* compulsions never questioned? He was an achiever, and he simply had to achieve—this was the end in itself. It wasn't really about money, although he understood that having money was certainly preferable to the alternative.

Still, sitting in the lobby of this club, he couldn't help but wonder about the wealth that surrounded him. There was nothing garish here, no ladies dripping with jewels and furs, and in fact a quick survey of the parking lot suggested the rich members favored earthy vehicles like a Subaru Outback or an ancient Volvo to a Mercedes or BMW at a ratio of roughly two to one. Yet there was still something in the air suggestive of the fact that these people could spare $65,000 for the club's initiation fee, plus who knew how much in additional monthly dues. Maybe Harry was just projecting, or maybe it was the gleam in the eyes of the kids who trolled the lobby, one of whom had just tipped over a ficus tree as he chased his brother and threw him to the ground. The boy didn't seem concerned about the dirt that spilled on the antique carpets, or his brother's bleeding head; even at age six he seemed to know that someone would come around to clean things up.

Harry wondered if he would even want to join a country club one day. One thing he vowed was to never be flashy. He would never build a house like the Kaluantharanas', for example, although he did wonder if perhaps a big house was a requirement if a person wanted to be a member of the ruling class. Perhaps a country club membership was necessary, too, so that a person could properly fete his fellow politicians or partners or CEOs with highballs and cigars and rounds of golf, which he made a mental note to learn to play. He imagined himself throwing salon-style dinner parties, where his brilliant, successful guests would sit around the table and discuss politics as if they were at a Brookings Institution seminar being televised on C-SPAN.

He looked around again for his interviewer and saw a large party of retired people headed toward the dining room. A few young families with toddlers were stationed in front of a huge illuminated aquarium, gawking at some brightly colored fish. The boy who had just knocked over the ficus tree tried to stick his hand inside the tank but couldn't quite reach the hatch. Harry saw some fit-looking women dashing through the lobby holding yoga mats. Still, he saw no one who looked like a Harvard alumni interviewer.

He returned his distracted focus to the newspaper, flipping to the sports section, where he noticed a profile about Verona's quarterback, who was being recruited by several Division I football powerhouses. This was remarkable because Verona, a school widely mocked for its lame athletics, began the season with a ten-year losing streak. Leonard Johnson seemed to be turning things around; Verona had managed a winning season so far and had just beat county champion Athens for the first time in history.

He heard someone call his name. He looked up and saw an extremely tall, thin (*lanky, gangly, awkward*) man with a shock of white hair leaning against the door of what appeared to be the bar.

"Are you Harry?" he asked.

"I am," Harry replied, disconcerted. Was this Mr. Kevorkian, and if so, had he been here this entire time? Had he already blown it? It had never even remotely occurred to Harry to check inside the bar.

"*AP* Harry?" the man asked, smiling. He approached with his hand outstretched.

Harry nodded wearily. How did the man know his nickname? This was definitely not auspicious. He walked over and shook his hand, which was as long and bony as the rest of him.

"I've heard about you," the man said cheerfully, patting him on the back. "A couple of your classmates mentioned you."

"Oh?" Harry asked hesitantly. Why were his classmates talking about him? Surely this constituted some sort of violation of privacy. But then, on the upside, his interview hadn't even begun and already he had made some sort of impression.

"Well, don't just stand there, my friend. Come on in and have a drink!"

Harry followed the man into the dimly lit bar and settled into a cavernous leather chair. A flat-screen TV was broadcasting the evening news, and he saw images of an explosion in Iraq, followed by what appeared to be a number of severely injured American troops being loaded onto stretchers. One of the soldiers grimaced in pain. He looked surprisingly young and strangely familiar, even though Harry almost certainly didn't know him. He didn't know anyone in Iraq, although a couple of his classmates said they were planning to enlist, either out of a sense of duty or as a way to help finance college. In the back of Harry's mind was the thought that if he didn't get into Harvard, maybe he ought to enlist, and then try his chances again in a few years. Surely a tour of duty would look good on his résumé. This idea had first occurred to him during a chat with the Marine recruiters who had been stationed in the school cafeteria just that week. Evidently, they were forced to relocate to the career center after a group of outraged parents insisted the Marines leave school grounds, fearful they were going to unduly influence impressionable minds, as if they were peddling Scientology or dealing crack. As it happened, there was a federal law that granted military recruiters access to public school grounds, so the best the parents could do in the end was tuck them away in a remote corridor where they'd have less opportunity to corrupt Verona youth. Harry had trouble grasping the crux of the argument: If these parents were opposed to reinstating the draft, didn't it behoove them to let kids join the military of their own volition? Or was it simply that these parents wanted a volunteer army composed of kids from a different zip code? He'd posed this question to Justin, but his friend just shrugged and said that Harry only saw it that way because he was a Republican.

Another glimpse of the television screen showed one of the soldier's arms had been nearly severed at the shoulder. Harry felt slightly ashamed of himself, being so focused on the brass ring when his peers were fighting and dying in Iraq. But Mr. Kevorkian's query cut short his moment of camaraderie.

"Gin and tonic, Harry?" the gaunt man asked, leaning back in the massive leather chair. His long fingers extracted a single peanut from the bowl in the center of the small table and deposited it in his mouth with a mechanical precision that made Harry shudder.

Was he really being offered a gin and tonic? Was this a trick question? Harry wondered. Perhaps some subtle test of his moral fiber? "Thanks, sir. I think I'll just have a Coke."

"Ha! I've never met a kid who said no to a drink. Roger!" he said, flagging the bartender, with whom he seemed possibly a bit too familiar. "Bring us a couple of G and Ts." *Gifted and talented*, Harry thought. Maybe this was a sign. A sign that he was getting a little soft in the head, thinking about things like signs.

"I'll have a Coke," Harry repeated, unsure if Roger heard him.

"So what shall we talk about first?" Mr. Kevorkian asked. He didn't seem to be actually looking at Harry, but was staring at a couple of striking middle-aged women waiting to be seated in the restaurant.

Harry shrugged. This was all rather confusing, and not at all what he had imagined. "When did you graduate from Harvard?" Harry asked, hoping this was an innocuous enough icebreaker. The books said to ask a lot of questions during your interview, and Mr. Kevorkian seemed to be suggesting Harry lead the way.

"Let's see . . . I married the year after I graduated, and I got divorced exactly one year ago, the day after our thirtieth anniversary. So you do the math if you think you are smart enough to go to Harvard!"

The bartender arrived with a fresh bowl of nuts and two gifted and talenteds. Harry reiterated his preference for a Coke.

"So you graduated in 1974," Harry said.

"Bingo. You *are* a bright boy. But being bright isn't everything. Do you know who my roommate was freshman year?"

"No, sir," Harry replied as he watched Mr. Kevorkian take a gulp of his drink. Harry stared at his own gin and tonic and decided that this *had* to be a test, but even so, he had no idea what the correct move was. He could just see the notation on his Harvard alumni interview notes: "Lacks spine." Alternatively, he could imagine this Dickensian Mr. Kevorkian character might scrawl an equally damaging "uptight" on his report. It was hard to imagine it mattered either way—from all that he had heard, alumni interviews didn't carry a lot of weight unless they were extraordinarily negative. Anyway, it wasn't as though drinking was not a completely acceptable aspect of coed life, even at a school like Harvard. He knew this because after he sent friend requests to a couple of former Verona students who had matriculated at Harvard, he was able to monitor their Facebook pages and keep cybertabs on their social lives. Alcohol figured prominently in almost every photograph, although he supposed it was possible this was not a very scientific form of analysis. People were more likely to break out the digital cameras when they were partying, as opposed to when they were studying alone in the library.

"Have you ever heard of Gordon Leka?" he asked.

Harry thought the name sounded familiar, but he wasn't sure why. He shook his head.

"Convicted in 1981 of illegal insider trading? Served ten years in federal prison and then wrote a memoir, *Ivy on the Inside*. Maybe you read it? Was on the bestseller list for months. Now that's one thing you can do with your Harvard diploma."

"Write a book?"

"No. Go to prison."

Harry wasn't sure how to respond to this. Mr. Kevorkian picked up his glass again and drained it in one long sip. Harry waited for him to turn this anecdote into some sort of question, or at least some pithy morality tale, but he only chewed noisily on an ice cube. Harry finally decided it was better to break the silence than to await the next prompt.

"Surely your diploma landed you in a better place, Mr. Kevorkian?" he asked hopefully.

The bartender returned with Harry's Coke and removed Mr. Kevorkian's empty glass. Harry pushed his untouched gin and tonic toward his inquisitor, hoping he wouldn't notice. This seemed to work; Mr. Kevorkian picked up the replacement drink and took a swig. "Do you mean literally or figuratively?" he asked.

Again Harry hesitated. In all of his boning up on interview techniques, all the time spent in front of the mirror fine-tuning facial expressions, he hadn't ever considered what to do if your interviewer is off-topic and a little bit sloshed.

"I guess either-or?" Harry replied wearily.

"Well, I'm fifty-three years old, divorced, my kids hate me, and I live alone in a one-bedroom condo in downtown Verona. On the upside, I run my own software business and I'm my own boss, so I can set aside time to do whatever I want. I'm one of Harvard's most active alumni interviewers because my schedule is unencumbered. And I can play as much golf as I want, so I tend to spend a lot of time here. That's the ticket, Justin! Be your own boss. And that's one thing a Harvard degree can do for you. Open doors. So you can be your own boss."

"I'm Harry," Harry said, although he wondered if he should really bother pointing this out, given that the interview did not seem to be going all that well. The serial position effect was not liable to do him any good if Mr. Kevorkian had seen so many kids that he couldn't tell them apart. It was only just occurring to Harry that there might be some other study, one that concluded there was an advantage to going *first* in any sort of contest, meeting the judge when he still had an open mind, a clean slate upon which it was possible to make an impression. Or in this case, even just a sober slate.

Mr. Kevorkian leaned back in his chair and yawned. Harry wasn't sure if he should keep asking questions, or just wait for Mr. Kevorkian to remember what they were doing here. He noticed for the first time that a manila folder lay on the chair between them and speculated that it might contain an evaluation form. Harry worried that at the rate they were going, Mr. Kevorkian was not going to be lucid enough to record his impressions of their meeting.

"Is that your folder?" he asked boldly.

Mr. Kevorkian looked at the chair. "It is," he rallied. "Thank you for reminding me. There are a few questions I just need to ask you. I hope you don't mind . . ."

Harry felt a rush of relief. Things were back on track. Now he could relate his well-rehearsed speech about his lifelong dream to go to Harvard and describe his summer internship working on legislation to remove environmental obstacles to offshore drilling. He could find a way to weave in a mention of his plans to one day run for office.

"I try to vary my questions, Harold," he said. "Some interviewers recycle their questions, but I like to be creative, to keep everyone on their toes."

"That's great," Harry said, unsteadily.

Mr. Kevorkian shuffled through his papers for a few minutes before finding what he was looking for. "Diversity, Harold." He paused to clear his throat. "Is diversity important to you?"

"Absolutely!" Harry said. "In fact one reason why I look forward to college is . . ."

"Whoops, sorry! That wasn't the question I meant to ask. I have a new one. I just thought of it today." Mr. Kevorkian paused and cleared his throat for what seemed like dramatic effect: "If you were a shoe, Harold, what kind of shoe would you be?"

"A *shoe*?" Harry asked. "Do you mean a type of shoe, like a sneaker or a boot, or do you mean a name brand, like Adidas or Reebok?"

"Whatever you prefer."

Harry was completely stymied. "A *shoe*?" he repeated, hoping some clever answer would come to him if he just kept stalling. He wasn't really a shoe person—he owned sneakers and dress shoes, and that was about it. He had outgrown his snow boots and thought he should probably get a new pair, especially if he was going to college in Boston. He had some dim memory of having bought a pair of flip-flops last summer, but he didn't know where they were. Perhaps he had left them at his father's apartment. He thought about girls' shoes—there was much more variety involved, what with their high heels, pumps, boots, Mary Janes, sandals . . . he didn't even know what half of the varieties of shoes he saw at school were called. Last year most of the girls wore cowboy boots; the year before, they all had fuzzy boots that looked like giant slippers. If he were a girl, he'd say he'd be a stiletto, if only because then he could say something about being sharp, but he didn't want Mr. Kevorkian to get the idea that he was somehow partial to girls' shoes. Mostly he felt like putting his head on the table and weeping.

A commercial flashed across the gigantic television screen: a bunch of wild and crazy coeds surfed on plastic discs through a flooded dormitory hallway, the point of which evidently was that Dell computers could withstand the rigors of college life. Harry could cope with just about any amount of work, but never with that level of immaturity. He stared at the feet of the kids on the commercial, but didn't notice any shoes.

"I suppose I'd be . . . um . . . a comfortable shoe," Harry answered at last, painfully aware that this was a completely lame answer. "As a future politician, I plan to spend a lot of time on my feet . . . Actually I already do, as I'm the Verona student body president," Harry offered, hoping he had at least strategically steered the conversation in a different direction.

"My kids would have gone to Verona," Mr. Kevorkian said sadly. "But they've moved to New Jersey with their mother."

"I'm sure they have good schools in New Jersey," Harry offered, glad to be back to the subject of Mr. Kevorkian's personal life. He couldn't believe how badly he had just botched the shoe question. Maybe he should have said a Birkenstock, but what did that imply—that he was earthy and practical? That wasn't really him. He could have said a Nike, because he liked the slogan, "Just Do It!" That at least showed a little gumption on his part, but that didn't seem quite like the right answer, either.

"Not as good as Verona."

"That's probably just as well. They'll have a better chance of getting into Harvard," Harry said. Then, realizing the irony of what he'd just said, Harry began to laugh.

Mr. Kevorkian stared at him strangely, and suddenly the hilarity of the entire situation hit Harry like a strong G&T, and his laughter grew louder, attracting the attention of the people at the next table, who turned and stared.

Roger the bartender appeared and looked at Harry worriedly before whispering something in Mr. Kevorkian's ear. Mr. Kevorkian then glanced at his watch and stood up.

"Time to wrap this up, Harold, my friend . . . Are you okay?"

Harry wiped a tear from his eye and tried to pull himself together. "Absolutely, sir. Thank you for your time."

"No, thank you, Harold. I'm glad we've had such an excellent exchange here. I wish you all the luck in the world at Harvard!"

Harry had no idea what to make of this last comment, but he was distracted by a more urgent thought as they finished shaking hands.

"A wingtip!" he said. "I'd be a wingtip. Elegant yet all-business . . . dark brown, or maybe black, well buffed . . ."

But Mr. Kevorkian was already stumbling toward the lobby, looking for the next victim, or perhaps just a bathroom.

○ ○ ○

MAYA HAD HEARD rumors that there were people living in other parts of the country, and even other parts of the state, who thought there were more important things in life than where you went to college. She assumed these were tall tales, as believable as the spontaneous eruption of crop circles in the Midwest, or the existence of UFOs. But Pam insisted it was true: she had spent the month of August on her cousin's farm in Wisconsin and reported back that people there rarely raised the subject of college, and when they did, it was typically in reference to sports. When Pam mentioned that she dreamed of going to Georgetown, for example, her cousin's face lit up excitedly: "Hey, isn't that the basketball school?" he asked. And when she mentioned a few small liberal arts schools she was also thinking about applying to, she was met with looks of pity. One of her younger cousins later explained that he thought a person only went to a private college if his grades weren't good enough to get into state. They evidently couldn't imagine a scenario in which a person would scramble together $40,000 a year to get a diploma unless they had no other choice.

Maya wished she could pack her own family off to a farm in Wisconsin for a summer of deprogramming. But to have any impact, the retreat would have to include *all* of her relatives, particularly the ones back in India. Her eighty-year-old grandmother was among the worst offenders. She had called Maya just that morning, and her very first question was about where she was planning to apply to college.

"What about Stanford?" she asked. "I know you keep saying your scores on these silly tests are not very good, but my neighbor's grandson goes there, and she says he got in because he was so charming at the interview. You are very charming, Maya. Just tell them about the time you won the spelling bee in sixth grade!"

Maya had not actually won the spelling bee in sixth grade—that had been her sister Neela. She had never won a spelling bee, or any sort of contest, unless you counted honorable mention in the beanbag race during school Athletic Day in second grade. Even if there was some correlation between spelling well and being a charming person, she suspected that no amount of charm could neutralize low SAT scores. In fact, the only instances she had heard of a kid being admitted on the basis of charm, alone, were when the kid's grandmother back in South Asia—or maybe also in South Florida—was telling the story.

Maya braced herself for her grandmother's next question, which she guessed correctly would have to do with swimming. "Anyway, your scores don't matter, Maya, because you are not only a terrific speller, but a swimmer!" In her darker moments, Maya imagined that the only thing she had ever done well was swim, and now she really wondered if she had ruined her life by sitting out the season. Certainly, she didn't miss the early mornings, nor did she miss the look of disappointment on the coach's face when she came in second place, or what she imagined were gentle but scalding scolds of her father in the stands. But she did miss the physicality of the water, the adrenaline rush in the seconds before the whistle blew as she stood in position, bent at the waist. She missed the smell of chlorine, and the camaraderie of girls in the locker room. It was true that her father had pushed her into the sport and that she found the workouts grueling, but the fact was she was a stellar athlete. She wondered if she would harbor the same vague resentment if, when she was a child, he had pushed her to play piano forty hours a week instead of swim. Would that have struck her as more acceptable simply because piano seemed a more worthy discipline? This wasn't exactly a hypothetical scenario, she had to confess, because in fact she had been provided with years of piano lessons and she proved practically tone-deaf, whereas the first time she hit the water she swam like a hopped-up fish.

The more time that passed since Mr. Joyce had left, the more she feared she had quit just to please him: he was always going on about his contempt for organized sports, which in truth began to seem less evil an institution with every e-mail that went unanswered. Had she misread him entirely? She had not been so delusional as to suppose there was ever the possibility of a relationship with Mr. Joyce, and yet his interest had seemed so genuine at the time. He asked her to come in after school on an average of once a week, and then he'd close the door to his classroom and read poetry to her in a seductive, gravelly tenor that reminded her of one of those NPR reporters her parents were always listening to in the car, delivering dispatches from faraway locales, cities with names as romantic as the disembodied voices. Once, he'd looked up from his volume of Keats and told her that she was special, that she was different from the other girls. No one had ever said such a thing to her before. And he agreed to write her a college recommendation even though she had not been among the first twenty in line, as long as she agreed not to tell anyone. When he told her this good news, he'd looked at her meaningfully, and he'd even touched her hair, or so she'd imagined. She could never decide on the many occasions that she relived this moment whether they had been on the verge of a kiss when Mike Lee entered the room, oblivious to the dim light and the suggestive positioning of the two bodies in the room. Mike begged Mr. Joyce to squeeze him in and write one more recommendation. His parents were going to punish him if he didn't get into Harvard, he pleaded, as Maya took a few steps back. Lately Maya wondered whether she had misinterpreted Mr. Joyce's affections, but most of the rest of the time she figured there was probably just no Internet access in Laos, and that he'd write to her if he was able. Another possibility was that he had been captured by guerrilla forces and was being held hostage, although that would presume there was civil unrest in Laos, something about which she was embarrassingly ignorant.

After the fight with her parents that morning about her decision to apply early to Yates, she instinctively headed to the pool. There was a big meet that day, and even though she was no longer on the team, she figured she'd cheer Pam on from the sidelines. She grabbed her car keys and headed out the door, so upset that she forgot to grab a coat.

As she drove the long stretch of Verona Boulevard, clogged with traffic even on a Saturday, she tried to deconstruct what had just happened at home. Until this morning, she thought she'd made progress in wearing down her parents' elitist attitudes. Her father had seemed to genuinely embrace some of the schools on her list, even if he was partial to larger institutions with Division I sports teams.

She had organized a recent trip entirely on her own, hoping that if her parents could just see a few of these schools they would understand they were legitimate institutions of higher learning. She wanted to take a second look at Yates, and as soon as they arrived at the admissions office parking lot, her mother let slip that she thought the campus looked more like a two-star ski resort than a top-50 college. She'd also commented unfavorably about the girl who greeted them in the admissions office sporting spiked green hair, with a tattoo of a dolphin on her neck, even though Maya insisted she was not really representative of kids at Yates, from what she'd observed.

Maya had set up her own appointments and interviews and even booked hotel rooms using her mother's credit card. She bought a road atlas of the Northeast, got directions from MapQuest, and took her mother's car in for an oil change in preparation for the trip. She had no idea how complicated it was to make the timing of tours and information sessions mesh with geographic realities, and had a new appreciation for her parents' logistical skills. She had to reschedule her tour of Bard three times, for example, so that she could figure out a way to see Union and Skidmore on the same day, and still have time to squeeze in second looks at Yates and Hamilton. She managed to work all of this in around a long weekend so that she only missed three days of school. When Maya first presented her parents with the itinerary, they resisted.

Her father grumbled about how they had already seen enough schools and, anyway, now that Maya had essentially ruined her chances of admission to a good university by quitting the swim team, she ought to just apply early to Chicago, where she at least had a double legacy, and be done with it. He also had another backup plan which he seemed almost deviously proud of: he thought Maya should apply early action to Tulane, on the grounds that since the hurricane had devastated New Orleans, it would be easy to get into. Maya was pretty sure that was not the case, but rather than argue she focused her energy on getting him to agree to the trip, pushing and pleading and pulling every guilt string in her arsenal. This worked, and once they hit the road, they had such a nice time together that Maya felt like she was in some sort of Disney movie and they should break into song.

Her father claimed to love some of the small schools they stopped at in southern Pennsylvania, such as Gettysburg, rich with Civil War history. And her mother—not someone who was easily amused—thought it hilarious that Dickinson had a mermaid for a mascot, evidently because the sculptor commissioned to create a trident for the bell tower had made a mistake.

They got a little bit lost en route to one school in the middle of nowhere in upstate New York and wound up in a town called Verona. They all had a good laugh about this, although Maya wasn't sure what was so funny. Even if the New York version of Verona seemed lacking in the spanking new amenities of its Maryland cousin, she suspected she might have felt smarter in a small town like this and could have lived happily without a dozen Thai restaurants and blocks of boutiques with price tags that even the Kaluantharana family thought absurd.

Maya liked Skidmore, notwithstanding the fact that her mother felt compelled to tell another mother in the admissions lobby that two of her other children had gone to Harvard, and one to MIT, but that Maya's scores weren't very good. Even though Maya was a very good writer, she explained, she had only scored a 3 on the AP English Language exam, but of course there had been extenuating circumstances as their tests had been lost. Maya cringed, but the other mother, who was knitting a poncho while her son was being interviewed, just nodded her head politely, as if this were acceptable information to share with a stranger.

Only in retrospect could Maya see that the seemingly happy road trip had been a complete sham, the last meal before the execution, to use the sort of overwrought metaphor that had probably earned her low marks on the stupid AP test, as well as on her English Literature SAT subject test. Her parents had plans for her education, and these did not necessarily involve consideration of Maya's wants or needs.

"I don't know what I did wrong," she heard her mother cry, a comment that had been the precursor to Maya's fleeing the house. "I didn't do anything differently than with her siblings. The pregnancy was very healthy, the delivery was problem-free . . ."

And then her father's reply, which she had hoped would be wise, along the lines of there being different ways to measure intelligence and about different human qualities being just as important as standardized tests: "Perhaps you did not spend as much time drilling her with the flash cards, Rita," he said. "Maybe since she was the last child, you were a bit worn out." At which point her mother ran upstairs and slammed the door.

An hour later, Maya could still hear her mother's choking sobs. She wanted to go inside and comfort her, but then she remembered that she was the source of the problem and went looking for her car keys instead. She was in the kitchen, rooting around the counters, when she realized the intercom was on and heard her father's voice piped into the room: "Look, Rita, it will all be fine. I didn't mean to upset you like this. Just be grateful that I upped our alumni giving last year to $1,000, so she will at least be able to rely on that. This is why I don't want to see her apply early decision to that awful Yates place. She will be cutting off her options if she gets in, and I'm certain she can do better even with her low, low numbers." Maya was at least grateful that they had fixed the bug in the intercom system that had their family conversations spilling out into the street for a few weeks when they'd first moved in, before AP Harry's mother had knocked on the door and mercifully informed them of the problem.

Maya didn't understand how her otherwise brilliant father could be so completely daft when it came to her college prospects. She was a world away from being able to get into Chicago, regardless of her parents' legacy or their recent donation, which while generous was probably tens of thousands of dollars short of flinging open any doors. Numbers-wise, she wasn't even a shoo-in at Yates, which was part of why she wanted to give herself a possible small advantage by applying early.

The application was ready to go. All she needed was the $75 application fee, the request for which had sparked the fight. For the second time in her life, not only did she question her father, but was considering an act of defiance. She could use her mother's credit card and simply not tell her what she was doing. She was ashamed of herself for thinking like this—she had never done anything even vaguely illegal in her life—and worried that she was already sliding down the proverbial slippery slope. One thing would lead to another, just like they told you it would in health class. If exchanging flirty text messages was the first step toward contracting a sexually transmitted disease, a bad decision about where to apply to college would probably lead to a life of future unemployment, then homelessness, and finally exclusion from family gatherings at holidays. Still, she didn't *feel* like a deviant.

MAYA PARKED her car at the far end of the lot at the aquatic center, where there were plenty of vacant spots. Although she had become somewhat more confident behind the wheel the last few months, she was still a bad judge of whether the SUV could squeeze between the painted lines and liked to leave a lot of room for error.

Her cell phone rang for the fourth time since she'd left home, and she finally fished it out of her bag and checked the caller ID. It was her mother, who had evidently left a number of urgent voice messages and had also sent a text message that read "pls pick up." Maya had to laugh— on the one hand, she was given strict instructions to never use her cell phone while driving; yet when her mother wanted to reach her, she was expected to be instantly available.

She swung her gym bag over her shoulder and headed toward the front door of the community center as she began to speed-dial her mother's cell phone. She had grabbed her swimsuit as an afterthought, figuring that after the meet ended, she would take a swim herself, just for fun. Events at home this morning had finally conspired to drive her back in the water, if only to blow off some steam.

She had just begun to climb the steps when Pam bounded through the door wearing her racing suit and flip-flops, goggles hanging from her neck. She had a towel wrapped around her waist and seemed agitated.

"Thank God you're here! I just called your house, and your mom said she didn't know where you were, but promised she'd track you down; but then she said you weren't answering your cell, and we're all kind of freaking out . . . Did you get the message? Do you have your suit? It's freezing out here!"

"Yes. And no. I mean I have my suit, but I didn't check my messages yet. What's going on?"

Pam startled her with a big hug. "I can't believe you have your suit. It's like a miracle. Vicki Thompson is sick. I mean really sick, like running a fever and throwing up. She just heaved all over the locker room."

"Yuck." Already Maya was reconsidering her swim.

"So the coach wants you to swim the 100 fly. This is huge. If we beat Naples, we go on to the state finals. Not only that, but a scout is here to see Vicki swim. I think he's from USC or someplace like that."

"Are you kidding? I can't swim! I mean, I haven't even been in the pool since spring. Literally. There's no way. You guys are better off just subbing in someone from another heat. And anyway, don't I have to be on the roster?"

"You are on the roster. Coach left you on there just in case something like this happened. You're on the reserve list."

"What? I can't believe he'd do that without even consulting me! I feel like no one listens to me sometimes, do you know what I mean? It's like I speak, and people pretend to hear what I say, but no one takes me seriously. Not even my own parents!" Tears began to stream down her face before she even realized how upset she was.

"Whoa, calm down. It's just a meet. You don't have to swim . . . But let's go inside and tell the coach. It's freezing out here."

AS SHE stood at the foot of the pool talking to the coach, Maya wondered if she should take some sort of assertiveness-training class. Pam once told her she was too nice—even when she said something mean, it came out sounding sweet—so she was trying to think of some way to get the coach to really listen to her when she said that she didn't want to swim. She had always been completely terrified of him, which was another reason she had quit the team. Her father could be frightening, too, but at least she knew that underneath his anger was unconditional love, and she could almost always wear him down, as she had with the recent college trip.

"Lane 5 at 2:10" was what the coach said when Maya approached him, and she knew that was probably the last word on the subject. "Let's see your best time, Maya. I know you'll be great."

The next thing she knew she was in the locker room, trying not to gag as she inhaled the trace odors of Vicki Thompson's vomit mixed with orange-scented Lysol. Then she was poolside, listening to a pep talk about channeling her inner strength and keeping her eye on the prize and not letting her school down and remembering the years-long rivalry with Naples. She felt strangely light, like she was having one of those out-of-body experiences she'd read about, and she found the whole thing vaguely entertaining. It occurred to her that these few months of distance from the team had possibly served her well. No one could expect much of her given that she was completely out of shape. She could only do what she could do. She heard the coach, but for the first time, his words had no sting.

And then she was in the pool, these strange events unfolding so quickly she barely had time to think. She felt oddly euphoric as she pulled herself through the water. She thought about teaching little Manju to swim, and then about what a jerk Mr. Joyce was. She understood all at once that she had been delusional in thinking that he cared

for her romantically. Still, she supposed he would disapprove of her return to competitive sports, and oddly that made her swim a little bit
faster. She thought about the University of Chicago, and how there could
not possibly be a worse fit for her than a school full of math and science
nerds in a city with long, gray winters. She wondered if they even had a
pool. Then she stopped thinking at all. She was so busy not thinking, she
had fallen into such a blissful rhythmic state of movement, that she did a
racing turn when she hit the wall at the end of the second length and was
headed for a third when she realized that the water was unusually still
and the crowd was roaring and people were screaming her name. She
pulled her head from the water and someone shouted her time. It took
her a moment to register the significance of this number. How was it
possible that all of these thoughts could have passed through her mind in
less than a minute? She had not only swum her personal best, but she'd
just set a state record.

She emerged from the water, dazed and blinded by a barrage of
flashes as photographers descended on her like paparazzi. The coach
slapped her painfully on the back a few times and told her she had always
been a star. She had no memory of what she said to the reporter from the
school paper, or the county paper, or from the sports section of *The
Washington Post*. She had no memory of what she said to the assistant
coach from USC, either, although she remembered what he said to her.
"Come on out and see us," he urged, pressing a business card into her
wet hand. "All expenses paid."

December

GRACE STUCK ANOTHER BATCH of cookies in the oven and turned her attention to the small television she kept on the kitchen counter. This was the good life, she thought, wondering what aspect of baking and daytime television watching stay-at-home mothers sometimes grumbled about. She recalled an occasional sense of boredom from her own few years not working, but in contrast to her current harried life, shuffling around the kitchen in an apron and slippers seemed like bliss. As it was, she had to call in sick to enjoy this one day of domestic solitude. She felt bad about the lie, but she'd used up all of her vacation days taking Harry to visit schools and was so desperate to putter around the house and get ready for Christmas that in a way, her need did constitute a minor ailment.

She set the timer for the cookies and then, noting it was almost the top of the hour, flipped the channel to CNN to make sure no disasters had occurred since she'd checked the morning headlines. She wasn't sure why she felt the compulsive need to stay abreast of the news—it wasn't like space shuttle disasters or missing young women in cities she had never heard of or even bloody insurgencies in distant lands had any immediate effect on her own life—but this was her version of religion, a penance to remind herself on a daily, and sometimes hourly, basis that she was lucky to be living the good life, even with its petty aggravations, here in bucolic Verona.

She tuned in just in time to catch the tail end of an interview with a group of kids who appeared to be about Harry's age. By the time she realized what this was, and what they were talking about, the psychic damage had been done. It was a rebroadcast of a news segment about the winners of some prestigious high school science award, and Grace had tuned in, as if by warped radar, at the precise moment the interviewer asked where each kid hoped to go to college. Was it too much to ask for some fluffy Christmas features, stories of heartwarming acts of philanthropy by the obscenely rich, or footage of politicians feeding hungry children? Truly, weren't there better things to talk about than college? She wanted to flip the channel, or turn off the television and put on Christmas carols, but some masochistic impulse caused her instead to turn up the volume. She privately bet at last three of them would say "Harvard," but their answers proved surprisingly egalitarian. Two of the boys said they hoped to go to Louisiana State University, one to University of Texas, one to University of Louisville, and the only girl said she had applied to the University of Alabama and really hoped she'd get in. Something told her they'd all be getting in. Not for the first time, she wished she'd had the sense to leave this town when she divorced, before both Lou and Verona had hijacked Harry's brain.

The dog began to bark, and Grace heard the familiar clanking of metal outside her door, heralding the arrival of the mail. She wiped her hands on the apron and headed to the front porch. She realized she had come to regard the mail as some quaint, archaic feature of life that while sometimes distracting with its alluring catalogues, and sometimes distressing with its overdue bills, was, regardless of its disposition, at least consistently unreliable. She had complained to the post office several times about the erratic service, to no avail. Days passed without delivery, and then she'd arrive home to a knee-high pile of post wrapped in twine, discreetly deposited in a corner of the front porch. Seemingly random pieces had been sliced open, then resealed with tape. When she finally went during her lunch hour to make a personal appeal at the main Verona depot, the postal supervisor promised that she'd look into it, but that Grace should understand that her regular mail carrier was experiencing emotional and family problems and that they were all trying to give him a little room.

Didn't they have any substitute postal carriers? Grace wondered as she drove home. Wasn't at least one Pottery Barn catalogue per week an inalienable right of life in the Verona zip code? In some weird way, she had begun to miss the junk. And she had been slapped with late fees three months in a row from various utilities. Eventually, she gave in to the new conditions and moved all of her banking online, which turned out to be much easier all the way around, and pretty much eliminated the need for her postal carrier at all. Not that she would add to his emotional problems by telling him.

She was sometimes nostalgic for the days when she had been on a first-name basis with her old mailman, the overweight, wheezy, and profusely sweaty Herb. When Harry was younger, Grace would sometimes send him to meet Herb with a glass of lemonade, and he would pause in the shade on their front porch for a few minutes and try to catch his breath. She had fantasized about a long relationship with Herb as though her life was a sitcom and he was part of the family, bringing envelopes containing plot twists each episode while a looping laugh track played in her mind. One day he would deliver something important, like Harry's acceptance letter to college, and they would all rejoice in Technicolor hugs. Instead, somewhat predictably, Herb had collapsed about five years earlier on his route in 100-degree heat; he was found stretched along the curb in front of the Rockefellers' house, with half the contents of his pouch spilled down the gutter. It was easy to find a metaphor for her suburban experience everywhere Grace looked, so the challenge was to not read meaning into every little thing.

After Herb, came a series of short-lived, mostly scowling replacements, none of them lasting much more than a year. Grace seemed to dimly recall that the last carrier was a friendly, slight man who she guessed was from the Caribbean. But she hadn't seen him in a few months. At least the delivery seemed to have stabilized in time to shepherd safe passage for a letter from Harvard, which was due to arrive any day, for better or for worse.

Meanwhile, today's mail brought a deluge of Christmas cards. Five of the day's cache contained the sort of seasonal missives guaranteed to quash any holiday spirit. She checked the cookies and turned the stereo to a London Philharmonic Choir recording of the *Messiah* before sitting down to read.

The first card was from her former boss, who had recently left NIH to take a position as the head of a Virginia-based biotech firm with a salary rumored to be in the seven figures. Grace deduced from the affected family photograph that the move had evidently caused him to reinvent himself from a haggard overweight research scientist to a wannabe member of the aristocracy.

> *Dearest Friends and Family,*
>
> *We hope this Christmas season finds you well. We are ringing in the New Year in Ireland at the behest of Bree, who was so taken with her reading of* Ulysses *in her rapid learner reading class that we are taking a self-guided tour of Joyce's Dublin. I write to you from O'Connell Street, the site of Lewers, where, as you may recall, Molly bought her silkette stockings . . .*
>
> *Our little family is well. Sixth grade has proven a bit dull for Bree, which is why we supplement her education with field trips. Our holiday excursion will continue with a swing through London, where she is interested in the Victoria and Albert Museum's collection of rare manuscripts. An aspiring novelist (as you may have guessed!), she plans to spend the summer honing her writing skills at a workshop at Johns Hopkins, led by last year's Newbery Medal winner, where she hopes to put her finishing touches on the historical novel that she has been tinkering with.*
>
> *Conveniently, her little brother will also be attending Johns Hopkins this summer. Gordon has been accepted into the "HeadsUp" program for preschoolers who show an innate predisposition for design and engineering . . .*

Grace couldn't force herself to read further. She was somewhat curious to hear about his new job, particularly since she had been contem-

plating a transfer to the private sector to help finance college, but not at
the cost of absorbing any more of this irritating family news. She thought
perhaps this letter might serve as Exhibit A in the case for not mixing the
personal and professional—it was better to have remembered him as a
good boss, a dedicated scientist, rather than as the blowhard he evidently
was. Still, she wondered about his wife, Anna, whom she had always
liked. The picture that graced the front of the card answered Grace's
question in just a glance. The family of five sat in a garish living room appointed with heavy velvet drapery and crystal chandeliers. The setting
looked so faux that Grace wondered if there was some special royalty
backdrop they rolled out at the JCPenney photo studio for an extra few
bucks. They were all wearing their Sunday best, but what was weird was
the stage direction that had each family member staring off in a different
direction. Only the baby looked straight into the lens, while Anna herself
appeared vague, directionless, a look of quiet desperation on her face.

Grace opened the next envelope, which she noticed had a return address just a few houses up the street. She paused for a moment to try and
think who that might be. The picture that dropped out of the card reminded her that she had not seen most of the members of this family in
years, since they had yanked their children out of public school in protest
of the sex education program, and that was back in the pre-condom-on-
a-cucumber days, when the health curriculum was rated G. The mother
seemed to leave the house each day to go to a job; Grace spied her in the
morning sometimes, dressed like a lawyer. From what Grace could tell,
the father stayed home with the girls, barricaded behind a spiked metal
fence that had gone up sometime in the last year, when a locksmith visited the house and installed four deadbolts on the front door. Grace
sometimes laughed at the level of paranoia indicated by this degree of security; other times she worried that they knew something she did not.

Just a brief glimpse of the letter was evidence that homeschooling
your kids did not insulate you from the general Verona madness, as she
was greeted with the news that their older twin daughters had just been
accepted early to Yale, where they planned to start a new order of an
evangelical student union. How could they possibly know this already?
She turned over the envelope to check the postmark only to realize they

must have been so eager to spread the Lord's good news on the college admissions front that they had hand-delivered the card that day.

Feeling vaguely demoralized, Grace went back to the kitchen to retrieve the cookies. The sweet, doughy smell emanating from the oven was reparative, and she considered feeding the rest of the cards to the flames as an act of further yuletide therapy before deciding that was not really the seasonally appropriate thing to do. Instead, she rotated the reindeer, which had come out looking slightly mutant, with a batch of a dozen elves.

Even though it was just her and Harry at home, Grace tended to go a little overboard at Christmas. She wasn't religious, but she loved all the holiday schmaltz, like the twenty-foot inflatable Santa that she anchored to the front lawn each year. She hated to overthink this thing that gave her joy, but she knew her enthusiasm for Christmas was almost certainly a response to having grown up with a Jewish mother and an atheist father, whose leftist politics and embrace of—or fierce insistence on— secularism resulted in an enforced boycott of all holidays. Even birthdays had been subdued, as if they were harbingers of some false faith.

As she prepared to begin icing a batch of just-cooled Santas, she thought she heard a noise. Grace froze, a tube of red icing poised midair, when she glimpsed a shadow. She clenched her fist tight, as if she was going to somehow frighten off an intruder by shooting him with sugared glop. She crept to the corner of the room, where the dog lay snoring loudly, and could see from that angle that the intruder was actually Harry, home from school, midday.

"What the heck . . . ?" she asked, relaxing her grip on the icing and wiping her hands on her apron.

"Geez, Mom. Do you think this music is loud enough?" Harry went into the living room and turned the volume down. "What are you doing home? You scared me!"

"Sorry, hon. You scared me, too. What are *you* doing home? It's not like you to play hooky." She realized she didn't know this for sure, since she was rarely home during the day. Still, it seemed highly unlikely that he'd become a truant at this late stage in the game. "Are you sick?" she asked, realizing that he did look pale and seemed a little shaky. She in-

stinctively headed toward him, her palm angled to press against his forehead.

"I'm fine, Mom," he said, gently waving her hand away. "Decisions
come online at 12:00."

She stopped her advance, startled. "I'm so sorry! I didn't realize . . ."
Harry had never mentioned this. She knew he would hear via regular
mail any day now, but it hadn't occurred to her that he would find out
first online. She tried to keep up but was evidently still very much a
Luddite.

Grace figured the best thing she could do was give him some space,
to pretend this was no big deal, and anyway the timer was beeping, indicating that the elves were done. "Just give me a holler if you need anything, sweetie. Do you want me to make you some lunch? A tuna melt? I
have cheese!" she heard herself say in a ridiculous singsong.

"Thanks, but I don't really have much of an appetite," he said, forcing
a weak smile as he turned and walked upstairs.

Grace cranked the music back up to distract herself as she returned
to baking. She iced another batch and had to admit that all the cookie
shapes were slightly warped. She must have added a bit too much of
whatever ingredient caused the shapes to bleed. Butter, perhaps? She
tried to stop her hand from shaking. After all these years, this last, long,
agonizing one in particular, it was hard to imagine the entire ordeal
might now be over. After all, he *was* a good student, he *was* Harvard material, and she was probably just being overly cautious in her pessimism.

If he wasn't accepted, a new drama was about to begin. She had been
treading a fine line between wanting to be sure he was on top of the details of applying to other schools and not wanting to nag him. Most deadlines were not until January, some even later, but he had only one week
left to get things organized at Verona, where the paperwork for sending
transcripts and recommendations had to be submitted before Christmas.
There was time, but it meant shifting into crisis mode.

Just last week she'd called Harry's new counselor to see if he had any
insights as to whether Harry was being reasonable about safety schools
and was so stunned when Mr. Kushner promptly returned her call that
she had trouble remembering what she wanted to ask. He actually took

the time for pleasantries, mentioning that he really enjoyed working with Harry and that he appreciated his "passion" for school. This made Grace smile. No one had put such a positive spin on Harry's academic aspirations since sometime in elementary school, when his aggressive jockeying to become bus patrol captain ushered in a long period of ambivalent relations with both teachers and school administrators.

Mr. Kushner confirmed that all of the paperwork had been sent to Maryland in time to make Harry eligible for admission to the honors program, but he admitted that was about the only sensible thing he'd been able to persuade Harry to do. He was still planning to apply to all Ivies, even though Mr. Kushner had brought the head of guidance into their last meeting to rattle off a list of top universities that would surely admit a kid like Harry and would even be likely to offer him money. But the only interest Harry had shown in these schools was to note, correctly, their *U.S. News* rankings, Mr. Kushner said, laughing. Grace was glad someone found this amusing.

Grace thanked him profusely. She was so grateful for his concern that she didn't want to hang up the phone, but after asking Mr. Kushner how he liked Verona—he had evidently just relocated from Texas for what he said were personal reasons—she couldn't think of anything else to say. Even if he was only a soothing voice on the phone, she felt for the first time in years like she had an ally in her campaign to protect Harry from himself. She was far more worried about his morale than about where he went to college, but he was too mature and generally self-contained to warrant a controlling, meddling mother. All she could really do was stay on the right side of involved. Even making this phone call without his knowledge had felt intrusive.

HARRY HAD been upstairs an unusually long time: almost ten minutes had passed, and she was starting to feel tense. Silence was not good. But then, silence was not necessarily meaningful—it was possible that he was just having trouble getting online, as their modem seemed to lose its signal almost as regularly as the mail did not arrive.

She decided to give it five more minutes before heading upstairs, but just then Harry came down, a half smirk on his face. He stopped short of the landing and sat down on a step. The dog, forgetting her size, tried to crawl into his lap, and Harry put his arms around her, stroking her head.

"Well?" she asked hesitantly. He seemed almost giddy, which could cut either way.

He was quiet for a moment, like he was looking for the right word. "Deferred," he finally said.

"Deferred?" she echoed. She had not really focused on this outcome: *Deferred*. Really when she thought about it, this was the worst possible news. Better to be rejected flat-out. Then he could at least move on with his life.

"Deferred is good!" Harry said, but it sounded like he was possibly trying to convince himself. "This means there's still hope!"

"Yes, of course there is," Grace agreed, walking up the stairs and sitting next to him. She put an arm around him and rested her head on his shoulder. The dog wagged her tail excitedly, like they were having a little party on the stairs.

"I've heard deferred is not that meaningful at Harvard. Actually, they say explicitly on the Web site that between 80 and 200 students who were deferred early action were admitted in the spring."

"That's right. Exactly." This was the time to bolster his spirits, not shove a reality check down his throat. While these were possibly impressive numbers compared with those at other institutions, where she'd heard "deferreds" were essentially polite rejections, it was still going to be better for Harry to psychologically move forward, even if his application was still technically pending.

"Anyway, this is probably because of the damn shoes! I should have said . . . I don't know, cowboy boots, or . . . I keep wracking my brain wondering what the right answer would have been. Loafers? Keds? Slippers?"

"What are you talking about?"

"Never mind. It's not important. It could have also been because of the new guidance counselor. I mean, how could he possibly know me well enough to write a good recommendation? That was probably it."

"He seems really nice, Harry. I think he'll do the best he can for you."

She wondered what this whole shoe thing was about. Was Harry finally cracking under pressure? She also wondered whether Justin Smelling had learned his fate yet—she knew this was a crucial bit of information, as likely to affect Harry's emotional state as the deferral itself. Did it make her a bad person to privately hope Justin was deferred as well? Evidently, this was on Harry's mind, too. "I'm going back to school," he said, glancing at his watch. "I need to find Justin."

Grace nodded her head. "Do you want a ride?"

"No, but thanks, Mom. I could use some air."

"I could use some air, too . . . I could walk you partway with the dog . . . ," she began.

Harry looked at her without expression, too polite to say no.

She wanted to walk with him and was feeling suddenly protective, like some feral mother with a newborn cub, but she stopped herself. "Actually, I've got some more cookies to deal with. I guess it would be better to just keep baking."

"Save me some cookies, Mom," he said, kissing her on the cheek.

"I'll make you an extra gooey batch of stars," she replied, tacking on the ridiculously sappy addendum "Stars for my star."

Harry gave a playful "oh shucks" sort of grin, and Grace worried that probably the stars would look less like stars than roundish blobs, and she hoped that, too, was not somehow meaningful.

○ ○ ○

OLIVIA PULLED her shawl around her, tight. It was so cold inside her office that she'd cut the tips off her gloves so she could shuffle paperwork without her hands going numb, and she'd taken to walking across the lobby to refill her coffee mug every twenty minutes or so just to keep her circulation flowing. Even her toes were tingling, despite being festooned inside three-hundred-dollar boots from Italy the likes of which had graced the feet of supermodels in recent pages of fashion magazines. Word from the Maintenance Department was that the furnace was on the fritz, but she had inside information that led her to suspect the frigid state of things had more to do with money than mechanics.

She had learned a few more juicy things from Ari, gossip delivered in a state of such intimate repose that the impropriety of his disclosures paled beside the sordid circumstances in which they were delivered. She couldn't claim a precise moment when it hit her, but it had slowly dawned on her over the course of the last few weeks that this had to end. Immediately. Or at least pretty soon. She felt truly on the brink of some great moral disaster, all these years of longing giving way to abject self-loathing now that Belle, evidently touched by the attempt to unload the cow necklace, had called her three times to suggest they have lunch, something Olivia kept managing to politely postpone.

Meanwhile, Ari had begun to stop by her house almost every night. Sex was especially invigorating now that she'd decided to leave him, but their lovemaking was frequently interrupted by calls and text messages from Belle keeping him apprised of household plumbing catastrophes and missing items in the larder, as well as general complaints about her tired, pregnant state. Olivia had once found being a witness to Ari's dysfunctional marriage darkly satisfying—she empathized with Ari's need to escape his taskmaster wife for a few hours each night. But this was beginning to make her sick, like she was no longer floating in some romantic gray area but was truly, officially, a wretch. As clear as this was in her head, there was something in her heart that still let him in the door each time he knocked.

"Have you read that book *The Tipping Point*, Livvy?"

She wondered if he could read her mind, or if it was just completely obvious that she was on the verge of . . . tipping. Everyone she knew owned a copy of that book, but she'd yet to meet anyone who had actually read it.

Oddly, this very subject had come up the previous evening (albeit in a slightly different context having to with the sad state of his own book sales) when she and Fritz Heimler went to dinner. She had been browsing in the Yates bookstore, unaware that he was giving a reading, and she took a seat in the back row. He spied her from the podium, and after he'd read three poems about the Yashequana that he said he'd written in an inspired flurry just that morning after discovering his own Yashequana blood, he suggested they grab a bite to eat. She wished she could like Fritz a little bit better, that she could have brought herself to kiss him when he moved toward her, lips first, rather than bursting into a fake spasm of coughs. But she couldn't work up a physical spark, even after a few stiff drinks. She didn't actually mind that he was pompous, frequently quoting from his own poetry, or that he mentioned his dusty Pulitzer at every turn, but she couldn't get beyond the debris that stuck in his beard when he ate. Perhaps if they attempted physical contact *prior* to a meal she might be okay. But maybe she was just making up excuses. Perhaps the only thing between her and a relationship with Fritz Heimler was the fact that he was available. Just because she didn't know how to straighten out her life didn't mean she was oblivious to the fact it needed fixing.

"Livvy?" Ari asked. "Are you awake?"

"Yes, sorry. Just thinking . . . No, I haven't read it yet. Why? Have you?" She loved it when he called her Livvy, the way the words rolled off his tongue made her able to imagine they were lying on a beach that hugged the Red Sea, drinking wine and eating things drenched in olive oil, as opposed to, say, huddling together under her comforter trying to preserve body warmth while ditching calls from his wife.

"No. I haven't read it either," Ari said.

She lay with her head nestled in the crook of his arm, playing with the army medallion on his chest and wondering where this conversation was headed.

"Do you know the Yeats poem 'The Second Coming'?" he finally asked.

" 'Things fall apart, the center cannot hold . . .' Why so cryptic, Ari?" Evidently something was about to crash for him, too. Although there was always the small possibility that whatever was crashing on his end could work to her benefit. Like maybe his marriage really was about to collapse. "What's going on?" she asked hopefully.

"I don't know, Livvy. It just feels like we've reached some sort of impasse."

"I feel it, too," she said, propping herself up on an elbow.

"Do you? This all just gets worse and worse. Just when I think we've got it under control, something even more unbelievable happens."

"What do you mean?" Maybe they were not quite on the same wavelength, after all.

"This Morgan Sterner business . . . Do you know Morgan Sterner?"

"I think I met him at Basil's party in August. That old guy who's the general counsel? He looked like he was about ninety-seven years old."

"He's only eighty-four, actually. He's pretty much retired, but he still helps Yates at some discount rate, given that he's basically senile. I guess we get what we pay for. He went on a four-week cruise beginning Labor Day, gave his assistant the month off, and forgot to have someone open his mail. So evidently no one paid the premium on our litigation insurance. Have you ever heard of such a thing? Surely this is it. Some incredibly little thing with consequences of biblical proportions. The tipping point. Now it's all downhill."

"Don't be absurd, Ari. Surely you're overreacting. They can't possibly cancel insurance over a late premium."

"They already did, Olivia. Anyway, that's just a symbolic problem. We'll get new insurance eventually. We just need to placate the Yashequana in the meantime. We quite literally cannot afford to be sued. At this stage we're dipping into the principal of the endowment just to keep the lights on."

"I thought the whole point of Basil being here is that he's some genius fund-raiser!"

"Well, he is, as it turns out. He's got a few deals in the works. I think he's got some Kuwaiti investor interested in underwriting a Middle Eastern studies program with some sort of side deal that also involves paying for squash courts in the new recreation center."

"The man's a real creative genius."

"Actually, he really is. He's got a few other things lined up, too. We've been out wining and dining people for months. I can barely keep up with him. He's got a lot of pledges, big things pending, but the threat of the Yashequana suit is keeping everyone from committing."

"Yes, I know . . . Everyone is totally obsessed with this thing. Fritz couldn't stop talking about the Yashequana last night. He said he's work-ing on a new collection of Yashequana-inspired poetry and that he was talking to Joshua Bear and thinks they might be distant cousins."

"Fritz Heimler? Last night? How is that possible—I was over here last night." He sounded both genuinely confused and encouragingly dis-tressed.

"The night is long, Ari. I was with him before you came over. At least he takes me out to dinner!"

This was not entirely true; Olivia had paid for the meal. When he wasn't talking about his poetry or his prize, he was busy complaining that he was broke.

"Of all the men in Yates . . ." He didn't finish the sentence, Olivia sus-pected, because it had no logical end. There were very few eligible men in Yates, which was perhaps part of why she'd wasted so many years of her life with the particularly ineligible man who was lying in her bed.

"Jealous, Ari? That's so adorable."

His cell phone rang, conveniently.

"Hello, darling," he said. "Yes, late meeting. I'm on my way right now. Milk? Sure . . . no problem . . . yes, I know, skim as well as 2 percent, sure . . . What's that? . . . I'm not sure I know which is which. Do you mean ones with the long oval tubes, or the ones with the squiggly shapes? . . . Okay, see you soon, darling."

"Sorry, Olivia. I've got to go. But I just wanted to tell you . . ."

"Rigatoni or penne?"

"What are you talking about? Listen, what I wanted to say is that this actually affects you, a bit."

"Oh, terrific! Am I invited to dinner? Then let's go with the penne."

"No, the financial crisis," he said, ignoring her. "Not to put too fine a point on it, but you might want to be a bit more observant than usual in your . . . shall we say, noting of zip codes."

"You mean keeping an eye out for kids with rich dads?"

"I'd try to be a little more sensitive about the wording of that sen-tence, but essentially, yes."

"Also, this is even a bit more awkward, something Basil mentioned this afternoon, having to do with this insurance debacle . . . Remember how that school in Virginia was held liable when a kid committed suicide? The judge ruled that since the student had made explicit threats, the college had a responsibility to prevent his death?"

"Yes, I vaguely remember that. Why?"

"Well, Basil wanted me to pass along the thought that, as I said, we quite literally cannot afford to be sued."

"Your point?"

"My point—or really Basil's point—is to just be careful. Keep one eye on zip codes and the other one on mental health."

"That's so incredibly sensitive of you, Ari."

"Hey, I'm a pretty sensitive guy," he said, pulling on his pants.

FRIGID TEMPERATURES and icy walkways had not kept a steady stream of protestors from gathering in the admissions office lobby each day for the last two weeks, edging things even closer toward some grand unraveling. They handed out pamphlets and sometimes joined hands around the base of *Yashequana Woman*, singing songs from the 1960s that didn't quite hold up. The question of whether the Yashequana tribe had a valid claim on land that included at least a fourth of the Yates campus seemed to barely factor into the agendas of the bunch of nut jobs who Olivia kept spying outside her office. Yes, there were two actual members of the Yashequana Nation among the protesters, but they were easily outnumbered by students from about half a dozen campus organizations evidently excited about having a cause, even if it had nothing to do with their particular mandates. Members of the Anti-War Union were there, for example, arms linked with representatives from the Pro-Peace Initiative, two groups that were famously at political odds despite the common interest their names might suggest. A few students wore Native American headdress and war paint in what struck Olivia as an almost certainly offensive stab at solidarity. But then, given that there were no actual Native American students on campus, they were possibly unaware that contemporary Yashequana were part of the great American melting pot, tending more toward suits and ties, or blue jeans and leather jackets, and that they typically did not pack bows and arrows when they paid routine visits to college campuses.

Vast resources had been thrown at raising the school's profile over the last few years. Even minor and completely insignificant references to Yates, both the university and the town, were routinely highlighted and posted on the school's Web site, including items such as the one buried in the business section of *The Yates Union-Ledger*: "Detection of anthracnose leaf blight, blamed on unusually humid weather conditions, is not expected to result in significant yield loss in Yates corn production next season." So it seemed ironic that the current mandate from upstairs was to keep the school's name *out* of the news, which was of course doubly rich now that Yates was in the news almost every day. The land claim was making national headlines, particularly since it mirrored the suit Olivia had vaguely recalled, the one brought in the 1990s which caused property values to plummet and title insurance to skyrocket when then U.S. Attorney General Janet Reno joined the side of the Seneca Indians in asserting that New York had no valid claim to land it had purchased from the tribe for $1,000 in 1815 because the state had failed to win approval from the federal government as was required by a 1790 land treaty approved by George Washington. Even though Janet Reno was long gone and the Bush administration had almost instantly severed itself from the litigation, this was ample evidence that the claim had to be taken seriously, especially since Joshua Bear's suit contained the additional allegation that Jeremiah Wheeling had negotiated the sale against a backdrop of unspecified criminal intimidation. No one was eager to dredge up the past at Yates, the unspoken worry being that the real history might prove even worse than the rumors.

Anyway, the latest bit of bad news—and there seemed to be a daily dose of it—had to do with *Yashequana Woman* herself, and once again cast Jeremiah Wheeling in a bad light. The Bear family was now claiming that contrary to the happy folklore that had the statue bequeathed to Yates as a gift of friendship from a Yashequana elder, Wheeling had acquired her in yet another sketchy deal in which he sold a parcel of land to the tribe that turned out to actually belong to Canada, throwing them into an international property dispute. Bear stipulated that the endearing story that had Jeremiah IV gifting *Yashequana Woman* to his good friend

FDR was also bogus: he claimed instead that the founder's great-grandson had lost her in a gambling debt to a close friend of one of FDR's cousins, who was later found dead from a self-inflicted gunshot wound. How the statue wound up in the White House basement was really anyone's guess, but the favored version at Yates—the one the tour guides were instructed to share with their charges—involved the adorable anecdote about FDR transporting her to the nation's capital, evidently enchanted by her busty physique, and Eleanor banishing her to the cellar for the same reason.

Actually, Olivia found these allegations to be a mild relief: she had expected Bear to unearth crimes much worse than property theft, which was at least socially acceptable, and even central to the whole raffish American narrative. Certainly, it was a lot more palatable than the ritualized murder or incest-related cult activities she had sometimes imagined lay at the heart of Yates's history.

That said, Olivia had recently begun to wonder if all of these rumors about Yates's past had been concocted just to add some mystique to the place. Maybe Jeremiah Wheeling had simply been an earnest if eccentric old potterer. Maybe he'd actually had a heart attack in the field where the freshman dorm now sat, and a wild animal had mauled him while he lay there, possibly running off with his hand. Evidently, a history student had incorporated this theory into her senior thesis last year, but the paper was a poorly written mess in which she too ambitiously attempted to weave this idea into the broader theme of the Kennedy assassination and general conspiracy theories in history. The college newspaper had written an article about her findings, but no one took it too seriously.

Controversy about the statue was just one of several related matters threatening to shift Yates into critical meltdown. That morning as she dressed, Olivia saw Fritz Heimler being interviewed on YNBC by Loretta Bear. Not only did Heimler proclaim himself to be a member of the Yashequana Nation—and a relative of Loretta's, to boot—but he was now taking their side in the land dispute. His revised family tree had him descended from a Yashequana great-grandmother who had supposedly sailed to Berlin with a handsome German tourist, his great-great-grandfather, in the late 1800s. As a consequence of this new information, with some looping logic Olivia didn't completely follow, he was demanding a pay raise.

IN FINANCIAL and legal terms the school might have been going downhill, but applications were pouring in at an unprecedented rate. Either the demographic bubble was seriously about to burst, or the constant mention of Yates in the news, albeit in a negative context, had increased its popularity even beyond the year it debuted at number 50. Or maybe it was just the lingering effect of having been mentioned on that MTV show, although the featured student, Garth, had just transferred to Ithaca.

Olivia had once fantasized—to the extent that she had cared—about being in charge, lording it over her own staff, having the final say. Now that this was a reality, however, she found herself missing Ray. She wished she could talk to him, to commiserate and let him know that she had underappreciated his leadership skills, his sense of calm, his quiet confidence. She wanted to tell him that now that she was dealing with Basil directly, she was beginning to understand why he'd cracked. It was possible that this was just a passing phase—she was long overdue for a physical, and during her last visit, the doctor had said something about her being "hormonally challenged." Whatever the cause, lately she found herself bolting awake in the middle of the night, fretting about the fate of some of the rejected kids, applicants who just a few years ago would have come to Yates and done just fine, but now, in this new competitive environment, were no longer so desirable. This empathy, coupled with her burst of moral consciousness about Ari, was really screwing with her mind.

In the past, she had browsed applications to see if something caught her eye with the same sense of spirit she brought to the sale rack at Bloomingdale's. There was simply too much to choose from, yet most of what she saw was pretty much the same. Essays had become so polished they were practically useless as a way to assess a kid's writing ability; she couldn't think of the last one she'd come across that hadn't read as though it had been vetted by a professional copy editor. Mostly she read

the essays only to keep a scoreboard of topics (character-building moments in sports; bonding with people from different cultures; Harry
Potter–inspired insights; etc.). But this season, a handful of essays had
actually burrowed their way into her psyche, a situation she found regrettable since only one of the authors was strong academically. Among the
highlights was a missive by a girl named Lindsey Greeley, whose mother
had died of ovarian cancer during the summer of her junior year. The essay had made Olivia actually *cry* on account of some treacly description
of the girl reading *Tuesdays with Morrie* to her mother on her deathbed
and the mother seeming to cling to life until the book was through. It
made Olivia mad at herself that she could read something so cloyingly
manipulative and wind up in tears. She figured she was almost certainly
just PMS-ing: sometimes she cried at the most embarrassing things when
her hormones were out of whack. When she read about the birth of the
new baby panda at the National Zoo in Washington, D.C., for instance,
she got all choked up imagining how gentle the 250-pound panda must
be when holding her tiny cub. She really hated herself at these moments,
and it was a relief when she returned to normal, as evidenced by her
clearheaded conclusion that Lindsey Greeley was no more Yates material
than the mother panda. Her scores were all in the mid-500s, her transcript was full of C's, and although Olivia had not read *Tuesdays with
Morrie*, she questioned the literary sensibilities of anyone who had.

Still, when she resolved to put the girl's application in the reject pile,
her hand began to quiver. Olivia reminded herself that she was not in
the business of charity. It was not her fault that the girl lobbed her best
shot too high. Blame her college counselor! Of course she could see that
the girl was from a large public school in an area not known for turning
out a lot of college-bound kids. She could also see from the computer-
generated chart that divided kids into regions and schools, that an unprecedented ten kids from her New Hampshire school had applied to
Yates, and certainly she was nowhere near the top of the heap. These
sudden surges in a school's popularity made up a whole subcategory of
the admissions game that she found fascinating. What mercurial, random
forces caused ten kids from the same school to suddenly apply to Yates?
Was it simply that one popular kid at the school declared his intent and

the rest lined up like sheep? Did the phenomenon involve the same herd mentality that had caused her to buy these stupid overpriced boots that were currently pinching her feet? She slipped Lindsey Greeley's application into the stack that read "deferred." She didn't know what was wrong with her.

This, together with about ten applications just like it, was beginning to make her appreciate her formerly limited powers as a lowly admissions officer. At least that had been like armchair punditry—she could rant and rave but ultimately she didn't have the final say. Each application was vetted by two readers, hard cases went to committee, and Ray made the final decision. Even though she had not been conscious of it at the time, she had allowed herself the luxury of being occasionally deliberately outrageous, knowing that Ray would ultimately make the right call.

There was one applicant who was causing her even more angst than Lindsey Greeley. She was the sort of kid who just a year ago Olivia would have accepted without hesitation simply because of her numbers; her scores were outstanding and her GPA was well above Yates's median, even with the suggestion of certain problems that had resulted in a slippage in grades. The girl's essay proved so powerful and raw that Olivia had a dream about her. The downside was that the author revealed herself to be a total head case. She remembered Ari's admonition to avoid this particular minefield, so it was hard to say whether she was fixating on this girl just to be difficult, or whether there was genuinely something compelling about her.

She had another theory, too. It had to do with all of her regrets about her stepdaughter, Amy, who had been close to this girl's age, and similarly disturbed, when she and Olivia parted ways. No matter how hard she'd tried to make amends over the years, Amy wouldn't let her in. At some level Olivia knew it was time to let herself off the hook; perhaps she wasn't the most morally upstanding member of society if you factored into any citizenship award a regrettable tendency to sleep with married men, but she had never meant to be the cause of anyone's suffering. In fact, she might have walked away from Preston had she been able to foresee the emotional consequences for Amy. Although then again, she might not have; no one seemed to appreciate that she'd only been twenty-two at the time! She'd beaten herself up about this for years, but that didn't resolve anything, or even make her feel any better.

She wasn't sure that she'd be doing this girl a favor by letting her into Yates. She tried to imagine someone on emotionally shaky ground spending her first winter away from home on this campus. The place was so isolated and gloomy even in spring that Olivia was surprised she had managed to weather all these years without slipping into a clinical depression, herself. Boosting morale was an ongoing student council mandate, which was the supposed excuse for the extraordinary number of silly theme parties they sponsored each year. One nearby university had one of the highest suicide rates in the nation, and while that was generally blamed on the intense academics and the sort of self-selective personality that attended the school, some of it, she suspected, was just geography. Now she'd been given a direct order to weed out kids whose profiles set off alarm bells. An author who implied, however subtly, that she was hoarding mail and ogling knives probably fell into the category of the great unhinged.

And yet, Olivia couldn't seem to let it go. There was something so familiar about this girl. She had to confess it wasn't only that this Taylor Rockefeller reminded her of Amy, but more to the point, she reminded Olivia of herself. One aspect of the connection was embarrassingly superficial—she loved the part about her mother being a wannabe Rockefeller. One of Olivia's most closely guarded secrets was that she had hung on to her ex-husband's name only because she liked to fantasize she had some relation to the Sheraton Hotels. It wasn't quite as glamorous as being a Hilton, but it was as close as she was likely to get.

But there was more to it than that: just as compelling as Taylor Rockefeller's brief personal narrative was the writing itself. The essay was a work of art, the most surreal, literary effort that she'd seen in her many years on the job. This girl was likely to create something powerful someday, if she managed to stay off the psych ward and out of jail. It was also a relief to read something edgy after suffering through her classmate's elegantly written but irritatingly earnest saga about teaching a tsunami survivor to swim. She had also mentioned something about lepers and broiler chickens, which made Olivia uneasy. She was already worried about bird flu. Was it a good idea to add leprosy to the mix? Naturally, a couple of the younger admissions officers loved the essay, and the girl's file had been flagged, her low test scores notwithstanding.

Two admissions officers had already read Taylor's application and voted to reject. Each application was stuck inside a manila folder, with a xeroxed score sheet stapled to the front. Readers were asked to assess a candidate in five categories on a scale of 1 to 5: academic transcript, standardized test scores, recommendations, extracurricular activities, and the vaguely titled "citizenship." While the Rockefeller girl had been awarded 4s and 5s in four categories, which was generally good enough to admit, both readers had given her 0s in the citizenship category. A single 0 in any category was generally enough to sink a score sheet full of 5s.

The citizenship category was deliberately vague and intended as a dumping ground: a way to reject a kid you didn't want to admit for reasons you didn't want to articulate. This was the category where an admissions officer could get rid of an otherwise perfect student because, say, she had received an off-the-record phone call from the applicant's guidance counselor explaining that while the charges had been dropped and the record was technically clean, it might behoove the Yates guidance office to know that the otherwise sparkling candidate had been accused of rape on three separate occasions.

Although Olivia had the power to overrule her subordinates, she had to use discretion. It seemed unlikely she could unilaterally admit this girl without raising eyebrows, possibly undermining her shot at being dean. Olivia set the folder back down on her desk and decided to postpone the decision until she swilled another coffee. Maybe she'd leave it to chance: if the coffeepot was half full, she'd admit her. A glance toward the lobby reminded her that there were other, larger problems than whether to admit Taylor Rockefeller, however. She paused to contemplate an amusing philosophical riddle that suddenly occurred to her: if twenty students simply declared themselves to be Native American, could the admissions office incorporate them into its minority enrollment figures? That would be a mighty impressive leap!

She could no longer stall; it was getting late, and it was probably best to get these few remaining decisions out of the way before the admissions office was completely overrun. A van was waiting to take the envelopes to the post office at 4:00 p.m., so she could dither for only so long. And decisions needed to be posted online, where they were theoretically available the next morning, although that was a whole other kettle of fish. Yates had only just been wired after two years of lobbying the state legislature to require the local cable company to provide service on the grounds that it was putting college students in this isolated sliver of rural New York at an educational disadvantage without high-speed Internet availability. Access was granted two years ago, and it was up and running and it worked great, when it worked, the caveat being that when it didn't work, they were on their own. Last time the system crashed, it had taken two weeks to get relief, and when the cable company came to fix it, they accidentally sliced through the wrong wires, severing electricity for three days. It was really impossible to stay on top of these things; now that high-speed service was available on every college campus in America, the kids all demanded wireless, the transition to which was causing the system to collapse with even more regularity. It seemed a given that by the time they got caught up with wireless, something new would have come along, like there would be some way to download information directly to the brain. At the moment, service was only sort of working, and it was possible that prospective early-decision candidates were simply going to have to receive their news the old-fashioned way.

Apart from Taylor Rockefeller and Lindsey Greeley, there were a couple of other candidates who were giving her indigestion, the case of Paul Kruzokowski among the most acute. Paul's situation was perplexing not because of his academic merits, which were entirely unremarkable, but because of the over-the-top sentiments his essay had produced among her peers. Paul had written an admittedly moving essay about losing his brother on September 11. He still had the voice recording his brother had left on their home answering machine when he realized he was stuck inside the towers. Paul's family thought he might have been one of the jumpers, and they spent days trying to identify him among the blurred images of falling bodies. His essay was the talk of the admissions office.

There was evidently a pool going, with the odds stacked against anyone in the office being able to read it without winding up in tears. Olivia had heard there was extra money riding on her reaction, so she locked her door and turned her swivel chair away from the glass wall when she read through Kruzokowski's folder. She hadn't cried, exactly, although tears did well. Still, she voted to reject. Even if she felt herself softening, Yates had a bottom line to maintain; this was an ascendant liberal arts school, not the Salvation Army. She had barked something to this effect when she handed the file back to the student intern, who began to cry on the spot. She wished these people would all get a grip.

Yet here was Paul, back to haunt her, with a note signed by the entire admissions staff urging her to please reconsider. Was it worth alienating everyone who worked for her by barring entry to this one boy? On another day, perhaps. But the whole thing, combined with all the racket outside her office, was giving her a migraine. Let him come to Yates: the more, the merrier! Who cared about a shortage of dorm rooms? She dropped Paul Kruzokowski into the accept pile, along with some other sob story of a girl who was a recovering alcoholic—another favorite of her colleagues—whose name she had already forgotten.

Now all she had to do was dispense with this Rockefeller girl, who was of no great consequence to Yates either way. Too bad there was no relation to the Rockefeller fortune—access to a deep pocket would have definitely tipped the balance. Olivia couldn't quite believe all the time she was spending agonizing about the fate of one not-all-that-remarkable, middle-class white girl from an affluent metropolitan suburb. Yes, her numbers would blend in nicely and would even nudge the median scores upward, but they had such a large overqualified applicant pool that there was no justifiable reason to admit someone who referenced knives in her essay.

Her desk was becoming a Ouija board; every time she tried to put the Rockefeller folder in the reject pile, her hand drifted the other way. The essay seemed a cry for help, and Olivia had the eerie sense that she was the intended recipient. She decided that the only way to handle this was to actually meet Taylor Rockefeller in the flesh. Interviews were not required at Yates—in fact, they were mostly discouraged as interviews sucked up precious administrative resources that they didn't have to spare. But they were held on rare occasions. Basil had recently decided to implement alumni interviews as a way to track down wayward graduates and make them feel involved, which in turn might get them to write a check, an effort which might help in the "alumni giving" category in the *U.S. News* rankings. But that was off in the future, set to begin next year.

She finally deposited the Rockefeller folder in the deferred pile, with a note scribbled on top that she should be scheduled for an interview if she happened to be in the area. As if anyone would happen to be in Yates, New York, in the dead of winter, a few hundred miles away from anything at all.

January

WHILE TAYLOR WAS STILL a little ambivalent about Mrs. Reiger, the college counselor down the street who her mother finally forced her to consult, she did feel sorry for her. It wasn't Mrs. Reiger's fault that she had been deferred from Yates, a school that, on the face of things, she should have gotten into. This didn't stop Nina Rockefeller from calling Mrs. Reiger a stupid cow, or threatening unspecified legal action, on the day the deferral letter arrived.

In fairness, Mrs. Reiger had actually advised Taylor against an early application to Yates for reasons Nina probably would have agreed with had they ever been able to engage in a civilized conversation. Taylor's profile placed her so far above the range of the typical Yates student that Mrs. Reiger urged her to use it as a safety school and aim a bit higher. Although she tried to steer Taylor toward some of the same more name-droppable schools that were on her mother's list, she seemed to have less twisted intentions, or at least Taylor got the impression that Mrs. Reiger really did want to help her maximize her options, rather than see her marry well. Still, Taylor was confident that she had made the right choice for the right reasons, regardless of whether Yates's Facebook provided a useful gauge of future social registers, which she gathered it did not.

Mrs. Reiger wore her graying blond hair in a loose ponytail and had three diamond studs through each ear. Her lips were painted movie siren red, but she wore Birkenstocks and drank herbal tea while chain-smoking Salems. Taylor liked the fact that she was hard to peg, that she was at once earthy and hard-edged, both in her personal appearance and in her no-nonsense attitude toward college admissions. The game was bullshit, she said—you could and would get a decent education at any of these schools—but why not play to win? This was what she kept stressing to Taylor in the privacy of the little office off her kitchen, where the years of accumulated cigarette smoke was so thick Taylor imagined she could feel nicotine molecules seeping through her pores. The smell made her vaguely nostalgic for her not-so-sweet grandmother, who battled emphysema alone in a studio apartment in Boston's Back Bay while obsessively watching CNBC, periodically removing her oxygen mask to suck on a Salem Light as she tracked every tick of her little bit of stock. They still owned the apartment, actually, and sometimes Taylor feared her grandmother's mostly unhappy life, particularly the chapter that involved a lonely, bitter death, presaged a glimpse of her own future. Still, Taylor liked that Mrs. Reiger smoked. It made her seem daring somehow, or at least very un-Verona-like, not just to risk her own health, but to have the guts to compromise the lungs that trafficked oxygen to some of Verona's brightest young minds.

Sometimes, when their conversations veered toward the personal, she wished that Mrs. Reiger was her therapist instead of her college counselor. There were things she longed to tell her, personal details that really did affect where she ought to go to college, in a way. But then these disclosures were even more private than her stupid tech-ed grade, which was an embarrassing enough piece of information to have sitting in an unlocked file cabinet in the house where her daughter possibly snooped at night.

The first time Mrs. Reiger rattled off the list of schools she thought she ought to consider, Taylor hesitated. "I'd need to learn a bit more about the bathroom situation," she said, quietly.

Mrs. Reiger threw her head back and laughed, her mostly gray ponytail bouncing up and down. "Taylor, you are such a wit! We need to somehow bottle this humor in your application so people can really get who you are."

Taylor wasn't sure how to respond to this. She wasn't trying to be funny, but was only expressing a sincere desire to not have to prance around naked in the bathroom in front of strangers, or to make awkward small talk in the morning when she brushed her teeth. And she still felt the need for this private hub, even if she hoped to have moved fully beyond the compulsion to paper it with certain items that belonged to other people. Regardless of her reasons, she didn't understand why no one took her seriously when she expressed concern about the bathrooms. Was this any more unworthy a consideration than caring about whether the campus contracted with Coke or with Pepsi, which was something one of her tour guides went on at length about at one school she visited in Pennsylvania?

One thing about Mrs. Reiger that really bugged her, though, and made her think that in the end she would not really make a great therapist was that they seemed to keep having the same conversations over and over. Mrs. Reiger didn't remember the bathroom concern from one meeting to the next, for example. And she kept asking her if she *really* wanted to apply early to Yates. She sounded surprised each time Taylor said yes, like this was the first time the subject had come up. Taylor had recently begun to notice that a lot of women her mother's age couldn't remember very basic things. Even some of her teachers kept repeating themselves, or worse, contradicting themselves. Like her multivariable calculus teacher, who assigned the same homework two days in a row, and then, on the last test, marked at least three problems incorrectly. Taylor wondered if perhaps all these people drank as many vodka tonics as her mother did, or if there was something in the Verona water supply that was causing every woman over the age of forty to lose her mind. Oddly, her mother complained about the same thing all the time, but from what Taylor observed, her mother's mental acuity was not much better than that of the people she accused. She speculated that if Mrs. Reiger were her therapist, she would have to begin every session by reminding her that she felt like she was living underwater and was sinking deeper every day.

So even though she was somewhat ambivalent on the subject of Mrs. Reiger, she'd been tempted to come to her defense when she heard her mother scream into the phone that day. A similarly ugly episode was now in progress, as Mrs. Reiger had evidently just sent a notice about the overdue bill. Taylor watched from the top of the staircase as her mother raved, punctuating each sentence by stabbing the air with the invoice. Now that the door to Taylor's bedroom had been removed from its hinges, she could see and hear everything that went on in the front hallway, where the house's only stationary telephone sat on a low table by the wall. Taylor wondered if her mother ever stopped to consider that the removal of her door by an apologetic handyman affected her own privacy as well. Now Taylor had no choice but to absorb all the household drama unless she kept her ears plugged with her iPod. Her father had been home for the last two weeks, and Nina railed at him pretty much nonstop about issues ranging from his domination of the remote control to his leaving wet towels on the bathroom floor. Just the day before, her father had bought himself an iPod, and he stopped by Taylor's room for a brief tutorial. It was the closest thing to a bonding experience they'd had in years. Now they both walked around the house in their private zones, united in their inability to hear Nina.

"I gave you explicit instructions to talk her out of applying early decision to that god-awful school," she heard her mother yell. "Given that you've ignored my wishes, I feel justified in refusing to pay this bill! As for your late fees . . . don't even get me started!"

Then a moment later, "What do you mean, 'It's not about *me*?' It's *my* money . . . Yes, you're damn right we'll have to take this to court! Believe, me, I will! I'm going to call my lawyer as soon as I hang up the phone. I have never been so embarrassed in my life! With her scores, to be rejected by a school I'd never even heard of? What kind of counselor are you?"

After Nina banged down the phone, she stormed upstairs, pausing at the threshold of Taylor's room to yell at her, too, but no words actually came out of her mouth. Taylor wondered if some great moment of reckoning had just arrived, when her mother had finally run out of things to say. Nina just stared at her for a minute with a confused look on her face that seemed more like sympathy than rage, but she left without speaking and headed into the master bedroom and slammed the door. Taylor heard her turn the lock, which made her relax a bit. Since her father had left an hour earlier after another door-slamming, foundation-rattling fight that seemed to have to do with the bank statement that had just arrived, this gave her some privacy for a while.

From what she gathered, Nina viewed this primarily as a botched financial transaction, but Taylor was actually rattled about the way this had played out. Mrs. Reiger had given her reasonably sound advice, and she knew she had only herself to blame for the fact that it was January and unlike many of her classmates, she didn't even have a safety school locked in. Taylor had ignored her suggestion, for example, that she apply to three schools with rolling and/or nonbinding early-action options. Mrs. Reiger had prepared a "menu" for Taylor that was divided into safeties and reaches, as well as "solid prospects." Taylor had not taken the list very seriously, as she was counting on a Yates acceptance. She thought she was being smart, identifying a school she liked, that she had reason to believe she could get into, and applying early, rather than choosing the approach of most of her peers, which was to use their early-decision applications to stretch. From what she had observed from her admittedly limited seventeen-year-old perch, it seemed to be the American way to always aim slightly higher than you should: to covet the jeans that cost twenty bucks more than you had in your wallet, or to lust for the unattainable boy. Proper consumer behavior seemed to dictate that you ask for the engagement ring that would break you from the start, so that you were already on the road to ruin when you bought your first house, which itself squeezed a monthly nut diminished by the luxury car. She thought she was being clever, and even virtuous, applying to a school within her reach, yet she'd been slapped with rejection. Or technically with "deferral," which she figured was really just a euphemism for rejection.

Taylor feared the Yates deferral foreshadowed more bad things to come, but she had rallied and stuffed her other applications in the mail before their January deadlines and was even working on one with a mid-February date. A couple of these schools sounded okay on paper, even if she'd never heard of them before, and they were not in exactly idyllic locales.

Nina seemed displeased with this game plan, embarrassed that Taylor was dipping her toes into the murky waters of *U.S. News* third-tier-ranked schools. She threatened to send her to an emergency "boot camp" in New York where, for $9,999, an expert would help her and ten other losers strategize about how to get into college now that they had blown the first round. Taylor couldn't bear the thought of having to spend a weekend with her fellow rejects listening to what she figured would be some slick con man supposedly salvage her future. Even though this deferral had finally motivated her to get the rest of her applications out, she still worried she might have messed up on the complicated legwork required to get her Verona documents as well as her SAT scores in on time.

She feared that whether her paperwork ever arrived at these various admissions offices was possibly beside the point. She should have gotten into Yates, so clearly something was wrong. Evidently, Mrs. Reiger had the same concern, because just after the first ugly shouting match with Nina, she called Taylor privately, on her cell phone, and urged her to apply immediately to Maryland, as well as to at least two other large state universities, speculating that they would be impressed by Taylor's numbers and would not be put off by whatever subtle things had seemed to trouble Yates. The problem was obviously with her essay. Mrs. Reiger said this without mincing any words. This was a crisis of college admissions, and not the time to be polite.

Mrs. Reiger, like Mr. Leon, seemed to intuit that Taylor's essay was not going to endear her to college admissions officers. Mrs. Reiger had also urged her to consider starting over; her own personal favorite topic had to do not with role models or favorite characters in favorite novels, but with community service requirements. Verona students needed to volunteer sixty hours in order to graduate, and Mrs. Reiger said that her clients (although Taylor couldn't help but think of herself as a patient) had a good track record of getting into college with essays that outlined the good deeds they had done. Taylor argued that no one would be impressed by her community service performance; she had logged her hours the summer between her freshman and sophomore years selling ice cream at a celebrity golf tournament at the Verona Country Club, ostensibly to raise money for the mentally retarded. Taylor had actually lined up a stint at a troubled elementary school in D.C., tutoring children with reading problems, and while her mother agreed in principle that this would look better on her résumé, she said there was no way she was driving Taylor to that part of town where she was certain they'd be carjacked and raped.

Taylor asked Mrs. Reiger how she might frame such an essay to evoke sympathy given that she'd not actually made contact with a mentally retarded person in her week of selling ice cream, and had also raked in about $200 in cash tips from the wealthy patrons who felt sorry for her standing in the blistering sun. Mrs. Reiger's eyes widened when she heard this, but she told her to improvise. Taylor wondered why everyone was so cryptic when they talked about college admissions. Why couldn't people just say what they meant? By *improvise*, did she mean *lie*? Or was she supposed to be creative and sort of *imagine* a scene where she manned her ice cream cart alongside an actual mentally retarded person, which she had not done, although she would have found that preferable to manning a cart beside Cathy Roberts, who yammered on nonstop about the different varieties of polo shirts the golfers were wearing and had herself come dressed in head-to-toe argyle.

Mrs. Reiger said no, she was certainly not suggesting that Taylor make something up, but she might consider writing about where all the money was going, or what the life of a mentally retarded person was like. Or she could write about the organization that sponsored the event— maybe she could even drop by and chat with someone there, to see if that sparked any ideas. Taylor gave it a whack, but she was certain that the resultant essay sounded as flat and insincere as the Mother Teresa essay, and both made her sound like someone she wasn't sure she liked. These rewrites made her think of the time her mother had forced her to stop at the makeup counter at Nordstrom, where a cute Bobbi Brown representative was offering free consultations. Taylor had reluctantly settled into one of the makeup artist's swivel chairs as her mother egged her on, and while she conceded that the relatively light application of eye shadow and lipstick looked good, she still couldn't wait to get home and wash the glop off her face. She wasn't sure about a lot of things in life, but she knew that she would rather take her chances looking and sounding like herself, even if the product was imperfect.

She sometimes worried it had been a mistake to rely on the limited supply of college information she had been force-fed over the years. It was possible there was a world of alternative options out there that no one ever mentioned. Even if not everyone had as warped an outlook as her mother, this was, after all, still Verona, where certain snobbish attitudes, particularly on the subject of education, were so pervasive as to seem the norm. All the college guidebooks lying around the house only touted what they called the *best* colleges and universities in the United States. The scattergrams she had access to provided information based only on Veronians' acceptance history, and as for her mother's holy grail of *The New York Times* wedding announcements, it went without saying that referenced a rather self-selective sliver of schools. When she really thought about it, she didn't want to go to the schools on the list Mrs. Reiger had prepared for her, regardless of how impressive some of them might sound. What she really wanted was to go to Yates. She had sat through dozens of tedious lectures by now, between all of the mandatory school meetings and the endless information sessions at individual campuses, and everyone told her to look for a school with that enigmatic right fit. She had found that at Yates, or so she'd thought; the only hitch was that they weren't so sure of the fit on their end, which was obviously kind of a problem.

It occurred to her only now, pretty late in the game, that she should have been more proactive in investigating schools. Just for the heck of it, she logged on to the Internet and did a Google search of "dorm rooms with private bathrooms" and—*voilà*—something called Okanagan College popped onto her screen, boasting more than one hundred single rooms mainly used by first-year students. There were also quads with single rooms, as well as studio suites and one-bedroom apartments. The only problem was that she was having trouble figuring out where Okanagan College was. She kept clicking on links, and it seemed she was gradually getting closer to an answer: the mission of the school was "to serve the educational and training needs of people from Revelstoke to Osoyoos." This sounded possibly like names of towns in Iceland. She didn't want to stay close to home, but Iceland was perhaps a bit extreme. A little more googling turned up the fact that the school was in Kelowna, which she eventually tracked to British Columbia, which she recalled from elementary school geography lessons was in Canada. Not so very far away, really, at least compared with Iceland! She got the sense, based on nothing more substantial than the vague mandate about training needs, that perhaps the school was not especially competitive and wondered if she might have a geographic advantage applying from the States.

There was also a school called Växjö University, with private rooms in *korridors*, which she guessed meant "dorms" in whatever country was in question. She liked the sound of this, she could imagine herself smiling every time she entered her *korridor*, and she was cheered by the pictures of the happy, healthy, coeds who all seemed to be riding bicycles. The school was located in Växjö itself, wherever that was. She found the lack of foresight by some of these Web designers kind of astonishing. It was like the people who called you and just started blathering, assuming that you knew who they were, or even like when someone on the phone identified herself as Eliza, when there were in fact at least ten Elizas in her graduating class, most of them named, as it turned out, for Elizabeth Bennett in *Pride and Prejudice*, or so they claimed. She figured it out eventually, but wondered how the heck someone sitting in Verona, Maryland, was supposed to know that Växjö was in Sweden.

The more she thought about it, a private room with a private bathroom in a very faraway place like Sweden or the part of Canada with weird Nordic names might provide a real solution to an entire host of problems. But applying as an international student required a lot of extra legwork, some of which she didn't entirely understand. She wondered who could help. Even under the best of circumstances, it took a couple of days to get an appointment with her guidance counselor. She did not especially want to talk to Mrs. Reiger about this, and anyway that was hardly an option after the way her mother had treated the woman.

She thought briefly of asking Maya Kaluntharana if she knew anything about applying to schools internationally. At least Maya had traveled to faraway places, even if she was American, but she doubted she would be of any help, and anyway she'd been avoiding her ever since the AP exam debacle.

AP Harry was perhaps a good person to ask. He knew everything about everything, especially when it came to college admissions. He knew offhand, for example, which schools required three, as opposed to two, SAT subject tests, and could rattle off a list of who offered nonbinding early acceptances, rolling admissions, and single-choice early action. She had seen the Excel spreadsheet he devised that listed the names of all seniors—where they had applied early, what their fate had been, and where they were applying regular decision. His information was limited only by the fact that about half of the students he surveyed refused to respond. He was able to fill in a few blanks with some detective work matched up against the scattergram program, which also listed the number of kids who had applied to each school, year to year, but this information was both anonymous and incomplete. Given that Taylor was one of the uncooperative, it seemed like it was probably wrong to ask him for advice. Besides, she had a hard time talking to Harry; even though it was stupid, all these years later she was still troubled by that confusing incident in his basement.

She needed to stop stalling. She wasn't about to get on a plane and go to some school in Sweden whose name she couldn't pronounce. Still, her episode of Google procrastination at least reminded her that college provided a chance to not only get away, but to get really far away, as in junior year abroad, and this made the prospect of matriculating somewhere, possibly *anywhere*, that much more appealing. Even if the odds of getting into a school once you were deferred were generally pretty slim, there, on the Yates deferral letter, was a ray of hope in the form of actual human cursive: "Please call us to arrange an interview." It had been over a month since the letter arrived, and she had yet to make the call.

Taylor pulled out her Princeton Review guide, *The Best 358 Colleges*, and read about Yates again. Median critical reading range 580–640; median math 600–640; median writing range 580–680. Her scores were comfortably above these numbers. Ninety percent of Yates's students were in the top 50 percent of the class. She was easily in the top 15 percent and until last spring, the top 10. She knew she had sealed her own fate by letting her grades slip at this critical juncture and then writing that stupid essay. She considered the possibility that her teacher recommendations had dragged her down, but this seemed unlikely—she was the quiet girl who sat in the back of the classroom and always turned her work in on time. The book said quite explicitly that interviews were not required at Yates, which was odd, but then some of these books were not as accurate as they claimed to be. She tried to log on to the Yates Web site to see if perhaps they had recently changed their policy regarding interviews, but the site was very slow and seemed possibly to be in the active process of crashing. Finally, her computer froze and she had to shut the whole thing down, which struck her as inauspicious.

After confirming that her mother was still locked in the master bedroom, Taylor went into the kitchen and dialed the number of the Yates admissions office, figuring she could clear up the mistake.

The woman on the other end replied as Taylor half-expected: "No, interviews are not generally required," she said. "Every once in a while, in unusual circumstances, we'll ask a student to come in, but it's not the norm. Unless . . . are you a junior? We'll begin administering alumni interviews next year."

"No, I'm a senior, and I have a letter here . . . It says to please call this number to schedule an interview?" The woman asked her to speak up, and Taylor had to repeat herself twice. Finally, the receptionist asked for her name and put her on hold for what seemed a long time.

"You did say you are Taylor Rockefeller, right?" she asked when she finally returned to the phone.

Taylor confirmed her identity, thinking that this was all kind of weird.

"Okay, great. Actually, our dean of admissions would like to meet you. When would you like to come in?"

The dean of admissions? It was like she'd really won—or really lost—the jackpot. Taylor hadn't realized she was supposed to actually come in. This seemed rather inconvenient given that she was a few hundred miles away and in the middle of exams.

"Um, whenever?" she replied.

"Okay . . . how about two weeks from Tuesday at one o'clock?"

"You mean February 13?"

"Yes."

"Um, sure. Great. Okay."

"Okay, do you need directions or anything? You've been here before, yes?"

"Yes," Taylor said. "I mean, no. I mean I've been there before. I'll find it."

She put down the phone and noticed that her mother was standing at the kitchen door. She had on her sable coat and announced that she was going to the grocery store and might be there a while, but that Taylor should remember she was grounded.

Taylor was not aware that she was grounded and thought that perhaps her mother, who was overdressed for Safeway and smelled vaguely of vodka, was confused. She was grateful that Nina hadn't asked her about the phone call, so she just nodded agreeably and then stood by the window until the car pulled out of the driveway. She waved to her mother even though she knew Nina wouldn't see her. The silver Lexus seemed a bit unsteady as it backed into the street, and she came just an inch shy of scraping the UPS truck, parked in front of AP Harry's house, where the deliveryman was approaching the front porch with what looked like a package.

There were several gashes in her mother's car, the result of scraping the side of the garage on a couple of occasions. Nina was a notoriously sloppy driver who in better days had simply replaced her car when it accumulated too many bruises. Now that money flowed less freely, she'd been forced to drive the same vehicle for three years. She frequently complained that it didn't smell new anymore, which had once been the first indication that it was time to upgrade.

Taylor watched her turn right, away from the main road that led to downtown Verona, and she wondered if perhaps her mother was actually going someplace other than the grocery store. She tried to picture her mother having some sort of secret life; she was not an unattractive woman, but it was hard to imagine her having a lover.

She stared wistfully at AP Harry's front porch. The desire to walk across the street and take a peek at the package that had just been dropped at his door was nearly overwhelming, but they were on stag-gered schedules during exams, so it was entirely possible that Harry was home. A moment later she saw him appear at the door and retrieve the package, mercifully relieving her of the dilemma.

Not that there *was* really a dilemma. She was done with the mail! She had a grip on the situation! It was wrong, it was illegal, and above all, it was pathetic to be unable to control this simple impulse. All she needed to do was stop her mind from drifting in this direction. It could be done; her mind no longer wandered toward the knife, even if she still kept it stashed in the bathroom, just for safekeeping.

She kept thinking about the confessions blog, about whether posting an entry might prove the final cathartic act, a public confession of sorts that would help end this misery, but that was not really her style. She liked to stand in the corner and observe, even in cyberspace.

Still, she wondered what others would make of her problems. She was a beacon of well-being compared with the kid who confessed, in the most recent batch of postings, "I'm such a looser I can't even manage to kill myself." This misspelled missive was accompanied by a picture of a bandaged wrist. Taylor wondered if this was the same person who had sent the earlier wrist-and-blade montage. She hoped it was, if only be-cause it seemed awful to contemplate that there was an epidemic of peo-ple toying with slitting their wrists. But this did not mean that she'd ever be the person in a position to write cheerfully, "I wish I could slow things down. Life is passing too quickly. The peonies just come and go." This confession was accompanied by a picture of flowers in full bloom. She found this even more startling than the bandaged wrist, in a way. How did this qualify as a confession? Were there kids out there that were *too* happy? And if so, what were they doing sitting at home blogging? She wondered if it was possible for one person to entertain both these sorts of sentiments and still function normally. Wasn't it a sign of higher intel-ligence to be able to keep two contradictory ideas in your head at once? It must speak to at least a not entirely hopeless state of mind to want to absorb every minute of life *and* contemplate ending it all with a slash of the wrist, which was not to suggest she was at either end of this extreme spectrum.

She heard a noise and turned back toward the window, where she saw the silver Lexus come barreling down the street, scraping its muffler on a speed bump before continuing on its way, now going the other direction. If even her mother was able to correct her course, this had to be a sign of hope, about something.

○ ○ ○

JOE KALUANTHARANA stood in the middle of the living room, holding a sharp surgical blade in one hand and a bottle of purple Windex in the other. If he were a different sort of man, Maya would have thought to take cover, even though she couldn't really imagine a scenario in which window cleaner figured into a murderous rampage, unless he was already anticipating the cleanup. Still, her father had been behaving strangely lately, and she had never before seen him wield any of his sacred medical implements in such a cavalier way.

His unraveling seemed to have begun just a few weeks earlier, when he stood in the same spot and theatrically shredded the Chicago rejection letter that had just arrived. He had always been a calm, reasonable man, qualities Maya appreciated and also recognized as essential for a surgeon. She couldn't help but feel responsible for pushing him toward the brink, and sincerely hoped his patients weren't also suffering trickle-down effects of her poor performance on the SAT. Perhaps she might have done better if she'd logged more hours with the workbook the tutor had given to her or spent the time before falling asleep at night memorizing vocabulary flash cards instead of wasting her time just reading novels.

"See if I ever offer them another one of my children," he had railed as he threw the bits of the Chicago rejection in the air. "See if I ever write them another check!"

Nearly a month later he was still muttering about the slight. Was his check not good enough? he'd asked rhetorically. Had his remarkable success as a plastic surgeon not brought enough glory to his former alma mater? They had never once profiled him in the alumni magazine, he complained, even though at least two of his clients were important politicians and he had just given the daughter of a well-known government lawyer a nose job. Instead, they had put on the cover of a recent issue a picture of another doctor, some young kid he had never heard of from the class of 1995, who reversed vasectomies at a clinic in northern California.

Joe in a foul mood was not a pretty sight, but at least these new, mercifully infrequent rages passed through the house as quickly as a summer thunderstorm. His shock over the Tulane deferral had caused a similar tantrum a week earlier, when he'd said he wished he hadn't given so much money to the Red Cross. Maya couldn't imagine what sort of magical thinking had allowed him to suppose that making a charitable contribution toward hurricane relief might have had a positive impact on the admissions committee at a private university, but she kept that thought to herself. At least he was able to let go of these disappointments pretty quickly, and for better or worse, he had already moved on to lusting over USC.

Joe had worn his new hooded USC sweatshirt almost every day since they returned, and while Maya was happy that he was happy, she worried that he was simply replacing one school with another, like a lover on the rebound. She was also worried because she was not sure that she wanted to go to USC. It was possible she was being narcissistic and this had nothing to do with her; perhaps he had fallen so hard for USC that he was willing to commit himself to wearing Trojan gear regardless of whether she even matriculated.

Bolstering this theory was the observation that in the same hand as the spray bottle was a USC decal; her father was evidently headed outside in 30-degree weather to swap the stickers on his car. Maya worried this indicated an even greater commitment than the sweatshirt, but then this was only a sticker, as opposed to a nonrefundable deposit, so it seemed best to remain quiet. Anyway, what was one more decal? The SUVs driven by Joe and Rita were so covered in advertisements for both colleges and now the various graduate schools attended by her siblings that Maya wondered how they could even see out their windows. Joe had gone ahead and applied a Chicago decal to Maya's car without asking her, but then, it was technically his car, so she didn't feel like she had a lot of say in how it was adorned. She had once heard someone say something about choosing your battles—they were talking about child-rearing techniques—but Maya thought this was good advice in handling one's parents as well, and she decided to let this one slide.

She still felt like she was missing some essential aspect of what it was that made everyone so obsessed with where they went to college. Yes, she liked certain schools better than others, and yes, she had cried when she received her Yates rejection letter (and she'd felt kind of stung that Tulane didn't want her, either, particularly after her father insisted that it would be a snap to get into, post-Katrina), but there were so many schools out there that were just like Yates, and she'd already been accepted to one of them, so she couldn't see the point of tearing herself up about this. She'd heard of one girl in her class who overdosed on Vicodin when she didn't get into Princeton and another who didn't come to school for a week because she was despondent about her deferral from Swarthmore. Maya had heard of one classmate who had locked herself in the Math Department office after learning of her rejection from Caltech; her parents had to finally come to school to coax her out so that the janitor could shut down the building for the night. Meanwhile, everyone was bragging about where they were accepted: it seemed like half of her class had come back from Christmas vacation wearing college gear as a not-so-subtle way of announcing their acceptances. Justin Smelling had plastered not one, but two Harvard decals on his car, lest someone view the vehicle from the wrong angle and somehow miss the news, which seemed unlikely given that he had also scanned his acceptance letter onto his computer and posted it on his Facebook wall.

Maya allowed that perhaps she was more bitter about her Yates rejection than she was letting on, but even Pam, who had gotten in early to Georgetown, found all this boastful behavior appalling.

Anyway, even if the ordeal wasn't completely over, she was in a very good mood. She had received an acceptance to Bard, where she'd applied early action; they had not required SAT scores, and she was a little bit giddy knowing there were people in the world who could see beyond her numbers, who could accept her for who she was. She felt suddenly like she could appreciate what it must feel like to be . . . she couldn't find a polite way to even think the thought privately, but to possess some horrible physical trait, to be a leper, for instance, and still find love. Her work was done, so far as she was concerned. The problem was that her father did not agree. Although he was sold on USC, he still thought she should use Bard's nonbinding early acceptance as a safety and toss another chip or two on the table—it was getting late, but at least a few schools were still in play through February. Maya saw enough of a problem without sticking any more applications in the mail since the real issue remained the same as always, with familial implications nearly worthy of Shakespeare: to swim, or not to swim. There was no other question.

The USC offer had raised the emotional stakes. She had always known that she wanted to go to a small liberal arts college—swimming for a Division I school had never been part of her dream, even before she quit the Verona team. But it was impossible to not be awed by how extremely unlikely this recent chain of events had been. How many second chances did a person get in life? It seemed like someone was trying to tell her something. Having a USC scout see her set a record when she wasn't even supposed to swim—this struck her as the college admissions equivalent of finding the golden ticket in your Willy Wonka candy bar.

She foolishly allowed herself to consider Mr. Joyce again: Was she going to let her future be determined by the interests of corporate conglomerates, he might ask, to be seduced by the promise of free Speedo bathing suits, by the mention of a possible Nike endorsement sometime down the line? But it wasn't about the perks, she would argue if they ever had this conversation, although it was becoming painfully clear that they never would. It was about being a good daughter, and yes, it was also a little bit about how nice it was to be wooed so aggressively.

The whole thing was driving her slightly crazy, even though she knew she was lucky to have such a privileged issue. On the one hand, she didn't want to be forty-five years old and wonder how life might have turned out had she not made some pigheaded decision at age seventeen. On the other hand, she didn't want to go to California, and she didn't want to swim.

Still, she had to confess that she had liked the school better than she'd expected. She and her father had had an extremely pleasant although very quick visit to USC earlier that week. Los Angeles reminded her in the most unexpected way of New Delhi—the congestion, the chaos, the pollution, the dry heat, and the palm trees. The only things missing were cows, although when they got lost driving in from the airport, they did end up in a neighborhood where some children were playing in the street with a goat, and it took her a moment to remember where she was. But mostly they saw the glittering side of LA, as the Athletic Department had flown them round-trip in business class and spared no expense in showing them the good life, including renting them an SUV that was so big Maya had trouble reaching the step to climb into the passenger seat. Among other things, the swim coach had organized a dinner at a gorgeous restaurant on the beach in Santa Monica with several other swimmers, and after hearing her concern about the school's size, he arranged a meeting for Maya with the head of the English Department, who she had to admit was pretty convincing about the small class sizes and the personal involvement of the teachers. She did find the campus surprisingly appealing despite the air of affluence and self-absorption of some of the kids she met, which lent it the same insular feel as Verona. But then she had to concede that most of the campuses she had visited felt like this, even the once-beloved Yates.

No matter how she weighed the pros and cons, she kept coming back to the fact that going to USC would make her father happy. Viewed through the lens of the sort of self-actualization stuff she was always hearing about, she knew it was wrong to be more worried about her father's feelings than her own. Was it possible this deeply embedded sense of duty was somehow cultural, even though she'd been born and raised in the United States to completely westernized parents? Joe and Rita hadn't had an arranged marriage, and certainly the subject never came up at home, yet Maya was of the belief that this was not the worst possible way to organize your life. It seemed to her entirely possible that you could learn to fall in love, both with a man and with a school. She really believed there was too much emphasis on happiness in general or, rather, on the idea that it could be attained through superficial means like going to the one perfect school, or living in the one perfect dorm, or being given a bid from the one perfect sorority. She thought that if you needed these things to be happy, then something was already missing inside. She was pretty sure she could make herself happy at any school, and even if she didn't want to swim, she could find a way to be happy doing that, too. Pleasing her father didn't strike her as the wrong reason for choosing one school over another. For one thing he was footing the bill, and even though she gathered they were pretty rich, at USC, with the athletic scholarship, there'd be a whole lot less to pay.

Her situation seemed pretty normal compared with a couple of the other stories she'd heard these last few weeks. The most widely gossiped-about incident had to do with Mike Lee, who had gone AWOL from his family after his father literally went berserk when he was deferred from Harvard. He evidently slammed Mike against the wall, leaving bruises on his face that were slowly turning yellow. He then he removed all of the televisions from the house and hauled them into the street, saying something about how Mike wasted time he should be using to study watching too many reality shows, which seemed a little bit extreme, given that Mike had straight A's and 800s across the board. He also forbade Mike to use the computer except under his supervision, and then only for homework.

Mr. Lee was evidently not persuaded by a phone call from the head of the guidance office, who tried to explain to him that thirty-one kids from Verona had applied early to Harvard, that nearly all of them had gleaming records, and that the deferral was in no way a reflection of Mike's abilities, but really rather a compliment, in a backhanded sort of way, to Verona High School: so many of its students were worthy of admission that even perfect kids like Mike didn't get in. He said that even taking Harvard out of the equation, so many kids had received deferrals from schools they ought to have gotten into that he and his staff were referring to the season thus far as a "bloodbath."

Mr. Lee did not find this helpful and kept going on about the long hours he worked at his store and the sacrifices he had made on Mike's behalf, all for nothing, in his estimation. The principal made a follow-up call to Mr. Lee to try to explain that there were many fine colleges in the

United States and that he was romanticizing the importance of a Harvard degree, but apparently she was not very convincing.

The night of the *American Idol* season premiere, Mike reportedly snuck out of his house and went down the street to Justin Smelling's, where he knocked on the door and asked if he could come in and watch TV. When Dr. Smelling saw the bruises, she sat him down for a long talk and asked if he would like to stay with them for a while, until his father calmed down. Mike readily agreed.

The police showed up about a week into the unofficial adoption of Mike Lee, sent at the behest of Mr. Lee, who claimed that the Smellings had kidnapped his son. But Mike had just turned eighteen, and evidently there was nothing his father could do to compel him to return. Within about a week, it seemed everyone at Verona knew that Mike was living with the Smellings, and after the second week, people stopped commenting about certain peculiarities, like the fact that Mike had begun to wear Justin's clothes, or that Dr. Smelling sometimes picked him up after school and drove him to his oboe lessons, which someone said she was paying for herself. They all just incorporated this into the norm, the way Maya had read about in her psychology class. Humans were an endlessly adaptable species: they created art out of suffering, and they ate one another in the absence of food. They also protected the young of the competitively insane, not that Dr. Smelling was herself a textbook example of healthy parenting.

There was another crazy story making the rounds, one that Maya could relate to. This one had to do with Marty Stoddard, who had applied early decision to Kenyon College and was accepted, but who was being offered a full scholarship to play football at Maryland. After all his years of playing multiple sports, he was evidently burned out and claimed that he wanted to concentrate on academics. His parents were said to be livid: it was not just the enormous amount of money at stake, but they had organized Marty's entire childhood around athletics, and it was a huge blow that he didn't want to play in college, especially since he was being recruited. Even though the Kenyon College acceptance was binding, the parents had spent several hours in the guidance office trying to release Marty from the agreement, which they claimed they had not known about. It seemed that while there would be no legal repercussions, it put Verona's reputation on the line and was frowned on by the guidance office.

While the Stoddards were in the meeting, Marty locked himself in a science lab and threatened to do something drastic, an act Maya did not completely understand now that she had purged her brain of chemistry facts, but which had to do with mixing a couple of compounds that were better kept apart. Later explanations of this incident at least solved the mystery of the five fire trucks that were parked for hours in front of the building for half the day.

In light of these incidents, Maya considered herself lucky that her dad had so cheerfully replaced one decal with another, literally whistling as he worked. She would take the next couple of weeks to contemplate her decision, but for now she could relax. As she flipped through the Bard catalogue she tried to imagine herself on the way to class, strolling past ivy-covered buildings as the leaves began to turn. She saw herself staring off into the middle distance of the sparkling Hudson River, thinking great liberal artsy sorts of thoughts. She imagined herself in the white studio on page 12, wearing a white smock and contemplating the white canvas with a paintbrush in hand, even though she couldn't so much as draw a tree and hadn't taken an art class since third grade. Or maybe she'd be like the girl sitting at her cello on page 13, a look of rapture on her face. She imagined bumping into the cute guy profiled on page 7, a sophomore, from Baton Rouge, Louisiana, who was throwing a Frisbee in the quad. She was so over Yates, and she'd let a healthy degree of anger replace the initial slap of rejection. It was their loss! In the grand scheme of things, she knew she had two good options, even if the schools were at opposite ends of the spectrum, about as different from one another as they could possibly be. Her heart leaned quite certainly toward Bard, but she also understood that making her father happy might simply be the price of admission.

February

BELIEVING YOU COULD conjure snow with childish, unscientific rituals was as foreign to Harry's way of thinking as some of the other goofy things his classmates did when they were young, like avoiding cracks on sidewalks or wishing on shooting stars, which he tried to explain time and again were merely pieces of debris entering the earth's atmosphere, glowing on account of friction. What puzzled Harry most about the hullabaloo over snow days was the notion of wanting to miss a day of school. When Taylor Rockefeller had called him one night back in third grade to urge him to wear his pajamas inside out and backwards, and to then call three people and pass along these instructions like some kind of telephone chain letter, his response had been a baffled "Why?"

The pajama ritual was supposed to bring snow, she'd explained, tacking on a bunch of circuitous stuff about wanting to go sledding and watch cartoons, build snowmen and eat marshmallows, and she'd even said something about having time to paint her nails. Harry couldn't understand why she would find any of this preferable to school, especially since they were scheduled to have a math test the next day; he had spent the night preparing and was pretty pumped up.

It was one thing for *kids* to want to stay home and play, but it had never previously occurred to him that adults might feel similarly. Once, when he asked his mother if she had ever heard of the strange practice of wearing your pajamas inside out and backwards, her face lit up. She had no idea they were calling for snow, she said excitedly, mentioning how grateful she would be to have the day off from work, assuming there was enough accumulation to shut down NIH as well. He found it disconcerting that when she stopped by his room to say good night, she had in fact been wearing her own flannel-checked pajamas with the seams and labels showing.

The officials in charge of deciding whether to cancel school in Verona County were notorious for making very bad calls. They tended to err so heavily on the side of caution that their decisions were frequently the subject of newspaper editorials, as well as the butt of jokes. The author of a recent opinion piece in *The Washington Post* wrote of the burden a day of cancelled school placed on families who could not afford child care. In December, a horrendous fire had sent three children to the hospital with serious burns when they were left home alone while their single mother went to work: she couldn't afford to take the day off, she said, weeping as someone shoved a microphone in her face, because they were already behind on their rent and were being threatened with eviction. That day, not a single flake had fallen from the sky. Just a couple of weeks later, a local television station had turned up the story of a woman who stuck her daughter in a storage locker while she went to her shift at McDonald's— another (no) snow-day-related personal catastrophe that resulted in the child's being hauled off by protective services, as well as in the loss of the mother's job. Why didn't the concerns of *these* families get factored into the snow-day safety equation? the author had asked. Perhaps because the county decision makers only cared about the welfare of people who drove the likes of four-wheel-drive Volvos—people who would be fine in the snow anyway, because they could afford cars outfitted with dual side air bags and child safety seats designed to withstand a mortar attack. The flip side of a season of overly conservative calls was that when too many snow days had been used up, threatening to shave days off spring break or cut into summer vacation, there was pressure to keep schools open and put the buses out on slippery roads.

Even Harry was surprised that school had not been canceled that morning as he made his way up the slick hill, where patches of invisible ice seemed to have formed overnight. It had only begun to snow an hour earlier, but already an inch had accumulated. He watched car after car skid at the same treacherous intersection. Harry had heard people joke that Maryland and D.C. drivers couldn't cope with the sort of weather conditions that people in the rest of the country dealt with routinely. He supposed this might be true—certainly he didn't drive especially well in the snow, but then his was one of the few families in Verona that did not have a vehicle capable of navigating frozen mountain passes outside Kabul.

Walking didn't seem a much safer proposition. His mother had been watching the news as he prepared to leave the house, and he overheard the meteorologist mention there was a 50 percent chance that the storm front moving in from Ohio might hit the Mid-Atlantic region and dump up to six inches of snow. He couldn't imagine what was behind the decision to open school. His mother joked that maybe the school superintendent, whose kids also went to Verona County public schools, had already purchased tickets to go to Aruba over spring break and didn't want to have to pay change fees on his reservation should the school calendar need adjusting. In defense of this somewhat risky call, however, was the fact that based on the weather forecasters' track record of the last several years, there were nearly 100 percent odds that the 50 percent chance of snow would never materialize.

Harry saw Mrs. Rockefeller's car slowly climb the hill. She began to skid as she approached the icy intersection and swerved into a trash can, which went banging down the street, discharging bits of greasy-looking garbage onto the pristine snow. A half-eaten chicken carcass landed at his feet. It took her a moment to regain control, by which time Harry had taken refuge on the middle of someone's lawn to avoid being hit. Taylor noticed him and rolled down the window to see if he wanted a ride, but she was actually laughing at the idea that anyone would voluntarily get in the car with her mother after this display of her driving prowess. Harry noticed that Taylor looked somehow different and wondered if she'd changed her hair color again, or maybe it was just that she was smiling, which caused a dimple to emerge on her left cheek. He entertained the brief, mostly subconscious thought that she was very pretty, something he'd forgotten once she'd turned so glum.

Harry spotted Maya up ahead, wearing a bright orange parka. His instinct was to run and catch up with her, but he hesitated; since receiving the Harvard deferral, he'd become somewhat less inclined to chase her down. He'd also been steering clear of Justin for the last few weeks, which put a significant crimp in his already spare social life. Harry had mumbled the obligatory congratulatory words to Justin, but he knew that he could have been more gracious. But then, Justin was being so in-your-face obnoxious about his victory that Harry was hardly the only one avoiding him. Now that the subject of college had lost its conversational appeal, he realized that he had no memory of how to engage in normal small talk. Still, he'd heard through the grapevine that Maya had been rejected from Yates, so he figured she must be feeling pretty depressed herself, a thought which brightened his mood ever so slightly. It was one thing to be deferred from Harvard, but imagine being flat-out rejected from Yates! As he took a step toward her, he began to glide on a patch of ice. At first the sensation was so strange he mused that it was almost pleasurable to lose control like this, but then the moment ended and he hit the ground, hard. A quick spot check of limbs suggested that he had not broken any bones, and he wondered if his too-heavy backpack had possibly helped cushion the blow. Standing up slowly, careful not to slip on the same spot, he brushed the snow off his trousers. He felt a little dizzy, but suspected that might be because his glasses had fallen off and everything was blurred. He noticed something brown sliding down the hill and realized he had lost his briefcase. He felt around in the snow for the glasses, but couldn't find them. He thought perhaps he ought to head home to see if he still had a spare pair, but decided it was best to press forward; he was only a block from school and he didn't want to miss the first bell. The only time in his life that he'd been late was when he'd spent the night at his dad's apartment and had had trouble persuading him to get out of bed in the morning to drive him to school.

He moved slowly toward the fuzzy building that loomed ahead, taking off his glove to massage the ache at the back of his head. He was startled when his hand came back red, smeared with blood. Again he debated whether to go home, but school was closer, and he figured that it made more sense to go directly there and assess the wound in the bathroom mirror.

Although he could hardly see anything more than a few feet away, it appeared to be a beautiful morning—there was very little traffic, and it seemed at least a few people in the neighborhood were giving themselves a self-declared snow day. A yellow Labrador retriever came bounding up to Harry, wagging its tail. Harry patted the dog on the head, accidentally smearing its fur with blood. He then made a snowball and threw it in the air. The dog leaped and caught it in his mouth, where it broke apart. Harry set his backpack down and lobbed another snowball in the direction of the dog. All he could really see was an impressionistic blur of leaping yellow and swirling white, which was actually quite beautiful. Harry had a strange thought: maybe he should relax and play with his own dog sometime.

As he approached the main entrance of the school, he felt that something was wrong. It wasn't just that, from what he could see with his limited vision, the parking lot was half-empty—he figured that many people, such as those students coming from the tonier sections of Northern Verona, as well as most of the teachers who lived in more affordable areas that required long slogs on the Beltway, very likely had trouble with the morning commute. But there seemed to be flashing bright lights in the area where normally only buses were allowed, and from what he could tell, a cluster of people stood outside.

Harry glanced at his watch and saw there were approximately four minutes until the first bell. He needed to stop in the bathroom to wash the blood off his hands. It appeared he was actually bleeding rather heavily, but he wasn't in any real pain. He vaguely recalled reading somewhere that scalp wounds tended to produce a lot of blood. He saw Maya in the crowd, and it looked like she was crying.

As he approached, he saw Taylor there, too, looking rather shaken.

"What happened?" he asked, pushing through a cluster of girls in pastel-colored fleeces.

"Harry, oh my God, you're bleeding!" she said, and he realized that he had just dripped a large splotch on Taylor's pale blue fleece. These whims of fashion seemed curious, the way the girls deliberately dressed alike. He didn't pay much attention, but every once in a while he would notice that pretty much every girl at his school sported some version of something or other, like freshman year it was the same silver heart dangling from a thick chain, and then, by the following year, the hearts were mostly gone and replaced by . . . well, he wasn't sure by what, as he was a little slow on this front, only just noticing that a recent preponderance of puffy down vests had given way to the fleece thing. He had always assumed the point of fashion was to make a statement of some sort, which he supposed Taylor did in her own way, with her ever-changing hair. He was too disoriented to really give this much additional thought.

"I'm fine," he said, trying to wipe away the blood but instead leaving a smear of red. Like a sloppy axe murderer, he had dripped his DNA across a two-block swath of town. "What's happened?" he tried again.

Taylor pulled a white scarf from her neck and began to wrap it around Harry's head. It was long enough for her to loop it twice, and then she tied it tightly while speaking. He found himself strangely touched by this gesture. "There's been an accident . . . ," she explained. "A garbage truck ran the light, or skidded or something. Smacked right into Justin . . ." Taylor started to tremble.

"Justin Smelling?" he asked. "What happened?"

"The cop won't say. He wants to talk to the principal first, but the word is that it's pretty bad."

Harry felt like he might actually faint for the first time in his life. Kids like Justin didn't get into accidents. He'd just been accepted to Harvard!

His mind wandered to his Excel spreadsheet, and he briefly contemplated what the outcome might be if Justin was removed from the Harvard acceptance list and a space opened up. Curiously, the thought did not make him happy so much as sick to his stomach.

"I need to see him," he said as he felt himself begin to fall. Taylor caught him in her arms.

"It's going to be okay, Harry," she said, rubbing his back in a soothing, circular motion. "Come, let's go inside and find someone to take a look at your head."

ON THE MANY previous occasions that Raymond Wiley had thrown a tantrum about a grade he didn't like, Mr. Leon threatened him with one of the very few weapons available in his limited, county-regulated, arsenal: if Raymond didn't shape up, he'd get an LOC, an acronym so familiar to the few slacker kids at Verona that it had become a verb, as in, "He's LOC-ing Health." Six absences would result in a Loss Of Credit for the class, sending Raymond to summer school and tarnishing his transcript, unless he was able to successfully appeal. Raymond was not a slacker, so the prospect of an LOC was usually enough to get him to turn around and slink back into his seat whenever he was about to walk out the door in protest of a less than perfect grade.

Harry had heard about the startling methods employed by some kids to get around the problem of an LOC. A forged note from a parent addressed to the attendance office usually did the trick, as long as you were prepared to field the follow-up call to verify the note's legitimacy. This was evidently accomplished by providing a phone number along with a scribbled postscript: *P.S. Please feel free to call me with any questions; it's best to reach me on my cell phone . . .* Then you provided the cell phone number of a friend, who was fully briefed in the details and prepared to impersonate your mother or father, and offer apologies along the lines of *Yes, of course, I'm so sorry Timmy keeps losing his notes for his orthodontist appointments. He's so absentminded!* in a convincing tone of voice. It was an old trick, but remarkably, it still worked.

This morning, however, even Mr. Leon was in such a state of despair about the accident that when Raymond threw his paper to the ground— an essay on Camus for which he had received a grade of 36.5 out of 40— Mr. Leon didn't react. All eyes turned to Mr. Leon, waiting for him to snap, but he just stared at Raymond, expressionless. When Raymond realized his theatrics were having no effect, he quietly picked up the paper and took his seat, and Mr. Leon resumed his halfhearted lecture.

Between the extreme weather and the shock of the accident, most everyone was just going through the motions, except for a few people on whom stress had the opposite effect, turning them aggressive. Two junior girls had such an ugly catfight in the hallway that a security guard had to separate them: they were at odds over which one was going to throw her name in the hat for editor in chief of the school paper next year. Applications for positions were due in a month, and already the newspaper staff could talk about little else. Word in the hallway had it that these two saw themselves as the leading contenders for the job. One of them was sure she was going to pursue a career in journalism and therefore felt that the other girl, who was only on the paper to puff up her résumé, was morally obliged to step out of the way.

Normally when the weather was this bad, the powers that be would close school early and send everyone back home. But conditions had worsened so rapidly that a counterintuitive decision was made to keep everyone in school until the end of the day, and possibly even longer, depending on how long it took to salt and plow the roads. For the first time in his life, Harry actually *wanted* to leave school. He had tried to reach Dr. Smelling but, not surprisingly, she wasn't answering her phone, and the several messages he left for her at the hospital went unreturned. He finally reached his mother at work. She agreed to come get Harry right away and take him to the hospital both to check on Justin and also to have a doctor take a look at his head, but then she called back half an hour later to say that her car wouldn't start, and AAA was reporting up to three-hour delays. Harry wished he could help his mother somehow. He knew she was pretty resilient, and he'd never once heard her mention being lonely or wishing she had a man around to do whatever real men did these days—climb on the roof to inspect the gutters, or at least hang a plasma flat-screen TV on the wall to watch football in high definition. Still, it would be nice if she had someone she could lean on, someone to pick her up from work when her car wouldn't start, or someone to bring her flowers and take her out to dinner once in a while, particularly since Harry imagined it might be possible that his brain was doing something dangerously weird right now, like swelling up or shutting down, and that she'd soon be on her own.

He contemplated trudging home in the snow, but he didn't want to be alone, even though he was having trouble tolerating the clusters of overly emotional girls sitting in the hallway, crying. Some were holding hands and praying. They were giving him his first-ever headache. He had never actually believed in headaches, and considered them the invention of hysterical women, but now he was going to have to rethink this position. The nurse, who had thankfully made it to school, was pretty sure the wound was superficial, but said he should watch for signs of a concussion, just to be safe. Harry suggested she put him through a series of exercises to be sure that he had not lost any of his mental acuity, but since she didn't know the elements of the periodic table, or even the order of former U.S. presidents, he had no real way to gauge the damage. She was able to effectively swab the cut with alcohol, however, and did seem confident in her pronouncement that he'd be fine. She insisted that Harry ought to take an Advil, and Grace, by telephone, agreed. Harry protested at first—he had not taken any form of ibuprofen since he was a toddler and was, in principle, averse to ingesting any drug liable to dull his thinking, but he finally gave in since they weren't doing anything very demanding that day, and anyway, the only thing he could really think about was Justin.

The part-time school psychologist was summoned to do some grief counseling. There had been no update on Justin's condition, just a rumor that he was in surgery, and a few people were evidently unraveling to an even greater degree than suggested by the drama on display in the hallway. Evidently, the psychologist didn't get very far before her car slid into a tree, however, so she went back to her home and set up a series of private phone calls with kids at Verona who felt the need for some telephonic counseling. Harry didn't believe in grief counseling any more than he believed in headaches, Advil, or the human ability to summon snow, but he was feeling very strange, and wondered if this might be a good time to reconsider his view of therapists. When he inquired, however, he learned there was a list of about forty-five people who had signed up ahead of him for a phone consultation. Still, he felt like he needed something, even if he couldn't say what, other than for Justin to be okay. Oddly, he felt like what he needed the most was some more time leaning his head on Taylor's shoulder.

He had just sat through thirty minutes of English class without really listening, and when he glanced at his composition book, he saw he had filled it with doodles. He didn't know that he knew how to doodle! His series of geometric ink shapes was oddly pleasing to the eye, and he thought that maybe when he got to Harvard he might indulge himself and take an art class just for fun. He also realized he had gone a record thirty minutes without even thinking about his Harvard deferral. He looked over at Taylor a couple of times, and she smiled. His face felt hot, and he wondered if he had a fever. Or maybe he really did have a concussion. But now he was thinking about Harvard again, so maybe whatever ailed him had just been temporary, and the vague depression that settled on him when he realized that he might be on his way to Maryland was perhaps evidence that he was basically okay.

○ ○ ○

TAYLOR KNEW SHE was socially awkward, but she had also observed there was no shortage of misfits in the world, an assertion she felt qualified to make after all the time she'd spent intercepting other people's confessions. Still, as the date of her interview at Yates approached, she feared she would ruin whatever possible good impression she might have made on paper by presenting herself in the flesh.

When she was conversing with someone, it usually seemed okay at the time: the other person would say something and she would respond, and sometimes the conversation acquired a certain momentum, and she might even manage something witty. That sort of magical, effortless rapport had occurred when Harry dropped by her house to return the white scarf she had used to bind his head wound and to give her an encouraging update on Justin, who was evidently out of intensive care and expected to slowly recover, even though he faced several surgeries to rebuild his shattered pelvis. They had spoken for a few minutes about other things, too, and she said something that made him laugh, although she couldn't remember what. He seemed to have lingered for a few minutes in the doorway as if he was waiting for something, and she realized later that she should have asked him in.

She was briefly elated after they spoke, but the euphoria was quickly replaced with a bad aftertaste. She had probably laughed at the wrong beat, or offered a facial expression that didn't match the tone of what was being said. In her darker moments, she imagined there might be some compendium of her conversational bloopers floating around in the universe that included her mumbled answers in class and the inarticulate voice-mail messages she had left over the years, as well as her pathetic stabs at relationships, all collected on DVD and advertised for cheap on obscure late-night cable stations.

And yet, she thought, it was actually Harry who had been acting strangely when they spoke on her front doorstep. He asked her what kind of shoes she was wearing, for example, and when she replied that they were just an old pair of moccasins that she'd slipped on when the doorbell rang, he'd asked her a lot of detailed questions, such as whether she was partial to wearing moccasins, and if she felt that her choice of shoe offered a window into her soul. She wondered if Harry was one of those boys with a shoe fetish and found it comforting to imagine that he might have some personal issues, too.

To seem normal to a Yates interviewer seemed a tall, if not impossible, order. She practiced trying to sound like a happy, confident girl as she drove, hoping no one would see her talking to herself. The road was mostly empty, and the sky was so dark she feared she might steer herself into a cosmic black vortex, some previously undiscovered Pennsylvania version of the Bermuda Triangle. She imagined herself gone missing; Nina would probably hold a press conference, hire a PR firm, and book herself immediately on her beloved *Larry King*. She hated to think of all the phony things her mother would say that would make her sound like the perfect debutante sort of daughter. She thought back to that jarring razor-blade confession, and it really did seem possible her mother would be happier if she disappeared. The thought was enough to get her to crack the window a bit to let in the bracing mountain air and help her stay alert.

She had already endured a few interviews without incident, even if she worried afterwards that she could have done better. In her experience it was nearly impossible to prepare, since the range of questions and interview techniques varied so widely. At a couple of schools all that had been required of her was to nod at appropriate intervals as she was bombarded with information, and then to ask a question or two that made her sound like she was seriously interested in the place—what sort of opportunities did the college offer for her to study music, was her standard query, even though she planned to leave her flute at home. On one occasion the interviewer asked her to identify the biggest problem facing her generation. She had rattled off a rehearsed answer about clashing cultures and religious strife and resultant acts of terrorism. In the end, however, she had not applied to any of the schools where she'd interviewed, so she had no way to assess her performance. She'd heard that these days, interviews were not really used as anything other than a way to weed out psychopaths, which was sort of a problem, since she was pretty sure that this was precisely why she'd been summoned to Yates.

Oddly, she was feeling very much unlike a psychopath for the first time in recent memory. She suspected that part of this was the cathartic effect of pretending to run away from home, even if she had every intention of returning by tomorrow. She had walked right past her screaming mother as she grabbed her car keys, and had delivered her words in a cool, direct manner. The application of Chanel Coco Red painted on her mother's lips was jarringly bright, and Taylor had come to know this shade as the first warning sign that Nina was hovering near the edge, like the color-coded warning system devised by Homeland Security. Taylor's declaration that she was leaving proved more satisfying than the way in which she usually spoke, a style which Dr. Zimmer once cruelly referred to as "passive-aggressive." She had told Nina that *she* was the one who needed help, and that yes, she, Taylor, had problems, but she couldn't get better in this toxic house. Nina's tears left tracks through the thick layer of foundation on her cheeks.

She had planned all along to tell her mother that she was going to Yates for an interview and to spell out in a rational manner the reasons that she felt the need to go alone. Unforeseen circumstances, such as her mother going berserk that afternoon, resulted in a last-minute change of plans, however. Nina had evidently seen a segment on the *Today* show that morning about teen sexuality, referring to one local incident in which kids engaged in sex at school. This resulted in a slash-and-burn foraging of Taylor's room while she was gone that day. Taylor couldn't imagine what her mother expected to find that might suggest she was having sex in the library stacks, and could only assume that because her mother was drinking more than ever, she had become even more irrational. This subject had come up once before, and she'd tried to explain to her mother that Verona was not really that exciting of a school, and in fact the general atmosphere might be improved by a little lunchtime fornication in the stairwells. But when she got home that afternoon, Nina produced Taylor's laptop as if she'd just unearthed evidence of mass orgies. Nina had turned the computer on—offering some comically illogical reason why she had done this in the first place—and had seen the background wallpaper of the wrist with the razor blade that Taylor had saved from the blog. This led to a somewhat incoherent rant about all that Nina had done for her over the years, and how much money she was spending to send her to a psychotherapist, and that all Taylor did in return was find ways to try to humiliate her.

As she drove, Taylor did feel kind of bad about her dramatic exit, and she even tried to leave Nina a message to let her know she was okay, but she couldn't get a signal on her cell phone. At the time, it had seemed better to just walk away, rather than attempt some rational response to a series of accusations that had more to do with her narcissistic mother than with a downloaded photograph.

The day's events made her even more determined to prove her worth at Yates. She so wanted to convince the dean of admissions that she was Yates material—even if she wasn't completely sure what that meant— that she had done something unprecedented and even a little embarrassing: she consulted the book her mother had given her for Christmas. Nina was always presenting her with these annoying guides to self-improvement, which typically had the effect of making her want to run out and get a tattoo or pierce something her mother would find objectionable. Normally she would have stuffed *Miss Manners' Guide to Excruciatingly Correct Behavior* where it belonged—in the bathroom with the neighbors' mail, or in the recycling bin with the *New York Times* wedding announcements, or possibly even in the fireplace. But for some

reason, she decided to flip it open to the section about interviews. She
read and reread one passage in particular:

> There is one social skill that can serve as your strongest asset in a
> job interview. In private life, it makes people fall in love with you
> and seek you for purposes ranging from honored dinner guest to
> spouse; and in business, it helps more than any other single qualifi-
> cation, with the possible exception of being the owner's eldest child.
> That is enthusiasm. A look of vitality and happiness, an interest in
> the world and an eagerness to participate in life comprise what is
> called charm in the social milieu; but in the working world it is
> called competence. One may practice such a look. It is chiefly done
> with the eyes. If they can be made to shine radiantly, the rest of the
> face will automatically compose itself into the properly attractive
> expression. Practice staring into the mirror as if you have fallen
> madly in love. Most people have little difficulty with this when they
> have thought it over . . .

Although it was so dark she could barely see her reflection, Taylor occasionally took her eyes off the road to try to catch a glimpse of herself in
the mirror to determine whether she looked as though she had fallen in
love. She was embarrassed to find that it helped to think about Harry. As
hostile as she was to the very idea of Miss Manners and excruciatingly
correct behavior, she had to admit that she looked like a different person
when she made an effort to look like someone not just capable of falling
in love, but of being loved in return.

She also appreciated that presenting herself well had as much to do
with the mechanics of her physical appearance as with some magical
gleam in her eye, so she decided to do something about her hair. Hair—
its color, texture, cut, shine, thinning, graying, splitting, bounce, and
silky-smoothness (or lack thereof)—seemed to be at the heart of just
about everything to do with personal presentation, a fact so easy to observe that she didn't need Dr. Zimmer to explain the various Freudian
aspects of her decision to have dyed her hair first purple, and then a variety of colors that all merged and blended incongruously into some in-

describably hideous color which she then highlighted with amorphous streaks. A week before setting off, she had bought a box of Revlon medium golden brown, which sounded like the sort of hair color that a healthy, well-adjusted girl might have. She considered herself lucky that the concoction didn't contraindicate the mucked-up foundation on which it was applied, and instead presented itself very much like the picture advertised on the box. It really was remarkable, Taylor thought, as well as vaguely depressing, to realize that the advertising people were not entirely wrong in their insistence that you are how you appear. Now that her hair was normal and she actually felt a little bit in love, she thought she looked not entirely unlovely for the first time in years.

She knew that colleges did not expect high school seniors to dress like corporate wannabes, but she also understood that she probably had more hurdles to overcome than most candidates. She had taken off the rack in her closet one of the many preppy oxford cloth shirts that her mother had bought her from Brooks Brothers, and paired it with a khaki-colored Banana Republic wool skirt. These had been sitting in her closet for more than a year, and she snipped the tags off both after deciding that they were still reasonably enough in style, even if they hung a bit loose on her frame. Practicing in her bedroom, she had pulled her new normal hair back in a ponytail, donned this outfit, and stuck a pair of small pearl earrings through her lobes. She found some nail polish remover and replaced what remained of the chipped blue enamel she had applied months ago with a light, sheer pink. The transformation was frightening when she thought about how easy it was to masquerade as someone so different from who you really were inside. She couldn't help but think what it must be like to be a suicide bomber posing as a happy member of society, or at least as a convincing commuter sitting on the train.

Sprucing herself up was one part of the challenge; the other was to physically get herself to Yates. She had never made such a long drive alone, but was sure that if she just handled things methodically, she could pull this off. She bought a map and also downloaded directions from the school Web site. She told her teachers that she would be missing a day of school—visiting colleges counted as an excused absence—and she even got the homework assignments in advance. She made a hotel reservation at the Yates Inn so that she could get a good night's sleep after the long drive, and then shower and dress properly before her interview.

Planning this expedition was a useful exercise in reinforcing her gut sense that she would be able to function much better in the world once she got out of her house. She wouldn't be the first girl in the world to go off to college with an unresolved problem or two. Look at all the girls in her class with eating disorders! And what about that girl who wrote *Prozac Nation*? She was slicing herself with a knife, ingesting various drugs, and giving blow jobs indiscriminately, and she still managed to get through Harvard! Anyway, she planned to take care of herself and would seek help from someone a bit more accessible than Dr. Zimmer once she got to college. At least a week had passed and she had barely thought about the mail. She hadn't put it out of her mind completely, but when she saw the little truck rumble down the street, she did not feel a quickening of her pulse. The first thing that registered was that the mail was about to be delivered; the thought of stuffing it all in her arms was only a tempting afterthought. Another thing she noticed was that the confessions blog was beginning to have less appeal, and she'd even found herself privately enraged by one of the most recent entries: "I'm jealous that my sister is in the hospital. She gets all the attention and no one even notices I'm alive," it read. That made her incredibly angry, and she wished the author of this entry might come along with her to visit Justin. There was nothing enviable about being sick; seeing Justin in pain made her want to go home and appreciate every minute of excruciating calculus homework, at least for an hour or two.

She could still relate to the picture that accompanied the depressing confession, however, which was the image of a boy floating in the air. No matter how much she improved, she thought she would always understand what it meant to feel somehow set apart.

THE WISDOM of this venture seemed less obvious the next day when she became completely lost. She had driven around in circles on icy winding roads for so long she was about to run out of gas, but that concern was overridden when the front end of the car became lodged in a snowbank after a botched U-turn. Pumping the gas pedal only seemed to cause the wheels to dig in deeper. There was no choice but to start walking and hope she wasn't too far from Yates. After trudging through thigh-high drifts for roughly half an hour, packing the inside of her boots with slush, it seemed she was getting nowhere. Unable to read several of the snow-crusted signs, she took at least three wrong turns. She was beginning to think it was a real possibility that she might actually freeze to death, so she tried to go back to her car to lean on the horn to summon help, but the keyhole had frozen over. She made this discovery just as she spotted fresh animal tracks belonging to something with extremely large feet. She thought about calling someone from the cell phone in her pocket to confirm that bears hibernated in winter, and that abominable snowmen did not actually exist, but she couldn't think of who to call in the middle of the school day, and anyway, now her battery was dead. What in the world had she possibly been thinking, making this journey on her own? She was a walking calamity.

Still, she was feeling strangely calm. She wondered, in an oddly detached way, if anyone would find her body before the spring thaw, assuming, of course, that the animal with big feet had not fully digested her by then. Just then a gnarly old groundskeeper with no front teeth passed by in an open Jeep and offered to give her a lift. She mused that this seemed like the prologue to a fairy tale that wouldn't end well, like "Hansel and Gretel," but with the children being sold into slavery. Still, she climbed in. As it turned out, she was already on the Yates campus, so she hadn't blundered quite as badly as she'd supposed. As the groundskeeper drove, he told her that he had grown up in Yates and had always wanted to go to the college, but since he couldn't afford it, working on the campus seemed the next best thing. He proved very sweet, and when he safely deposited her at the admissions office exactly on time, she added his acquaintance to the list of reasons why she wanted to attend the school.

She swung open the door looking far less presentable than intended, but no one seemed to even notice as she stomped her boots on the rubber mat in the doorway and wiped about an inch of snow from the shoulders of her coat. Her failure to attract attention possibly had to do with

the commotion going on just behind the reception desk, in the small ro-
tunda where Taylor had first spied the statue that had so intrigued her.
Three men were studying *Yashequana Woman* from various angles. One
had a tape measure; his face was scrunched in concentration as he made
notations with a mechanical pencil on a small pad he pulled from his
pocket. Another was in the process of erecting a barrier around the
statue with duct tape and rope. Taylor noticed that there was a mound of
dirt and clay and ripped-up linoleum at the base, and realized that there
was some attempt being made to remove the statue. Someone who
looked possibly like a student circled the periphery, taking pictures with
a digital camera.

The girl at the front desk must have noticed her staring. "Don't
worry," she said, "it's just one of those days around here!" She offered to
take Taylor's coat. "You look a little bit cold. Can I get you some hot
chocolate or something?" she asked.

Taylor looked up at her, suddenly terrified. It was one thing to fantasize about talking her way into Yates, and another thing entirely to be
here. She mumbled an answer, not even sure what she'd said. She tried
to remember that she was someone else now: she was a person with a
look of vitality and happiness, a person with an interest in the world and
an eagerness to participate in life. She was a person who looked like she
was in love, a person worthy of admittance to Yates University. At least
that's who she thought she was. Or was she really the awkward girl with a
messy mind who would be better off going to Okanagan College? Maybe
Yates was not remote enough, and her dark personality was better suited
to some even colder, icier climate than upstate New York had to offer. Of
course, when she thought about it, every Canadian that she'd ever known
seemed remarkably well-adjusted, and certainly far sunnier in disposition
than she was.

"I'm sorry, I couldn't hear you," the girl said, leaning closer. "Surely
you want something hot to drink to warm yourself up? You look half
frozen."

Miss Manners would probably advise her to accept the offer, even
though she would discourage a response that involved simply nodding
her head. The sound of the jackhammer that had just resumed tearing

through the floor was suddenly so deafening, however, that there was no point in even attempting a polite exchange. The girl motioned again that Taylor should relinquish her coat, which she did, but she kept the scarf and wrapped it tight around her shoulders like a shawl, her eyes locking for a split second on a spot of Harry's faded blood.

The girl took the coat and returned with hot chocolate. "So, are you here for a tour?"

"Oh, no! Sorry. I am Taylor Rockefeller," she replied in a way that seemed not quite right. For one thing, she was shouting to be heard over the commotion, but the problem had more to do with her declarative tone, like she was introducing herself as the Elephant Man, insisting she was not an animal.

The girl told her to have a seat. Taylor settled herself into one of the elegant chairs in the corner and pretended to concentrate on a Yates catalogue for a few minutes although she was too nervous and distracted to absorb any information. After a few minutes, a skinny woman with dark brown hair that framed a string of pearls approached and shouted over the drone of the jackhammer, "I hope you aren't too cold. Our heat is on the fritz." The woman also had a white scarf draped around her shoulders, and they stared at each other for a moment, absorbing the meaningless coincidence. Taylor was pretty sure she'd seen her last time she'd visited the school.

Miss Manners whispered in her ear that she ought to stand up and shake the woman's hand, and she obliged. "I'm Olivia Sheraton," the woman said. "Come, follow me to my office. Watch out for all the mess. We don't want you to trip and fall and sue us!"

Taylor wasn't sure if that was a joke, but she followed her down the corridor, carefully stepping over bits of torn-up concrete. Each office that they passed was chock-full of file folders and papers, and the entrance to one hallway was nearly impassable with cartons of what appeared to be more folders. Taylor wondered if these were all applications, and if so, it seemed a small miracle that amidst all this chaos anyone had even noticed who she was, never mind summoned her to Yates. When they reached the office, Taylor was instructed to sit in one of the chairs facing Ms. Sheraton's desk.

"I'm so sorry to have asked you to come all the way here," the woman said. "I confess it's a bit unorthodox. We don't normally require interviews, but something about your application struck me as . . . well . . . *unusual*."

Taylor really did not want to have this conversation and thought that maybe if she just remained very quiet the discussion might shift away from her and toward something more uplifting, like current movies, or even inroads in eradicating certain communicable diseases in third-world countries. She studied the woman's houndstooth wool suit and high heels. She looked more like a lawyer in a stuffy firm than a dean at a scruffy school.

Ms. Sheraton walked over to a space heater in the corner and kicked it so hard that a couple of books fell off the credenza. "Damn heat," she said, returning to her swivel chair and opening Taylor's file. She smiled but it looked a little forced. Then she began to stare. "I have to confess you are not what I expected," she said after a few awkward moments.

Taylor hesitated. "Probably you thought I'd have, like, greasy purple hair and blue nail polish or something."

"Yes, something like that, although I'm not sure, exactly . . ." Someone knocked on the door, interrupting the thought.

"What?" Ms. Sheraton snapped.

The door inched open and a person who might have been an admissions officer began to speak but quickly retreated when he realized she was in a meeting.

Ms. Sheraton mumbled something about the fact that the door was possibly closed for a reason and that he might have thought about that before knocking. She seemed kind of scary, and what had survived of Taylor's small burst of confidence was rapidly dissolving. Over Ms. Sheraton's shoulder she could see it had begun to snow again, which made her remember her car, and the fact that she needed to call for help. She wondered if it was snowing at home, and whether mail trucks were equipped with four-wheel drive. They seemed light and not very aerodynamic, and she realized that she had never considered how well they performed in the snow.

Ms. Sheraton again cleared her throat as if she was about to speak, but something evidently caught her eye in the hallway. Taylor noticed that a man was standing outside the office; he held his thumb to his ear and his pinky to his mouth, evidently encouraging Ms. Sheraton to call him. She scowled and swiveled her chair in the other direction.

"The thing is . . . ," she began to say, and then paused again, looking back toward the hallway. The man was gone. Ms. Sheraton seemed so distracted that Taylor wondered if she should volunteer to come back another time. She wondered who this woman was, if she had a husband or children, if this man in the hallway was possibly her boyfriend. Taylor didn't notice any pictures on her desk, but she did see a bunch of little horse statues. She picked one up. It was made of a cold, smooth stone that felt oddly soothing in her hands. The woman's eyes widened, and Taylor felt a wave of panic. She couldn't imagine what in the world had compelled her to touch this woman's personal property.

"Sorry!" she said, setting it back down, carefully.

"No, it's okay. Do you like horses?" She seemed to brighten at the possibility.

"Not particularly. I mean, I don't *dislike* horses . . . I'm just not that into them."

"Do you ride at all?"

"No. I'm so sorry. I'd like to learn to ride someday. It's just that we live in the suburbs, and well, I guess it just never came up." She felt as though she might cry.

"No, no. Don't worry. It's not a requirement. I was just curious. You remind me of someone and . . . well, never mind. Let me get right to the point, Taylor. The thing is, you are a very strong candidate, despite a slip in grades that I'm willing to overlook, but I have to say there was something disturbing . . . I'm just a bit worried about . . . there were certain implications of . . . the admissions committee felt that . . ."

"I know!" Taylor said, leaning forward in her chair and interrupting. "I know that was the wrong essay. Lots of people advised me not to send that essay, but they were all telling me to write stuff that just didn't seem right, like Ms. Reiger wanted me to write about my community service project, but all I did was sell ice cream at a celebrity golf tournament and I'd be lying if I told you that I learned any lesson other than that there are a lot of rich people in Verona with a lot of nice golf clothes. And Mr. Leon wanted me to tell you about my favorite character in my favorite novel, but that didn't work either because she was kind of . . . not mentally in a good place . . . and that would have also set the wrong tone . . . so he wanted me to write about Mother Teresa, and I tried, but that was just, like, totally insincere . . . but what I really want to say is that I've had a bad year but I'm going to be okay. My mother is really messed up, she and my dad barely speak to each other, and I'm starting to think she's an alcoholic, and she took the door off my bedroom, and she wants me to go to college only so I can marry a rich man, and she's really into this whole Rockefeller mystique thing, even though we are totally not related, and anyway this issue that was going on with me is much better . . ."

Miss Manners reminded her to lift her chin in the air and catch a gleam in her eye and look like someone who was in love, which she did. And then she remembered Harry. "There was this horrible accident at school last week, and our friend Justin was nearly killed, but he's going to be okay, and he's going to go to Harvard, but it made my friend Harry realize that there are more important things in life than where you go to college, and, like, I realize that, too. But the thing is, I really want to go to Yates and I just have this sense that if I could only go here, I'll be fine. I mean, I'm trying to say that I'll be fine, period, because I am feeling so much better, but I'm also trying to say that if your concern is that I won't be fine, I will be fine."

"Breathe, Taylor," Ms. Sheraton advised, leaning back in her swivel chair and laughing. "What is it that attracts you to this place?"

"I don't know, so many things. I love that amazing statue over there," she said, gesturing toward the hallway, "and I know that you have a great English Department, and oh my God, it's just awesome that Fritz Heimler is on staff. We read his poem about the radioactive sheep in my English class."

Ms. Sheraton's expression turned momentarily sour. "Actually, you should know that they are removing the statue as we speak; that's what all this noise is about. It's on its way to Washington, to the Museum of the American Indian. I'd say we'll be lucky if the whole building doesn't collapse—in fact, there are structural engineers coming in today to reinforce the beams or something—but that's another story. And, well, you probably ought to know that Heimler, well, there's a little bit of controversy. We're trying to work things out, but there's the possibility he might resign. We're hoping that won't happen, but it's better you should be fully informed."

"Oh." Taylor paused, confused. "Well anyway, there are other things I love, like for one thing, there are hardly any other schools that still have all-girls dorms. I mean, I know that's very old-fashioned of me, but I think there's just something appealing about not having all this potential sexual conflict in a dorm. And I'm really attracted to the thought of having a single room."

"It's just gone coed. We had to turn it into all double rooms because we had an extra-large freshman class this fall, and the trustees just voted to permanently increase the size."

"Oh . . . well that's still okay, because there's something about this place that I really love anyway, even if I can't say what right now, off the top of my head . . ."

"I don't suppose it was that cute Garth guy on MTV, because you ought to know that he's transferred."

"That's okay," Taylor said. "I didn't think he was that cute anyway. I just had that feeling they describe in all the books? Like, this is the school that just clicked for me. Oh, I know another thing! This old groundskeeper who just gave me a ride in his Jeep. Ernie, I think his name was. He was really sweet."

"Oh yeah, Ernie. He is pretty sweet. I suppose that's a good enough reason to want to come to Yates."

Taylor couldn't tell if she was kidding. "Listen, I mean, I'll be fine, I'm going to go to college and I'm going to be fine, I promise, even if I go to Okaganan. I'd just really like to go to Yates. I could tell you some more things about myself. I play flute, I like to paint, I plan to be an English major . . ."

"Okaganan?"

"It's in British Columbia."

"Oh. Strange, I'm not familiar with the school. Anyway, tell me, what's your favorite novel?"

"The Bell Jar?"

"I love that book, especially the scene where she goes to the lunch at some fancy hotel and everyone eats . . . what was it, shrimp salad? Maybe lobster salad? Or caviar? Something fishy anyway, and then everyone gets food poisoning and throws up for the entire day."

"Oh my God, I know! I haven't eaten either crabmeat or caviar since I read the book!"

The man appeared outside the window again and rapped lightly on the glass with his knuckles. "Anyway, we're all set. I think this is enough to work with."

"Enough?" Taylor asked, worriedly. It seemed bad to leave things on this low note, with a shared fondness for food poisoning. "Can I ask you something?" she said, feeling suddenly bold.

"Sure. Go ahead."

"This person that I remind you of, is that a good thing or a bad thing?"

Ms. Sheraton's face seemed to soften. "At first I thought you reminded me of my stepdaughter, but the more I thought about it, and really, now that I've met you, you remind me of . . . well, this is really kind of awkward, but you remind me a little bit of me."

Taylor smiled. She couldn't quite believe she'd asked this question any more than that she'd elicited this weirdly personal response.

"Just promise me that if you come to Yates and you feel yourself slipping, you'll come talk to me."

"I promise I will," Taylor said.

"And promise me something else."

"Anything."

"Promise you'll come talk to me even if everything is fine."

March

OLIVIA LIKENED THE ANNUAL March admissions meeting to the academic equivalent of a sausage factory. You didn't really want to see what went into making up your would-be diverse, wishfully egalitarian, incoming freshman class any more than you wanted to watch pig intestines run through a meat grinder.

She used to think Ray was joking when he said he felt dirty after stumbling, shaken, out of the conference room each year. Now she wished she'd paid more attention to the evidence that Ray was breaking down. He once said that he'd tried to scrub himself clean by standing in the shower for two hours, long after the hot water had run out. He'd shown her the patches where he'd rubbed his skin raw, but she figured he just had a bad case of eczema and was kidding around. He'd also mentioned on several occasions a recurring dream about torching the admissions building. Given that Olivia frequently had the same dream, she had failed to grasp the significance.

She privately feared that after an admissions season spent sitting in his chair she might wind up shattered herself, but really what she came away with after these few months was an appreciation for the fact that Ray wasn't cut out for the job, whereas for better or worse, it suited her just fine. The horse-trading that went on in the admissions office bugged her for precisely the amount of time it took to complete the transaction.

True, she'd allowed herself a brief lapse in the instance of Taylor Rockefeller, but this was really just evidence that she was right for the job. She
could make the tough calls without losing any sleep, yet she could bend
the rules when something moved her sufficiently, which to her credit,
didn't happen very often. She would make an excellent dean of admissions and was prepared to prove that today.

She was feeling very clearheaded now that the latest bout of panda-
weeping and empathy for underachieving candidates had passed. She
didn't know what caused these periodic outbreaks but figured it probably
had something to do with the slow drying up of things in her ovarian region, which she preferred not to think about. Or maybe it was just that
summoning the tremendous amount of willpower required to quit Ari
had unintended effects, not unlike the way a reformed smoker sometimes puts on weight. She had not yet completely kicked the habit; she
still thought about him every waking moment, but she'd managed to turn
him away at the door last night when he'd shown up with a bottle of wine
and a fistful of flowers, even though she wanted nothing more than to
throw him against the wall in a violent fit of passion. In any event, things
seemed to be stabilizing: she had just pulled the picture of the mother
and baby panda from her desk drawer, and mercifully she'd seen nothing
other than a couple of dumb furry animals.

A new sky-blue cable-knit sweater that she ordered online had just
arrived, and it went just as nicely as she'd imagined with the pleated
beige wool skirt she'd bought last year. This seemed a good choice of
outfit for the meeting, stylish yet professional, and just cheery enough to
suggest she was someone other than herself. She wondered if Ari would
notice, then reminded herself that she wasn't supposed to care. She held
a steaming cup of black coffee in her hand, which always felt like a hope-
ful thing—the first sip of the day seemed as promising as the first
glimpse of daffodil buds peeking through the earth, even if all these
years of experience were proof that her morning optimism would wither
faster than those fledgling flowers in a Yates spring snowstorm.

She was the first to arrive in the conference room, and she settled
into a seat at the far end of the table and opened her folder. She'd been
studying the day's agenda with the same level of scrutiny she brought to

bear on The *Daily Racing Form*, and had already formulated a strategy. Foremost, she'd decided that she had no real problem with giving a nod to the two spectacularly dumb athletes the athletic director was so aggressively lobbying to admit. After all these years, she'd come to the conclusion that dumb athletes were an important part of the mix. Yates did have a football team, after all, and even if they were not very good and played schools of equally pathetic ability, the school still needed a few good men to stick in uniform. Besides, if a college campus was supposed to be a microcosm of society (she wasn't so sure about this herself, but she'd heard the assertion espoused by various progressive scholars), this meant that a bunch of kids were naturally going to fall to the bottom of the academic heap. In the view she had recently come to embrace, you might as well let the bottom-feeders be happy, so why not layer that tier with the sort of boys who were content to drink heavily and give themselves concussions on the football field? Studies showed that these kids typically did just fine in life—they made a lot of friends, earned college degrees regardless of their GPAs, and had so much fun at Yates that they'd even be inclined to make large charitable contributions, someday. Of course this was a closely guarded private view; to her admissions colleagues she moaned about the compromises she was forced to make to accommodate the Athletic Department, and how the world would be a better place if a liberal arts college could conform more closely to some platonic ideal of a learning environment.

Another highlight of the meeting was sure to be the arm-wrestling session over the fate of Simone Atkins, the uninspiring niece of the head of the Philosophy Department. Simone was a terrible student who had made so little effort on her application that she had sent it in with no less than ten blatant grammatical errors. Olivia had overruled a committee recommendation to admit her early decision, and her mother had called the admissions office at least twenty-five times since December to urge them to reconsider. Meanwhile, Neal Atkins, who had been at Yates for thirty-five years, was threatening to quit. Olivia personally saw this as a win-win situation—the girl had nothing to recommend her *and* this was a rather expedient way to get rid of dull Neal and breathe some new life into the mediocre Philosophy Department. Evidently, either Basil or Ari

did not see it this way, however, as Simone's name was second on the
punch list, after the two dumb athletes, who'd been grouped as one.

She figured there was probably more to the story, something almost
certainly to do with low faculty morale; if you weren't going to increase
their pay, which Basil was not yet prepared to do based on his calculation
that salaries were currently not *hugely* below the national average, you
could at least give a minor break to their relatives by allowing them the
opportunity to pay $40,000 a year to come to Yates. Otherwise, there was
no rational explanation; if the plan was to quietly try to jack up the numbers, there was no room to bend the rules for a girl like Simone. Basil
had told Olivia without mincing words that she had to be selective in dis-
pensing her humanity, to give lucky breaks where they counted most. As
a case in point: she was prepared to cede on item number three and admit the Kuwaiti investor's daughter, even though the girl had been forced
to repeat a year at her private New England prep school after failing four
classes junior year, and from what they had learned, she had applied to
sixteen schools and had not been accepted to a single one. Olivia thought
this demonstrated real range in her decision-making process—she understood the importance of squash courts!—and that she should be ap-
plauded for taking her interim dean of admissions gig seriously.

She got what Basil was saying about the whole legacy thing, too.
"Smart parents produce smart kids," he informed her, "so why so much
hand-wringing? Of course, Yates is not starting with an alumni gene pool
that boasts a lot of brain surgeons," he added, smirking, possibly forgetting that he was a Yates alumnus himself. Anyway, fidelity to the school
was not really the point; one category in the rankings was the rate of
alumni giving, and coaxing a donation from someone whose kid had been
rejected was a thankless proposition, Ari once told her. Hearing him
complain about the distasteful aspects of his job was the only thing about
the relationship that she didn't miss.

Basil had also impressed on her that she ought to set aside any moral
problem with the idea of creating space for the children of the super-
wealthy, assuming they were willing to make a substantial donation to the
school, and it made him slightly crazy to hear critics excoriate the reser-

vation of spots for the financial elite as a form of reverse discrimination. If you were going to abolish affirmative action, they railed, you had to first get rid of legacy. What did these people think kept institutions of higher education financially afloat? *Tuition?* he'd asked. Given the financial crisis at Yates, Basil told her, she was lucky to still be drawing a paycheck. Let the children of the superrich come to Yates as long as they could foot the bill and write a few supplemental checks, or help build a state-of-the-art recreation center, and possibly toss in an oil rig along the way.

She took a few sips of coffee and reflected that the color of the new sweater was already seeming a little too bright—normally she dressed in earth tones with a particular enthusiasm for certain darker shades of gray, but she thought she might try to lend a little cheer to the drab, windowless conference room.

The only way to do this job without driving herself quite literally mad was to accept the fact that life simply wasn't fair. Take being female, for example, which came not only with built-in inequities such as having to be the mother in any childbearing arrangement (where was that father panda, and couldn't he stick around long enough to even pose for a picture?), but with a skewed ratio of girls to boys applying to liberal arts schools; women were at a disadvantage before they knew what hit them. Even with a deliberate attempt to correct the imbalance, Yates was still top-heavy with girls, who outnumbered the boys by a 3–2 ratio.

She thought Basil's suggestions were generally in poor taste and went against the grain of the sort of values a place like Yates was presumably founded on, assuming of course that it was founded on something other than murder and incest. But once she got her mind around the fact that they were playing the same game as always—they were simply using a shinier deck of cards—she was back in fine form. The rules, even if they skewed advantage, were reasonably transparent, and frankly she saw a certain beauty in the way things worked. Life might not be fair in America, but at least the system had produced a lot of choice. If you didn't like *U.S. News, Washington Monthly* had recently begun to produce its own list of rankings based on schools' commitments to things like public service and social mobility. If you couldn't get into Yates because of some fluke inputting error, you could probably get into a least two schools in the *top fifteen* at the *Washington Monthly* list that you had probably never heard of. Every school came with bragging rights of some sort. There were "hidden Ivies" and "little Ivies," and any number of Southern schools were known as Princetons of the South. Yates could just start calling itself the Princeton of Upstate New York and no one could really argue. Another option was to start your own list and put yourself at the top. It was a great country that way.

Olivia saw Ari coming down the hallway and braced herself. He looked stunning in a somewhat crumpled yellow oxford cloth shirt, more casual than usual with an open collar and a bit of stubble on his chin. She wondered if something was wrong that was causing him to forget to shave and press his clothes; perhaps slamming the door on him last night had been a little harsh. But actually, he had a smile on his face and he looked pretty happy. He was carrying a stack of folders under his arm, balancing a steaming cappuccino in a giant Yates mug. He kicked open the door, nodded at her, and took a seat at the other end of the room where he yawned and put his feet up on the edge of the table. She looked at him, but he wouldn't meet her eye. She was about to apologize for having possibly been overly hostile last night, but Basil entered the room just as she began to speak.

"Everyone have enough coffee?" he asked cheerfully. "Number two pencils sharpened? Ready to begin?"

Ari laughed like he truly found this funny. By the time it occurred to Olivia that she ought to feign amusement, the moment had already passed. She really needed to do a better job of pretending to like Basil if she wanted to keep this job.

"All right," Basil said, rubbing his hands together like he was about to dig into the house special at Yates Steaks, "Let's take Simone Atkins . . ."

"I say just let her in," said Ari.

"But . . . ," Olivia began hesitantly. She had planned to begin the meeting by showing everyone what a good sport she was, letting in the two dumb athletes. As for Simone, she was prepared to hold her ground.

She and Ari had a conversation about this back in December! She'd been worrying the buttons on his shirt, as she'd recalled, her lips pressed to his neck, leaving a dark red ring of lipstick that she half hoped Belle would see. Ari had claimed he felt even more strongly about rejecting this Simone girl than Olivia did. One good piece of advice that Ray had given them both over the years, the bottom line in these sorts of troubling situations, was that when push came to shove, a kid had to be able to do the work. It didn't behoove the kid to come to Yates and suffer academically in order to please whoever it was who was pulling strings or writing the check on his or her behalf. (Unless, of course, the check was extraordinarily large.) There was the related fact that if they couldn't keep up, they dropped out, affecting the rankings, as Arnold Hutch had indelicately pointed out at Basil's summer barbeque.

"It's not worth it, Olivia. It's too ugly, the repercussions."

"Yes, but I thought you agreed, Ari. Remember how you said . . ." Actually, what she was remembering was that she had just begun to loosen the knot on his tie when the subject first came up. He'd been wearing one of her favorites, blue with small cherries in the background.

"I know what I said, but I've just reconsidered. It doesn't behoove you to alienate your own faculty, even if they are tenured dead weight."

"Excuse me, did you say that it doesn't behoove *me* to alienate *my* faculty? What exactly did you have to say about this? Do you remember your choice of words, Ari? You said you'd met Simone Atkins and that she was dressed like a slut and . . . I believe you made the observation that she had fat thighs . . ."

"I'm sorry," Basil interrupted, "but this seems to be getting a touch unprofessional. I happen to agree with Ari, in this case, Olivia. And I don't usually say this, but I think you should just let it go . . ."

Olivia was almost shaking, not about Simone Atkins per se, but about Ari's switch of allegiance.

"Ditto for number two here, our Saudi friend," Ari began.

"She's Kuwaiti, I believe," said Olivia. "But of course I defer to you. You know that part of the world better than I do."

Ari shot her a hostile glance. "Excuse me. I misspoke," he said.

"I have no problem with her, I might remind you, Ari," Olivia contin-ued. "She's on the list because every single admissions officer voted to re-ject her. You were the one who said . . ."

"Honestly, this one is a no-brainer. She can come to Yates if she wants to come to Yates. I don't know what she's even doing on this list."

Basil nodded his head in agreement.

"I said I agree!" Olivia shouted, banging down her folder, her coffee splashing over the rim. She'd come through the door in her cheerful blue sweater with a perfectly good attitude only to be ganged up on like this.

"Listen, Olivia," Basil was saying. "Given the current Yashequana sit-uation, we really have no choice but to admit this girl. Her father has promised to help underwrite the scholarships."

"Yes, I understand completely," she said, trying to sound more concil-iatory. "But, what are you talking about? What scholarships?"

"Ari, I thought you said you were going to tell her about . . . Have you told her . . ."

"Basil, sorry. I actually stopped by to talk to Olivia last night, but well, she slammed the door on me. Actually, Olivia, you hurt my finger!" he said, holding up a slightly bruised thumb.

"Listen, I don't know what's going on here, but I can tell you it's a good thing Ari's leaving or we'd have to get to the bottom of this."

"*Leaving?* What do you mean, *leaving?*"

"Sorry, Basil, I really planned to have this conversation, but well, as you know . . . ," he said, producing his thumb again.

"Ari is going back to New York," Basil said. "He's going back into banking. Can't say I blame him."

Ari pulled out a business card and slid it across the table.

"You already have business cards?" she asked, her voice cracking.

"They just arrived, yesterday. Seriously, Olivia, this is what I wanted to talk about last night. It's really for the best. I'm sure you'll agree once you get your mind around this. Anyway, New York isn't so far. Come see me, we'll do lunch."

Their eyes caught briefly, and she realized he was serious. She thought about this for a moment—she could do with a trip to New York, perhaps over Memorial Day weekend. "It's a huge loss for the school," said Basil, "but we understand. We can't compete with those kinds of salaries and Belle—Ari's wife—is pregnant and . . ."

"What's this about the scholarships?" Olivia asked, changing the subject before saying something else she knew she'd regret. She reminded herself to behave like a proper dean of admissions, whatever that actually meant.

"Ari, you didn't tell her about the Indian boys, either?"

"No, Ari did not tell me about the Indian boys," Olivia said calmly.

"It's nonnegotiable, Olivia," Basil said, looking vaguely afraid. "Just hammered out last week."

"No point in including the interim dean of admissions in the conversation," Olivia quipped, already losing the struggle to be pleasant.

"You'll be admitting ten Native American boys from a private school in New Mexico on full scholarships," Ari said, ignoring her. "It's part of the phase one negotiations. It's good for the school, Olivia."

"Just any old ten boys? And what about ten girls?" she asked. This seemed as good a time as any to become a feminist.

"Yes, ten girls, too. But there doesn't seem to be a private girls' school that Joshua Bear has identified and insisted on, so those will just have to come through the regular transom. We can grandfather these changes in next year, since we all agreed it's a little late to start soliciting applications for next fall."

"Did you say *full* scholarships?"

"Yes."

"Super! And this will be coming from . . . oh, right. Kuwait. Makes perfect sense to me."

"Fortunately for you, Olivia, that's not your concern. Anyway, the Yashequana are putting up some money, too. They're doing quite well, and some of that will go toward underwriting a new arts center which, over time, we're hoping, will generate its own income."

"Is that all?" She had to admit this was not the worst solution to an entire host of problems.

"Not quite. Then there's the Native American Studies Department."

"I thought we were adding a Middle Eastern Studies Department."

"We will, eventually. The investor has agreed to put that on hold for now—we had a little leverage given the difficulty his daughter has had in the admissions arena. He was amenable to seeing the need for Native American studies as the more urgent matter. This all worked out rather conveniently, actually. Fritz Heimler needed a little incentive to stay on. Now he'll have his own domain."

"Wait, are you saying Fritz Heimler will run the Native American Studies Department?"

"He'll soon be a Bear, so that will make it a little less awkward."

"Pardon me?"

"So as soon as the paperwork is finalized, he'll be Fritz Bear. Now that he's retraced his roots . . ."

"It's not a name with much . . . poetry, is it?" Still, she brightened at the thought. At least Fritz wasn't leaving her, too. Maybe she could try a little harder. Did Native American men typically sport beards? She thought not.

"Anyway," Basil said, "as long as we're on the subject of transitions, it seems that Ray has asked to extend his leave a bit longer. Our lawyers tell us that even though, according to the terms of his contract, we could terminate his employment at this stage, we would be better off not putting ourselves in a potentially litigious situation."

"Yes, so I've heard."

"So what I'm trying to say is that we're still pretty much in limbo, and wondered if you'd be willing to stay on in your current role. You've been doing an excellent job—the numbers, at least, are terrific . . . Although I might suggest that you take a little more time to make your colleagues feel . . . shall we say, less intimidated, to create a possibly more collegial work environment. Maybe you could host some sort of admissions party. Have a buffet or a luau or something festive to celebrate the end of the season. And of course we're hoping . . . or rather, I'm hoping, you'll allow us to consider you for the position should the job open up . . . There will be a national search, of course. You should know that it's not automatic . . ."

"A luau?"

"Whatever suits you, Olivia. It doesn't have to be a luau."

"I see, so you're basically asking me to stay on in a job another year with no guarantee of the future while suggesting I hold a luau for my colleagues who, by the way, don't like me. I'm not really a luau sort of person."

"I get that. Luau was the wrong idea. But you are being a little touchy. Have an admissions *tea* then. Anyway, Olivia, you are missing the point: the important thing is that the numbers are just spectacular. Have I told you that already?"

"Yes, I've heard you mention that before. What if we changed the title?"

"What do you mean?"

"Maybe you could call me *acting* dean of admissions."

"*Acting?*" Basil seemed to hesitate, but Ari nodded his head.

"Okay, Olivia, anything you want."

"Anything, Basil?"

"Well . . . I suppose not quite," he stammered.

◯ ◯ ◯

"GREAT NEWS!" Nina called excitedly. Grace was already turning the corner at the end of the block and gave no indication that Nina had successfully caught her attention. A noise overhead caused Nina to look up, where she saw a burly, bearded, half-naked man standing in his boxer shorts, leaning out his bedroom window. "It's six o'clock in the morning, lady, so would you please do me a favor and shut up and get your fucking dog off my lawn," he yelled in heavily accented English.

Nina gave him the finger and shouted something to him about his unneighborly behavior and urged him to buy some curtains for his monstrosity of a house so that she wouldn't have to suffer the indignity of seeing him every time she walked down the street. "In America, we don't shout at our neighbors," she informed him. "We are a civilized people. Maybe you ought to go back to Iraq."

"Iraq?" He hesitated, sounding genuinely confused. "I'm from Colombia, lady!" He then said something in Spanish that she couldn't understand.

"Okay, whatever!" she said, now energized by this exchange. "They're having a sale at Next Day Blinds. We could take up a neighborhood fund to help you pay." Money, however, was evidently not the problem; not only was his house even larger than the Kaluantharanas', but it was outfitted with turrets, a faux moat, and four garages, in front of one of which sat a brand new Bentley. He seemed finished with this exchange and closed the window without further comment.

Nina resumed shouting Grace's name, moving toward her. Even when she was within a few feet of her neighbor, Grace still didn't respond. Nina finally realized that she had headphones stuffed in her ears; in her more paranoid moments she wondered if everyone she knew was deliberately tuning her out. At least the dog could hear her, although even this was becoming an increasingly less fulfilling relationship. Every half block or so he would simply lie down, sometimes in the middle of the street, ignoring her commands. She'd have to pick him up in order to continue, which was becoming difficult given his weight, so sometimes, instead, she'd just give him another treat to get him moving again.

"Oh, hey, Nina," Grace said, finally taking notice when the dogs began to snarl at each other. "You're up early . . . And look at you, you look so nice!"

"Yes, well . . . seize the day, etcetera!" she said, trying to give the impression of a person who might actually want to seize the day, etcetera, rather than have a drink and crawl back into bed. "Actually, Wilson and I have a meeting with the marriage counselor at eight o'clock." She couldn't quite believe she'd just blurted that out, especially since Dr. Zimmer had recently advised her that she was under no obligation to share with other people every single thought that passed through her head. Still, she continued to think of Grace as her hypothetical confessor; Nina hadn't actually told her anything all that personal over the years, yet she often found herself wondering what Grace might think or do in any given situation.

She and Wilson had been to see Dr. Zimmer twice. While Nina didn't have much faith in the process of marriage counseling, Dr. Zimmer had convinced them both that they were on the verge of—or really in the midst of—a serious crisis with Taylor, and that in his opinion they were almost entirely responsible for her troubling behavior. Nina continued to find it impossible to believe that she had anything to do with Taylor's problems—really there was absolutely no history of mail-hoarding in her family!—and yet that horrific picture of the wrist and the razor blade continued to haunt her: "I think my mother would be happier without me around," the words on the confession read. Nina kept wracking her brain about this. How could Taylor think such a thing? She was always inviting her to lunch, offering to take her shopping, suggesting matinees at the Kennedy Center, visits to art galleries, high tea at downtown hotels, proposing all sorts of highly sophisticated mother-daughter outings. Really, Taylor was the one who seemed unhappy to be around *her*!

But as the hours ticked by on that awful day when Taylor seemed to have run away, Nina found herself back in her daughter's room, sitting on her bed, supposing it might be possible that she was not the most enlightened mother in the world. By 2:00 a.m. she was in shatters; she called the police, but they said that it was too soon to file a missing person's report. By 3:00 a.m. Nina was back on the computer staring at the razor blade, drinking and weeping. The steak knife still sat in Taylor's bathroom, and under the sink was a new pile of mail. As she sifted through it she noted with relief that it was 100 percent junk: at least Taylor had weaned herself off taking anything of importance, and in fact could be considered to be providing a public service by relieving people of the temptation to order overpriced items from their Williams-Sonoma catalogues. Then she saw something worrisome, a dozen small bottles of some sort of liquid that she feared might indicate Taylor had drifted back to the more traditional kleptomania that began that awful summer at camp and which was, in retrospect, a harbinger of all her recent woes, clearly something Nina ought to have taken more seriously at the time. Closer inspection revealed that all she had just stumbled upon was a collection of free samples of cooking oil sent by Safeway through the mail.

I think my mother would be happier without me around. The sentence rattled her even more than the gruesome still life of wrist and razor blade, and by 5:00 a.m. on the day after Taylor's disappearance she had called Dr. Zimmer's office and had him paged. He agreed to squeeze Nina in that morning, and after an hour-long emergency session, he urged her to come back with the reluctant Wilson. Coaxing him into the car was going to take some doing; but she knew him pretty well despite their recent estrangement, and in a surprisingly successful maneuver she confiscated his BlackBerry and threatened to run it over if he didn't get in the passenger seat immediately. She had just been bluffing, but it worked, and also provided a helpful window into her husband's soul; at least he was still capable of passion, if only for his PDA. After two hour-long sessions with Dr. Zimmer, they were already having a small break-through that involved acknowledging they both loved Taylor with the same level of intensity that they brought to hating one another.

"Great news!" Nina repeated. Grace seemed a bit slow to inquire about the great news, but she finally rallied.

"What's that, Nina?"

"Taylor got into her first-choice school," she exclaimed, but then she froze, worried that she had just violated some rule of etiquette. She had only recently come to understand that there were various ways of broaching this topic and that most people preferred the one that in-volved subtlety. You exchanged a bunch of niceties before pretending to stumble onto the question of where the other person's kid was going to college, as if the subject had come up quite by accident. Nina thought this was pretty stupid, and personally, she didn't see what was wrong with stopping her car in the middle of morning rush hour traffic to yell to peo-ple she hadn't seen in a year and inquire about their kids' fates.

Fortunately, Grace didn't take offense, and her face even seemed to brighten. "Yes, I heard from Harry that she got into Yates. I'm so happy for her. I really loved that school. I wish Harry had applied."

Nina stifled a laugh. As if AP Harry would ever have gone to Yates. Although she had to admit that she didn't really know what was going on with Harry beyond the fact that Taylor seemed to be spending a lot of time with him, often sitting on his front porch and talking into the evening, sometimes taking long walks with him around the neighbor-hood. Nina wondered if "taking a walk" was really a euphemism for less innocent teenaged behavior, yet a nosy neighbor on the street behind them reported seeing Taylor stroll past her house with Harry every night this week, and she mentioned how sweet they looked together. When

Nina asked if they were dating, Taylor replied that no one *dated* any-more, and then she rolled her eyes.

Nina had always taken pride in having a hand in just about everything that went on at Verona, but in truth she didn't know what was going on with her own daughter. It was maddening that Grace probably knew more about the Taylor/Harry situation than she did, but this was one more thing that Dr. Zimmer had suggested she do—step back and be a little less controlling, and give Taylor a little more room.

Nina decided it was best to change the subject to something about which she was at least somewhat better informed. "I hear that Maya—whatever her last name is—was offered an athletic scholarship to USC. Can you believe that?"

"Yes, well, she's pretty amazing. She's set a state record or something. Harry says she's conflicted about swimming but decided in the end to go. She can always transfer, and she can always stay there and just decide not to swim, although I suppose then she'd have to give up the scholarship."

Nina was tempted to point out that she thought it was wrong that foreigners—rich foreigners, at that—should be taking scholarships from taxpaying Americans, but she stopped herself, realizing that the Kaluan-tharana family probably did pay some form of taxes even if they were from some other country, and she reminded herself again that she was not supposed to give voice to every thought that passed through her head, which was turning out to be much harder than it sounded.

"Someone said at the last PTA meeting that three kids got into Har-vard," Nina tried, thinking this might get Grace talking. She'd asked around, but oddly no one in attendance that night knew the outcome of Harry's application. "Shannon Rodgers said she thought it was four, but Lena Bell said no, she was sure it was three . . ."

A van drove by delivering newspapers, and the driver expertly tossed one that slid right between them as they stood at the foot of a long brick driveway, causing both dogs to bark.

"Is that right?" Grace asked. "I suppose that's about what you might expect."

"Yes, I hear that Angie Lee, Justin Smelling, that black actor boy, and then I don't know who the other might be, if there is another . . ."

Grace still didn't react, so she had to assume this meant poor Harry didn't get in to Harvard. She suddenly felt sorry for Grace—a single mother living in that slightly shabby house, surrounded by all this wealth. Poor Grace would probably have to work at her crappy government job until the day she died to pay Harry's tuition, wherever it was he wound up. Grace was an attractive woman; Nina wondered if there was something wrong with her that caused her to remain single all these years. She pitied them both, mother and son. At least Taylor had gotten into her first-choice school, and frankly now that she got her mind around it, Yates didn't seem all that bad.

"What about Dartmouth, or Yale or Princeton? Have you heard who got in where? Do you know what happened to Mike Lee?"

"I heard he's been offered a scholarship to Boston University," Grace replied. "Harry said he's very happy—he wants to study communications and they've supposedly got a good program. Evidently, his dad is still pretty angry, but at least with the scholarship now he says he can afford to send the little sister to Harvard. She's only ten years old, the poor girl. Can you imagine the pressure? Listen, I've actually got an early meeting so I'm gonna jog home, if you don't mind. I've still got to shower and change and be at work by eight o'clock. Have a great day!"

"No problem," Nina replied. "I'll jog along with you!" But then she realized that she was wearing high heels and that the dog was fast asleep at her feet, so she said goodbye.

She stood for a moment, watching Grace fade into a bouncing speck. She tried to prod the dog awake with a few jabs of her pointed shoe, but he merely groaned and readjusted his position, edging even further into the street. Two young mothers pushing strollers approached, parting in order to steer clear of the sleeping dog. A little voice emerged from inside the tightly drawn hood of a pink down parka.

"Look at the silly doggie!" she said.

Nina smiled. "He *is* a silly doggie, isn't he? He's taking his morning nap in the middle of the road!"

"Get up, doggie. Get up!" the girl cried.

Nina bent over to pick up her fat beast and felt a rogue tear slide down her cheek. She'd been so consumed by Taylor's progress at every turn, from what preschool she attended to where she went to college, that it was really just occurring to her that her own stroller-pushing days were over, and her dog-walking days were not likely to provide a very satisfying substitution. Still, there was a little bit of mothering left to do: Taylor was going to need help getting ready for college, and there were graduation plans to be made. Maybe Taylor would like to plan a party at the club! Really, when she thought about it, there was quite a lot ahead— trips to the Container Store and Bed Bath & Beyond; another long car ride to upstate New York during which they might bond; parent weekends to attend; not to mention large checks to write, which was going to require a bit of creative financing. There was plenty of work, and she made a private vow to try to get the next part right.

"Can I pet the doggie?" the pink parka–clad girl asked.

Nina bent over the stroller, and the girl squealed with delight as the dog ate the Cheerios clutched in her tiny hand.

She found herself laughing and crying simultaneously as she touched the back of her hand to the child's smooth cheek. The young mother shot Nina a worried glance and began to push the stroller away, moving quickly down the hill.

○ ○ ○

GRACE COULD see subtle changes in Harry. True, she had just noticed a spreadsheet on his desk that appeared to calculate the odds of getting off the Harvard wait list, and she had also noticed a GRE study guide among his pile of books, and yet he seemed, if not exactly carefree, like he was no longer carrying around a great weight.

She set down a shopping bag full of old clothes and books and pulled a pair of woolen gloves from her pocket. The twine handles of the heavy bag were cutting into her raw, chapped hands, and her fingers were numb from the cold. It was a familiar time of year, that slog of the transitional season when she frequently found herself underdressing despite knowing the temperature, perhaps subconsciously thinking that leaving off a layer of clothing might somehow summon spring. Harry, too, had left his coat in the car, even though it was only in the mid-40s.

"Just two more trips, Harry," she shouted as she wrestled a large bag of old linens into the charity bin in front of the hospital. Grace had been slowly sorting through closets, getting a jump start on spring cleaning, a task roughly ten years overdue. She assumed this compulsion to get organized, to literally clean house, must have something to do with the enormous and mostly unspoken changes looming just a few months away now that Harry was officially going to college. She tried to methodically stick things into bags without sinking into a sentimental black hole as she remembered the history of each item. She refused to dwell, for example, on the gorgeous hand-embroidered tablecloth from Turkey she had purchased on her honeymoon that despite being spun through countless hot water cycles with all varieties of bleach, still bore a red blotch from the anniversary dinner with Lou that ended abruptly when he smashed a bottle of expensive Bordeaux on the table for reasons she could mercifully no longer recall. It was best to just sort through these items without getting overly emotional, to come to terms with the fact that it made sense to get rid of some of the musty linens stuffed in her dining room buffet that she had not used in years.

This was what she had managed to collect on the scavenger hunt of her adult life, and that was that. It wasn't as though she'd ever especially wished for more—she had no delusions of grandeur, no aspirations to be a member of the British royal family, or to be featured on the pages of a glossy magazine, or even to be feted as a world-famous malaria researcher. She was mostly happy with her job and with her life, even if things hadn't turned out quite as she'd imagined. And yet she felt at a certain remove from who she was, at least on paper: a middle-aged, divorced American woman with one grown son. A law-abiding woman who paid her bills on time so long as they arrived in the mail, who worked long hours but didn't complain, whose great wish for the future, apart from seeing her son thrive, was to maybe take a longer than usual vacation and do something exotic, like ride horses in Spain, or even see for herself one of the countries where her life's work had some relevancy.

After three trips to the charity bin, she and Harry began a looping journey to Justin's hospital room. Grace wasn't sure why Harry insisted she come this afternoon. She had visited Justin just two days ago. She'd felt the need to just stop by and say hello, to plant a kiss on Justin's cheek, even though Harry tried to persuade her that he'd be too out of it to care. Then, oddly, Harry had called her at work this morning, suggesting that she leave a couple of hours early and meet him at the hospital. At least it was a good opportunity to have Harry help unload these bags that she'd been driving around with for a couple of days.

Justin had been here all week, recovering from a third surgery to his left hip, and they had just randomly reassigned his room without notifying anyone. Finding him involved climbing several flights of stairs and making treks down long, winding hallways, including a quick dash through a wing labeled INFECTIOUS DISEASES, while they both held their breath. They kept poking their heads into different rooms, which proved rather awkward, and in one case they had to stop to assist an elderly man with limited English who they thought wanted them to flag down a nurse, but really just wanted them to retrieve the television remote, which had slipped under the bed. Along the way they ran into about five of Harry's classmates, with each of whom he stopped and chatted warmly. Grace watched as he even hugged Angie Lee, and remarkably the subject of college had not come up once, although he did ask a couple of people about some math problem that he was stuck on. He was sure there was something wrong with the formula, he said, and he'd stayed after school trying to find the statistics teacher, but he'd already left for the day. Grace kept begging him to let it go. He was already into college, and besides, no matter how poorly he did on the quiz, he was still going to get an A for his quarter grade. For once, it truly didn't matter.

Tucked under Harry's arm was a present for Justin. After a few days of contemplation, he decided against purchasing the two award-winning Mensa games he had consulted Grace about. He'd narrowed the list down to Octiles and Da Vinci's Challenge before rejecting those in favor of the multivolume *In Search of Lost Time*, which was evidently the name of the new translation of *Remembrance of Things Past*; he had no interest in reading this book, he'd explained, but he'd heard others go on about it and figured it was very "literary," something he said Justin would no doubt appreciate, and then he'd mumbled something under his breath about Harvard and his critical reading score that Grace chose not to hear. She wasn't sure if he was asking for advice, but she offered it all the same, suggesting Justin might like something a little less demanding while he was in the hospital recovering. She was pleased to see Harry go deliberately lowbrow and purchase the first season of the television show *24* instead. Harry and Justin had always considered it a badge of honor that they were about the only kids at Verona who hadn't dedicated every Monday night of their high school careers to watching the show, but he told Grace that they had recently decided it might behoove them to make a stab at cultural literacy before heading off to college. They had tried to watch an NCAA basketball game last time Harry visited, although as soon as Justin nodded off, Harry confessed, he'd flipped off the television to begin his homework.

Grace hated hospitals—she had spent too much time in this very same one as each of her parents passed away one year apart—but somehow Harry's light mood and all the jocular conversation in the hallway made the place seem less grim. When they finally found Justin, Grace had to wonder if she had ever seen so many bouquets of flowers jammed into a room. He'd been stashed at the end of the maternity ward: evidently the previous night's derailment of a local commuter train en route to Union Station had caused a massive shortage of rooms. She could only imagine that at least some of these flowers were left over from the last occupant, although that seemed, if not unethical, at least unsanitary. Perhaps *that* was why people were always dying of infection in hospitals— germy flowers. All the ribbons trailing from the ceiling full of balloons practically obscured the sight of Justin propped in his bed, chatting with a man in a gray tweed jacket. Grace wondered if that might be Mr. Smelling, but he seemed an unlikely match for the much older-looking, dowdy Dr. Smelling.

Harry smiled and headed toward the bed, shaking hands with the man, who now stood, revealing himself to be quite tall. He had a gray-flecked beard, which made him appear both wise and benevolent, like her idealized version of a rabbi. "Oh, hey, Mr. Kushner," Harry said, walking over and enthusiastically clasping hands with the man. "What are you doing here?"

"I'm just keeping the seat warm for you, Harry. Although I should warn you that I may have worn Justin out with all my witty banter."

Justin smiled weakly. Even his normally taut brown curls looked droopy; strings of plastic IV tubes merged inside his arm and Grace assumed at least one of them must be pumping him with sedatives. She walked over and smoothed Justin's hair and gave him a kiss on the cheek, and then she greeted this Mr. Kushner person, trying to figure out who he was, and why his name was familiar. She had a weird sense of déjà vu, like she'd met him somewhere before.

Harry also seemed thrown off by the presence of this Mr. Kushner person, and was acting a little weird. "Why are you here? Where's Mrs. Ruiz?" he asked, but the question sounded stilted, like Harry was reading from a script.

"Mrs. Ruiz was here yesterday, and anyway, I happen to like the kid even if I'm not his counselor."

"Oh! You're Harry's counselor!" Grace cut in. "I'm Harry's mother! We spoke on the phone once."

"Of course," he said. "Mother of the famous AP Harry. I must say I was expecting something more . . ."

He stared at her for a minute, which was mildly unnerving, and Grace felt a bit self-conscious as she anticipated his choice of words. He finally landed on "severe."

"Um, I'm guessing that would be a compliment, then?" she replied. "A very backhanded compliment, of course."

"Yes. Well, let's call it a straight-up compliment, just to get off on the right foot here. Definitely less severe than I would have guessed. You strike me, in fact, as being . . . or at least looking . . . rather *unsevere*."

"*Mild . . . gentle . . . tender . . . sensitive . . .* ," said Harry. "*Sympathetic . . . warm . . . tranquil . . . serene . . .*"

"Enough of that already, Harry!" Grace scolded. She hadn't meant to snap, but the whole thing finally clicked. She was being set up. This was sweet, and she knew she shouldn't be angry, but she really wished Harry wouldn't meddle in her love life. She'd felt like she needed to join a support group after the last two dates he'd arranged.

"Ouch," said Harry. "Of course she *is* capable of severity, as you can see."

"You'll have to fill me in sometime, just for professional purposes, on what it's like being the mother of AP Harry. I might want to do an anthropological study on what makes the beast tick," he said, punching Harry playfully on the shoulder.

"Why don't you two go downstairs right now and get a cup of coffee. Maybe Justin and I can watch an hour of this insipid popular television program. Are you up to that, Justin?"

Justin nodded his head, but Grace got the feeling he'd be asleep within moments.

"You can spend an hour talking about me," Harry proposed. "What could be more delightful?"

Grace looked at Mr. Kushner, and he shrugged. There was no graceful way out of this, and besides, she had to admit she felt strangely attracted to this man. "I was going to grab a bite anyway. It would be nice if you'd join me. I'll even treat if we don't mention Harry's name," Mr. Kushner joked.

"I suppose that sounds like a pretty good deal," said Grace. "Justin, don't let Harry do any more homework. He's already studied all weekend, and he needs to take a break . . . do you hear me, Harry? Watch some television!"

"Yes, Mom," he replied. But he was already unzipping the backpack that she hadn't realized he'd brought.

"I don't think he can help it," said Mr. Kushner. "How about you just catch Justin up on what he's missing and then watch the show?" he suggested.

Grace found herself surprised by this good suggestion: she wasn't used to having anyone help moderate Harry's behavior. It was nice to have someone else guide him, even if it was only for the amount of time it took to down a latte, and who could say, maybe there would be a second cup.

Epilogue

MAYA SOUNDED PRETTY HAPPY as she described her future room-mate; the girl was a tennis player from Miami, and they discovered that they liked a lot of the same music. They had already agreed on a color scheme—blue and light blue—so that they could buy the right linens. Harry tuned out right about then. *Linens?* Had he possibly misheard this? He'd been given his roommate assignment and had exchanged obligatory e-mails with the boy, who was from some boring Verona-like suburb outside Baltimore, but all he'd learned about Jeff Martinez was that he planned to major in biology. Harry couldn't imagine what more he needed to know about his future roommate. Certainly, he didn't care what color blanket he planned to put on his bed. He wondered how it was that girls drifted off on such bizarre tangents. Did these subjects come up naturally in the course of conversation, or was there some list of talking points distributed to kids at private universities? He was about to ask Maya this question when he saw smoke coming from the direction of the Rockefellers' house.

"Holy mother of . . . that looks like a *fire!*" he yelled. Harry dropped his briefcase and ran, then tossed his backpack on the Rockefellers' front lawn to further lighten his load. He left Maya standing across the street near the curb.

"Taylor?" he shouted, as he approached her house.

He had just seen her a few minutes ago in English class. She'd smiled at him from across the room, and he looked around for her after class, hoping they might walk home together. He wanted to ask her something, like maybe if she was thinking about going to the prom, and maybe if she was, if she maybe wanted to go with him but she didn't really have to . . . it was just a totally random spontaneous idea and maybe he wouldn't have asked at all when the time came.

As Harry ran toward Taylor's house, he felt again this strange emotion that was something like . . . *love* would definitely be vastly overstating it, but he felt extremely concerned about Taylor's well-being and imagined himself racing into her burning foyer and bounding up the stairs to rescue her, carrying her out to safety just as the stairway crumbled behind them. He couldn't help but entertain the thought that this might make a compelling supplemental essay for the packet of materials he planned to submit to Harvard later this month, in the hope that he'd eventually be moved off the wait list.

Even if he didn't get in, which he was beginning to accept as a real possibility, he was still in good spirits. He'd done a little more research about the honors program at Maryland and decided that it was definitely in ascendance. A retired professor from the Math Department had recently won the Nobel Prize, so it couldn't be full of losers. He didn't actually feel like a loser—he'd been offered a full scholarship, and he'd decided that a full scholarship at any school was just as impressive as being let into Harvard, if you had to pay your own way. Maryland wanted him so badly they were willing to cover even the costs of his room and board. It seemed like a no-brainer. But he still couldn't help but wonder what other people thought. If he didn't *feel* like a loser, was it possible that he was one, anyway? Was there some actual definition of being a loser, some particular threshold of failure, or was it truly only a state of mind?

He was worrying about whether he was really capable of breaking down the front door if need be—it always looked so easy in the movies—when he realized that the smoke was not coming from inside, but rather seemed to be emanating from the backyard. He opened the back gate and saw a huge plume of smoke coming from the barbeque grill, where the flames were leaping dangerously high. For a brief moment he was cheered by the thought of spring, of hamburgers on the grill and fresh sweet corn. But then it occurred to him that the unusual smell was not suggestive of slowly charring meat.

"Taylor?" he called. He began to walk toward her, hesitating when he noticed that she was feeding bits of paper to the flames.

She glanced up, and the look on her face was serene. She wore her hair in two long braids, which made her look even younger than her seventeen years. Her wrists were heavy with silver bracelets that made a soft musical clanking sound as she moved her arms back and forth between the grill and a huge stack of papers.

"Hey, Harry!" she replied, smiling.

"What are you doing?"

"I'm moving on," she said.

"Oh." Harry was confused about the meaning of this, but then he didn't seem to understand about half of what she said, as she used a lot of metaphors, as well as elliptical references to books with which he was unfamiliar.

"I'm just about done. Hope you don't really need any more of your college crap."

"What do you mean?"

"I mean I'm burning your Washington University catalogue, if you don't mind."

"I never applied there."

"I know. That's why I'm burning it."

"Okay. Whatever . . ." He had no idea what she was talking about, but as long as they were already having this weird conversation, he figured this was a good time to just blurt it out. "Hey, Taylor, I know it's really dumb and everything, but do you want to go to the prom with me?"

He thought the prom was a pretty silly thing, a huge distraction and the catalyst for a lot of ridiculous drama involving girls gossiping in the hallway for weeks at a time and endless Instant Messenger traffic, or so he'd heard. It was also, in his view, an enormous waste of money; Verona parents had raised something like $30,000 for last year's post-prom party, and they had given away door prizes that included free laptop computers, supposedly as a way to keep kids from devising their own post-prom activities that would presumably involve the ingestion of drugs and alcohol, something Harry couldn't deny was true. Last year three kids had wound up in the hospital with alcohol poisoning, and someone still placed flowers each week at a particularly dicey intersection near the school where a car full of inebriated girls had crashed head-on into a tree years ago.

But then, Harry knew he was not a fair judge of these things; he was of the opinion that weddings and bar mitzvahs and elaborate sweet sixteens were a waste of financial resources, and sometimes as he was digging into an entrée at one of these events, he liked to calculate the interest that might have accrued over a rate of thirty years if the money had been invested in municipal bonds rather than squandered on pastries in the shape of swans. He'd never understood the point of the little party bags full of dime-store junk, and frankly he didn't even understand the fuss his mother made at Christmas. The lights on the tree were a fire hazard, and the inflatable Santa was unbelievably gaudy. But it seemed to make her happy, and he supposed this was important in some intangible way.

Taylor poured what looked like some kind of cooking oil into the barbeque grill, and the flames leaped so high that she jumped back, screaming. "Hey, be careful, Taylor! That's a gas grill! You're going to blow up the neighborhood!"

"Prom, Harry?" she asked, wiping smoke from her eyes. "That's so sweet!"

"That *is* sweet," he heard another voice echo. He turned around and saw Maya, holding his briefcase.

Maya must have sensed his discomfort. "Sorry," she said. "I didn't realize. I was just making sure everything was okay, because when you saw the smoke and . . ."

"That's okay," Taylor said. "Everything's fine. I'm just doing a little purging here . . . So the prom, Harry . . . I never thought you were the type . . ."

Harry felt a little defensive, like these two friends were mocking him when he'd finally, for the first time ever, worked up the nerve to ask a girl out like this. "You don't exactly seem like the prom type either, you know," he said.

"No, you're absolutely right. I'm hardly the prom type."

"You should so totally go with him, Taylor. You would make the cutest couple ever," Maya said.

She seemed utterly sincere, and Harry suspected that Maya was perhaps the only person he knew who genuinely did not have a dark side, even if both girls had begun to giggle uncontrollably all of a sudden.

"Okay, forget it," he said, heading toward the gate. "I'm glad you're okay, Taylor. I was just checking 'cause I saw the smoke. I'll see you guys tomorrow."

"No, wait, Harry. We're just kidding around. I'd love to go. That would really be awesome," she said, smiling.

"Come here a sec . . . Can you guys give me a hand?" She passed Harry a pair of tongs and gave Maya a long metal spatula. "I've got so much stuff to get through here, if you could just help me out . . ." She handed them each a thick stack of papers that looked kind of like junk mail. Harry wasn't sure what he was doing, but he stuck some coupons for Giant Foods through the grill, even though he thought his mom might be able to use the one offering a significant discount on steak. The leaping flames were oddly mesmerizing. He dropped a copy of someone's AARP newsletter into the grill and watched it burn slowly. Then he set fire to various credit card solicitations that he couldn't help but notice were addressed to neighbors up and down the street. He wondered briefly if he might go to jail.

The next item in his stack was an old copy of *The Washington Post*. He was about to stick it in the flames when a headline caught his eye. It had to do with the opening of a new Wal-Mart store in Arizona, where eight thousand people had put in applications for 525 jobs. Harry wondered if this number could possibly be correct. He took a step back from the barbeque grill to take a second look.

"What's wrong, Harry?" Maya asked.

"I don't know . . . I mean, this can't be right. There must be a typographical error or something in this article. Otherwise, it would have you believe that, statistically speaking, it is harder to get a job at Wal-Mart than to get into Harvard."

"We might as well all just pack it in right now, Harry," Taylor said. "I mean, seriously. Why don't you stop worrying about that sort of stuff and have some fun. It's over. You're done with all this college stuff. Relax! You had the right idea a minute ago. Let's get dressed up and go to the stupid prom."

"That's only a 6 percent acceptance rate . . . ," said Harry.

Taylor grabbed the newspaper from him and let the edge catch fire. She handed him a magazine. "Here, Harry, burn this. It will feel good."

Harry looked at what she'd placed in his hands. It was the newest edition of *America's Best Colleges*. It had a mailing label on the back, addressed to the father of a boy who was a junior at Verona and who lived down the street.

Harry stared at the magazine for a moment, feeling unsteady. He was tempted to open it, to see if Maryland still held the same rank in the list of national universities. He wondered where Harvard had landed this year, whether it was still tied with Princeton for the top spot, and whether he would have been better off applying there instead. He wondered if Taylor had cracked it open to see if Yates was still hanging on at number 50, or if he was the only one who cared. Not that any of this mattered, he reminded himself.

"Just stick it through the grill," Taylor repeated. It sounded like an order.

He looked at her for a moment, unsure of what to do. He dipped the corner of the magazine through the metal bars, hesitantly.

Then he let go, and watched it burn.

Acknowledgments

Although this is entirely a work of fiction, I sought the wisdom of a few people along the way. Any slant on the subject is entirely my own. Alan Cafruny at Hamilton College, Dean Charles Deacon at Georgetown University, Jon Keates at Occidental College, and Jay Mathews and Valerie Strauss at *The Washington Post* all gave generously of their time, as did Robert Morse at *U.S. News & World Report*, who kindly answered a few questions and is in no way responsible for my interpretation, or possible misinterpretation, of the way things work.

Material on cutting and obsessive-compulsive disorders was gleaned from *A Bright Red Scream*, by Marilee Strong; *Obsessive-Compulsive Disorders*, by Fred Penzel; *Cutting*, by Steven Levenkron; and *Kleptomania*, by Marcus J. Goldman.

Thanks to Becky Wald, Jessica Stadd, and Jane Kepler, who chatted with me about tours, dorm conditions, and competitive swimming, and to Jane and Emma for letting me claim their "urban rap." Thanks also to Trustman Senger, Liz Kastor, and Emily Bliss for suffering through early drafts, and to Rose Lichter-Marck for presumably much more help than I'm even aware of. I've surely won some cosmic lottery in getting the chance to work with Melanie Jackson and Sarah Crichton on this book, and with my husband, Steve Coll, in this life.

A NOTE ABOUT THE AUTHOR

Susan Coll is the author of the novels *karlmarx.com: A Love Story* and *Rockville Pike*. She lives outside Washington, D.C., and she and her husband are the parents of three children, either college-aged or about to apply to college.